The Populist

By the same author

The Régime Change Man

The Régime Change Man (The Long Version)

The Plutocrat

Rory Harden

THE POPULIST

Black Spike Books

www.populistbook.com
www.roryharden.com

Published by Black Spike Books

US First Edition

Version 1.00

ISBN 978-1-910665-17-6

Cover photo of iguana in Costa Rica by Nancy Crockett.

For Bonnie Crockett

"I only know what I believe."

- A famous statesman.

CHAPTER 1

Deserts are beautiful, but deadly. In return for peace, purity and perfection, you accept danger. Bonnie DiAngelo had forgotten that, or else she had deceived herself.

An unending emptiness can fill the soul and seduce, or seem to. But the void can kill you without a thought, as if you were a careless visitor from another planet. And no desert is truly empty — not even the great deserts of Africa.

But they were the most beautiful of all. And the most dangerous.

A blast of canyon dust stung her eyes. *Someone save me from myself*, she thought. *Where are you, Leo?*

"Get down, Bonnie, get down *now!*"

Leo, the eco tycoon and seismic sophisticate from Costa Rica, whose advice and itinerary she had bought into, but now regretted, had tumbled from his donkey and lost his ridiculous hat in the process.

"Up *here!*"

He meant up by the red, vulcanized walls of the canyon — and this time his counsel was sound.

All ahead was commotion: The loaded-up camel trains; the attendant mules and donkeys; the Tigrayan salt merchants and their Afar guides and guards, rifles bouncing on their backs — all charging towards them. The Saba river canyon narrowed here, so the risk of meeting this dusty, panicky exodus head-on was too great.

She lost her donkey, but found Leo in a sandy cleft, dusting off his hat. The din rose and the dust blew up with it, filling the canyon like an overheated vacuum cleaner.

"What's happening? Where's Sam?"

"I don't know. Sam's over *there*. Somewhere."

On the other side of the canyon, out of sight for now — gone for good? Sam (not his real name, they knew, but the boy had tact) was their guide, a subtle young Afar hipster with trad-style goat-butter ringlets and the latest sneakers. When he'd made enough money, he'd told them, he would travel to America. Would he be allowed to take his AK-47?

1

The slow-motion stampede went on. Animals collided. The camels' economy-sustaining cargo — the salt blocks slung like paving slabs at their sides — cracked and shattered. Leo's donkey — understandably, she thought — considered the odds and voted with its hooves, propelling Leo into the rear of the cleft where, once again, he parted with his hat.

"We should have done this by Jeep," she said.

"If you ride in a..." – Leo paused to catch his breath — "...in a four-by-four, that is not an *eco adventure*."

Well, okay, he had a point. She imagined the pitch she would make to her discriminating clients at her next Adventure Travel Evening.

Here you have a camel train. It travels through the canyon, down the escarpment to the salt flats at Lake Asele. They've been doing this for two thousand years, maybe much longer. Ignore the rifles and the footwear and it doesn't look any different. You've got the local people, the Afar. Very exotic. Read what these British explorers from the nineteen-thirties have to say about them. Pretty scary, right? See the picture of the sixteen-inch curved dagger? That's what they used. On their enemies. And *foreigners*. Don't worry — *laughter* — they're not like that now.

And *there* you have a Toyota Land Cruiser. Which is more romantic? Which picture do you want in the brochure?

She shuffled back into the shade of the cleft. The sun was high now, and the canyon was heating up — not quite to the 120 degrees they'd been told to expect on the salt flats, but hot enough.

"This morning," she said. "Did you hear it?"

"Yes. I heard it."

The journey to the salt flats by caravan took three days. It began, half-way down the escarpment from the highlands, in the salt-market town of Berahile, a purposeful settlement of red-brown gravel, stone walls, tin roofs, recycled plastic sheeting and wonky electricity poles. Here they had parked their Land Cruiser, rented in Addis Ababa, under the supervision of Sam's uncle and next to the pen where he kept his goats.

The trail ran to the north through tiny villages comprised of circular wood-and-palm-thatch huts and then, turning to the east, entered the Saba river canyon. Twisting its way down the escarpment, the canyon eventually issued out into the Danakil desert. Here, in a zone spanning Eritrea to the north, Ethiopia in the center and Djibouti to the south, lay the Danakil depression. In it, one could encounter, at fifty meters below sea-level, and at a volcano called Dallol, the hottest place on Earth. It was official.

So someone had decided that the hottest place on Earth was going to get hotter.

It was going to happen anyway, but Bonnie DiAngelo, burning up under the Ethiopian sun on her sixty-second birthday, was not willing to flame out quite yet, and saw no good reason to hasten the final conflagration.

Who needed this? Not the proprietor of Eco Adventures of Brookline, Massachusetts, who, contemplating another down year with her frazzled accountant, had been urged to seek out new destinations, the old ones having gone either out of fashion or into the op-ed columns, or both. What did the clients want? Not the fiery birth-pangs of democracy, for sure. Nor boredom in placid Botswana again; they'd seen the wild dogs, and the hyenas, and then there was the dollar-cost. Find somewhere exciting, Bonnie — the real Africa. But safe. And not too expensive.

So here she was, excited for sure, high up in the mountains of north-eastern Ethiopia. And it might have worked, it really might. But down there in the Danakil depression, she now felt sure, the desert was on fire.

It had not been their intention, on this trip, to visit Dallol, or Erte Ale and its uniquely permanent lava pool, or the geysers, or the hot springs, or the faults and fissures — much as Leo might have wished. This would have necessitated vehicles and equipment (Bonnie's clients were not youngsters) and would not have been *eco*.

Instead, their destination was a dusty outpost called Hamed Ela, located on an outcrop above the desert and the salt flats, where the camels rested and the salt merchants paid their taxes. Here they would determine whether Bonnie's clients could sensibly undertake the final hike to the flats to observe, at first hand, the hacking-out and levering-up of the salt and the fashioning of camel-sized blocks, all by hand, all very ancient and all without a carbon footprint, if you didn't count the camels.

But this morning, after two nights under the empty Ethiopian skies and just after tea, they had heard something — far off and in the direction of Hamed Ela. There had been a conference of merchants and guards. Quite a discussion, in fact. She'd approached Sam while Leo was finishing his tea and observing the debate. Any problem? No, Sam had said, the caravan would proceed as normal. He hadn't looked happy, so she'd pushed things a bit. Bandits? The Eritreans? The possibility of being kidnapped by Eritrean bandits was the only convincing danger that her research had turned up. (I mean, *really*, she imagined telling her clients — in Botswana you can get *malaria*, you can get *eaten* by *crocodiles*...)

But those sounds were explosions, she thought now. Big ones. Not bandit-sized ordnance.

The donkeys and camels were right to panic. She and Leo would have to turn back.

For perhaps another fifteen minutes she sat immobile, blinking the dust from her eyes, until the tide of men and animals began to abate. She became aware that Leo, behind her, had taken out a notebook and a GPS and was scribbling furiously. What was he writing? A demand for a refund on the donkeys? Instructions to his plantation managers to put more eco logos on the coffee bags? Notes for his big speech at the climate conference?

Probably the latter: She was the cynic, not he. At the conference in Cape Town — most likely the last one ever, he'd said, considering the way the others had gone — would he give them the pitch he'd rehearsed with her?

Drought and politics. Put them together, what do you get? Think back to the nineteen-eighties. But the politics didn't *cause* the drought; rainfall in the highlands is unreliable. Now consider this. Two thousand years of sustainable industry in the hottest place on the planet. Yet by the end of the century it's too hot for people, too hot for camels. It's the first totally uninhabitable place on the surface of the Earth. It's Venus. And up in the highlands it's one big political drought. And sixty million people live there.

And so on.

The few hardy stragglers remaining in the canyon passed by without acknowledging her, but, on the far side, cross-legged on a ledge, staring across at her in calm concentration, was Sam, the precocious Afar entrepreneur who, she remembered, hadn't been paid yet.

She attracted Leo's attention by swatting at his ankle.

"Hey. Better head back, I guess."

Leo pursed his lips and adjusted his hat — a voluminous custom-made job, donated, he claimed, by a fan in New Mexico. Why wear an abomination like that when you had such thick, lush black hair?

"We should consult with our guide."

"Sure." Keep things on the up-and-up, as Leo prefers.

By the time they reached the center of the canyon, Sam was already there, cleaning the dust from his rifle. The kid seemed to have lost his cool; he looked embarrassed.

"Our caravan..." – he waved a sorrowful arm in the direction of Berahile — "...has gone. I am sorry."

"No, no, not your fault," she said. "It's only twenty minutes. We can catch up, right?"

Sam looked her up and down. Beautiful dark eyes, she thought — but do they have to look so dubious?

"Maybe," he said, in a tone that meant *I don't think so*.

She looked at Leo. Come on, Mr. Sustainable Business Leader of Costa Rica, 2009 — show us some leadership. Leo fiddled with his GPS.

"We are *here*," he said, with conviction.

We certainly are, she thought. He gave his GPS some thumb action.

"Hamed Ela is *there*. Four or five hours."

"You think we should go on? But —"

"It's two and a half days back to Berahile. We have no food."

"The villages —"

"Still too far."

She turned to Sam but the look on his face, translated, read what-can-I-tell-you and no-good-options and reminded her, for an absurd instant, of that last session with the accountant.

"Well, fine," she said, "but something — I'm telling you, *something* blew up down there. That can't be good."

For a moment no one spoke.

"Sam," she said, "do you know what happened?"

Sam shook his head, slowly. Didn't know or didn't want to speculate?

"We should go to Hamed Ela," Leo said. "Hamed Ela has not blown up." He let out a sigh and stowed his GPS carefully in his cargo pants. "They have huts and they have camels. What could blow up?"

Well, in his annoying way, he's settled it, she thought. But what's he so uptight about? What does he know? Nothing, probably, but the rugged-and-sensitive stuff can be hard to keep up when you're not feeling in control and you can't

4

easily get someone on the end of a phone who's seen your picture on magazine covers. But, be fair, Bonnie — would you want to be here without him?

"Let's go," she said.

With the briefest of smiles in her favor, Sam took his rifle in both hands and stepped out in front. They began to walk.

She slipped on her super-dark sunglasses and fell into a rhythm. Exploding camels? Of course not; give him that. But what was the hidden agenda, if there was one?

Leo, of course, had never lacked an agenda. Land reform, capital controls, carbon trading, sustainable energy — two decades of this, combined with the hair, the smile and the irresistible allure of the enlightened capitalist, had been enough to earn him the unpaid job of pin-up or poster-boy for the New Latin American Economic Model. His reputation ran high in such circles. And in Europe, and the better sort of coffee shop in Brookline and the Back Bay. Perhaps a little too high? Washington certainly thought so. But what a crazy town that was, these days! You had to laugh. Well, no, actually.

And serious-minded Annie, Bonnie's daughter and only child, wouldn't be laughing either, though she might have done once. Before graduation, perhaps — before she set off to save the place from itself? That, surely, had been a joke. Did she laugh at all these days? Well, dumping your husband wasn't so funny, especially when you tell everyone it's not just personal, it's political. And then you copy his hard drive and mail it to the Feds. But you could get another husband — even, God help us all, a conservative. Dumping your mother was worse.

Was there an explanation? You could say it was simply the politics of the new generation gap, as the weekly magazines, high as ever on demographics, would have it.

But was it? For that fleeting, sunny interlude — Bonnie's Rich Period — during which the condo in Brookline had pretended to be worth more than two million dollars, you might easily have understood the frustrations of a twenty-something researcher for a lobbying firm who made thirty-five thousand a year.

Yet Annie hadn't seemed frustrated by her mother's transient wealth so much as Bonnie's refusal to celebrate it. Annie had rejected her mother's politics for a stunted ideology that seemed childish and secretive. And, despite Mom's hopes, she wasn't going to be growing out of anything anytime soon because, at twenty-nine, she was scarily committed, and implacable. Leo, of course, understood how Bonnie felt about her daughter, but maintained a strict neutrality — a deliberate and, it seemed, highly sustainable detachment.

You're rambling, she thought. Brain too hot? Hyperthermia? Let's hope not. We want to see Hamed Ela — intact and with all its camels.

She tapped Leo on the elbow.

"You know what? We *do* have food. I have Oreos in my pack. Want some?"

He did. And, in deference, he left unsaid what she heard anyway: Oreos are *not* food.

On they went. It got hotter.

But look, she thought, if it wasn't the camels exploding, then... Vulcanicity? The Afar Triple Junction: Three faults defining a triangle that was sinking into the Red Sea. Cracks everywhere, eruptions. Leo would know. But he hadn't said anything.

Not camels, not volcanoes, not the bandits. Well, then: Unavoidable conclusion? Military activity. A sensitive subject in these parts, and not just because of the endless, pointless animosity between Ethiopia and Eritrea, something about which the clients would have to be gently educated — mind those cameras, people, especially in Addis. So... Military activity?

She felt the dullness of defeat begin to seep into her soul. Coming here had been a big mistake. She had really screwed up. This was going to be a problem; this was going to be a huge waste of money — real money, not pretend — that she didn't have.

She should have looked at the map a little longer. What would her former son-in-law have told her?

He would have told her that there were (a) war zones; and (b) War Zones, capitalized, the latter being ours. But she knew this. South Sudan was a war zone, still category (a). Mali and Somalia fell into both categories — she wasn't going to argue about it. The Maghreb — looking more and more like (b). Yemen, definitely (b). Tanzania and Kenya, not there yet but heating up. Egypt — freed up and then locked down, but for how long? Iraq, Syria, give me a break. Then all this talk, even from her daughter, about the Greater Persian Region. And Djibouti — what the hell went on there? Was she supposed to keep up with all this?

No. But Leo did, didn't he?

Hotter, flatter, brighter, wider — the canyon went on. But at length they stumbled out on to plains of sand and gravel. Now visible, far off in the haze, under a vacant and trembling sky, was the outcrop upon which Hamed Ela crouched.

A hot wind blew up. They covered their faces and picked up the pace.

CHAPTER 2

This was one hell of a party to crash. How long would he last? The name on the photo ID he wore around his neck on a red ribbon was not his own. Nor was the picture, though it resembled him somewhat.

He did not represent the real-time embedded-systems software development corporation whose Head of Business Development he purported to be. That corporation did not exist, except as a figment of cyberspace. And it was only recently that a friendly science teacher had explained to him, in seventh-grade terms, what real-time embedded systems were. He hoped that none of the corporate tech-heads he'd already spied in the Laptop Lounge (you weren't allowed to bring your own) would expect him to converse on the subjects of "multi-threaded error-handling", the "apartment model" or "interface negotiation".

And he knew that, back at the office, a pool had been established and bets taken on how quickly he would be unmasked and ejected. He had a reputation, after all, for clumsiness, accidents and fuck-ups. And he had only taken on this job because no one else had the nerve. What a bunch of wimps. Risk, he had tried to explain, was not just for the capitalists.

Which was why he had infiltrated himself into the Unmanned Aerial Dynamics Expo, Fair and Picnic.

So far things had gone well. He had mispronounced his fake name to the security guys on the way in, and misspelled it on the non-disclosure, but they hadn't noticed. Nor had they spotted the latest edition of The Liberal — with his face on the cover! — that he had forgotten to remove from his bag. A battery of detectors, scanners and sniffers had been negotiated almost without incident. He had broken the lock on the cubicle in the men's room, but hey — it wasn't like they couldn't afford a new one. And he had brushed against a model of an in-flight refueling tanker, which obviously hadn't been secured efficiently, and sent it crashing to the floor. Fortunately, the room had been empty. No one was interested in tankers. They were interested in drones. As was he.

And so, in order to plausibly resemble a man legitimately interested in the world of drones, dronedom and droning, he had, under instruction from

Katherine, his boss, cut his hair way short, shaved properly, bought a tie, borrowed a suit, rented a black Mercedes, collected his bogus credentials and driven down to South Carolina, to the thousand-acre compound or campus which had been constructed in the foresty middle of nowhere by an outfit called Fair Meadow Solutions. FMS was a private company — very private — and appeared to be descended from the deliberately unpronounceable and now defunct Qfw Corp, which had been split up following various foreign embarrassments. An earlier and only slightly different set of foreign embarrassments had led the briefly notorious Military Logistics Group to change its name to Qfw. But so what? Business was a constant process of evolution and improvement, right?

Yet, in truth, Jefferson Crockett (Jeff Crock to his friends and his rather more numerous enemies) was unhappy with the mission. As he followed the crowd into the lecture theatre and edged his way along a row near the back, trying very hard not to step on anyone's toes, he couldn't help but dwell on the reasons why.

For one thing, that issue of The Liberal in his bag was to be the last ever produced in physical form. Katherine had lost money to that Ponzi bastard in New York and couldn't afford to subsidize it any more. Advertising? Forget about it. Back in Katherine's office they'd cased the competition. Ads for aerospace, anyone? Agribusiness? Private banking? The Global Faith Initiative of... Well, at that point he'd slammed his coffee mug down on the table and the handle had snapped off. There would be no big-ticket advertising. And besides, that magazine with the Faith Initiative ad — look at the shit they were writing about the so-called Greater Persian Question. Fuck off, Katherine!

And so, from now on, he would be an investigative *blogger*. He'd better start getting used to it.

He selected a seat between two dark suits who didn't look like tech-heads.

Moving on, then, there was the more personal question of his *obsession*. Yes, he knew it was an obsession, and a particularly unhealthy one, too, according to the wisdom of the times. Like an all-consuming addiction, or a self-inflicted wasting disease, it was eating him up. Everyone said so. Some spoke of it with concern, rather more with mockery. Those who loved him — a small band, admittedly, but dedicated — tried to distract and soothe, to sympathize and share his pain. Others... Well, just wait around and see what happened the next time someone told him to his face to *get over it*.

The lecture theatre was military-media-center spotless, corporate-hospitality plush and clammy with Bible-Belt air-con. He calmed down a bit.

Basically, drones were fine. Drones were important. Something had to be done about drones. But there were *War Criminals* at liberty, folks! Walking around free. Taking money from dictators. Talking on the TV. Setting up Foundations and Initiatives. Getting rich. Giving speeches about Africa. War Criminals! Don't we care any more? Doesn't it matter? A little thing called justice? *No evidence*, you say? Are you kidding? Oh, *that* sort of evidence. Fine. I'll get it. One day. I'll get it. You'll see.

So, anyway, added to the obsession and the *blogging* thing, there was the Annie issue. But there wasn't time to fret about that because the top-of-the-bill speaker had come on and was cranking up his laptop — a specially-licensed one, presumably.

Jeff reconfigured his long, lanky frame into a comfortable shape, reached up to brush back his hair, realized it wasn't there any more, jabbed his neighbor with his elbow — oops, sorry! — then breathed out heavily and perked up his ears.

The speaker, a Big-'n'-Tall customer who would have resembled an Italian opera singer but for his ginger buzz-cut, waited for the audience to fall silent.

Someone dimmed the lights. A hush fell. All Jeff Crock could hear was the huffing of the air conditioning.

With operatic flair, the speaker threw his gaze from one side of the auditorium to the other, nodding, as if checking off each of the twelve hundred or so attendees against a mental list. Then he must have activated a secret switch, because the cinema-sized screen behind him lit up in blue. Oh shit, Jeff thought, PowerPoint time. A click of the mouse and the first slide appeared: "The Future," in very big letters. How exciting. Another long pause. What a tease.

And then something odd happened. Up came a photograph. There was the minutest pause — just long enough for a cartoon double-take — and then a collective "Whoa!" went up from the crowd, followed by the sort of applause you got on a reality show finale where the winner's family and supporters took up the first ten rows. Jeff studied the photograph. Yes, he'd done his homework. He knew what it was. Two wings, long cylindrical body — fuselage? Tail fin. The bulges and insect-antennae that gave it the sinister vibe that everyone expected. It was a drone. What a surprise. Why the commotion?

His neighbor leaned across.

"That's something, don't you think?"

"Certainly is."

"Haven't seen anything like that before!"

No? Jeff looked the screen again. It looked like a perfectly ordinary drone, positively humdrum, as drones went. He'd seen lots of pictures exactly like this one.

"No," he said. "It's so... What would you say it is?"

But his neighbor didn't seem to be listening.

"This is huge!"

What was huge, exactly? Well, perhaps ginger buzz-cut would spell it out; he had begun to speak.

But it was no use. Jeff's mood plunged. It was all jargon and he couldn't make any sense of it. Extended parameters. Battle space matrix. Remote capability modes. Automatic target profile sensing. Strategic-tactical duality. Enhanced this. Enhanced that. Of course, he would have smuggled in one of those tiny digital audio recorders, for later consultation with experts, but these people had a detector for everything.

Quite soon, to his surprise, it was all over. There were no more pictures. The room emptied in a buzz of excitement. Well, he still didn't get it. He took one last look at the image before the screen went dark. What was he missing? Well, fuck it, there was condensation trickling down his neck; he needed to get outside and get some air. Wait a minute — wasn't there supposed to be a Fair and a Picnic? Perhaps the drive from Brooklyn hadn't been a waste after all. He made a dash from the auditorium. Then immediately returned to fetch his bag.

J eff Crock stood in the parking lot with upturned face and secretly stole himself some pristine, early fall, Carolina sunshine. The aroma of pine forests infiltrated his nostrils and a gentle breeze probed his defenses. Camouflaged birds in the parking lot's landscaped margins exchanged coded messages. From undercover, somewhere nearby, came the cryptic cries of children, whose hidden meanings evaded him.

He shook himself out of his reverie. Katherine had been right about the car. The parking lot had voted, and black was its color — SUVs, Limos, Mercedes. His second-hand white Prius, with its provocative decals, would have been noticeable.

But what about those children? He followed the sound of their voices, tip-toeing, since there were no footpaths, across the red earth of the parking lot's floral borders and around the side of the main building, a low reflective-glass hangar almost completely obscured by banks of shrubbery.

At the rear of the building he found lawns, tents, a major catering operation, an inflatable castle and the children. Well, of course — the Picnic. A picnic in the lap of the Flying Death Robots? Why not? They probably had cook-outs at Los Alamos, desert notwithstanding.

But whose children? The employees', presumably. Even for drone people, automation, cybernetics and remote control only took you so far. He'd noticed a day-care center in the main building and a "Family Administration" wing. The building on the far side of the lawns resembled a school. And was that a supermarket next to it? Quite the little self-contained community.

He tracked the scent of barbecue to its source and loaded up; drones made you hungry, he had to conclude. All frivolity aside, though, what had he accomplished here? They're unveiling something new, Katherine had said, find out what it is. Well, it was same-old, wasn't it? With a bit of enhanced this and a dash of enhanced that. Typical corporate product hype. Find out which countries they're operating in, Jeff. Who really controls them, who owns them. Where's the investment coming from? Who are the buyers? These were tough, relevant questions — which he clearly had little chance of answering.

He took up his paper plate of pulled pork, snatched a plastic fork and set off to investigate the tents.

They turned out to house the Fair portion of the proceedings. Drones, it was interesting to learn, were like cars. They came with many options and accessories. For example, satnav was generally standard, as you'd expect at this price point in the market. But you could opt for *premium* guidance. And while undercoating didn't really apply, you were free to select your color of choice. Disks — SSD or Sata II? Tires — these cost more upfront, but you'll get your money back after fifty missions.

But the most important add-on package a buyer had to consider was what shit they wanted to drop on people.

The options were extensive.

As he turned to walk back to the parking lot, he felt that familiar knot of disgust in his stomach. Unhappily, these days it always came with an unwanted soundtrack — Annie's voice repeating "Are you sure this whole thing isn't just about *you*?" For Annie, righteous anger was always suspect. She was a grown-up; she did the cost-benefit analysis before involving her emotional resources.

Sensible. Pragmatic. And, he felt he had learned at length, cold. He had come up with the come-back too late: "Well, if you don't *feel* these things, maybe it's really all about *you!*"

"Sir!"

Someone was hailing him.

"Sir, would you like to try?"

Try what? Try again with Annie? Oh, whatever.

"Just step inside, sir."

He allowed himself to be guided into the last tent in the row. Inside he saw nothing but a large video screen at one end and a Barcalounger recliner at the other.

"Take a seat, sir."

He sat.

"May I?"

He handed over his pulled pork.

"Make yourself comfortable."

"Thanks."

"Here's your phone."

He was handed a touchscreen cell phone.

"Okay. That's your app right there. Just tap and we're away."

"What?"

"Just tap, sir."

He tapped. The video screen came to life. He was looking down at a desert, as seen from beneath the nose of a drone.

"Use your cursor keys, sir. Blue button to lock on, red button to fire. Take your time."

What the fuck?

"Here comes the target. Steady, sir..."

He wasn't in the mood for stupid bullshit video games. He stabbed his thumbs randomly against the touchscreen, jumped to his feet and flung the phone down on the chair. Then he stopped. Jesus Christ, that was realistic — a rocket had torn away from the drone, smashed into the desert and a huge cloud of smoke and dust was rising up.

"Gee, a miss, I'm afraid, sir."

"Wow. Almost like the real thing. I guess."

"I'm sorry, sir?"

"Looked almost real."

There was a pause and the moist Carolinian air seemed to chill.

"It *is* real."

"Really! No shit. You mean I actually... But where..."

He became aware that his photo ID was now an object of interest. He covered it casually with his hand.

"Let's just say it's in a very big, hot country."

"Okay."

"Ah, sir, would you mind just waiting here a moment?"

Yes, he would.

"Sorry, gotta go."

11

He fled the tent, dodged around behind it, and made for the crowds at the barbecue stand. After ten minutes of ducking and lurking it seemed safe to conclude that he wasn't being pursued. A mild elation suffused his ramshackle frame. He would have *something* to tell Katherine after all. They're *phoning it in* now — can you believe it? He could hardly wait to get back to Brooklyn and *blog* about it. Or, better still, he could get out of here, pull off the highway and *blog away* from his cell phone. Was there any way he could get hold of that app? Presumably it wasn't available in the App Store.

No, forget it, he thought. His luck had lasted way longer than usual; it was time to leave. And he would have done so, right then, if he hadn't seen three black SUVs emerge from the forest, drive across the lawn and head for the row of tents. Across the lawn! This had to be someone important. He felt something that he experienced only on very special occasions — a pang of pure political lust. Oh, who could it be! Let it be... No, not him, let it be... Well, he had to find out. But the cars had stopped outside the last tent in the row. He wasn't going back there again. He needed to loiter inconspicuously and wait for the cars to return.

He decided to hide behind the inflatable castle.

Very quickly, he realized that this was a bad decision. Someone was tugging at his sleeve. It was a small girl, aged about nine.

"Why are you hiding?"

"I'm not. I'm just getting out of the sun'."

"There's more shade on the other side."

"I prefer it here."

"But your head is in the sun."

"It's the rest of me I'm worried about."

"Your head's more important. You'll get heatstroke."

"No, I won't."

She pulled a skeptical face and changed her line of questioning.

"Are you here for the picnic?"

"Amongst other things."

"What's your name?"

"My name's Jeff. What's yours?"

"Amelie."

"Hi, Amelie. Having fun?"

"Yeah, I guess."

"Does your dad work here?"

A shade of defiance colored Amelie's face.

"No, my mom. And I'm prohibited, uh... I'm not allowed to say where my dad is."

Prohibited? It was a warning sign, but recklessness overcame him.

"Really? That's weird. Why not?"

She thought for a moment then shook her head.

"I'm not allowed to say why not."

"Huh. Who says?"

Another moment of thought — and a frown of anguish.

"No, it's okay. I get it," he said. "Is your mom here now?"

A nervous pull at her hair.

"She's gone to get more wine."

"That's good."

"Do you want to come on the castle?"

He surveyed the scene. There were other grown-ups inside, bouncing grimly away, so it was probably all right. Good cover, too. And he could still observe the motorcade — he might even get a better view on a good bounce.

"Sure."

They climbed in and the bouncing began.

And it would, Jeff Crock felt convinced, have been good, clean fun, had not Amelie and her little friends decided that the only thing better than bouncing was bouncing *into* harmless, truth-seeking *bloggers* and flipping them upside down. Eventually — and, on reflection, predictably — things got out of control and he found himself lying face-down on the grass with Amelie sitting on his shoulders and shrieking with delight.

Then a pair of elegant designer sandals came into view. Amelie dismounted.

"Mommy's back!"

Jeff looked up at a tall woman in a pale shift dress, a dark bob, and enormous sunglasses. She was holding a large glass of white wine.

"Who's your new friend, honey?"

"That's Jeff."

"Good to meet you, Jeff. Hope Amelie didn't hurt you there."

"No, no. We were doing great."

Actually, he was pretty sure he'd bruised his ribs.

"Oh..."

Amelie's mom had spotted something.

"Sweetie, hold that for mommy."

She gave her glass to her daughter and picked up something from the grass.

"You lost your..."

She was reading his photo ID.

"What was your name again?"

What *was* it?

"Actually, Jeff is a nickname. It's Burt. Burt... Burt *something*."

There were some words, he mused, that, in his experience, women were able to shout much louder than others. "Security" was one of them. By the time he had struggled to his feet, men in black baseball hats and bulky bomber jackets were converging on him from all sides.

And at that point, the motorcade returned, slowed, and then stopped to see what all the fuss was about. Down went the tinted windows. And, focusing in on the back seat of the middle vehicle, Jeff Crock experienced, full-on, what in other walks is called the money-shot.

A face pinched but hard, sagging but resilient, tanned but off-color. Eyes full of tension, rimmed around with corruption. Full, pale lips. Rich, bad teeth. Superfluous hair. Belligerent bones.

War Criminal Number Two.

And as he felt his collapsed frame sing with suffocating electricity, a single repeating phrase rang through his brain.

This is huge!

CHAPTER 3

T he escarpment dimmed from scorched brown to volcanic black as the sun retreated across the peaks of the Ethiopian highlands. To their relief, the desiccating wind dropped, the air cooled and they felt becalmed.

Then, as they stumbled their way, breathless, into Hamed Ela, they saw that the village, like a ghost ship on a fossilized sea, had been abandoned by its crew.

Together, at Sam's insistence and six steps behind him, they went from house to house — huts, really, Bonnie DiAngelo thought, but homes to the people who lived in them and had left in such a hurry. Meals abandoned, clothing discarded, money — the salt taxes? — left uncounted.

It was a rapid evacuation, she thought, but not a panic. Valuable animals had been rounded up and herded out. No one had been left behind. It was what you did when you woke up and found — or heard — Military Activity on your African doorstep.

"Where did they go, Sam?" she said.

The boy was running his hand along the doorframe of a hut and wrinkling his nose.

"Sam?"

He looked up and gestured to the north. "I think that way."

Leo looked disconsolate, verging on angry, like a business leader who'd made the wrong call and lacked any means to pretend otherwise.

"Well," she said. "I guess we spend the night here. Maybe we should get on the sat phone and —"

"It's not working," Leo said.

"Why not?"

"I don't know. No connection. Satellite not found."

"Oh. Maybe in the morning."

"Maybe. Where's Sam?"

"He's right over —"

But Sam had vanished. *That's it*, she thought. Here it is, that dumb, random, binary fate that still ruled in the uncapitalized half of the world: You're alive, you're dead, it's just a probability thing, nothing personal — completely impersonal, in scientific fact. But then, no; it was vanity. She ought to stop dramatizing herself. Sam's gray shadow was beckoning them on, towards the east and the edge of the outcrop. They followed.

And down on the plain, torn perpendicular to the trail that the caravans took to the salt flats, was a great longitudinal scar of red, black and yellow rock, now turning brown in the weakening light.

For a minute or so no one spoke. It was hard to judge the scale of the thing at this distance, but it was huge.

"So what is that?" she asked, but got no answer. "Leo?"

But Leo was staring at Sam. The boy's head was tipped back, his nose wrinkling again.

"Smell something?" Leo said.

Sam nodded.

"Know what it is?"

A shake of the head.

"Me neither."

A pause.

"Go a bit closer?"

Another nod. The two men started down towards the plain. She hesitated. What could they smell? Her senses couldn't match theirs. Did she want to find out? She could just wait here and... No. She'd be sitting here in the dark, her flashlight would die after an hour and then what? Better to bust her ankle within shouting distance than slip away in silence. Sure, she was fit for her age. All the same...

*

B y the time they reached the scar, the light had almost gone. Leo had taken out his flashlight; she did the same.

There had been an impact. Something very large had smashed into the ground and traveled some distance — how far, it was impossible to tell in the gloom. But, from the way that the rocks and gravel had been scattered, Leo said, the trajectory of this object was clear. It had come out of the north-west. He took out his GPS and marked their position carefully.

"Did you mark the village?" she said.

"It was already marked. Do you have your camera?"

"Yes."

"Can you take pictures?"

"What of?"

"Everything."

"Okay."

"Except Sam. We'll leave him out of this, yes?"

"If you say so."

So now she was official expedition photographer, but no portraits, please. And if Leo thought any plane-crash images were going in the brochure, well, they weren't.

16

Now Leo took the lead. She followed, and Sam, without a flashlight but apparently able to see in the dark, became their rear gunner. After a hundred yards or so they began to find wreckage.

"This," Leo said, pointing. A *blip* on the GPS.

She photographed a shard of gray metal with rivets along one edge.

"And this," he said, working his flashlight like a fashion-shoot director until shadows were minimized and the object rendered in sharp relief.

She photographed a steel plate covered with dense, black numbering.

"Here." *Blip.*

Some kind of circuit board, with trailing wires.

"And here."

A small, black box — a computer hard drive? Everything in small pieces, she thought. Fragments. Unsurvivable.

They progressed: Sam silently on guard, barely visible behind them; and Leo, darting from side to side, flicking his flashlight; and herself, sweating despite the cooling air, snapping his pictures and now thinking the unthinkable.

"Leo," she said. "Wait. Should we be doing this? The passengers..."

He stopped.

"No, no, no," he said, all at once flustered, as if there'd been some silly mistake. "No passengers. You were worried. I'm sorry. You thought I was going to make you —"

"Yes, but the crew?"

"No crew."

"No crew? Then what —"

"Unmanned."

"Unmanned what?"

"Aerial vehicle. Drone."

Yes, she thought, a *drone*. You saw pictures of them in the New York Times. They looked like toy gliders. *This* was not a toy glider.

"You can tell that?"

Leo was firm.

"Yes."

She waited for him to explain. Realizing that he had to say more, he seemed to improvise. Sam, immobile, listened from the gloom.

"No seats, no baggage, no fabric. Other stuff. I know a bit about planes, so... I knew it wasn't a plane."

"But it's — it must have been so big."

Unexpectedly, Leo laughed, loudly.

"Yeah! It's big, my God."

Bodies or no bodies, she thought, survivors or no survivors — this had to end. She wasn't in this business, and neither was Leo, was he? What usually happened to people who photographed Military Activity? And not just any old Military Activity, if Leo wasn't talking out of his ass.

"Leo, I don't like this. Let's go back to the village and wait for help."

Leo lowered his flashlight.

"Okay, you're right. I'm sorry. This is just so... We'll go back. Just a hundred meters more, okay?"

17

She shone her flashlight in his face.

"Okay. But no more photos."

"No more photos."

They moved on, Sam lingering ever more obscurely behind them.

But now, what had been merely frightening became, by turns, both sinister and absurd. Large, shiny-metal tanks, with hosepipes attached. A *Wholefoods Market* recyclable eco-bag full of glossy corporate literature. A shower head. More plastic pipes, like spilled guts. A copy of *USA Today*, from three months ago. A mobile phone in a pretty, pink case.

With great care, Leo picked the phone up by the strap attached to its case and examined it under his flashlight. Then he brought it close to his nose and sniffed at it. Apparently satisfied, he removed the phone from its case.

"Does it work?" she asked.

"I don't think we should find out."

With his flashlight wedged between chin and shoulder, he popped the back cover off the phone and removed a memory card. Then he slipped the cover back on and positioned the phone exactly as he had found it.

So what did he want to be now, she wondered — a spy?

"What do you suppose is on that?"

"Could be anything."

Right, she thought. Friends and family. Vacation snaps. Account numbers. Porn. Facebook crap. Military secrets.

"Do you know what you're doing?"

"Most of the time."

Most of the time.

"So whose drone is this?"

"I'm assuming it's yours."

"Mine?"

Leo removed the memory card from his GPS. Then he took out a glasses case from his cargo pants, opened it and removed a pair of sunglasses.

"One day we'll all have them. Give me the card from your camera."

She gave it to him. He pried up the inner lining of the case with his thumbnail, slipped all three memory cards underneath, and packed the whole thing away again.

"They're getting cheaper, better, bigger. So why not?" He paused. "Well, maybe not *this* big."

Great, she thought. Drone wars everywhere and ours are the biggest. But could she smell something here? Something musty and organic?

"Let's go back now, Leo."

"Sure, okay, let's go."

Sam stood off to the side in the dark, and their little expedition reversed itself in silence.

And what, she wondered, was Sam thinking? Interesting question. How did he feel about having his desert despoiled like this? What kind of tip or bonus could make up for it? Was he angry? Probably. She wanted to apologize to Sam for the alien garbage in his unspoiled wilderness and, well, just the whole concept of it, really — the parceling up of the globe into *commands* and the sheer un-neighborliness of it all. Eco Adventures prided itself — herself — on its light footprint and sensitivity. Crashing military hardware into your host's backyard wasn't on. At least it hadn't hit the village. No, it hadn't, and yet...

"Leo."

"Yes?"

"Why did the villagers leave? The crash site is a long way from —"

"They were afraid of something."

"That smell?"

"Maybe."

"There was more than one explosion."

"I think it shot off some rockets or something. Before it crashed."

"Why?"

"I have no idea. Maybe it got lost."

"They send these things over Yemen from Djibouti, don't they?"

"Yes. But this one is not from Djibouti."

"Where, then?"

"Good question."

"It's probably an accident, though?"

Leo muttered something that she couldn't make out. She dropped back and fell in step with Sam. He seemed surprised, but pleased.

"I'm sorry, but that's all wrong," she said, with an emphatic gesture. "That's really too much. What a mess we make, sometimes — honestly!"

So there she was, apologizing for America. Could you do that? ("*Never!*" she imagined she heard someone say loudly, over the horizon). But just this once, on the quiet, between herself and this boy... Well, she wasn't the President. So there.

"I think people ought to see this land," she went on. Sam smiled at her. "I mean, not too many. Sustainable." A nod towards Leo. "So fragile."

"People are fragile," Sam said.

"Yes, people too." Fragility everywhere.

"It's hard to live here."

"Even so, it's a special place."

Sam looked at her.

"Where are you from?"

"Boston."

"Is that a special place?"

"Uh, well, maybe. It's different. I suppose it depends —"

"To you?"

"It's home, so..."

"I think I will go there one day."

"You should."

And then, unprompted, he began to describe for her the terms under which life was conducted in this brutal, burning, fragile void: The ever-present drought, relieved perhaps in the two short rainy seasons; the lack of permanent vegetation, except for one river valley in the extreme south; the imperative of following the rains; the impossibility of following them when politics closed the borders; the diet limited to not much more than whatever the goats could provide; the presence of bandits in the north and hostile tribes in the south and clan rivalry everywhere; social customs, such as the filing of teeth; the remoteness of the government; the memory of famine in Tigray in the highlands; the regular loss of valuable animals to the drought; the occasional discovery of antiquities, which excited foreign experts; the joys of a marriage linking two families, and thus two villages; the unpredictable pleasures of meeting visitors like herself.

And, finally, in short, he wasn't *that* upset that she'd littered his ancestral domain with smart, but now useless, war-fighting technology.

"Thanks," she said.

They pressed on, their pace slowing. Bonnie felt the glow of Sam's dissertation and the hideous excitement of their discovery slip away, to be replaced by exhaustion. Then, at the point where they were to turn west to climb back up to the village, she remembered that it was her sixty-second birthday — and fatigue turned to light-headed elation. Much was survivable, after all. Things might drop out of the sky, but, if they didn't blow your head off, you were fully entitled to keep right on.

Leo was looking at her.

"I haven't forgotten, you know. When we get there, we shall celebrate. I'm carrying something special."

He tapped his backpack.

Perhaps you are, she thought.

"I'm too tired."

"You'll be able to rest soon."

But then, as they crept up upon the last ridge before the village, she heard the thumping of the helicopter.

CHAPTER 4

The helicopter, though large and plainly military in character, Bonnie DiAngelo thought, lacked confidence in its identity; it bore few markings. No flags, no insignia, no numbers — just an aggressively abstract logo of no obvious import. Perhaps it had been borrowed from a movie studio.

While it maneuvered to land — too close to them, surely — they sheltered from its downdraft and blazing lights behind one of the abandoned huts. When the whirring sandstorm subsided, she looked for Sam. But this time the boy had given himself up fully to his ancestral night — rifle, sneakers and all.

The helicopter's engine cut out and its blades coasted to a stop. Somehow this told her that they weren't simply going to be offered a lift. Leo's hat had blown away, but he made no effort to retrieve it.

"Stick with me," he said, as if he thought she might prefer to join Sam on his midnight run.

From the helicopter there came the squeaking of doors and the clattering of steps. In the dim square of the doorway, a slight silhouette appeared. As it edged towards the top of the steps, the helicopter's external lights revealed desert boots, black pants, a loose white polo shirt and a young face, tanned, confident and curious. One very careful survey of the terrain from his vantage point, a leap and a bound, and he was with them.

"Just the two of you?"

Leo nodded. British accent, she thought. And not so young; blond hair turning to gray, receding at the temples.

"Not three?"

"Just two," Leo said.

No pictures of Sam, he'd said earlier. Not just cultural sensitivity; a precaution.

"Only we thought we saw... Well, that's okay, then. Now *you*," he said, pointing at Leo, "...are Mr. Vargas? All the way from Costa Rica?"

"Who are you?" Leo said.

"And *you*... Are Mrs. DiAngelo. American. Very good. No doubt you'll be wanting a lift, and that's fine, we're all set up for that and it won't cost you a penny. Just the two of you. Good."

He rubbed his hands together, like a father conscripted for after-school taxi duty and determined to evince enthusiasm.

"We'll get going shortly. Just a few details first."

"Our plan is to spend the night here," Leo said. "But I would like to know who you are."

"Here? But they've all gone!" Arms spread wide in mock incredulity. "You can't stay here."

"Our caravan will return tomorrow."

"It won't, you know. It won't."

"Why not?" she asked.

He turned his smile on her.

"The thing is, they've declared an exclusion zone. The government. The Ethiopians."

He let her absorb this fact.

"So, obviously, nobody's coming in or out. That's all there is to it, really."

He folded his arms, as if resting his case.

"An exclusion zone?" she said.

"On your little expedition," he said, "you must have noticed it. Bit of a mess, down there, isn't it? We could see you on the infra-red, with your little torches. And on the thermal imaging. All two of you."

"So that whatever-it-is that crashed — that's yours?"

"We're just part of the clean-up."

She decided to test his patience.

"Well, so you say, but who are you?"

The smile collapsed on one side.

"My name is Andrew, Mrs. DiAngelo. I work for a company, that through a long chain of contracts and connections and so on and so forth, that I won't bore you with right now, is ultimately acting for and responsible to your very own State Department."

"Oh, them..."

"And — I hope you don't mind my saying this — but a woman of your intelligence — Princeton, no less! — who knows her way around Africa, keeps up with current affairs and has a daughter who works in the defense industry, ought to recognize a national security emergency when she sees one."

"My daughter works in the defense industry?"

Leo touched her elbow gently.

"Where are you going to take us?" he said.

Andrew turned back to Leo, the smile gone now.

"Back to base. For fuel. Then we'll see."

"All right. We'll come with you."

"Great. Splendid."

A big sigh.

"Now, before we all hop on — electronic devices. What have we got?"

He looked from Leo to Bonnie and back to Leo, as if they were children who might or might not have presents for teacher.

"Cameras? Anyone?"

"I have a camera," she said.

"May I?"

She gave him her camera. Expertly, he opened the memory compartment.

"There's no card in here, Mrs. DiAngelo."

"I just filled one up."

"Mm. You were going to put a new one in later."

He pointed to the helicopter.

"To be perfectly honest... I'd really prefer *not* to ask for help here. Yes? I want everything electronic. Cards, phones, the lot."

They removed their packs and emptied their pockets. With impatient dexterity, Andrew inspected and discarded, examined and confiscated. When it was over, Leo's glasses case was not the first thing Leo picked up, and it was not the last.

Andrew seemed satisfied. The smile perked up again at both corners.

"You will, of course, each get a receipt. Especially for Mr. Vargas's satellite phone and his GPS, which happen to be very expensive models. Very nice indeed. So, I think we're ready —"

He broke off because two men in fatigues had jumped from the helicopter. They ran to the rear of the craft and crouched in the darkness. A searchlight snapped on and swung its beam in the same direction.

Andrew swore under his breath.

"You two wait here. What the hell —"

He ran to the helicopter. Bonnie could hear the sound of racing engines. Leo grasped her hand and tugged her towards the nearest hut. A set of yellow headlights appeared in the gloom, then a second, brighter pair. The grilles of two trucks flashed in the searchlight. Rifle shots rang out. Leo pushed her into the hut and rolled in after her. She heard Andrew yelling and swearing.

They crawled to the back of the hut. Leo pressed her to the floor and folded his arms over her head. The battle outside was ragged and ill-disciplined, like a middle-of-the-night firework binge conducted by a drunken neighbor.

The helicopter engine began to whine. Shadows jumped and the noise of the trucks reeled around behind them. A gale of sand and grit blasted into the hut as the helicopter rose and the shadows flickered again.

"Stay down," Leo rasped in her ear.

She stayed down. The pounding of the helicopter receded, fading into the sky to an insolent salute of pot-shots. For a moment there was quiet. Then came the crunching of tires at their door. A slam, some footsteps and a sarcastic rap on the doorframe.

The bandits, she thought. After all this, the bloody bandits. Taking advantage of a *national security emergency*. Then a voice.

"Anybody home?"

An American accent. She felt Leo fall away from her.

"Are you..."

"Am I what?"

"Are you kidnapping us?"

"Why no, ma'am. My name's Jay and I'm rescuing you."

CHAPTER 5

O wing to the treachery of the over-active and under-parented Amelie, Jeff Crock (real name Jefferson Crockett, fake name Burt *something*) had been zapped, dragged out, roughed up, shaken down, harangued, insulted, accused, intimidated, coerced, compared to Hitler, belittled and, worst of all by far, threatened with a law suit by a rich and aggressive corporation of mysterious ownership that was, by all appearances, on the best of terms with war criminals.

Then, on the way home in a second (and much cheaper) rental car, the black Mercedes having been impounded — and, for all he knew, dismantled — by Fair Meadow Solutions' forensic security, he found himself detained and questioned at length by the Border and Immigration Joint Security Task Force, which had woken up and decided that this was an ideal day for conducting a "routine sweep" along the interstate. Coincidence? This despite his elongated stature, his unyieldingly Caledonian complexion and a passport convincing enough for Fair Meadow Solutions' finest.

Plus, he would have to break the news about the Mercedes to Katherine.

And yet, it had been a good day.

Why? Well, what could you really do to someone for sneaking into a *picnic* and bouncing in an inflatable castle? The threat of a law suit was a joke. And he didn't have a beard, so they couldn't plausibly allege that his intentions towards the picnic were terroristic. Weirdly, they hadn't mentioned the lecture he'd attended. But he had been forced to sign an agreement to remain silent about his adventure (yeah, right!) and had been given to understand that he was going to be under heavy surveillance from now on. By what or whom wasn't stated.

But the thing was this: He'd gained an invaluable piece of intelligence. War Criminal Number Two — henceforth just Number Two for short — was into something that smelled real bad. Or good, depending on your point of view.

Global Faith Initiatives, unpaid diplomacy, book royalties to charity — it was all bullshit, a smoke screen. Open your eyes, people! Number Two might no longer be in a position to start any more wars — *might* not — but it was obvious that his addiction hadn't been cured. Why else would he be hanging out at the drone factory? What new martial fantasy had drawn him there? Would any wedding party anywhere in the Developing World be safe if he were not stopped? And what if there was a money connection, too? Cash being the other thing Number Two couldn't get enough of.

It would be tough to persuade Katherine to sanction a proper investigation. But, since he was sitting in her Upper West Side office, right across the desk from her, and although she was beaming at him in her I-cope-with-difficult-kids way, it was worth a try.

He let her have it.

"It was definitely him. This could be huge. We've got to go after it."

"Well, he *is* in the country. Someone's giving him a medal."

Another one!

"No! Who is it this time?"

"Oh, I don't know. The Florida Realtors' Association?"

"Shit!"

"All right, Jeff. So you saw him there. And it's not on his public itinerary, so it looks a bit sleazy. But what else have we got?"

"But *why* was he there? He's working for someone else, that's what I think. I mean, he's basically a gofer, right? Doing the dirty work for the real boss?"

"Well..."

"Needy guy, too. Needs the praise, the applause, the fucking medals. Wants them to let him into the club."

"Look, Jeff —"

"You should see the crap they drop from these drones. Oh! And you know what? You can do it from your phone now."

"Your phone?"

"Yeah, I did it myself. There's an app. You can see everything on the screen. You can actually fly the fucker, and then it's just tap-tap-boom!"

"That's certainly a story, you're right about that. Pity we can't back it up."

Out of Katherine's sight, Jeff Crock's right foot began, unbidden, to flail in righteous agitation.

"I think there's a conspiracy," he said.

"But there's always a conspiracy, Jeff," Katherine said, her voice softening into tell-it-to-Mommy mode. "The world runs on conspiracy these days. We both know that, don't we? Our job is to be selective. That way we can make a difference. Can't we, Jeff?"

"I think I should follow him back to London."

"London's very expensive, Jeff."

"I thought England went bust."

"Even so. And besides, you've kind of blown your cover already, haven't you?"

Jeff's foot stilled itself. She wasn't buying it. The more reasonable she got, the more obvious it was.

"And there was definitely nothing special about this new drone?"

"No."

"And yet it got quite a reception, you say?"

"Yeah."

"Why was that, do you think?"

"Fuck knows."

"Think back. Remember what you saw. Visualize. See it again in your mind's eye."

Here we go, he thought. We'll be doing yoga in a moment. Katherine's problem was that she put too much emphasis on intellectual speculation and thought experiments, and not enough on, say, hacking people's email or going through their trash cans.

He blamed the parents.

Katherine was the fifty-ish but young-looking daughter of celebrity academics who — once their book on preserving American values while achieving self-worth and financial security in a China-dominated world had become first a blogospheric sensation and then a Hollywood franchise — had parachuted out of their ivory tower and into talk-show heaven. Now retired, they spent their days island-hopping around the Caribbean, with more style than caution. Katherine had been left with her grandparents' now-Ponzified money, a finely-developed sense of the ridiculous and the obligation to uphold the family's intellectual tradition.

"I've got nothing," he said.

"Oh well."

There was a pause. Katherine brushed her shoulder-length blonde hair behind her ears.

"Tell you what, Jeff."

He folded his arms and put his head on one side.

"What?"

"You're going to like this. And it involves foreign travel."

So there was a budget, after all.

"You know there are certain places I can't go, right?"

"Central America."

He unfolded his arms and sat up.

"Go on."

This sounded promising. There had been a series of failed right-wing coups in Central and South America, accompanied, like rice and beans, by the usual protestations of disinterest up north. But something was definitely cooking down there, and it was only a matter of time, conventional wisdom held, before some faux-populist businessman ate an elected leftist for lunch.

"Costa Rica."

Nice place, he thought. Rainforests, tree frogs, volcanoes, pineapples, coffee, palm oil, turtles, business-friendly government low down on the list of possible coup targets.

"So what's happening down there?"

"Someone is constructing a kind of private resort for Americans only."

This was hardly news.

"And?"

"It's one of these gated, high-security places."

"It would be."

"Yes. But it goes much further than that. My sources say that it's positively fortified. And it's enormous. And no one can figure out who's really behind it."

"Fortified?"

"Like something out of Baghdad. Only much prettier, obviously. Nice landscaping."

It was intriguing.

"Costa Rica doesn't have an army," Jeff said.

"No. Don't really see a connection, though."

"Guess not."

"Could just be paranoia and too much money."

"Possibly."

"Or you could go down there and take a look for yourself."

He considered. It was probably just the tax-exempt folly of some billionaire survivalist who'd been tuning in too often to Freedom News Network. But he hadn't had a foreign vacation in a long while...

"Well," he said, drawing out the word to great length in order to tease her, "I'll go down there if you really think it's worthwhile."

"I think so, yes. Thanks, Jeff. I'll set things in motion. Can you be ready to ship out by Thursday?"

"I guess so."

"That's really good of you, Jeff."

"No problem. Are we done?"

"Almost."

Katherine's eyes narrowed, indicating that she was about to enter painful-truths mode. Shit, he thought.

"Jeff — the war criminal thing? You know I agree with you, don't you? Wholeheartedly. In every detail. Well, pretty much. But, well, I know you've heard this before, but don't you think it's really time, at long last, after everything that's happened, after all the arguments and all we've been through and all the moving on and so forth — isn't it time you were over it?"

There was a perfectly good filing cabinet in the photocopier room next door, and there was no reason, he felt, for not going in there right now and vandalizing it severely. The only thing that prevented him from following this course was iron self-control — and the memory of what had happened last time. The drawers had jammed and the whole thing had ended in an ugly mob scene involving crowbars and chainsaws.

"Nnngh!" he said.

"Just think about what I've said."

"Yes, Katherine."

"Well, there we are! We're done."

Jeff unclenched his fists and rose carefully from his chair.

"Oh, one last thing," Katherine said. "I've been getting phone calls. Did you take the Mercedes back?"

*

I n the event, Katherine was understanding about the Mercedes. Perhaps she had feared for her filing cabinet.

Jeff stumbled on to a number 2 train and, under cover of darkness and stopping only to collect a six-pack from a bodega, dragged himself home to his rented one-bed on the extreme northern fringe of what he regarded as the Official Park Slope Gentrification Zone. His mood was one of equable trepidation. This turned out to be prescient. His apartment had been ransacked in the most blatant, condescending and by-the-numbers manner. It was not the first time. He cleared a space on the couch, yawned and flopped down.

All his top-secret material was stored securely off-site. That went without saying, so this petty intrusion was just meant to piss him off. Actually, right now he didn't have any top-secret material worth the name. But the principle applied.

He turned on the TV and flipped, as he often did, to Freedom News Network. Some people might have diagnosed in this act a psychological weakness or disorder — narcissistic self-pity, perhaps, or masochism, or a complex involving the fetishization of victimhood and the desire for self-abnegation. He called it research.

Unusually, they were broadcasting from Europe — it looked like London. He turned the volume up.

Some civilian dumb-ass, it appeared, had fought off an attacker and saved the Prime Minister from injury. The PM's security detail had, it seemed clear, fucked up royally, and this guy had jumped in. What a hero! (Although, looking at his flabby, vacant face, you had to wonder if he'd had any idea what he was doing.) And then — get this — he'd spent half an hour — *half an hour* — berating the PM about what was wrong with the man personally, his government, the country, and the world in general.

And the PM, out of gratitude, embarrassment, and an acute awareness of the PR peril of his situation, and with the cameras rolling, had stood there and taken it. Sensation! The whole, brain-dead, right-wing rant. Incredible! The Brits were totally screwed. No wonder they'd gone bust.

And look at this: The guy's name was *Dolt*. John Dolt. Come on, this was too much. And now, according to mallet-headed Flint Gunner, FNN's man on the scene, the question everybody's asking is *Who is John Dolt?*

Give me a break.

He turned off the TV, headed into the bedroom, shook the tangled clothes and scattered books from the comforter, disrobed and climbed into bed.

Who the fuck was *John Dolt?*

Nnngh.

CHAPTER 6

J ay Percival, it seemed to Bonnie DiAngelo as she struggled to decode the shifty résumé he gave her, wished to represent himself as some kind of renegade American spy with a self-awarded license to roam Africa and cause trouble. He claimed "good friends" in South Africa and contacts everywhere.

And his companions, six of them, were indeed bandits.

But, Jay explained as they rattled and careened their way across volcanic deserts to his operating base of the moment in the midst of an aerially-unremarkable Eritrean village, banditry was not always all it was cracked down to be. These guys, for example, had always treated their captives well and handed over the goods promptly upon payment. Local employment opportunities were poor; but, for now, these six were employed by *him*, so everyone was happy. He was a one-man economic stimulus and much respected in the village.

So everyone was in good shape, Jay insisted — except, of course, Leo, who had been hit in the back by shrapnel and was in pain though not in danger. His *guys* had not had the best training, Jay conceded. He was very sorry.

Jay was a like a wild animal, she thought, a little long in the tooth but still vital, a nervous and probably reckless predator with clear, restless eyes, a hunter's brain and all manner of instincts, some unnamable, on call. This picture of Darwinian exuberance, however, was contradicted by the fact that he wore slick, black dress shoes, like a fashion-conscious lawyer; and that, underneath the dust and sand, they had surely been recently polished.

As soon as they arrived in the village, the trucks were camouflaged with wooden fencing and palm thatch. No privacy anywhere any more, Jay told her. A sky full of spies, for all eternity. Then Leo was taken away for treatment and Jay asked Bonnie if she would be interested in knowing what the hell he was up to.

"Yes."

"Then come this way."

He led her to a hut full of electronic gear and batteries.

"Have a seat."

She sat down on a palm mat, the only seating available.

"Tea?"

"Definitely."

He produced a vacuum flask and a plastic cup.

"I make it before we head out, and it's here waiting for me when we get back. Never used to like tea until I came here. This is yours."

She took her tea and drank. It was as strong as creosote.

"Okay," he said. "So you're a travel agent?"

A little respect, please, she thought.

"Eco Adventures. For educated travelers."

"I get it. Light footprint and all that. No littering."

"That's it."

"Been in this part of Africa before?"

"Not really."

"But you've been most places."

"Except the war zones."

"Right."

He paused.

"You say you rescued us," she said.

"From Andy."

"Andrew?"

"That's the guy."

"Who's going to rescue us from *you?*"

He laughed.

"That's good. A day like the one you've just had and you still have your sense of humor. When was the last time you were in a gun fight?"

"Never."

"A new experience. That's why you travel, correct?"

"Correct."

He laughed again, softly, and drank his tea.

"I actually don't know much about you," he said. "Just what I got from listening to Andy." He tapped his stack of equipment with his well-fitted toe.

"We didn't know if we would get down there before Andy. Wanted to take a look at the drone. Didn't have time, as it turned out. But at least we got you."

"Do you know what happened to Sam?"

Something snapped on, she thought — one of his animal instincts? He put his tea down.

"Who's Sam?"

"Our guide. He disappeared. Just before the helicopter landed."

A pause.

"Local?"

"One of those young Afar guys. Rather sweet."

"Never heard 'em called sweet before. You didn't see him go?"

"No."

Jay sat back, tapped his chin with his fist and made a show of pondering Sam's fate — a performance for her benefit?

"Don't rightly know what to do about that for now." He sighed. "Andy didn't see him?"

"No. Except on his *thermal imaging*."

"Oh, for sure. Got all the toys, Andy's people. Most likely had a surveillance drone tailing the big guy."

Well now, she thought, was a good time to find out exactly what sort of trouble she and Leo were really in.

"*Andy's people* — who are they?"

He sniffed and rubbed his nose.

"Private contractors. It's all private contractors, now."

"Not the government?"

"Who's the government?"

Was that an answer or an attitude? She put her tea down.

"I think that's all I can drink. A bit too strong."

"Really? I'll bear that in mind when I fix breakfast."

"Thanks. How about telling me why you *rescued* us?"

"Yup. Okay. One moment."

He reached over to his equipment and punched in a number on a keypad.

"Time to change frequency. Now, why did I rescue you from Andy? Seems like a fairly harmless guy, right? Kind of officious, maybe a little — what's the word? — smarmy? Didn't threaten you or anything, did he?"

"Maybe a little."

"Okay. Guy's probably feeling the pressure. Did he say where he wanted to take you?"

"His base. To refuel. Then..."

"They didn't need to refuel. They could have flown to Asmara. Or Djibouti. Sana'a. Khartoum, Addis."

"Oh."

"And this base of theirs, well, I'd like to know where it is, because that's one of the things my boss is paying me to find out. I don't suppose Andy happened to mention..."

"No. Who's your boss?"

"One of Africa's elder statesmen. One of the good guys. You won't have heard of him."

"He wants to find out about this drone thing?"

"Hates the idea of 'em flying over his house."

She pictured a dignified, but indignant, Mandela-type standing on his back porch, waving his fist at aerial intruders — and found herself laughing.

"But it's good you didn't go with Andy," Jay said, "because Andy's got some pretty questionable friends, and *their* friends are even worse. And, the way it works these days is, if you've got a problem you don't want to deal with, you can hand it on to someone else. And maybe the someone else will hand it on, too. No telling where you're going to end up. Until it's too late and nobody's responsible because they all asked for and were all given *assurances*. With me?"

She wanted to say "yes", but no words came.

"I guess you are," he said.

Jay poured himself more tea.

"You saw their new toy."

"Some toy."

"Exactly. Don't seem to working quite right yet, but there you go. And they don't want anybody to know about it."

"But I do. And so do you."

"They don't know about me. Let me ask you this. Would anyone be surprised if you went missing in Africa and never showed up again?"

"Me? Maybe not. What about Leo?"

"Mr. Vargas, the prominent global citizen, who's pro-business but wants to save the three-toed sloth and the rainforests, especially *his* forests, and also abolish poverty. Even I've heard of him. Guy's got a bit of a reputation. Something for Andy's friends to get their teeth into. You need to understand we're talking about people who can't tell the difference between a Costa Rican businessman and Fidel Castro."

She remembered what she felt when she first met Leo, just after he opened that original little hotel of his, up near Arenal, and she brought in his first big group: Here's a man who wants to make a lot of friends — and influence everyone.

"I guess he can command publicity," she said.

"You bet. Does he have a camera?"

"No, but I do."

"Okay, here's the question I've been itching to ask you. Don't let me down. Did you get pictures?"

"Yes."

"Have you still got them?"

"Yes."

"Where are they?"

"Leo hid them. With his glasses."

"Bonnie, you are one hell of a travel agent. Let's go see."

*

"**Y**ou found *what?*" Jay said, starting up his laptop. Leo, propped up against sacks of camel fodder, stiff but alert, she thought — and probably sizing up Jay the freelance intel man for a role in one of his *agendas* — described the homely junk they'd found amid the wreckage of the drone.

"*Corporate literature?*" Jay said. "Did you read it?"

Leo reached inside his shirt, drew out a thin, glossy flyer and offered it to Jay.

"Green Lake Robotics," Jay read. "*The world at your robotic fingertips.* Huh. Or under your robotic heel, I guess. Depending. Green Lake? New gang to me. And there was a cell phone? You got that, too?"

"One moment." Leo took out his glasses case and removed the memory cards. "GPS," he said, handing the cards one by one to Jay, "pictures, phone."

Jay plugged the phone card into his laptop and began clicking and typing.

"Encrypted. Going to need some help on that. So these people aren't complete idiots. Not to the point of leaving their laundry or their lunch inside the freaking drone. Maybe they're really busy? Can't keep up with demand?"

He plugged in the GPS card.

"Okay, good. Now let's see the pictures."

Bonnie shifted her position so that she could see the screen but Jay turned it away from her. Why didn't he want her to see her own pictures?

Jay's face assumed a look of cold, cat-like intensity as he clicked slowly through the images. At the end he paused and glanced up at Bonnie, without changing his expression. Then he looked down again and clicked through the pictures, slowly, a second time.

"The village was completely empty, wasn't it?"

"Yes," she said.

"And you looked pretty much everywhere?"

"Everywhere."

"Nobody left behind."

"Nobody."

"The wind," Jay said, "was blowing pretty fierce all day, wasn't it?"

"We felt it in the canyon."

"Uh-huh."

There was a moment of expectant silence. Come on, Jay, Bonnie thought, let's have some intelligence, let's have your analysis. And then, not to be ungrateful or anything, but let's talk about how we're going to get out of here and go home.

"So what do you think?" Leo said.

Jay turned his computer off. "What I'm thinking," he said, "is, why are Andy's friends building giant crop-spraying drones? And why are they sending them out over the desert?"

"Crop spraying?" she said.

"That would be the innocent explanation. Trouble is, it don't make sense."

"Chemicals?"

"Think about it. Think about that wind."

"But… That would be illegal, wouldn't it? I mean, apart from —"

"Oh, yeah. Big time."

"So how can they —"

"Okay, look," Jay said. "Let me ask you something, the two of you. What's your position on the Greater Persian Question?"

Don't go political on us, she thought. Don't talk about *chemicals*. Just tell us when we're going home.

"What do you mean?" Leo said.

"Instability," Jay said, rubbing his eyes. "That whole region. It spreads out from the center. This isn't what *I* think, it's what *they* think. You stomp down on trouble here, it pops up over there. It's all connected. It's like whack-a-mole. Very frustrating. Such a lot of trouble finding the bad guys. Mountains every-where. So many places to hide. You know roughly where they are, but not exactly. To get lucky you need a tip-off. You send out your drone, let loose with the precision ordnance. Week later, it turns out some guy had a grudge against his neighbors. It's not working, is it? Bigger thinking is required. What if you could sanitize a whole mountain or a whole valley?"

"This isn't possible," Leo said.

Jay shrugged. "Maybe it *is* just a crop-sprayer."

For a moment no one spoke.

"Jay," Bonnie said, "whatever it is, it isn't *our* business."

"It isn't?"

"We just want to be done with this. We want to go home. We're grateful, I guess, but..."

Jay collected the memory cards and zipped them into a pocket.

"You want to go home. Not so easy."

"Why not?"

"Andy knows who you are. He can't be sure you don't have pictures. He's not going to let it rest."

"We could destroy the pictures right now."

"I'm not going to do that. Wouldn't make a difference anyhow."

She looked at Leo, but Leo said nothing. Why the reticence? And, really, why did such otherwise useful men still have to be boys, too — with their little empires, wars and agendas?

"Well, what are we going to do then, Jay?" she said.

Jay looked at Leo and tapped his pocket.

"Want me to make you copies, Mr. Vargas?"

Leo nodded.

"Leo!" she said. "What are you doing?"

"I'm just doing my job, Bonnie."

"Your job?"

"Mr. Global Citizen," Jay said. "Doesn't need the money. Does it out of a sense of duty. Not quite like me, but we're on the same side, I guess."

Leo and his agendas, she thought — his secret bloody agendas. *All* the way down that canyon, when they could have turned around; *all* the way across the desert. People had shot at her. She'd almost been poisoned. She couldn't go home. What would the accountant say?

"Leo, you didn't tell me *anything!*"

"No. I'm sorry. It was a mistake."

Well, she'd never heard him say *that* before.

"So, then, I want to hear from one of you," she said, "what exactly I'm supposed to do."

Jay looked at her.

"Don't worry," he said. "I've been thinking about that."

*

In a still, graceful, Eritrean dawn, as the sun began to warm the distant slopes of the Ethiopian escarpment, and the Great Rift cracked open and the Afar Triangle sank into the Red Sea, Bonnie DiAngelo, the American travel agent, said goodbye to Leo Vargas, the Costa Rican entrepreneur, eco-saint and spy.

Fittingly, Leo was in disguise — dressed up from head to toe like an Ethiopian camel-hand, and not unhappy about it, either. According to Jay, the sky was full not only of stars, but also spies, and you just wouldn't believe the resolution they were capable of, these days.

Jay's bandits had gone into the goat-trading business and had marshaled an authentic and convincing assembly of animals and supplies. Now, as they receded into the west, Bonnie saw Leo raise a hand. She waved back.

36

Get home safely, you lying bastard, she'd told him. *Of course*, he'd replied; *see you in Brookline.*

That they had to separate was obvious to Jay. Didn't they see the logic? Well, yes, she supposed she did. Leo and his precious cargo — computer memories, not goats — would wend their way up into the highlands, perhaps to Mek'ele. Or else to some other town — it was best not to know — from which Leo could take a bus to Addis. Buses were a great and fun way, Jay insisted, to hide from the all-seeing sky. Jay had a contact in Addis who would help Leo with his onward journey. Leo should return to Costa Rica, that being the safest place for him, and resume his preparations for the Cape Town conference. Oh, and he should remember to store those memory cards somewhere super-safe.

As for Bonnie — and Jay's attitude here irked her — she was a little more of a *problem*.

"Well, I can't stay here," she said.

"No, you can't. Nor me. Where shall we go?"

"Can't we go to Addis, like Leo?"

"I think we're out of goats."

"No, seriously —"

"Seriously, we need to go someplace else. South, I think. Most likely going to need my support systems. Ever been to Namibia?"

"Yes, it's beautiful."

"Also a long way. Obviously, we're not walking. Not even from here. Pardon me for mentioning it, but you're not as fit as Leo. Plus you're going to be a lot more obvious."

"Sky full of spies."

"Yeah."

Jay was teasing her, she thought. He had a shelf full of plans and he'd pulled one out the moment he'd seen her.

"So," he said, "we'll wait for a dark, cloudy night. Then we'll take the truck to Aksum. Then we'll buy a plane. Could be a rough ride."

"Rough ride?" she said. "The truck or the plane?"

"The truck *and* the plane."

Was this man brilliant, or exasperating — or both?

"What do we buy a plane with?"

"Cash. Don't worry, I'm loaded."

"*How* are you loaded?"

Jay smiled and shrugged — the way, Bonnie thought, pretty teens did when challenged about their beauty.

"The years of the gold-rush," Jay said. "A while back now. We used to hand out suitcases full of money. There was more than I could use. I got stuck with it. Tell you more on the trip."

"I think you should."

A de-frocked, felonious, CIA chuck-out with a redacted history, she thought. How far should she travel with him?

"Are you serious about Namibia?" she said.

"I had a farm there," he said, his voice lower. "But it got blown up. Long story. Had some friends round at the time, and... Well, I bought another one. We can go there."

Okay, she thought, we'll go to your farm. The one that hasn't blown up yet.

"There'll be some stops on the way," he said. "The plane can only go six hundred miles, max. We'll need a little help from Walter."

"Walter's your *elder statesman?*"

"He is."

"How do you contact him?"

Jay grimaced.

"Unprotected radio."

"I guess those spies in the sky have ears, too?"

"They do. But they're not always listening."

"Can't use a phone or the net?"

He shook his head.

"Totally bugged."

"So," she said. "When do we get a dark and cloudy night?"

"I'm hoping," he said, "tonight."

CHAPTER 7

This was going to be a glorious day. His luck was about to change. The light squeaking through his filthy blinds told him that a warm, sunny autumn day had dawned and, all in an instant, a great, big, high-definition panorama descended on him like a vision: Droplets of dew strung along the A40, at the end of his road; sunlight bouncing off the mirrors of the amiable old minibus he drove for the Super Westway Limousine Company; happy pigeons celebrating his good fortune up on high, perched on his corroded guttering; the morning air still scented with the perfume of last night's extravagance at the Mega Kerahi Kebab; the city shaking off its night sweats in anticipation of a New Day and a new man to command it; London lying back and waiting for it. For him.

The question was, would they be there?

John Dolt slipped out of bed, adjusted his underwear and approached the did-it-himself double-glazed window of his ground-floor bedroom. Would they be there? He was sure they would; you could tell when your turn finally arrived, when the golden envelope denied to so many flopped down on your doormat. He pried the sticky slats of the blinds apart — and there they were! Hordes of them. Shoved up against his window, crushed between the minibus, the skip and the van, taking up every square foot of the heavy-duty concrete he'd put down in place of the useless garden; staring with understandable distaste at the frontage of the house (originally pebbledash, but painted over so many times that it looked like the house had bad pores). There was even a satellite truck blocking next door's driveway.

Good, he thought. But the van was a bit of a concern. He didn't want it damaged. It was quite new — only four years old — and he wanted to keep it nice. Would this media mob respect it? It was an important asset, and essential to his various enterprises. You could get two three-piece suites in there, or a dozen gas boilers. What if they took pictures of it? Would they blank out the license plate? Suppose they photographed what was inside? He tried to remember what *was* inside. Well, it was probably okay.

Now, it wasn't like he was emotionally attached to the van. You just had to have one, didn't you? He liked it, didn't love it. Not really a pride-and-joy sort of thing. It was a white Jobba van. It got the job done.

So there they all were, waiting for him. This was his moment. How should he stage his appearance? To what profitable end could he leverage his sudden celebrity? Hadn't really given it enough thought, had he? So much excitement yesterday — and so little time in which to formulate a media strategy.

His first thought, which had occurred to him just after he finished his little chat with the Prime Minister and was being ushered away for a separate chat with a lot of policemen and some anxious blokes in suits, was *springboard.* He could use his unexpected encounter as a springboard into a TV career. It was the sort of thing that happened all the time. He couldn't sing — not even, he was sure, with the assistance of computers — but he could go on an island. Or... Well, he could go on an island, or whatever.

But wait: Your white van man was a realist, was he not? Bloody well had to be, didn't he? Was Dolt over forty? Yes. Was he overweight? Well, a little. Pretty face? Nothing special; a bit pasty and droopy, to be honest. Hair and teeth? Some investment required. Overall televisual appeal? Despite his strong chin and persuasive blue eyes, his squat stature, tufty gray-brown hair and fast-food physique argued for an emphasis on personality. Narrative or back-story? Well, his personal odyssey all the way from an Essex council estate to half a house just off the A40 contained plenty of grind and angst, but lacked that essential spark of tragedy. And when he asked himself what hurdles and setbacks he'd overcome, the answer was: Same as every other bleeder round here.

So he had no strategy. Yet it was essential that he grasp this opportunity. Perhaps he could probe the experts outside for tips? He took another peek through the blinds. This time they spotted him. The uproar was immediate.

"He's up!"

"John! Come out and talk to us!"

"What time d'you call this?"

What time was it? Ten o'clock! And he had a minibus job at eleven — transporting a girls' lacrosse team from Maida Vale to Heathrow. Shit! Could he blow it off? What, and get on the wrong side of Hamid at Super Westway? No chance. But what an idiot he was. Why hadn't he set the sodding alarm? He was going to fumble his one-and-only.

But John Dolt was at his best when under pressure — hadn't he demonstrated that yesterday? He conceived a plan. A quick shower was necessary because, for some reason, he stank. He would dress in the clothes that Hamid preferred him to wear, but which he never did. Then he would step outside, issue a brief statement, give them his mobile number and offer to grant interviews to selected outlets later in the day. After that, he would jump in the minibus and set course for Maida Vale.

It was *still* going to be a glorious day, and there was nothing that these girls or their stupid lacrosse could do to sabotage it.

In the shower, he reviewed, as if in slow motion, his triumph of the day before.

The scene was the Big Builder DIY Warehouse. He'd piloted the Jobba all the way down there on a mission from Lescek the bathroom guy to acquire a large quantity of the cheapest tiles possible that weren't plain toilet white. He hadn't really noticed at the time, but now it was obvious: Big Builder had stepped up their security. Normally, their dozy staff didn't have wires coming out of their ears. And they usually couldn't care less about the portable satnav that he never failed to remove from the Jobba; on this occasion he'd been required to demonstrate it.

After that, he'd gone straight to the bathroom section. But all the tiles, by Lescek's standards at least, were ridiculously expensive. It was very frustrating. And he'd already been on the verge of exasperation, what with the upstairs neighbors moaning about not having room to park their Micra; the council threatening him on account of the skip; letters from the VAT; the insurance about to run out on the Jobba; and Tamsin and Tamara, his daughters, constantly texting him about the latest lies their bloody mother was feeding them. Frankly, he'd been close to the edge.

And another thing that had been close to the edge — the edge of the crappy Big Builder Warehouse mile-high shelving, that is — was a pallet of plastic toilet brushes. This had been key.

Why, of all the dreary dumps in London, had the man, or his top political know-alls, chosen Big Builder DIY? A cheeky grab for the working-class vote? Some pathetic we're-all-in-this-together-but-you-have-to-do-it-yourself stunt? Whatever it was, it hadn't been planned properly. The warehouse had not been cleared of customers. Presumably, a lonely stroll with the managing director would not have provided the images required.

Anyway, just as the Prime Minister approached the very aisle in which John Dolt, oblivious and consumed with tile-rage, tottered on a Big Builder value-priced ladder, it happened.

Some nutter had come charging out of the garden section, armed with a battery-powered hedge-trimmer. Now, whether or not the PM's security blokes had been distracted by Big Builder's end-of-summer sale bargains — some of which were quite tasty, to be honest — Dolt couldn't say.

But they hadn't moved fast enough. And, if Dolt's foot hadn't slipped on the value-priced ladder's non-slip step, then the toilet brushes would not have tumbled, the crazed assailant would not have been felled, and the Prime Minister would have been — well, not toast, perhaps, but certainly topiary.

He, John Dolt, was therefore a hero. That this was merely an accidental side-effect of the dearth of affordable tiling in North London would forever be his secret.

At the time, however, he had not been so sanguine. This, too, had subsequently played out to his advantage. Because, as he rose from the warehouse's greasy floor, incensed and in pain, Dolt had been minded to vent at the first person he saw. That person just happened to be the Prime Minister.

It had taken a little while before Dolt had realized who he was talking to.

Then he'd really let rip.

As he thought about it now, in the shower, he was conscious of a certain embarrassment. Did he really believe all those things he'd said? Hadn't some of it — too much? — come straight out of the tabloids? Wasn't a lot of it just the jaundiced natter you heard in horrible pubs like the Britannia Arms in Wembley and the Royal Fusilier in Cricklewood? Stuff that crawled into a guilty hole at the back of your mind when you found yourself talking to Hamid or Lescek? And some of it had come out of nowhere at all, it seemed — what, after all, did he, John Dolt, know about terrorism or international banking? Bugger all, actually. So where had all those fiercely-argued opinions come from?

It was a mystery. But he was all showered now and there was no time for idle speculation. He toweled off and began to hunt for his limousine-driver's uniform.

Of course, the police had been quite taken with him. Less so their slick-suited and wary friends. But never mind *them*. He'd been the toast of the station, and not just because of the facts he'd placed before the PM on the subject of law and order. The cops had explained to him that certain formalities had to be gone through and, so long as he wasn't a terrorist or an extremist or an anti-war protestor — and they were quite sure he was none of these — then it was perfectly all right to *talk to the Prime Minister like that.*

They'd given him a ride home; declared the Jobba free of suspicion and restored it to its rightful place next to the skip; and two of the cops had even joined him at his table at the Mega Karahi — for his own protection, they said.

The limousine-driver's uniform was creased and crinkled, but still preferable, in the circumstances, to the cargo shorts and Big Builder fleece he would probably have worn otherwise.

He grabbed his wallet, keys, phone and satnav, grasped the handle of his front door and prepared to embrace his destiny. Then he cracked the door open and they were upon him.

"John! Over here! John!"

"John — is there anything at all you *don't* regret saying?"

"Tell us the truth, John — we can handle it!"

"Give us a quote on migrants, John! Tell us what you really think!"

"What've you got against the Germans, John?"

"John! We need some pictures of your missus!"

"Where're you going to put all the people you want to round up?"

"John! Do a rant for us! Do one now!"

"What exactly have you got against VAT? And tiles?"

"What was all that stuff about banking?"

"Don't look now — some scroungers are stealing your van!"

"John — d'you really think the Prime Minister's a wanker?"

"*John! John! John!*"

*

D olt realized very quickly, as he flung the minibus along the silky streets of Little Venice, that in becoming a Public Figure he faced something of a learning-curve.

Take, for example, his reception at the hands of the mob, as he emerged from his half-a-house. It had not been, as he had anticipated, that owed to a plucky everyman who spoke truth to power. Far from it. They had been rude and sarcastic. He had been mocked. And yet when they showed him the headlines in their papers, the tone could not have been more different. *DOLT THE HERO! DOLT TELLS IT LIKE IT IS. DOLT SPEAKS FOR ENGLAND.*

How did you explain that?

Another skill he would have to acquire was how to deal with intruders, hangers-on, groupies and such-like. The minibus had filled up, despite his protests, with some of the more aggressive members of the mob. He'd told them about the girls and the lacrosse, but that had only encouraged them. They yelled questions and obscenities at him as he maneuvered the minibus past flower vans and badly-parked Range Rovers.

What's more, if he checked his mirrors — as Hamid constantly urged — he could see an entire procession of cars and vans on his tail, with the satellite truck bringing up the rear.

Two of his back-seat questioners proved insistent. One was small and weasely, with raked-back curly hair. The other was much larger, taking up two seats, and had a head like a breeze block. This giant sounded American. The two seemed to operate as a team; one shouted questions at Dolt while the other intimidated the competition.

Dolt tried to answer their questions but, stressed-out with negotiating traffic-calming measures and preoccupied with not mowing down what passed for café culture in Maida Vale, he could not address the perplexing issues they raised with the consideration such topics merited. Instead, he fell back on the more instinctive mode he had employed with the Prime Minister. It didn't seem to matter, though. His responses were met with uproarious approval.

"Nice one, John — like it!"

"What did the guy say, Nige?"

"He said this country was built by people like him, Flint."

"He wants his country back. Guy's a friggin' patriot, Nige. You got patriots in England?"

"Yes, Flint."

The school barged into view and Dolt's heart sank. There were the girls, milling about in front of the gates, talking — quite possibly to each other — on their little phones; and there was the lacrosse gear, piled up high on the pavement — it would present a weighty challenge to the minibus, but he'd coped with worse. So far so good. The problem was the mothers: They'd illegally parked their people-carriers and four-by-fours on *both* sides of the street and there wasn't room for the minibus to squeeze through, let alone park.

Dolt cranked his window down and addressed the nearest conference of mothers.

"Excuse me, you're going to have to move," he said.

No response from the mothers. Dolt yanked on his handbrake and revved his engine.

"I *said* you're going to have to *move*, okay?"

Still no response. "Right. Here we go," Dolt muttered to himself.

"What'd he say, Nige?"

"He's mildly pissed off and he's about to make an executive decision, Flint."

Dolt dismounted from the minibus and approached the mothers.

"Oi! Excuse me! Whose car is that?" he said, pointing out the offending vehicle with what he calculated to be low-to-moderate aggression. They stopped talking and looked at him.

"That one!" Dolt said. "The big BMW."

"That's mine."

"Well, you're going to have to move it, aren't you?"

"Why?"

"And the Lexus and the thing behind that."

"Why?"

"Because I can't get the bus through, can I?"

"Why not?"

It wasn't that Dolt was inexperienced in these situations; it was just that they never got any easier. It made him sympathize with the troops in the War Zones.

"Because there isn't enough room, is there?"

"Why not?"

"Because..."

But Dolt knew the threshold of cluelessness when he saw it. The discussion would proceed from mere physics into the realm of the moral and political. He wasn't going there.

"Look," he said, "you've *got* to move it. That's all there is to it. *And* the Lexus *and* that big ugly thing behind it."

"It's a Porsche, you stupid little man!" someone yelled.

Dolt ignored this insult with great insouciance and pressed his case further.

"If I can't park, then no one's going anywhere," he said, folding his arms.

"Why not?"

"I'm not loading up the bus in the middle of the road."

"Why not?"

Word of the confrontation must have spread back down the procession because Dolt now became aware of a semi-circle of spectators at a respectful — or safe — distance behind him; there were microphones above his head and cameras looking over his shoulder.

"Because that is further than I am prepared to go."

Strictly speaking, this was not quite a lie. The truth was that mid-carriageway embarkation of minors was against regulations — regulations that Hamid, unaccountably, was keen to enforce. And, until his other enterprises began to transition from the investment to the profit phase, Dolt could not afford to lose his employment with Super Westway. If the present scene were not being broadcast around the world in real time, he would have offered up his usual case-closer: "There's nothing I can do, it's the Health and Safety." But he understood, all too horribly, the storm of derision that would have erupted over him were he to invoke it now. And how could the man who, fewer than twenty-four hours earlier, had *told off* the Prime Minister in blunt and unflinching terms now be seen to weasel out of a tight spot in ignominy?

Of course, not all of those petty rules so dear to Hamid were entirely stupid. Even amid the present gridlock, a poorly-applied handbrake or an undisciplined maneuver could cause injury. But this was not a time for hair-splitting or logic.

"I pay your bloody wages!" someone told him.

44

This was stretching a point at best, Dolt felt. The remuneration that trickled down to him from Hamid's keenly-priced contracts was modest.

"Bloody little council bureaucrats with their gold-plated pensions!"

Why did they think he worked for the council? Dolt operated exclusively in the private sector. As for pensions — *what's a pension?* he thought satirically.

But, more to the point, didn't they know who he was? Hadn't they seen him on TV? Why did they think the cameras were here now? Something didn't add up. And he wasn't sure what to do next. He just knew he couldn't back down.

"If *you* don't want to move it," he told the BMW-owner, "*I* will. Give me your keys."

This provoked a reaction that ran a little beyond his intent; he might as well have said "Give me your daughters." And it was now that things threatened to slide into anarchy. The noise level went up and the mob consolidated in front of him. Faces turned red. Even the lacrosse girls looked up from their phones. Then at his shoulder he heard two familiar voices.

"What's he gonna do now, Nige?"

"He's going to make a stand, Flint. He's going to remind them who he is."

Yes, Dolt thought, that's *exactly* what he's going to do.

He put a foot on the minibus's shiny offside front tire, levered himself up on to the hood and, in the manner of that revolutionary bloke in some film who hopped on the front of a speeding loco, leaped to a perch on the roof rack. Once stabilized, he took a deep breath and began his oration.

"Right," he said. "You lot. Shut up and listen."

The racket subsided a bit.

"I am John Dolt!"

It subsided a bit more. He repeated the line, slowly, and with emphasis on the *am*.

The racket all but dissipated.

"That's right," he said, calmly and at moderate volume. "My name is John Dolt. And nobody — *nobody!* — is going to tread on me. Understand?"

Dolt scanned the crowd. Frozen looks and open mouths told him they were beginning to.

"Didn't you see me on the telly last night?" Dolt continued, accusingly. "Don't you get it? See *them?*"

He pointed at the media caravan which, to the sound of distant honking, still blocked the road behind him for a hundred yards or more.

"Why d'you think *they're* here? Because of me. Because of what I said, right?"

He noticed a lot of mouth-to-ear whispering going on in the ranks. What was the matter with these people — didn't they watch TV? Didn't they read the papers?

"I'm not going to repeat it all now," he said, reasonably enough since he wasn't sure how much he could actually remember, "but I will say this. This country is dying. It's bleeding to death. Why? Because of the *takers*. They take, and they take, and they take. They never get enough. They take what's rightfully ours. Yours. Mine. Someone has to stand up for this country and say *enough!* And that is what I did, right? *They* —" Dolt pointed vaguely towards the top of a nearby block of flats. "— *they* don't get it. The so-called elites..."

Were the elites merely so-called or were they actually elite? Something to ponder later.

"...the elites don't get it. Do they? I mean, I had to tell the bleeding Prime Minister myself!"

He thought this was a good crack, but no one laughed. He pressed on.

"We've got to get back to basics. No more hand-outs! No more bureaucrats! No more wasteful spending! No more coming over here and expecting the best this country has to offer!"

A queasiness arose in Dolt's stomach. Had yesterday's eloquence deserted him? Were these exhortations honest prescriptions or mendacious slogans? A voice below him piped up.

"Bravo!"

It sounded like the creature known as *Nige*. And with this, the mood of the crowd seemed to turn. A smattering of applause rang out. It was time to bring matters to a conclusion.

"And so it is in that spirit that I call on you now to *move those cars!*"

And they did.

The BMW woman resisted, but was prevailed upon by her peers. A space opened up at the curb and Dolt was able to dock the minibus. Things then proceeded smoothly. The girls boarded the bus. Their mothers, giving Dolt a wide but respectful berth, bade their daughters farewell, good luck and don't give those bloody foreigners an inch. Cameramen crouched in order to flatter Dolt with imposing angles. He felt his back slapped in congratulation.

No one, of course, offered to help him load the lacrosse gear on to the roof rack. But that didn't surprise him.

Then the media pack, having caught wind of another soccer sex scandal, wished him well and took their leave. The rest of the journey to Heathrow was uneventful. The roads were as passable as could be expected, delays amounting to no more than a single bomb-scare at Hangar Lane and a small riot in Hounslow.

It was only after he'd unloaded the last piece of gear at Terminal Five and was climbing, sweatily, back into the fraying driver's seat that he noticed he still had two passengers.

"I bet you're glad *that's* over."

"What?"

"I'm Nigel and this is my associate Flint. Flint's with Freedom News Network, very big stateside. You've probably heard of *FNN's National Security Bunker Hour with Flint Gunner?* You haven't? We'll get you some DVDs."

"Nigel?" Dolt said. "Nigel fucking who?"

"Nigel Weese. You might have seen the name here or there."

Weese started in on a kind of *curriculum vitae*, in which he claimed to have contributed *major ground-breakers* to everything from The Star to The Statesman, whatever that was.

"Hang on," Dolt said. "Why are you still on my bus?"

"Well," Weese said, "isn't the question really, don't you want everyone to be on your bus?"

"What?"

"You're a star, John. Don't you want to make a career of it?"

Dolt considered. It was already well past lunchtime and he was no nearer to going on an island.

"Depends, doesn't it?"

"Of course. *Everything* depends, doesn't it, Flint?"

"You betcha."

"My point is that it's all very well being a three-day wonder. I mean we've seen it all before, haven't we? Opera singers, pop stars, balloon boys, roller-blading hamsters, third-party political leaders. But how often is it *sustainable?* Don't get me wrong, John — you've got talent. He's already gone viral, hasn't he, Flint?"

"Sure has."

Viral?

"But what you're going to need," Weese went on, "is professional management."

"Management?" Dolt said. If this was a scam and they were going to hit him up for cash, they could forget about it.

"Now you're probably thinking," Weese said, "being the perspicacious sort of chap that you are..."

Perspicacious?

"...is this going to cost me anything? Could it possibly be a scam or ruse?"

This Weese had a funny way of talking. What was he getting at?

"Well, let me be clear," Weese continued, "it absolutely is not a scam. Is it, Flint?"

"Hell, no."

"You will not have to contribute a penny. We have all the investment we could possibly need lined up already."

"Investment?"

"For your campaign."

"Campaign?"

"Yes. And your staff, your advisors, your spokes-people. Your web site, your blog, your online video, your social media presence."

Social media?

"Your magazine articles, your books, your merchandise."

Merchandise?

"Your lecture tour, your think-tank events, your town halls."

Town halls?

"Your old-media placement, your image consultants, your pollsters."

Image consultants?

"The lot. All you need to bring to the party is your own, pure, naked talent."

Talent?

"You see, I was thinking," Dolt said cautiously, "that I might go on an island."

Weese roared with laughter. The mallet-headed giant, Gunner, joined in.

"No, no, no, John," Weese said, blinking away tears. "You've got to think much, much bigger than that."

"I do?"

"Oh, yes."

Weese took a moment to regain his composure.

"Now, then. What do you say? Are you in?"

Dolt hesitated. Whatever they intended to do with him, it didn't sound like it involved wearing stupid clothes or eating something disgusting. And, bus-top homilies aside, the day so far had been less than glorious. So perhaps it was worth going along for the ride.

"Well, all right, then."

"Brilliant. You're going to make history. Come with us."

Gunner and Weese clambered out of the minibus. Weese strode off to hail a black cab.

"What about the bus?" Dolt asked.

"Screw that," Gunner said.

CHAPTER 8

John Dolt, bouncing with deftly-concealed apprehension on the flip-down rear-facing seat of a black cab as his two newest best friends in the world contemplated him with what could not, at this stage, have been buyer's remorse and was probably only chagrin at the likely fare, hurtled back into the almost-heart of not-quite-first-class power, delayed only by disturbances in Hammersmith.

During the journey, no one spoke; and Dolt was able to conduct a subtle deconstruction of his partners' demeanor.

Gunner, the American, was too large for the cab and had made no attempt to fasten his seat-belt. Well, all right, nobody except Hamid bothered with petty regulations any more, and Gunner was sufficiently well-wedged not to fear the bang on the head that Dolt or Weese might have suffered. But it was more a question of attitude. Gunner wore the kind of expression — disgust surmounted by suspicion — that told of outrage on tap and a readiness to stiff the driver if the ride or the scenery weren't up to scratch. With his menacing wide-body chin, energy-pack chest, deep-set night-vision eyes and blast-resistant forehead, he resembled a Humvee in a suit and khaki wind-breaker. And when he made eye-contact — a little too often, Dolt felt — it was like being shoved through a full-body scanner. And yet, intimidating though all this was, Dolt suspected that Gunner's was not the presiding intelligence in the cab, and he was, if you wanted to put it that way, a couple of polls short of a trend.

Weese, by contrast, slumped in his seat with low-lidded satisfaction, like an unfit alligator that had caught its lunch but couldn't be bothered to eat it yet. His eyes moved constantly but his gaze never fell on Dolt. Advertising some slippery cogitation, his tongue poked about inside his mouth. Lip-licking and teeth-sucking betrayed the relishing of schemes. He was scruffily dressed in expensive and outdated clothes — a double-breasted suit with floppy lapels and a stripy shirt in too-thick cotton with those cuffs that you had to fold over. He wore a mushroom-colored raincoat that looked like it had never been cleaned; there was a penumbra of grime where his greasy, raked-back ringlets brushed his collar. And Dolt recognized a fellow smoker: Weese had dull, grease-paper

skin, corrugated lips and cloudy eyes. Moreover, Dolt felt, here was a lifer —
someone who would never give up; someone who thrived on poison and would,
out of spite, live on into a vigorous and rotten old age. He, John Dolt, was quitting
today. Yes, he really meant it this time. It was propitious. If that was the word.

They hadn't told him where they were going. Posh hotel, trendy studio or bijou
boot camp? It turned out to be a townhouse in Mayfair.

On arrival, Weese argued with the driver over a hand-written receipt while
Gunner made sure that any thought of flight on Dolt's part was moot.

"This is where it all starts," Weese said, tucking his receipt away. "Make us
proud, John."

"You heard the guy," Gunner added.

Together, they turned from Dolt and set off on foot, Gunner taking a straight
and unyielding line along the pavement, Weese dodging street furniture and
oncoming pedestrians, and jogging to catch up with his lumbering partner. A
double-act, Dolt thought — and one of the weirdest ever.

But before Dolt could speculate further on this most special of relationships,
he became aware that a pair of blonde girls in tweed suits had issued from the
townhouse and were now busily occupied in shooing him indoors.

Bemused and curious, he permitted them to escort him to a large, first-floor
room with a fireplace and a chandelier. Here, he was parked in an executive-style
chair in front of a twenty-seater conference table, given a small bottle of water
and a paper cup, and abandoned without further instruction. A cup of tea would
have been nice, but these didn't look like the sort of girls who made tea.

Everything went quiet, except for the distant humming and banging you
seemed to get in every office. He sat alone and pondered.

So what manner of establishment was this? Property prices around here were
bonkers, despite the economic crisis. Who could afford it? The pale-blue
paintwork, elaborate moldings and ceiling-mounted motion-detectors weren't
much of a clue. There was a portrait of some craggy-looking bloke standing in
front of an American flag, but Dolt couldn't put a name to him.

He spun slowly in his executive chair, subjecting the conference room to a
pitiless examination — it was the sort of thing he did as a matter of course
whenever Lescek tempted him with a new bathroom job. Then he saw something,
way off in a far corner.

With a nonchalant glance at the winking red lights on the motion detectors,
he rose from his seat and strolled over. It turned out to be a magazine stand
loaded with glossy brochures. He picked one up.

Atlantic Affairs Institute, he read, *Protecting Values in a Changing World*. Fair
enough, he thought; you couldn't argue with that, as far as it went. *Executive
Director, Lord Aylsham, OBE*. Never heard of him, Dolt thought. Of course, you
never did hear of these people — not unless they got caught molesting teenagers
or swindling the tax-payer, and probably not even then. Aylsham? Dolt's brain
wound backwards through a decade of tabloids. No, nothing.

He flipped through the brochure: A lot of boring text full of abbreviations,
acronyms and numbers, broken up by pictures featuring groups of well-dressed
people in smiley poses. The people were interchangeable, but the backgrounds
varied — mostly flags, but also churches, fighter jets and oil refineries.

Dolt didn't know what to make of it. Weese had told him he was a "star" and had specifically highlighted his "pure, naked talent." So where were the agents, the cameras and the leggy presenters? Why was he in some boring *Institute* instead of an edgy TV studio? Who was this irksome git Aylsham — who wasn't even famous?

Dolt sat down again and drank his water from the bottle. It tasted of... Well, he couldn't really identify it. Something floral. He opened the brochure at the last page. On the inside of the back cover was a picture of the former Prime Minister — the one who never seemed to go away — shaking hands with some skinny, sharp-faced geezer with wavy hair. According to the caption, this geezer was Aylsham. The ex-PM grinned at the camera with cheery fanaticism. Great, Dolt thought, bitterly — if *he* comes in here now, I've got a few bleeding things to say to *him* as well.

But when the door opened it failed to admit any such dignitary — just one of the tweed girls and a tall, nattily-dressed man with chubby cheeks, an over-generous forehead and hair slicked back like an upper-class duck's arse. It was important to note, Dolt observed, that this bloke's suit, while very double-breasted indeed, looked, unlike Weese's, to have been bought that morning. And, not that Dolt was an expert, of course, but there was something about this baby-faced thirty-or-forty-something that screamed *butler!*

The tweed girl exited and the butler closed the door by jabbing it with his heel. But he didn't advance into the room. Instead, he locked his gaze on Dolt and held it for an uncomfortable fifteen seconds or so.

Dolt wasn't having this.

"I," he said, airily, "am John Dolt. Who are you, then?"

The butler, not picking up on Dolt's annoyance, actually seemed to chuckle.

"*Who is John Dolt?*" he said, as if struggling to contain himself. "Who indeed?"

"Look —"

"I'm sorry." The butler shook his head like a wet dog emerging from a pond. "Forgive me." He strode forward and held out his hand.

"My name's Gideon Reeves. I'm to be your Personal Assistant."

Well, this raised a number of issues, didn't it?

"Gideon?"

"Yes."

"*Gideon?*"

"That's right."

"No, mate. I don't think so."

"You don't think so?"

"Nobody's called *Gideon.*"

"I am."

"You can't be. Trust me."

"But I am. Really!"

At this point Dolt's phone tinkled. "Hang on a mo," he said. It was a text message from Hamid, who wanted to know where Dolt and the minibus were. He was assuming, of course, that they were in the same place. "*still @ hrow,*" Dolt texted back, accurately enough. By now, he speculated, the minibus would likely have attracted attention. But that was a side-issue.

"*Gideon's* no good, mate. Sorry."

"Oh."

"Got any other names?"

The butler raised his eyebrows, butler-style.

"Well, as a matter of fact, my *full* name —"

"Thought so," Dolt said. "*John Dolt.* Two syllables, right? Does what it says on the tin."

"Right. Exactly. Good point. Um..."

But Dolt had made a decision. Despite the fact that he wasn't going on an island; that he wasn't in a TV studio; that he was still wearing Hamid's stupid uniform; that he hadn't had a cup of tea; that Hamid was hassling him about the minibus; and that this idiot *butler* had been sent to wind him up — despite all that, he was going to be nice to the fucker.

"Did you say you were my personal assistant?"

"Yes."

"Well, I think we should talk about *that*. We'll come back to the name."

"Yes, good idea."

"Well, then. Get stuck in, shall we? What is this place? Why am I here? And, speaking of this and that, and taking everything into consideration, and so on — what the fuck is going on?"

The butler appeared emboldened.

"Excellent questions, all. And I shall endeavor —"

"No, no. Don't endeavor. Just spit it out."

"Yes, of course. Now, we want to welcome you here to the Atlantic Affairs —"

"Wait."

The butler frowned.

"There's one thing I want from you," Dolt said. "And we're not going any further until I get it."

"Ye-es?"

"I want a cup of tea."

*

T hey must have made the tea with the same water they put in the bottles because it tasted like leaves. But Dolt didn't care. He had asserted his authority over the butler, whom he had decided to think of, for now at least, as *Reeves*, and had acceded, late but with grace, to Reeves' handshake. Now, with his feet up on the conference table, Dolt listened in earnest as his Personal Assistant outlined what he seemed very pleased to call the *Big Picture*.

"You're just the person we've been searching for," Reeves said, pacing the length of the conference table with what looked to Dolt like the wary but confident enthusiasm of the teenage heir about to set out on his first illegal hunt. "When we saw you — when we *heard* what you had to say, and the way you said it, well — we *knew* we had to have you. It was *that* special."

"Glad you think so," Dolt said. This contradicted what his mother had often told him, but he was comforted to learn that she had been wrong after all. Yes, it was one more sadness to add to her tally, but it didn't matter now.

"...the right person at *precisely* the right time," Reeves was saying.

"Go on."

Reeves needed no encouragement. The western world was in a ferment, he said, waggling his fingers in illustration. But also a funk. Political leadership had failed and people knew it.

"I know it," Dolt said.

"Yes, you do," Reeves said.

Ordinary people were frustrated. They felt put upon, oppressed — even tyrannized, you might reasonably say. Dolt wondered how someone called *Gideon* went about tapping the mood of the masses, but didn't interrupt. So to whom, Reeves wanted to know, were the people to turn? To the elites? No, the man — or, indeed, woman — in the street knew that the elites were corrupt and self-serving.

"I know that," Dolt said.

"Yes, you do, don't you?" Reeves said.

He went on to describe, in terms that Dolt didn't fully understand, the nature of the prevailing power system and its roots in the nineteen-thirties and nineteen-sixties. It was hard to follow, though Reeves had obviously thought about it a lot, and made his case with impressive intellectual and emotional fluency. A great many things connected up, when you thought about them, apparently, and it all pointed in one direction. The era of big government was finally at an end, brought down by its own contradictions, and the people were yearning to throw off the yoke of progressivism. Some bloke called Wilson was originally to blame — not Harold, surely? — but he'd had a lot of helpers, both evil and deluded, down the years. Nice, Dolt thought — although the "big government" stuff was a bit lame. As for progress, that used to be a good thing, didn't it? Just went to show.

Now most people, Reeves admitted, might not sit up all night analyzing things quite so — another chuckle — *forensically*, but they felt it in their bones.

"I understand it instinctively," Dolt said, slyly.

"Of course you do," Reeves said.

He had warmed to his thesis now, and Dolt leaned back and rocked in his chair as Reeves spun argument after argument, linked theory and anecdote, quoted from unimpeachable academic studies, cited rock-solid polling evidence, appealed to constitutional authority and promised to show Dolt some simple graphs that proved just how wealthy the average citizen would be if the government only got out of the way.

"I find it all totally persuasive," Dolt said.

"I knew you would," Reeves said.

"It's common sense."

"I know."

Reeves now turned to current events. If you looked at them in context, he claimed, there was only one conclusion you could draw. The financial crisis, the economic crisis, and all the other crises — moral, political, ethical, constitutional, jurisprudential, medical and religious — they all derived from the same root. And the protests, demonstrations, riots and disturbances you saw on the streets — well, same thing. And that thing was: Liberty. Or, rather, lack of it.

"What about the environmental crisis?" Dolt said. "You missed that one."

Reeves seemed to deflate a notch. He shook his head.

"No, no. There really isn't one. The market —"

"You haven't seen my house," Dolt said.

"Ah, yes — your house..."

Reeves looked at his watch.

"What about the War Zones?" Dolt asked.

"Comes under Liberty," Reeves said, absently. "Um, look, John — we seem to be running a bit late here. My fault. Got a bit carried away, you seemed so interested... We've got some arrangements to make and you've got some people to meet." He took out his phone and attacked it with his thumb. "Yes, better get a move on. Ready to get started?"

Dolt held up a hand.

"One thing," he said.

"Yes?"

"You said you're my assistant."

"Absolutely."

"What are you assisting me with?"

"Oh, *that!*" Reeves straightened up and puffed out his chest. "That's easy. You, John, are going to be the leader — the *de facto* leader, I should say — of the New Patriot Movement. The British version, that is."

Dolt lifted his feet from the table and planted them deliberately on the floor. He was about to speak when his phone chirped again. It was another message from Hamid. Did Dolt know why armed police had staked out Hamid's office? He sounded distressed. "*r u jokng*?" Dolt texted back. Immediately a voice call came in from Hamid's office number. Dolt hit the reject button. It was of course, the wrong thing to do, but this wasn't the time. Then again, an unattended vehicle at *hrow*, owner's name *Hamid*... Well, old Hamid could talk his way out of anything, couldn't he?

"Reevesy?" Dolt said, noting with satisfaction the butleresque twitch of his assistant's eyebrow, "This job. This leader of the whatever. I'm assuming there's some..."

Reeves spread his arms wide.

"Look around you. Money's no object."

"Not where patriotism and what-have-you's concerned."

"Precisely."

Dolt sipped the dregs of his tea. Its bitter, woody taste clung to the roof of his mouth. He swallowed.

"So... How do we get started?"

"How would you like to start?"

Dolt considered.

"Well, I'd like to get out of these bloody clothes, for one thing."

"A new outfit. Of course. How about a complete makeover? It's on our list of possibles. Up to you. You're the boss."

Was he? It seemed unlikely. And yet here he was, in a super-posh West End post code, with his own butler-cum-personal assistant, contemplating untold — and, so far, unspecified — riches in some poncey *Institute*, whose drains he would

54

hitherto have been unqualified to de-clog. But they — whoever *they* were — needed him. What choice was there? None, really. He wasn't going to be the lovable clown on the island, the one who spiked people's drinks and danced in a grass skirt; he was going to be the *de facto* leader of the New Patriot Movement.

But *Gideon* and his pals, whoever they might be, would be well-advised to tread carefully. *Who is John Dolt?* Give him power, tell him he's the boss — and you might just find out.

Another text message arrived from Hamid. Dolt deleted it.

"Let's do it," he said.

*

T he rest of the day was a blur, but it was a blur — and Dolt had experienced a few — like none he had known. It began, like so many of the great adventures, with the sense of possibilities just within grasp.

Dolt might be surprised to learn, Reeves said, as he himself had been, that many of the great men of history were autodidacts. An autodidact, he further explained, was someone who, not needing or, as in Dolt's case, not having had the benefit of a formal education, taught himself what he needed to know. But — not to worry! — Dolt wasn't going to be on his own. Reeves and the staff at the Institute had lined up, at short notice, a panel of expert mentors who would clue Dolt in on everything he needed to learn. A mentor, Dolt gathered, was someone who told you stuff and kept on telling you until you got it.

Today, Reeves announced, Dolt would meet his mentors. And there would also be a reading list, but Dolt wasn't to worry too much about that because the experience of the New Patriot Movement in the States was that the public responded better to conviction than to book-learning. Though that didn't mean, Reeves warned, that Dolt wouldn't be required to point out the War Zones on a map or quote the exact amount of cash owed by each ordinary family on account of the deficit. No problem, Dolt said; his work had often required him to study maps — the A-to-Z, for example. And he was good with figures. You had to be when you worked with people like Lescek the bathroom guy. Reeves looked reassured, Dolt thought.

"I think, then," Reeves said, "we'll start with economics." They ascended to a book-lined study where a bat-like woman with short, black hair, pointy shoes and the soulless eyes of a debt-collector instructed Dolt to consult the works of Hayek and Laffer. Therein he would learn that taxation, its inherent immorality aside, not only sapped the spirits of entrepreneurs and rewarded the feckless, but also diminished government revenues the higher it rose. Dolt noted that this seemed odd. He was told he had much to learn.

"Next up," Reeves said, "domestic policy." They descended to a basement library where a tall, sunken-eyed, bald man of about seventy, who wore a tight polo-neck shirt and resembled a zombie vicar on his day off, complained to Dolt that the problem with actually having an established religion was that you couldn't campaign on the basis that the constitution, contrary to the leftists' claims, not only didn't forbid it but actually embodied it. And the result was, nobody took said religion seriously.

"Sure," Dolt said.

"That's a bit advanced, Norman," Reeves said. "Keep it simple, will you?"

"Yes, all right."

Had Dolt heard of Malthus and Bentham? No? Well, he was going to. But he should remember that neither of these philosophers had imagined the day when the government would insist that *he*, Dolt, should pay for *his*, Norman's, retirement and upkeep. Dolt felt that someone, at least, ought to pay for Norman's medication, but kept that thought to himself. There followed a short lecture in which it was proven that pretty much anything Dolt could come up with in terms of public expenditure was unaffordable.

"Thanks, Norm," Reeves said, giving Dolt a furtive glance. "Lastly, and perhaps most importantly... Foreign policy." Once again they ascended, this time to a large attic containing an over-sized snooker table and a brusque, sixty-ish American in a gray suit and walrus moustache.

On closer inspection, the snooker table turned out to be a map of the world. The walrus produced a laser pointer. See here and here and here? Dolt looked. Yes, he thought — the War Zones, shaded red. There were more of them than he had realized. The walrus nodded. And this? The walrus traced out an area outlined in purple. Dolt shrugged.

"The Greater Persian Region," the walrus said, with a meaningful flick of his moustache.

Dolt looked at Reeves. Reeves narrowed his eyes and met Dolt's gaze. Dolt, not wanting to feel left out, bit his lip with great shrewdness. To be honest, though, he had no idea what he was being shrewd about. *Greater Persian Region?*

The walrus moved on to an analysis of what he called the *global threat environment*, touching on asymmetric warfare, host country alliances, preemption thresholds, dynamic surge doctrine, resource depletion, emerging powers, the Long War, public perception conditioning, enhanced techniques and new advances in battle-space management. In sum, it appeared, the globe itself was a threat. It followed that such a threat had to be confronted. Dolt, still nursing the queasy suspicion that something significant had passed unspoken, asked about diplomacy. The hairs in the walrus's moustache seemed to stand on end.

"He means the public media strategy," Reeves said, stepping in pre-emptively, as it were.

The walrus directed his laser pointer at Dolt, locked on and began to advance.

"I think we'll leave it there for now," Reeves said, hustling Dolt towards the door. "It's an awful lot for John to take in. In one sitting, I mean." He opened the door and pushed Dolt through. "Much obliged, Dick!"

Outside in the corridor, Reeves slammed the door shut but kept a grip on the handle. With his other hand, he grasped Dolt by the upper arm.

"Well, that was a close one," he said. "You know what happened the last time someone used the "D" word in front of Dick?"

"What?"

Reeves hesitated.

"Actually, never mind. My fault entirely. Should have warned you. Will you forgive me?"

"Yes, but —"

"Good. Now — my office. Ready to make a dash?"

The door handle rattled. Reeves held it tight.

"Ready."

"Ground floor. On a count of three."

*

S afe from incoming walruses in an armchair in Reeves' office, a small glass of sherry on the three-legged table at his elbow, Dolt felt it was time for a reality check.

"Reevesy?"

"Yes?"

"Are you sure you've got the right person? I mean —"

"Well, of course, I know what you're going to say." Reeves sipped his sherry and shook his head with what Dolt took to be calculated ruefulness. "They're a bit of a bunch, aren't they? Eva, Norman, Dick. Especially Dick. But you have to make allowances for them, John. They're not like you and me. They're intellectuals."

"Thinkers, you mean."

"Exactly. Not like you. Not men of action." Reeves took a pensive sip. "Possible exception of Eva."

Perhaps it was the sherry, but Dolt felt himself warming somewhat towards his personal assistant.

"They frightened me, Reevesy."

Reeves put his sherry down and leaned forward, elbows on knees, chin on fists.

"I know, John, I know. Frankly, they scare me sometimes. They don't get out much, you see. Makes them a little too intense."

"Yeah."

"But they're really just there to help you. You're the important one."

"Am I?"

"Of course. No question. Have some more sherry."

Dolt gave himself a top-up.

"But politics, right? I'm not sure I can —"

"No, John. Don't you get it yet? You're the *anti-politics*. You stand for the common man. For common sense. Now, Eva, Norman and Dick — of course they're all facts and figures and theory and so on. That's fine, as far as it goes. But it's all useless without someone like you, who, um, has the ability — the very *rare* ability — to put it into language that *real people* can understand."

Dolt thought about this. It was true that he could put things in language that real people were able to understand. But was that really so rare? He took a sip of sherry. Perhaps it was. Why would Reeves lie to him?

"Well, I suppose so, but..."

Reeves took a deep breath and held it.

"You know what?" he said, at length. "Let me show you something." He reached under his chair and pulled out a hardback book. "Look at this," he said, handing the book to Dolt. "Signed copy."

The book's jacket depicted an intensely-groomed, blonde-haired woman of perhaps forty-five who dressed in expensive and conservative attire — blouse, pearls, red tailored jacket and black skirt. Her hair fell in self-conscious tendrils to her shoulders and she wore steel-rimmed glasses. The expression on her face struck Dolt as one of cultish self-exaltation backed up by freight-train neediness.

But what really impressed him was the monstrous machine-gun she held across her chest. And the two hooded captives who knelt at her feet. The book's title was *Exceptional* and the author's name was Amber Pike.

"Heard of her?" Reeves asked.

"Um..."

"She's one of the leading lights — some would say *the* leading light — of the American New Patriot Movement."

"Ah."

"This is her autobiography. Written by an old friend of mine, actually."

Dolt studied the book's jacket.

"Is that really her gun?"

"No."

"Does she have a gun like that?"

"No."

"Did she really catch those two terrorists?"

"No."

"Are they terrorists?"

"No."

"What are they?"

"Actors."

Dolt paused to take this in. He flicked the pages of the book. There weren't that many of them and the print seemed quite large.

"So... This is her story?"

"Yes."

"Is it true?"

"Not really."

"So... She's just a big fake?"

Reeves drained his sherry glass.

"John, it's a bit late in the day to start investigating the nature of reality. Or, indeed, the uses of mythology. The point is this. She's just like you. She came from nowhere, and the intellectuals and the professional politicians all looked down on her. But — like you — she *connects* with real people. She knows how they feel and she knows what's bothering them. She's had her problems — her family, I mean, my God! — and she knows that real people have the same problems. Just like you. Do you follow me?"

"Sort of."

"She's not a *fake*, John. She's authentic. Like you."

"But you said the book —"

"Is fake, yes. Mostly. It's just something she had to do to play the game. You know that sometimes you have to play the game by the opposition's rules, don't you?"

Dolt thought of his dealings with Hamid and Lescek, and of a lifetime under the thumb of one dumb authority or another.

"Yes," he said.

"You know that the game's rigged, don't you?"

Dolt permitted himself a bitter laugh.

"Yes."

"And you know that there's no such thing as a level playing-field or a fair fight?"

"Yes."

"And that to understand the nature of the prince, one must be of the people?"

"What?"

"Forget that one. The point is, Amber knows all this, too. Read the book and you'll see."

Dolt opened the book near to the beginning and began to read. Amber had wanted to build a deck at the back of her house so that her children could play there in safety. But she had been swindled by a corrupt contractor whose political contacts protected him from prosecution. To get her money back and rebuild the deck — better than ever! — for her children, and, indeed, her disabled neighbor's children, Amber had run for the office of mayor. Dolt skimmed pages of adversity, hardship, calumny, mishap and betrayal to read that Amber had won office, cleaned house and built the deck.

"Bullshit," Dolt said.

"Yes, but *inspiring* bullshit, John."

"Yeah, but —"

"Look at her now. She's the most, let's say, motivating force in America. And she's worth millions."

"Millions?"

"Millions."

Reeves topped up his sherry and sat back in his chair. Dolt did likewise. Amber Pike, he thought, might just have got something figured out. And so too, perhaps, had Reeves.

"If you and I are successful," Reeves said, "you'll be meeting her. Perhaps sooner than you think."

"Really?"

"Absolutely. And I'll tell you this. She'll respect you."

"Will she?"

"Yes, she will. Not like those women at the school."

So, he knew about that?

"They didn't respect me."

"They did not."

"But they *will*, won't they?"

"That's right, John. They will."

Dolt finished his sherry.

"Well?" Reeves said.

"Well what?"

"Ready to start building that deck?"

Dolt closed the book.

"Yes."

CHAPTER 9

J ohn Dolt had never been a sherry drinker. Consequently — and partly because of the rapport that, bizarrely, he seemed to have struck up with his new personal assistant, whose butler-smooth style and sympathetic manner had, Dolt was forced to admit, utterly seduced him in the end — he had misjudged his intake. Thus it was that, cocooned in a warm and woozy numbness, Dolt found himself transported to an undiscloseable central London hotel of startling kitsch and international ritziness.

He had presumed that the day's work — a long and arduous day, at that — was over. He was wrong.

In the "business den" of his suite, described in the room guide as "styled by Groot-Karlo as a comment on African-inflected Swiss modernism," Dolt held bleary court before a succession of advisors, consultants and other suitors, all of whom claimed to be acting under instructions from Reeves, and most of whom resisted Dolt's declaration that *he* was the boss here, not *Gideon* the bloody butler.

The first thing Dolt learned, from Des, his security consultant, who claimed a "special forces" background but looked like a bricklayer, was that there was no way he was going back to his half-a-house — styled by Dolt as a comment on Big Builder — just off the A40. And that wasn't all. The house had already been secured and was about to undergo decontamination.

"Decontamination?" Dolt said. "Are you having a laugh? It's not *that* bad."

No, Des explained, he meant merely that all compromising materials had to be removed and destroyed. Before Dolt's enemies could access them.

"Enemies, you say?" Dolt said, half-consciously emulating his personal assistant's cadences. "What rubbish! I'm extremely popular. Reevesy said so. I'm going to be a national treasure."

Des scratched his nose.

"Drugs?" he said. "Porn? Guns? Stolen goods? Dodgy receipts? Pirate videos? Unlicensed TV? Illegal pets? Financial documents of any description? Embarrassing medication? Letters from girlfriends? Boyfriends?"

"No, no, no," Dolt said. "None of that."

Des looked skeptical.

"We'll find it, you see. It's just that you could save us time."

Dolt shook his head — and then stopped because he felt dizzy.

"Nothing."

"If you say so. Got a computer?"

"Yes."

"We'll get you a new one. Who's your ISP?"

Dolt told him.

"Good, we can take care of them. Got any mobiles?"

"Yes."

"How many?"

"Only one."

"Hand it over."

Dolt gave Des his mobile phone, which Reeves had made him turn off prior to their encounter with Eva, the vampire economist. Des turned it back on and tapped away.

"Know anything about a minibus?"

Dolt groaned.

"Maybe."

"Would that be the one blown up by the army at Heathrow?"

"What!"

"Don't panic. It's already taken care of. We'll get you a new phone. Make sure you set the PIN. Now, then. Money..."

Des unfolded a laptop and proceeded to unpick what he called Dolt's "entire financial infrastructure," which, he said, would have to be rebuilt from the ground up.

Finally, as Des shut down his computer and prepared to leave, Dolt raised the issue that had been bothering him.

"So, um, where am I living, then?"

"Here."

"What, in this hotel? It's eight hundred quid a night!"

"Yeah, but it's secure."

"But —"

"In year or two, when they're finished with you, you can buy yourself a fucking mansion in Surrey. Or, in your case, perhaps Essex. Sound good to you?"

"*Finished* with me?"

But Des was gone, to be replaced by Jacqueline, who must have been waiting outside the door.

Jacqueline wanted to know if Dolt was up for a little fashion show, because she just knew he was going to be excited when he saw the sample outfits she'd brought with her.

The prospect of binning Hamid's miserable uniform for good certainly appealed but, Dolt found, the practicalities of disrobing and then dressing again in his sherry-sozzled condition occasioned more embarrassment than excitement. But Jacqueline — even more than Des, it seemed — was made of stern stuff. Just get it all off, she told him; she'd seen things that no sensitive stylist ought to have seen. It was a hazard of working with politicians. *But I'm not a politician,*

Dolt wanted to say, but couldn't because his head was wedged in the neck of a too-tight cashmere sweater — *I'm the anti-politics!*

Ultimately, however, knitwear was rejected. So, too, were a series of business and leisure suits. Some people just weren't suit people, Jacqueline lamented. Sorry.

So his final catwalk turn from his safari-chalet kitchen to the den found Dolt kitted out in mid-blue jeans — not quite designer but definitely better than high-street — plus open-necked shirt and a sports jacket that was mildly tweedy but not too structured. For footwear he was given lace-up ankle boots that hit a mark somewhere between upmarket petrol-head and military reservist. The overall effect, Jacqueline declared, was that of a successful self-employed artisan — a plumber, say — togged up for a Friday night out with the wife and the nice couple down the road.

"Fine," Dolt said, wondering to himself whether Jacqueline could tell him what line the average successful artisan would take on the Greater Persian Question. "Looks really good. Thanks."

"Glad you like it," Jacqueline said, gathering up her samples and shoving Hamid's uniform into a bin bag. "I'll get to work on outerwear. Formal's still a problem, but I'm sure there's a solution."

And then there was Roberto.

"No," Dolt said. "It's nearly fucking midnight. I'm not having a haircut!"

"Ah, but, yes you are, you see — Mr. Reeves, he made himself very clear, you know. And, of course, the facial."

And so it went on.

Step by step, ever wearier and blearier, Dolt observed himself as if from slightly outside his own body as he was stripped down, tarted up, made over, reconstructed, and generally re-engineered from the ground up. Reeves' words echoed through his muddled brain: *You're the important one, John; they're just here to help you.* Yeah, thanks, *Gideon*.

And so Dolt's personal private banker explained how money would be deposited, discreetly, in an account in the Cayman Islands; and how Dolt, if and when it was deemed appropriate, might access it.

His publicist asked for a few authentic details of his early life that could be woven into an affecting narrative that would engage the public. Dolt thought of Amber Pike and her fake autobiography and made up a couple of heart-warming anecdotes.

An earnest young man in an ill-fitting suit and under-developed goatee, who said he was Dolt's Director of Communications, offered Dolt his choice of *vox pops*, to be inserted in his speeches as he saw fit. Baffled at first, Dolt quickly realized that these were prefabricated encounters with members of the public in which Dolt would claim to have met a *blank* in *blank* who told him *blank*, where the first *blank* was a type of person; the second, a boring provincial town; and the third, a politically-slanted fairy tale. Thanks very much, he said.

An aggressive young woman in a very tight-fitting suit and over-developed make-up, who said she was Dolt's Political Advisor, insisted on giving him the low-down on the state of the parties and the hidden fault-lines within the government and the cabinet. Dolt, she said, was to use this information to out-flank just about everyone from the right, and to boost his populist credentials. But Dolt was too tired by this stage to point out that (a), he was already popular; and (b), he wasn't political, he was *anti-political*. Sure, he said. Out-flank, no problem.

The next few visitors passed by in a haze. Someone showed him some graphs. Someone else wanted to know about his travel preferences. A dentist called to make an appointment, and left looking grim. Another young woman wanted to walk him through his engagements for the next week, but decided to call back in the morning. A messenger arrived with a golden envelope — but no, it wasn't golden, merely buff — which contained a fancy, embossed invitation to a Global something-or-other.

Then, last of all, Dolt's personal lawyer asked if he wouldn't mind signing *here* and initialing *here* and *here*. Sure, Dolt said, whatever, thanks very much — and signed his way through a stack of documents without reading a word.

And then, as he tumbled into his emperor-sized bed, having shed his new clothes, splashed water on his new face and run his fingers roughly through his new hair, he fell into a deep and refreshing slumber.

At what point this gentle sleep turned to terror he couldn't say but, waking again in a shivering sweat at four in the morning, breathing heavily and still battling the demons of the night, he gave himself up to one solemn vow: Never would he, John Dolt, agree to go unaccompanied to any lonely mountain cabin owned by the famous American rabble-rousing faker, Amber Pike, no matter how *exceptional* she turned out to be.

Troubled and disoriented, he reached for the bedside lamp and flicked it on. As his eyes began to focus, the first thing he spotted, nestling on top of his zebra-skin coffee table next to his stainless steel mini fondue set, was the golden envelope — and the odd thing about it was that, in this light, it really did look golden. He stumbled over, picked it up and shook it. The embossed invitation card tumbled out.

Global Faith Initiative, he read. *Uniting Humanity for Peace.* There was an address in Kensington and a web site, but no phone number. The invitation itself was written by hand in broad, slopey strokes: *Love to get your input, please come on Friday.* There followed an unintelligible signature. This minor mystery resolved itself only when Dolt read the very small print at the bottom of the card. The *Global Faith Initiative*, it appeared, was a wholly-owned subsidiary of the foundation formed by and modestly named after the former Prime Minister — the one who kept coming back like a toothache and was on chummy terms with Aylsham, the supremo of Atlantic Affairs.

What to make of this? Dolt put the card down and toyed for a moment with the fondue set. The former PM wanted Dolt's *input?* He wanted Dolt to help him unite humanity for peace and profit? No, wait — it was just peace, wasn't it? Curious, all the same.

He wandered across to the windows in the business den, slid them open and stepped out on to the balcony. The chill of the night air shivered him into wakefulness. The city, too, seemed alert, watchful and ready for action, despite the hour. Probably storing up energy for another day of ire and recrimination, plus a load more *disturbances*, Dolt thought. A police car screamed past in the street below and faded away into the city's sleepless hum. Looking down, Dolt could see the hotel's security patrol flashing their torches and checking their equipment; Des, the consultant, would no doubt approve. The whirring of a helicopter came from above, but the night was full of low, restless cloud and Dolt couldn't locate it. As it retreated, the angry strains of an argument rose up from one of the hotel's lower and slightly less expensive rooms. Then a gusty wind picked up and Dolt retreated to his den.

This, he realized, was his new world; this was how the glorious day ended. He had won his freedom from Hamid and Lescek; from the A40 and Big Builder; from all the threats, demands, debasements and impositions of white van land; and, with any luck, from all those sodding arguments about invoices. He had a personal stylist, a Director of Communications and, apparently, a bank account in the Caribbean. All compromising materials were to be destroyed by his security people; the process of decontaminating his life had already begun. Would this process extend to Tamsin and Tamara, his daughters, or to Victoria, their irreconcilable mother?

Gone were the Jobba van and the half-a-house, replaced by rented luxury and Reeves the butler. Dolt, the accidental tribune of the people, had, almost at the moment of his alchemical rant — turning bile to gold — been separated from them. Not that the people, in his opinion, were that much to write home about, anyway. And as for *humanity*...

Certain that the opportunity for sleep had passed, and fearful in any case of a repeat visit to Amber's cabin, he padded into the entertainment lounge and activated the LED 3D Ultra-HD multi-satellite system.

The foreign news channels came up first. Flicking through them, he was at first horrified, but then, by degrees, ever more amused to view his confrontation with the lacrosse mothers in Mandarin, Hindi, French, Russian, Italian, German and a bunch of other languages, some middle-eastern, that he couldn't identify. The BBC had shut down for the night — a cost-saving measure, apparently — but from the remaining English-language stations he gathered, variously, that the PM (the current one), responding to accusations from the Leader of the Opposition, had insisted that he had indeed taken Dolt's criticisms to heart and was planning a National Symposium, to which Dolt himself would be invited; that measures were to be stepped up against the disturbances, now widely believed to be fomented by a shadowy figure known only as *Red Ron*; that there was no evidence that the Government had knowledge of a coup said to be imminent in South America; that Amber Pike's book of children's stories was number one in the best-seller list; that a new strategy in the War Zones was expected to bring rapid improvements; that the financial markets approved of the government's fiscal policies and weren't too worried about the disturbances; that the economic crisis had unexpectedly worsened again; and that the Big Builder home improvement chain had gone bust only a month after its chief executive had retired to Costa Rica. Inadequate customer demand was blamed.

Dolt turned the TV off.

Got out just in time, he thought, as he sank into his leopard-and-chrome sofa, picked up his signed copy of *Exceptional* and began to read.

65

CHAPTER 10

J efferson Crockett — or Jeff Crock, as he had long been known, cordially and otherwise, in the small and embattled world of American left-leaning investigative journalism, and would no doubt continue to be, at his new and degraded perch in bloggerdom — had been right to surmise that Katherine, his kindly boss at The Liberal, had managed, despite the efforts of New York's finest Ponzi artists, to preserve a budget for overseas investigations.

He had been wrong to presume that it would be adequate.

Thus, it wasn't long after he touched down in bustling, sweaty San Jose, that he discovered that the only vehicle he could afford to rent was a clapped-out Suzuki jeep with a canvas roof. Even then, he was forced to skimp on insurance.

Naturally, the Jeep lacked satnav, so Jeff had to fall back on the maps Katherine had given him. The ones he'd left on the plane. Eventually, on his third pass by the airport, a weary traffic policeman had taken pity on him and set him on the right road.

And so, by the end of his bone-rattling journey to the sleepy, bay-side town of Puerto Jiménez, the only significant settlement on the hot, humid and remote Osa peninsula on Costa Rica's Pacific coast, and having realized that this was a place that anyone with any sense — and any budget at all — *flew* into, Jeff Crock had shed any illusions he might have entertained of enjoying a cushy, free vacation. And the Jeep had shed its top.

On a shady street at the edge of town, next to a tree full of iguanas, he found a backpacker hotel whose owner, a dreadlocked Canadian of indeterminate age called Eric, agreed to rent him a private room for US dollars, cash, plus a little help around the outdoor bar. They drank a couple of Imperials together to cement the deal, and then Eric offered to help Jeff unload his Jeep.

"Traveling light, huh?"

"Yeah," Jeff said. "Best way." Especially if you found you needed to make a quick exit, which had often been his experience.

Eric looked interested.

"So, maybe you would like to rent some gear?"

"Gear?"

"To take down to Cabo Matapolo."

"Cabo…"

"Yeah, the waves, man. I figured you took the top off your Jeep to make room for —"

"Surfing?"

"Cabo Matapolo, man. Surfers' paradise."

Jeff Crock had never surfed. He had learned at an early age that all sports were dangerous sports.

"Not really a surfer," he said, retrieving his single, small bag from the back seat of the Jeep.

Eric looked him up and down.

"Guess not," he said, sadly. "Tall guys like you… So I guess you're hiking the Corcovado?" He peered into the back of the Jeep. "Bring your own tent?"

"Corcovado?"

Eric took a careful step back from the Jeep.

"The Corcovado," he said. "Forty-one thousand hectares? The only tropical, primary lowland rainforest in the world?" He raised his hand and made a gun-like gesture. "It's just over there."

Jeff looked. The hills beyond the town were indeed forested. But had he detected a change in the atmospherics here? Try a little enthusiasm, he thought.

"Rainforest, you say? Gee, that sounds interesting."

Eric took another step backwards and folded his arms.

"You know," he said, "the local cops and I, we have a very good relationship. And there's no way I…"

At the word "cops," Jeff realized, a little late as ever, that he might have a problem.

"Problem?" he said, facing the issue head-on.

Eric ground his heel in the dirt and shrugged.

"I mean, come on, dude. You're not surfing, you're not hiking, you're not paying six hundred dollars a night to sunbathe at the friggin' eco lodge. You don't have a camera, so I'm guessing you're not here to photograph the scarlet macaws."

"I *do* have a camera," Jeff said, producing his trusty compact spy-camera.

"I mean a *serious* camera. Okay, look. I don't want any trouble, so what's the deal?"

"The deal?"

He was tired, of course, but Jeff had to ask himself how it was that the same crack operator who had bluffed his way into the heart of the military-industrial complex had now failed to infiltrate a hippy flophouse.

But then he realized what Eric was getting at.

"You've got the wrong idea," he said. "The deal is… Not what you think it is."

"Gonna have to do better than that, man. Otherwise…"

"Otherwise what?" Jeff said, picking up his bag and taking a delicate step towards Eric.

"Otherwise, I'm going to have to charge you for that beer. And ask you to move on." Eric pointed at Jeff's bag.

"Whatever kind of shit you're doing, I can't have it here."

Jeff stopped and put the bag down again. There was nothing else to do, he felt, and he didn't really care at this point.

"There's no shit," he said. "Really. No shit at all. Look for yourself."

"Sure?"

"Go ahead."

Eric unzipped the bag and picked through its contents as Jeff shifted his weight from one leg to the other in dull humiliation. It took longer than he expected; clearly, Eric was more diligent than he looked.

"I guess you're clean. Sorry about that."

"Not a problem."

Eric bit his lip, a look of judicious circumspection on his face.

"I guess I'm still kind of curious as to why you're here..."

If you thought about it, Jeff reasoned, it might not be a bad thing to get on the right side of a clued-in local who had a good relationship with the local cops. Local cops — more so even than corporate lawyers, private security goons, and Katherine's budgets — had been the bane of his professional life.

"You know what?" he said, wiping the sweat from his brow with the hem of his T-shirt, "I think I'm going to tell you. Let's go back to the bar."

*

J eff Crock cracked open another Imperial. "And so," he said, having regaled Eric Lapierre, his curious host, with the PG-rated rendering of his illustrious career, including the episode in which he had exposed the off-shore tax evasions of a bailout-seeking bank CEO, and not forgetting the time he bugged the antebellum boudoir of a distinctly pro-bellum southern senator, to the dismay not just of the defense-contracting industry but the family-values crowd as well, "it's really all about this place called Rancho Colorado."

Eric choked on his beer.

"What?" Jeff said, and waited for Eric to recover.

"You're here about *that?*"

"That's right."

Eric decided to splutter a little more.

"That's a crazy place, man. You want to stay away from there."

Since this was precisely what Jeff didn't want to do, he sipped his beer and settled on an indirect approach.

"Sure, if you say so. But it's right around here, isn't it?"

"No, it's the other side of the eco lodge."

"Oh, okay. Only I couldn't see it on the satellite maps. I zoomed in but..."

"It's only been there eighteen months."

"The maps were newer than that."

"Well, that's weird then, isn't it?"

"Yeah."

Jeff took another long draw on his Imperial.

"But *you* know where it is."

"Uh-huh."

Another pause.

"So this rainforest — this..."

"Corcovado."

"...Corcovado. Must be a pretty special place."

"It's a national park. Global importance."

"Right. So how do you get to build a thing like Rancho Colorado in it?"

"Good question."

"Must have been protests."

Eric looked at Jeff as if he were an idiot.

"Well, duh. That eco guy was all against it. But if *he* couldn't stop it, then..."

"Which eco guy is that?"

"Leo Vargas. Owns the eco lodge. Very big on the environment."

The name sounded familiar. Vargas — was that the guy who was threatening to shake up the big conference in Cape Town?

"Does he live here?"

"Mostly. He went off to Africa. Should have been back by now, but I haven't seen him around."

Vargas was clearly someone to talk to. Jeff would have to track him down. But wasn't he also some kind of businessman with political pull?

"So, Eric. This Vargas guy. You're sure there wasn't some deal —"

"No, man. He's for real. Listen, where're you from?"

"Brooklyn."

"Okay. So how much of your energy — your electricity — how much is renewable?"

"Uh, not much, I'm guessing."

"We get eighty percent. It's all hydro."

"That's good."

"The temperature goes up, we get less rain."

"Not so good."

"Up in the Monteverde — the cloud forest, okay? Maybe the cloud level is going up. It's going to dry out. Maybe all the tree frogs are gonna die."

"That's bad."

Eric waved his empty beer bottle in Jeff's face.

"And down here, we got the ocean. And if that warms up, maybe this forest starts putting out more CO_2 than it takes in."

"Don't want that."

"So, you've got to understand. This is where Leo is coming from."

"Got it. You a friend of his?"

Eric put his beer bottle down and scratched the back of his head.

"No, he's not a big fan of the, uh, surfing community."

"Bit of a prig?"

"Maybe."

Jeff tipped his chair back and looked up at the tree that shaded the bar.

"What kind of tree is that?"

"Wild plum."

"Ah."

Jeff studied the tree.

"Those iguanas?" he said.

Eric looked up and inspected the tree as if he'd never seen it before.

"What about them?"

"Do they ever fall down?"

"Sometimes."

"Another beer?"

"You paying?"

Jeff considered. He was extracting some useful info from Eric, so this conversation counted as work. It was, therefore, expense-able.

"Sure. Break 'em open. *Dude!*"

*

J eff Crock lay awake and sweltered on the creaky single bed that comprised most of the furniture to be found in his private room, which, as a seasoned traveler, he was able to identify as an improvised lean-to that served partly to shore up Eric's kitchen. The remainder of the furniture, a wooden chair with a fraying seat, supported a grimy electric fan that puttered to itself to little effect.

Yet Jeff felt content. Somehow, the effects of the beer and the humidity canceled each other out, transporting Jeff into a state of lucid doziness. The thickness of the atmosphere softened the fecund sounds of the night and, despite the thinness of Eric's mattress and the pokiness of its brittle springs, Jeff felt almost as if he were floating on a forest of clouds.

How long this sense of well-earned serenity lasted, he could not say. But it ended when the roof exploded.

Of course, the roof did not explode; it merely sounded that way. And the cavernous *rat-a-tat* that followed couldn't have been the rending of tropical thunder or the ripping of fire-crackers, although it resembled them at first.

Jeff snapped into consciousness and then froze, waiting for his war reporter's brain to haul itself back online.

Then it happened again.

He jumped to his feet, tripped over the fan cable, picked himself up and ran outside. A minute of squinting in the gloom and the whole thing became clear.

Reaching down to a point about two feet above the tin roof of Jeff's lean-to was one of the thicker branches of the wild plum tree. The iguanas had selected this branch as their on-ramp of choice in their plan to penetrate the open skylight on top of Eric's kitchen. The two-foot drop from the branch to Jeff's ceiling appeared to be something they took in their ungainly stride. How did they get back up? Jeff wondered. Well, it wasn't his problem and, fuck it, he'd probably have done the same thing in their situation.

He decided to sit outside in the comparative cool of the night until the last of the iguanas had taken the plunge. While he was waiting, he would review his evening with Eric. It had turned out to be quite productive, once the beers got rolling.

Not only did Eric know where Rancho Colorado was, he also knew how to get there. Presumably, Eric said, Jeff was thinking more in terms of slipping in through the tradesmen's entrance than of rolling up to the front door and ringing the bell? Exactly, Jeff said. Residents, according to Eric, arrived by sea-plane or helicopter; because of the terrain, or perhaps for security reasons, there was no airstrip. Supplies and staff came by boat, although employees lived on site for months at a time. Of course there wasn't really a back door at all, but there were tracks through the forest which had been used by the heavy construction equipment, and some of these might still be passable. You'd need a four-wheel-drive, but Jeff had one of those, didn't he?

Jeff had wondered if the Suzuki did, in fact, have four-wheel-drive and, if so, how you turned it on. Go on, he'd said.

Well, Eric said, for a small consideration, he'd be prepared to guide Jeff along these tracks and make sure he didn't get lost, or eaten by jaguars or molested by tapirs. Jeff would be responsible for fuel and all incidental expenses. Fine, Jeff said. He managed to negotiate the "small consideration" down to two hundred dollars, which was most of what he had in his contingency reserve.

But didn't Eric have other guests to care for? No, Eric said. Jeff was his only guest. The global economic downturn had impacted the surfer community badly, and the only people down at Cabo Matapolo these days were the *trustafarians*, who had their own beach houses.

There was one more thing, though, Eric said. Once they got close enough, Jeff was on his own. Because the people inside Rancho Colorado were totally crazy, man. Crazy as in wing-nut, rightist politics? Jeff suggested, humorously. Well, maybe, Eric conceded — but mainly crazy as in *armed and extremely crazy*. Did Jeff have a gun? No. Did he want one? Probably not. Well, at least he'd been warned, hadn't he? Yes, Jeff said, he'd been warned.

Actually, there was one thing he *did* need, Jeff said. One of the problems of being an investigative reporter — or blogger — these days was that it wasn't enough merely to be intrepid. You almost had to be invisible, too. Any place worth busting into was pretty much guaranteed to have wall-to-wall, twenty-four-hour, smart HD surveillance. Some kind of head-to-toe disguise was required; could Eric provide such a thing? You mean, like a burqa? Eric said. It didn't matter, Jeff said, so long as it didn't cost more than twenty dollars. He was sure he could come up with something, Eric said.

To seal the deal, they'd cracked open two more beers, and then the conversation had taken a darker, more philosophical turn.

Something, Eric felt, was *up* in Costa Rica, and Central America in general. On the one hand, you had the ever-revolving rumors of coups and plots — one month here, another month there — and the general feeling amongst ordinary people that they were being manipulated, prodded, sized-up and bamboozled. What, more than ordinarily? Jeff wanted to know. Yes, Eric said — much more so. And then, on the other hand, the economic colonization of the south by the north — of which he was himself a tiny part, he was ready to admit — seemed to have moved into a new gear. In addition, the new Latin American politics of people like Leo Vargas, snobby elitist as he might well be, had been pushed back, and yet no one could say precisely who was doing the pushing. Usual suspects, if you ask me, Jeff had said, but Eric didn't look convinced. And don't forget the plight of the tree-frogs, he said; America had practically written climate-change denial into its constitution. Not quite, Jeff said.

And if you wanted a perfect symbol in which all four of these baleful trends coalesced, what could serve better, Eric demanded to know, than *Rancho Colorado?* What indeed, Jeff said.

Then, hoping to lighten the mood a bit, he'd asked Eric whose turn it was to be top of the bill at the coup-of-the-month club. Venezuela, since you ask, Eric had replied.

The mood hadn't lightened.

Not until they'd consumed a couple more beers, that is, and Eric had gotten out his acoustic guitar and played a medley of Neil Young tunes.

Jeff glanced at the roof of his room and noted with satisfaction that the last of the iguana raiding party was about to make its leap. From inside the kitchen came the sounds of clattering pots and smashing glass. Jeff took a depth breath of perfumed night air and went back to bed.

*

T he damage to Eric's kitchen couldn't have been all that bad, because Jeff's breakfast of rice, black beans, eggs and fruit, served on papaya leaves, was delicious. That Eric harbored suspicions was clear — *are you sure you didn't hear anything, man? Not a thing*, Jeff had lied. But this night of the iguanas hadn't jeopardized the mission. Jeff was pretty sure about that.

Eric had taken the Jeep and gone off to fuel up and gather supplies. While he was away, Jeff found a spot near the jacarandas in Eric's back yard that had passable cell phone reception and checked his messages.

Most were from Katherine. Jeff hadn't forgotten about the limit on the corporate Amex card, had he? No, he certainly hadn't. Was Jeff picking up anything on the street regarding Venezuela? It was fortunate that Jeff happened to be in the region; a shame that the budget didn't stretch to Caracas. Just the usual rumors, he replied. Katherine had sent him a link to the social media mumblings of some guy called John Dolt. Dolt? Oh, the dumb-ass Brit who'd gone to the trouble of saving the Prime Minister only to turn around and rip him a new one. Why did Katherine always think these morons were so hilarious? He clicked though and read the latest post:

> Talked to a plumber in Norwich. Told me the migrants want to take his job, but always b@ll#cks up the work. More for him! Socialist stimulus!

Well, Katherine was famous for her sophisticated sense of humor. Frankly, it did nothing for him.

Lastly, and most importantly, Katherine wanted to know if Jeff had heard anything about a local notable called Leo Vargas. Right ahead of you there, Jeff thought. Vargas had been in Ethiopia, but had not shown up at a meeting connected to the Cape Town summit. No one seemed to know where he was. Katherine included a link to a news report of a light aircraft crash in the region of Ethiopia where Vargas had last been heard of. Who was in the plane? There were conflicting accounts. Could Jeff find any friends, family or associates who could clarify? Well, perhaps, but it would have to wait until after his assault on Rancho Colorado. And another thing, Katherine said: Why such a huge exclusion zone for one little Cessna? Yes, Jeff thought, that would be weird, wouldn't it?

And then there was the message from Annie. This was, to say the least, unexpected. The subject was "stuff." He sat and thought about it for a minute. No, he decided, this was not the right moment for Annie's *stuff*. Perhaps later, after he'd cased Rancho Colorado, submitted his findings, and felt relaxed and carefree.

By the time he'd typed in his replies, Eric had returned. He looked strangely pleased with himself.

"Are we cool?" he said.

"I think so," Jeff said.

Eric laughed.

"Awesome. Let's roll."

The Suzuki, it turned out, did have four-wheel-drive. In fact, it was stuck in it. So no worries there. Eric took the wheel, pointed the jeep in the direction of the hills, and the two men — the hippy surfer and the subversive veteran — set out to confront the forces of paranoid plutocracy.

It was like something out of *Star Wars*, Jeff thought.

CHAPTER 11

U nder heavy, colluding clouds and a blind night sky, Bonnie DiAngelo stole back across the border, from Eritrea into Ethiopia, in the company of Jay Percival, a one-man spin-off from America's global enterprise, whose shiny shoes and cat-like tread betokened the kind of light footprint that any right-minded eco-traveler ought to have admired. Nothing so kind, she thought, could be said about the state of his pick-up truck, which was a mess.

Sand, plastic bottles, and miscellaneous rubbish; dead batteries and bullet cases; papers spilling from folders — secrets? And something that might have been a hand grenade. Freelance spying was clearly a dirty business. When she moved one of the rubber mats, she found forgotten hundred-dollar bills underneath. What *would* the accountant have said?

The journey was difficult and soul-wearying. Under a veiled and indifferent moon and craftily-dimmed headlights, she could barely tell a pothole from a crater; a dip from a crevasse; a sandy ledge from a dune. Jay's face had lost all its customary animation; he was driving the desert and the desert didn't care for it.

At dawn, they reached the foot of the escarpment, and stopped for breakfast — black tea, goat's cheese and flatbread. The first rays of the morning began to glint off the truck, filthy though it was.

"Now they can see us," she said.

Jay pointed to the west.

"We'll go along that canyon," he said. "Should be pretty well hidden. When we come out at the far end, we'll just be traffic."

The canyon by day was no easier than the desert by night. They crossed the river bed and then crossed it again. Each time she thought the truck would stick on the bank, but it never did. Three times they had to stop to shift rocks from their path. She realized that Jay had never driven this route before; perhaps no one had. He had picked it at random.

The heat built and by mid-afternoon they had burned most of their fuel and exhausted their water supply. More encouragingly, Jay proclaimed an absence of airborne watchers. What chance of spotting them? she asked. Actually, not much, he said.

At dusk, they reached a village, where Jay exchanged tea for water and emptied the last can of gas into the truck's tank.

"Wake me in an hour," he said, tipping his seat back.

*

When she woke, they were driving on a surfaced road and the truck's lights were bright.

"Where are we?"

"On the road to Aksum."

"Good."

Aksum was the kind of place she should have stuck to all along: A scrappy little city of no small prettiness and high touristic aspiration, with all the myth and history required to back it up. Famous for its *stelae*, its obelisk, its ancient kingdom, and, if you wanted to believe the local Orthodox Church, custodian of the Ark of the Covenant.

"Sleep some more," he said.

She did.

*

Beside the weather-beaten hangar of a scenic flight company adjacent to the airport, Jay told her to wait in the truck while he conducted business.

"Let's see if they really meant it," he said, pulling a shopping bag full of dollars out from under his seat.

Twenty minutes later he returned without the bag.

"Seems they were going to sell it anyway," he said. "It's worn out. These guys are not the smartest businessmen."

"But you gave them the full price anyway?"

"Good to have friends."

"Or buy them."

"Well, that was what the money was for in the first place, you know? Your tax dollars at work."

She laughed.

"Funny. Here's a question for you."

"Okay."

"I can get on a plane here — not *your* plane, a nice, big one, like *that* one over there. And I can fly to Addis. Then to London. And on to Boston. Why shouldn't I just do that?"

With what seemed intended as exorbitant patience, Jay brushed his dirty, blond hair out of his eyes.

"Got your passport?"

"As a matter of fact, I have."

"Money?"

"No. But you seem to have plenty."

He paused and gave her a look that seemed to say *I know you're not serious,
tell me you're not.*

"Not worried about Andy?"

"Perhaps he's not the threat you imply."

Jay turned on the truck's shortwave radio and punched in some numbers.

"Had to talk to him anyway," he said. "So..."

The radio buzzed and clicked and then a deep, slow, regretful voice came
through.

"That must be Mr. Percival. How are you today, Jay?"

"Fine, Walter. Listen, I've got to keep this short. I'm taking route B down to
your place, okay? Do what you can, yes?"

"I'll do what I can."

"I'm going to need your computer guys."

"I'll wake them up."

"And I've got Mrs. DiAngelo with me. Mr. Vargas's, uh, friend. She's not
worried about Andy. Keep it short but tell her, will you?"

A fuzzy, over-modulated sigh seeped from the radio. And Bonnie listened as
the African elder statesman she'd never heard of asked her to please believe that
this man, *Andy*, was truly the worst of the worst. And she could ask Mr. Percival
if she really wanted to know.

"Please go with Mr. Percival," he concluded, plaintively.

"Thanks, Walter. Be seein' ya!"

Jay turned the radio off.

"Well?"

"Okay. So tell me."

"I'll just run down the highlights."

And here they came: Private military companies; mercenaries; secret contracts
and illegal weapons; mayhem-for-hire and off-the-books assassination; privatized
kidnapping and out-sourced murder; extra-judicial thuggery and goons gone
wild; black sites and torture; and, the ultimate reason for all of this, the immense
amount of money that accrued to Mr. Andrew Willoughby-St. John and his
enterprises.

"Enough?"

It was enough.

"So where's our plane?" she said.

"They're getting it ready. Get out and stretch your legs."

*

J ay's taxpayer-funded impulse purchase was an ancient four-seater Cessna.
It was not fitted with an emergency parachute; nor did it, as far as Bonnie
could tell, benefit from GPS navigation. Instead, it had brown, fake-leather seats
and ashtrays in the doors.

All this seemed to matter less when she looked down on the roof of Africa —
the jagged, green mountains of the Ethiopian highlands — and wondered how
much her customers back in Massachusetts might reasonably pay for a similar,

but safer, view. Whether Jay had learned to fly at the expense of the CIA, or of African elder statesmen, or — improbably — had shelled out for lessons himself, the results were not impressive.

Bonnie remembered a flight across the empty desert mountains of Northern Namibia, up into the Hartmann Valley, the home of the Himba. Her destination had been a lonely and otherworldly lodge that sat on the bank of the Cunene river, looking across to Angola on the other side. (The lodge had since been refurbished to plutocratic standards and was no longer worth offering to Bonnie's clients. The price of a single night there would buy you a small Volkswagen.) And, on that occasion, her pilot had been a tiny, eager South African girl who must have been at least twenty-one, but looked fourteen. It had been a nerve-testing ride. But the girl flew better than Jay.

The plane, needless to say, had only one working headset, so conversation was difficult. Jay asserted, with reckless enthusiasm, she thought, that he intended to fly down the rift valley, skirting Addis, and refuel near Lake Abaya. They would then cross — without observing the niceties — into Kenya. He would aim for the southern tip of Lake Turkana, refuel again near Nakuru, and head on to Lake Victoria. There would be an overnight stop in Tanzania, and further refueling in Zambia before they snuck into Namibia via the Caprivi strip. And there would be some sneaky, low-level flying because there was no guarantee as to how many strings Walter could pull or how many radars he could jam.

How many times, Bonnie wanted to know, had Jay flown *route B* down into Walter's stoic but tender embrace? First time, Jay said. I knew it, she thought.

Her voice began to crack up; it was simply too much for her to shout over the noise of the plane. Jay, however, had become talkative. Was it the excitement of the mission — conveying a bewildered travel agent across half a continent? Or the result of sitting in an Eritrean hut for longer than the average covert-action man would prefer?

Things were likely going to get rough, Jay said. And, no, he wasn't talking about his flying. Was Bonnie following the elections? Which elections? The US campaign, of course. Well, if Bonnie felt turned-off, he could relate to that. Problem was, the incoming administration — Jay, like everybody else, could see which way things were going — didn't know what it didn't know. Worse, it didn't think it needed to. You had a whole bunch of people who hated everything about the government except the military. And, by the way — Bonnie might not know this but it was true — the intelligence services were effectively a part of the military nowadays. You only had to look at the funding and who reported to whom. Now, back in *his* day, spies weren't expected to wear combat boots — but he was digressing.

You'd got this trillion-dollar machine, he said. It was slipping out of control. Look, you had generals on the talk shows, making policy; and then letting their guard down in the speakeasy and dining out in the private sector. People back home were too busy avoiding foreclosure to keep count of the War Zones.

"There's no money for nothin'," Jay said, "but we need all the drones we can get. They're profitable. They're the future of warfare, and warfare is therefore our future. And then, in come these yahoos. This is what they're thinking to themselves: Hey, if war is the only path left to greatness, we'll take it, and — *shit!"*

He was looking out to the left and above at another plane in the distance.

"No, come on, you guys aren't that good."

"Who is it?" she said.

"It's no one."

They had emerged from the mountains into the valley; she could see roads and settlements. Jay banked the plane and took it lower.

She looked out of her side window and realized that the other plane was much nearer than she had thought. Jay put them into a steep, twisting descent.

"They don't like flying too close to the ground," he said. "If they're using a satellite link, there's a delay — they can't react so fast." Down they went, until Jay leveled out close to the valley edge.

The other plane, she now realized, had come very close. And it wasn't a plane at all — it was small, unpiloted and remorseless in its attentions.

"Another new model," Jay said. "Kind of fast. Hang on."

He pulled the throttle out and climbed sharply. She felt the plane judder. When they evened out, the drone was ahead of them. As she watched, it accelerated and cut across their path.

"Turn around," Jay said. "They want us to turn around."

"Is that thing —"

"Armed? No. Not this one. Just for spying."

"So what do we —"

"Ignore it. Get down at Abaya. Figure out route C."

He was flying at full power, and too low, she knew. Could they even make it to Abaya?

The drone made another looping pass in front of them.

"Shit! That thing is *fast.* They want us to go north, fuck 'em. Not gonna do that, I think."

The plane hit some turbulent air and she felt her seat drop away beneath her.

"Getting hot. Better go up a bit."

The drone followed them up and cut across their path again — closer this time.

"Why won't they take *no* for an answer?" Jay said, pulling the plane higher.

She looked out of her window to the right.

"Jay? What is *that?"*

Before he could answer, a streak of gray smoke tore across the sky in front of them and exploded in a ball of white light. For a moment she was blinded; Jay must have been too, because the plane banked sharply to the right and began to yaw, before she felt him correcting it. When her sight returned, what she saw, directly in front of them, was the underside of a silver-gray plane about the size, she thought, of a 737, perhaps larger. But when it banked to turn north, she saw that its shape was angular and elongated; that it had no windows, and no cockpit; and its wings were loaded with weaponry.

"*That,"* Jay said. "Is what you found in the Danakil. *Jesus.* The size of it."

He eased off on the throttle and fumbled under his seat for a bottle of water. She opened it for him and he drank, slowly. So what did he do now? Get Walter on the shortwave? She watched him drink: His face had lost its tautness and his head seemed to have sunk into his shoulders — the look of the cornered cat, she thought.

And if the little drone's big brother had wanted to shoot them down — well, it could have done so easily, couldn't it? So what did it really want? Her?

Jay handed her his empty bottle.

"I am truly sorry, Mrs. DiAngelo," he said. "But we will have to go north after all."

He banked the plane in a tight circle. Ahead of them and receding into the distance was the big drone.

"We can't keep up with that," Jay said. "I guess the little guy will keep us company."

They climbed high above the mountains, following the small drone. Jay slumped in his seat and said nothing.

She thought of Leo, and wondered where he was now. Holed up in Addis? Safely off-limits on a scheduled flight to London, in the unwitting company of two hundred human shields? Jay had been right to send him off on his own. He would *do* something. Even so, it was hard to believe that Leo, or even that unseen mastermind Walter, could match the capabilities of Mr. Andrew Willoughby-St. John and his faceless flying corps of robots.

She lapsed into a semi-dream of fearful deserts and death-dealing computers, wondering what Annie would say when she found out her mother had been kidnapped by cyborgs.

Eventually, they turned towards the sun and left the mountains behind.

"Sudan," Jay said. "This is ridiculous. There's nothing here. It's all desert. It's the Sahara. We're going to run out of fuel."

An hour later they did.

Jay brought the plane down between longitudinal dunes. Its wheels dragged in the sand and the plane slid to a halt on its side, its wing snapped. But they crawled out unhurt.

As they stood and watched, the small drone descended and circled them three times. Then it turned to the north-west and faded into the orange glow of the sunset.

Jay kicked at the sand.

"Libya," he said. "They've gone to fucking Libya. That's just great. What a perfect place for them." He started towards the plane. "I'll check the radio."

When he returned, he looked embarrassed — but in the grimmest way possible.

"No good?" she said.

"No good."

"So what now?"

"They know we're here. They know we're not going anywhere. They know we'll be dead in two days."

"Only two?"

Jay looked at her.

"It's just a question of whether they come back. Or not."

CHAPTER 12

Jeff Crock was not happy. Not happy at all. He could tolerate derision; he could endure denigration; he could even suck it up when Very Serious People mocked his *naïve emotionalism*. But there were limits.

"It's a fucking gorilla suit!"

"Hey, you said twenty dollars. It was only fifteen."

"You paid fifteen dollars for *this?*"

"No, you're only renting it, man. Come on, it's perfect! Nobody's gonna recognize you in *that*."

Eric Lapierre, hotelier to the hard-up hippy surfer community, reckless off-roader, and Jeff's guide to one of the ecological marvels of the world — the Corcovado rainforest of Costa Rica — seemed to be enjoying himself.

"What can I tell you, they're all out of burqas in Puerto Jiménez. Sold the last one just before I got there."

"You fucking idiot."

"Look, what did you expect?"

"I don't know. Maybe a jumpsuit and a ski mask. Not a *fucking gorilla costume*. It doesn't even look like a real gorilla!"

Eric climbed on to the hood of the jeep and peered ahead through the forest.

"I think we're nearly there. And what has verisimilitude got to do with it?"

"Is this about the iguanas?" Jeff said.

Eric scratched the back of his head and squinted into the trees.

"What about them?"

Jeff hesitated.

"Nothing," he said.

"Listen, think about it," Eric said, jumping down again. "The gorilla is *perfect*. You're a big, lanky guy. You move in a — no offense, dude, okay? — funny kind of way. Very recognizable. The gorilla's going to disguise that real well. Plus when their security guys see you on the playback, they're gonna freak. It'll be *hilarious*."

This was true, Jeff thought. And he did have a distinctive gait; perhaps Eric had a point there. But it was still a *gorilla suit* — and a gorilla was going to sneak, inconspicuous and unnoticed, into the super-secure, high-tech citadel known as Rancho Colorado? *Shit!* But what choice was there?

He picked the suit up by the shoulders and held it against his chest.

"How d'you know it's my size?"

"Supposed to be adjustable."

"All right, fuck it, help me get it on."

"Sure thing. Got to be careful with the zip, they tell me."

Jeff sat on a fallen tree and undid the zip that ran down the back of the suit.

"Where'd you find it, anyway?"

"Elementary school. They use it to teach kids about wildlife. Donated by Leo Vargas."

"Figures. Here, hold my camera."

Jeff struggled into the suit. As expected, it was hot and itchy.

"Okay, let me put the head on," Eric said. "There we go."

Jeff peered out through the gorilla's eyes. Actually, it wasn't that bad. And he certainly felt well-disguised.

"And the camera..." Eric said, taking a carefully-framed snap with the spy-camera before hanging it around Jeff's neck.

"You look great. Turn around for me? Perfect. Oh, wait — your zip's undone."

Eric yanked up on the zip.

"Yeah, that's fixed it. You're all set."

All set? Jeff thought. He was in a gorilla suit, in a rainforest, in Central America, and he was going to break into the secret bolt-hole of hostile billionaires. Yes, he was *all set*. Whose idea was this, again? Oh right, *Katherine*. Well, their next little debriefing was going to be interesting.

"Do the walk," Eric said.

"What?"

"Do the gorilla walk."

"Fuck you, Eric."

"Just trying to help, man."

"Yeah, right. Which way is it?"

Eric pointed.

"Go into the forest over there. Keep heading west."

"West?"

"That way — towards the sun. It's maybe five hundred meters."

"Where are you going to be?"

Eric indicated the track they had driven down.

"Back there a little way. Just off the track. Guess I'll camouflage the jeep a bit."

"And you're going to wait for me, right?"

"Sure."

"I don't know that I can get this thing off on my own."

"Don't worry about it."

"Okay. I'm going, then."

"Okay."

"See you later."

"Yeah. Good luck."

Jeff paused.

"You're sure this wasn't about the iguanas?"

Eric shrugged.

"Nah. Stupid iguanas."

Let it go, Jeff thought. He raised his hairy hand in a gesture of farewell and set off into the forest.

There was something, he quickly realized, about wearing the suit that made you want to walk like a gorilla. He gave in to the urge, bent forward and began to swing his arms. The creatures of the forest seemed to respond: Gangs of parrots gathered in the tree-tops to observe his progress; troupes of spider monkeys followed him at a distance; a mob of coatimundi, coming upon him unexpectedly, reversed themselves and fled, tails in the air. Owing to these distractions, it seemed no time at all before the greenery gave way to the grim outer walls of Rancho Colorado.

By all appearances it was, as Katherine had suggested, an enormous structure. No attempt had been made to camouflage it, blend it in with its surrounding, or soften its aesthetic impact: The walls were gray concrete, about twenty feet high and topped with coils of razor wire that were just beginning to rust. It looked impenetrable. Katherine had described it as "fortified," true; but he'd assumed a certain exaggeration. Not even a real gorilla, Jeff felt, could have broken in. And no sensible gorilla would have gone near it. What to do?

Staying within the forest — ominously, all vegetation within twenty yards of the walls had been razed — he made his way first to the south and then, where the wall changed direction, to the west again. The land began to slope down and, about twenty minutes later, he began to hear the sounds of the ocean. Pressing on and pausing at intervals to cool down, at length he stumbled out on to a beach. Here, the wall turned north to run along the upper margin of the sand. With the trepidation of a lowland gorilla scouting a poachers' camp, he crouched, peered around the corner, and immediately noticed two things: First, that the wall stopped abruptly only ten yards away; and, second, that about a hundred yards beyond, the beach was populated with a dozen or so sunbathers, all decently equipped with loungers, towels, laptops, gaily-colored gazebos and white-uniformed attendants.

A commotion erupted in the trees above him. He retreated from the beach and looked up. A flock of bright-red, yellow and green birds were conducting some kind of raucous town-hall meeting. The famous scarlet macaws, perhaps? They were certainly disputatious. He waited for them to fall quiet and then crept back to the beach. It was time for some spy-camera action. He raised the camera to his eye and realized there was a problem. The spy-camera did not have a screen. It had an old-fangled viewfinder. The gorilla's nose got in the way. All his pictures would have to be taken in portrait mode. He sighed and zoomed in on the nearest occupant of the beach.

If it were only the case, he reflected, that the FBI focused its activities on the corporate-criminal class, rather than, say, honest dissidents and bearded loons, then they would surely have had to develop specialized facial-recognition software. These guys all looked the same. If you'd seen one country-club bonus-bagger, you'd seen them all, pretty much. The chubbiness of the cheeks;

the amplitude of the chins; the smoothness of the forehead; the Gorbachovian hair. You also had the rotundity of the stomach and the hairiness of the legs, though presumably the FBI could take those for granted. But which specimen was this? He zoomed in further.

Well I never, he thought — it was Landon Carter, the former boss of Regal Realty, the mortgage broking company, who had unexpectedly stepped down to spend more time with his family shortly before an equally unexpected, and fatal, write-down in the company's assets. Was his family here, too? There was no sign of them. *Click!*

He scanned the beach and selected his next target. *No way!* But, yes, it was — it was Morrison Tweed, the coal-mining tycoon, whose mineral empire had caved in almost as fast as one of his mines. Supposedly, he'd been lost at sea following a mysterious fire on his yacht. And yet here he was. *Click!*

All his resentments towards Katherine began to fade. She'd been on to something, after all. This was almost too sweet to be true. It was like picking chocolates from a box. Well, except that these chocolates would cost a fortune and give you heartburn.

He began to take aim at the next sun-worshipper but stopped because something heavy and squelchy had landed on his head. He froze. For a moment, he wasn't sure what to do. Cautiously, he looked up. The macaws were ripping fruit from the trees, eating the bits they fancied and throwing the debris to the ground. No doubt they believed the macaw god had given them the Earth to exploit.

Back on the beach, he focused in on his third target. Target number three was reading a book. Jeff couldn't make out the title, but the cover featured a sinister-looking man in a dark overcoat and white scarf. And target number three was — *oh no, you didn't!* — that guy whose hospital corporation had suffered cardiac arrest shortly after its Chief Financial Officer had undergone arrest of a different kind on account of a monumental Medicare fraud. What was his name? Elliot Tucker. But wasn't he in a coma in Switzerland? Must have been one of those after-dinner comas. *Click!*

The other beach folk were too distant to be identified, but Jeff snapped them all anyway. He retreated into the forest and sat under a tree that, as far as he could tell, contained no macaws.

But now what? He had some fantastic material; Katherine would be impressed. Yet how tempting was it to try for a little more? Very tempting, was the answer. After all, how often did he find himself in a situation such as this? He'd invested fifteen dollars in the gorilla suit. How could he not attempt to maximize the return on his investment?

He took to his hands and knees and crawled along the beach to the point where the wall ended. Then he looked up.

Jesus Christ, he thought — if Kubla Khan had had the budget, the architects, and a tropical location, this was the kind of thing he might have fantasized about. Terraces, lawns, formal gardens, fountains, pools, rows of palm trees, tropical topiary, panoramic decks with floral plantings and umbrellas, an outdoor restaurant... And a golf course? *Click!*

Golf buggies trundled along landscaped pathways. Nobody seemed to be walking. Beyond the upper terrace were wide, multi-story buildings in glass and pale stone cladding that resembled offices. Dotted around the edge of the golf course were what Jeff took to be private residences. These differed stylistically; some, in Jeff Crock's opinion, lacked taste. A French chateau on a Costa Rican beach?

He took a few more pictures and wondered if Leo Vargas, the tree-frogs' friend and would-be savior, had seen what he was looking at now. How much water did this place drain from the rainforest? What did they do with their waste? Where did they get their power? The huge satellite dishes on top of the office complex suggested they were using a lot. Did the chateau guy leave his air-con on all day?

Now, these were all pertinent questions, but the most pressing was this: How did a gate-crashing gorilla get from the beach to the office buildings without causing a scandal? He considered this for a few minutes until he realized that the answer had been parked before him the whole time.

Just the other side of an ornamental pond, a green-uniformed gardener had abandoned his electric mini-truck. Puffs of smoke rising from distant bushes indicated that he had elected to go on a break. The mini-truck had an enclosed cab. It was, Jeff decided, sufficient for his purposes. He crept up to the truck, opened the door, plucked the gardener's hat off the seat and jammed it on his head. Then he slid in, closed the door softly, and eased his foot on to the accelerator pedal. Nothing happened. He located a parking brake under the dashboard and released it. The truck lurched forward into a flower bed. Unable to locate a reverse gear, he ploughed on through to the far side, traversed an outdoor chessboard, scattering pawns and toppling the white queen, and re-joined one of the main pathways. Then he steered an indirect route uphill, aiming for what looked like the main lobby of the office complex.

At the top, he loitered for a moment behind some shrubbery to check his surroundings. All the action seemed to be on the beach. The zone adjacent to the glass-fronted lobby was deserted. Slowly, he drove out in front of the main doors and glanced in. He saw a woman sitting at a reception desk. She looked up from her computer and stared back at him. *Oh shit*, he thought. But when she raised a hand and gave him a friendly wave, he realized that the sun was in her eyes and she couldn't see him clearly. He waved back and then, chancing happily on the gear selector, reversed slowly out of her line of sight.

Well, that was one close call. What next? On the far side of the lobby was a distinct and imposing section of the building. Glass-fronted like the lobby, it had double-height floors, and was situated directly beneath the satellite gear. Since the sun was currently his friend, Jeff figured he could risk a look. He drove forwards past the lobby. The receptionist looked up again but this time she didn't wave. Jeff gave her a casual salute all the same.

He pulled up alongside the double-height section and peered in. What he saw would have taken his breath away if the increasingly fetid atmosphere inside the gorilla suit hadn't already done so. Rows of desks, computers, banks of screens, men and women in suits and headsets, huge monitors full of financial data and news feeds, vast TV screens all tuned to news stations — Freedom News, most prominently — a tumult of activity, and such a hubbub that Jeff could hear it plainly through glass, truck and gorilla fur.

The scene resembled a Wall Street trading floor, and also the super-villain's lair at the end of a James Bond movie.

It was too much for him. Without thinking, he stepped out of the truck and advanced to the glass. No one seemed to notice him. He raised his camera. *Click!* He snapped away for about thirty seconds and then his instincts kicked in and a funny feeling came over him.

What exactly was he watching here?

The computer monitors showed data from the major South American financial markets. The news networks all carried live feeds from the same city. Crowds, riot police, tanks, tear-gas. Some of the men and women in headsets seemed to be talking to the armed men in masks who appeared on the big screens at the far end of the room. The city was Caracas, Venezuela. These bastards were directing a coup in Venezuela! Fuck!

Frantically, he took more pictures. But then something ominous happened. The light dimmed. His shadow vanished. A cloud had passed in front of the sun and his cloak of invisibility had been snatched away. In a panic, he jumped back into the truck and reversed at full speed towards the lobby. Then he shifted into forward and took off downhill. In his rear-view mirror, he saw the receptionist stand and reach for a phone.

Taking the same short-cut on the way down as he had on the way up, he demolished the black king, barreled through the flower bed and came to a halt in the ornamental pond. Slipping on a rock as he exited the truck, he plunged backwards into the water. He stumbled out of the pond and staggered towards the beach. The gorilla fur had soaked up pond water and was now incredibly heavy. As he loped into the forest, he heard raised voices and barking dogs behind him in the distance. He was beginning to suffocate in the suit; it *had* to come off, disguise or not. The only thing that mattered now was running away — as fast as possible.

But the zip was stuck. Not only that, but the flap at the back of the gorilla's head had got caught in it. Neither the suit nor the head were coming off. *Fucking Eric!*

He stumbled into the trees. Something squishy hit him on the shoulder and he heard the macaws mocking him from on high. Lungs aching, he ploughed deeper into the forest, on and on, away from Rancho Colorado and into the deep green of the Corcovado.

When he could run no further, he rolled under a bush and lay on the ground, chest heaving, head throbbing. Immediately, he noticed a sharp pain in his right knee. And a minute or so later he realized that something else was wrong. He grabbed at his mucky, matted chest with his hairy hands. The spy-camera was gone. It had fallen off in the pond. *Bastard Eric!*

He felt the fight go out of him. His heart sank at the same time as it hammered at the inside of his ribs. What a fucking disaster. He was lost. He couldn't walk any more. What else could he do now but lie here and let happen whatever was going to happen? Would Eric come and rescue him? Yeah, right. He'd already got his two hundred dollars; Jeff should have kept a hundred back. No, those Rancho Colorado fuckers were going to find him, and then... *Shit!*

He closed his eyes and let his hairy arms fall to the ground. Coups, he thought. Yes, he knew a little bit about what happened in coups. Guatemala, El Salvador, Honduras, Pinochet in Chile. Soccer stadiums, mental hospitals, abandoned mineshafts, special houses for the daughters of trade unionists, shock therapy for the economy and anyone who doesn't know what's good for them. The stained iron bed-frame. The steel ring in the cement floor.

The nausea was too much. He opened his eyes. A dozen sets of beady eyes stared back at him from the thickening gloom. Startled, he sat up. The coatimundi took off into the dark, tails aloft.

He sank back down and closed his eyes.

When he opened them again, Eric was standing over him with a fearful look on his face and a flashlight in his hand.

"For fuck's sake, man," he said. "Take the fucking suit off. You look like shit."

CHAPTER 13

If Jeff Crock had been a real gorilla, he reflected bitterly, then the conversation about to ensue between himself and Eric Lapierre, the hippy hotelier, would have been cut very short. As would Eric's disgusting dreadlocks.

Jeff hauled himself to his feet.

"The *zip*," he said.

Eric shone his flashlight in Jeff's face.

"What about it?"

"It's stuck."

"Stuck?"

"Stuck." Jeff took a deep breath and then spoke with quiet purpose.

"Get me out of this thing, Eric. Do it now."

Eric seemed to get the message.

"Oh. Okay, then. Turn around."

Jeff turned. Eric began to yank on the zip, to no effect.

"Huh. You know, you're right. It *is* stuck."

Jeff took another deep breath and counted to five. Then he turned to Eric. Eric took two steps back.

"Eric?"

"Yes?"

"Go get some tools from the jeep. Do whatever you have to do."

"Right. Uh..."

Jeff peered into the forest. Lots of trees, he thought. No jeeps.

"Eric?"

"Mm?"

"Where's the jeep?"

Eric shook his head with some emotion.

"They torched it, man."

"What!"

"I told you they were crazy. I had to run. If I hadn't —"

"It's burnt?"

"Yeah, totally."

Shit! Another vehicle loss to explain to Katherine. What about the insurance? He'd waived everything. He'd be lucky if he was covered for theft by three-toed sloths. Had he left anything in the jeep? No, for once he'd been careful. He'd hidden his passport and other valuables at Eric's. His phone and a small amount of cash were in his pocket, under the gorilla suit. Yes, he'd forgotten to turn the phone off, and it was impossible to operate it with the suit on, but there was no reception in the forest and thus no problem. Well, except what the hell to do now. This was all Eric's fault, wasn't it? Including the loss of the spy-camera and its deliciously incriminating evidence.

Some venting was in order, and he would have let fly right then, except for the look on Eric's face.

"Eric?"

Eric brushed the hair out of his eyes and lowered his flashlight.

"They've got guns, man. Dogs. They're in teams. They're out there, looking for us."

Guns, Jeff thought. Dogs. Teams. Teams of what? Ex-paramilitaries from Columbia? He became aware of a trickle of sweat running down his spine. This was a predicament. He needed help. What he had was Eric.

"Um, Eric. How'd you find me?"

"Followed the howlers."

"Howlers?"

"Howler monkeys. They make this sound. You know, if they see something they don't like."

"Huh. Interesting. How long —"

"Hours."

"You could have just gone —"

"Couldn't abandon you, man."

It was easy to misjudge people, Jeff thought. Here was Eric, dozy slacker that he was, risking his life for sake of a casual acquaintance and two hundred dollars.

"Got to take the suit back. Paid a deposit."

Paid a —

But Eric was laughing, in a nervous sort of way. Jeff felt tears well up in his eyes, and there was nothing he could do about it; the fur on his hands was matted and stiff. The teardrops dribbled unmolested down his cheeks.

"I don't know what to do," he said. "What do we do, Eric?"

"Well," Eric said. "Let's see. Have you eaten?"

"Eaten?"

"You know, like dinner?"

Jeff wondered for a moment if he'd died under the bush and all this were some post-mortem hallucination.

"We'll go to the eco lodge," Eric said, coolly, as if he'd considered the yacht club and rejected it. "I know Isabel. She's, like, the hotel manager."

The eco lodge. Leo Vargas's deluxe yet bio-diverse resort. A promising place to hide from vengeful paramilitaries? Doubtful. A likely source of info on Vargas? Possibly. A good spot for dining? Apparently. Somewhere suitably equipped for the removal of gorilla suits? Definitely.

"We can get to it through the forest," Eric said.

"Let's go."

Eric hesitated.

"You look like you're limping. It's maybe five miles. Think you can make it?"

"Sure."

"We need to keep off the tracks. Could be tough going."

"No problem."

"Okay. One thing before we go."

"Yes?"

"I just want to say I'm sorry."

"Sorry?"

Eric sighed.

"About the iguanas."

Oh, *that.*

"Yeah, me too," Jeff said. "Me too."

They began to walk.

*

Isabel liberated Jeff from the gorilla suit by melting its nylon seams with the mini blow-torch the lodge kitchen kept ready for action in case the executive chef — a stern proponent of local cuisine, she explained — ever lifted his ban on crème brûlée. Relieved, if a little scorched, Jeff then permitted Isabel to apply surgical reinforcement to his injured knee. Next, Isabel brought food and drink, and Jeff complimented Eric on his culinary discernment. After that, Isabel had taken Eric aside for questioning, at length and in Spanish, and Jeff had jumped — or, rather, hobbled — at the opportunity to check out the lodge.

It was impressive. The main building was a tall, spacious, open-sided construction of timber — sustainably harvested, no doubt — with a thatched roof. It contained the dining area, a library, a bar, a gift shop and the front desk. A spiral staircase ascended to a viewing gallery. The lodge sat on the upper slopes of a small hill, wrapped around by forest but with views down to the ocean. Elevated boardwalks on the southern side led to the swimming pool and the guests' bungalows. To the north, a rustic suspension bridge controlled access to what appeared to be a private function room — built on stilts and also thatched, naturally.

Jeff helped himself to a beer from the bar, flopped into a cushioned wicker chair and opened up his senses to the tropical dawn, which now proceeded to do its stuff, as it seemed, for his sole benefit. The ocean shimmered from indigo to turquoise. Sunbeams squeaked between the fronds of palm trees. Parrots, macaws and toucans got down to business, picking up where they had left off the day before. Lizards and geckos vied for basking space. Down at the swimming pool, a white-jacketed attendant began to remove last night's leaves.

Not too shabby, Jeff thought. If you could afford it. But not a patch on Rancho Colorado.

Exhaustion, injury and a second beer took their toll, and Jeff slipped into a tropical slumber. Unbidden, a dreamy pageant played out before his eyes.

Exiled from his dominions on account of yet another video sting and political stitch-up, Jeff had set sail for some mythical island or other in search of ideological tranquility. Not having had the budget for a decent boat, of course, he wasn't surprised to find himself shipwrecked and washed up on a beach of pink sand. And, what do you know, it's the very island he was seeking. But what's this? Someone's flattened the island with concrete and erected a gated community for vanished billionaires only. If Jeff doesn't move along instantly, the least he can expect is Armed Response, if not a surgical drone attack. And who's this strange, deformed creature who wants to lure Jeff into danger?

But it wasn't a strange, deformed creature; it was Eric, shaking him awake. And it looked like he had news.

"They're *here*," he said, his eyes bulging.

Jeff sat up.

"The Columbians?"

"Columbians? No, man. Some of the big wigs. From Rancho Colorado!"

"Why would they be here?"

"They're having breakfast."

"Oh, well, that makes perfect sense. I guess their refrigerator was empty and they —"

"No, man, listen. They're having a breakfast meeting in the Pelican Room." He seemed to be referring to the function room on stilts. "Some important politico flew in from Washington last night. Isabel told me. It's like a secret summit, man."

"Why can't this *politico* just go to Rancho Colorado?"

"Isabel doesn't know."

"What about Vargas?"

"Isabel says he's missing. This Washington guy only booked in after he disappeared."

"What's his name?"

"Isabel says Douglas something."

Douglas. Jeff felt a subtle knot form in his stomach. Not *that* Douglas, surely? Hardly the sort of company Vargas would welcome, one would surmise.

"What else does Isabel say?"

"She says put this on."

Eric handed Jeff a thick cotton safari shirt in eco-friendly olive green. It carried the lodge's branding — a fake-heraldic rosette featuring a smug pelican.

"I don't need a new shirt."

"You do, man. Trust me."

Jeff noted that Eric, too, had been re-outfitted to Isabel's specifications. Ordinarily, he would have disputed the need to look like the Tall One in some god-awful buddy vacation movie, but his brain was racing ahead with schemes and stratagems, and fashion issues were moot. He swapped shirts.

"Okay, here's the plan," he said.

"Plan?" Eric said. "No more plans, dude. Your two hundred bucks is all gone. No offense, but you're on your own. I just wanted to give you the scoop. I've got a hotel to run."

Hotel was way too grand a term, Jeff felt. But he didn't want to alienate Eric.

92

"But you haven't got any guests," he pointed out.

"Iguanas are missing me."

Jeff felt a lip-pursing urge but resisted it.

"Look, I've got more cash," he said, omitting to mention that he'd stashed most of it at Eric's place.

Eric scratched his ear.

"Something's telling me this is a big mistake," he said. "However, let me ask you this. How much?"

"Another hundred?" Jeff said, calculating that Eric would probably settle later for eighty.

"And what do you want me to do?"

"Help me bug the meeting."

"Yeah, that's what I thought."

Jeff waited while Eric considered.

"Iguanas'll be good 'til tonight, right?"

Eric sighed.

"I guess they will. Got the hundred on you?"

"Not really. I need to borrow an audio recorder. Mine got wet."

"Figures. Come on, let's go to Isabel's office. See if you can sweet-talk her."

*

I sabel, for her part, didn't care whether Eric and his idiot friend wanted to bug the entire forest. And yes, she had a digital audio recorder they could borrow, if they must. She didn't care about stupid, clumsy Americans in gorilla suits. It was a matter of supreme indifference to her whether or not they fell into ponds. Rancho Colorado could slide into the ocean for all she cared; in fact, she wished it would. There were only two things that merited her concern. One was what had happened to Leo Vargas. The other was the menacing *Yankees* who'd taken over her hotel.

"What's menacing about them?" Jeff wanted to know.

Isabel launched into Spanish. Eric translated.

They wore suits and ties, despite the humidity. And sunglasses, day and night. They never went anywhere alone. One of them — the *boss* — was always guarded. They were brusque with the staff and didn't leave tips. They all had *guns* — except the boss. Isabel didn't know how they'd managed to book themselves in; they'd just showed up one day on the system. They'd arranged a special day-long boat-trip today for the other guests, and hadn't allowed any of them to opt out. And they'd taken it upon themselves to give the staff — except for herself, Felix and José — an unofficial day off.

"And the boss is called Douglas?" Jeff asked.

"Douglas Moreland."

"Oh fuck."

Eric gave Jeff a look.

"Why'd you say "fuck," Jeff?"

Well, there wasn't time to run down the entire charge sheet, was there? Among the highlights: Services to the petro-chemical-mercenary complex in

Africa; *pro bono* attorney to the enhanced techniques crowd; subverter of all that was fine and decent in what was left of the American constitution; enabler-in-chief to War Criminal Number One.

"Because he's one bad, dude, Eric."

"Uh-huh. Are we bugging him?"

"You bet."

Isabel intervened to point out that the Yankees would be getting out of bed soon, and Eric and Jeff, should they wish to pursue their lunatic plan, ought to get out of her sight and take up position in the jungle-filled gully underneath the Pelican Room.

"And watch out for snakes!" she added.

The jungle provided good cover, Jeff noted, and appeared to be snake-free. There was only one problem. The floor of the Pelican Room was way above them — so high up, in fact, that the chance of overhearing anything was slight.

"We need a long pole or stick," he said.

They hunted in the undergrowth. Eric located a length of bamboo.

"Good," Jeff said. "Give me your shoe-lace."

"What about *your* shoe-lace?"

"Velcro."

"Shit."

Eric surrendered his laces. Jeff tied the recorder to the tip of the bamboo pole.

"When they come, I'll turn it on and hold it up."

"Brilliant."

"So now we wait."

"Yeah."

They waited. Then a thought occurred to Jeff.

"Eric?"

"Yes?"

"How do we get back to your place?"

"Ha! Don't worry. I got the key to Vargas's personal transportation. Found it in Isabel's office."

"What is it? Jeep? Land Cruiser?"

"Dunno."

"Hmm."

"Shh — they're coming!"

There were six of them, by Jeff's reckoning — five men and one woman. And two more big guys on guard outside the door.

"Here we go."

He turned the recorder on and raised it up towards the floor of the Pelican Room.

After a minute or so, Eric whispered in his ear.

"How d'you know if it's working?"

"Yeah, good point."

Jeff lowered the recorder. A quick rewind revealed that it wasn't working. All they had was an indistinct hubbub.

"Need to get closer," Jeff said. He studied the woodwork above them. The Pelican Room had been constructed in a deliberately rough-hewn, rustic style —

for extra eco-friendliness, presumably. There were gaps between the floorboards. In one place, there was just enough space.

"Over here," he said, easing his way through the jungle until the gap was overhead. Luckily, it appeared to be underneath a table — the breakfast buffet, perhaps.

"Now lift me up."

"What? You're too big."

"Oh, come on!"

"*You* lift *me* up."

Jeff pointed at his bad knee.

"All right, fuck it. Get up."

And so, with all the style of trainees at a cheap circus, they formed a wobbly human tower. But then, with NASA-like precision, Jeff guided his secret probe through the launch window and into hostile space.

Above, in the Pelican Room, it sounded as though the pastries and the pleasantries had come to an end and something more rambunctious had begun. The breakfast party seemed to turn into a celebration. Champagne corks popped. Toasts were proposed and drunk. Cheering and foot-stamping ensued. Jeff couldn't make out much of the conversation, but "Venezuela" came through clearly enough. Jeff couldn't quite hear what had become of that most fortunate country's former president, but whatever his fate had been, it occasioned much merriment. "Where in the world is Leo Vargas?" someone yelled, to general amusement. There came the sound of furniture-shifting. They were pretending to look for him. What a hoot.

Then things got quieter. Someone was going to make a speech. When it began, Jeff recognized the speaker at once. Long, sinuous sentences, full of passive aggression. Questions posed, left to hang and then answered. A tone aggrieved and disingenuous, coy yet vindictive. Wheedling belligerence. It was the way that Douglas Moreland always talked.

Of course, something had to give. It might have been Eric's back, but, not so surprisingly, it was Jeff's luck. His phone emitted the loud, chirruping noise associated with the arrival of a text message. Clearly, it had recovered from its dunking in the pond and was eager to make up for lost time. And Vargas's guests, Jeff should have realized, expected Wi-Fi with their wilderness.

Everything went quiet. Jeff swayed on Eric's shoulders. Then all was commotion. Eric ditched Jeff into a spiky bush. Jeff's bugging pole fell against a palm tree and the audio recorder went flying. Eric took off downhill into the jungle. From above, Jeff heard the shouting of orders and the banging of doors. He plucked himself out of the bush, spotted the audio recorder on the ground, snatched it up and plunged into the undergrowth.

Eric was fast, but Jeff had long legs. Despite his bad knee he caught up with Eric at the entrance to the lodge's eco-friendly, educational gym trail.

"No time for that now," he said, wheezing.

"Fuck off, Jeff. I'm out of here."

"Don't be like that. It's okay. We'll take Vargas's car and head back to your place."

"Those are mean-looking guys back there!"

"Yeah, they are."

"You're being too cool about this, you know?"

"Kind of used to it. Come on. Parking lot's hidden round the back."

"Shit!"

They fought their way through ferns and creepers, past the camouflaged water tanks and smelly but ecologically-sound waste-water swamps, to the parking area behind the lodge. There were pickup trucks, service vehicles, trailers and four big, black SUVs with Texas license plates.

Eric seemed at a loss.

"Which one is Vargas's?"

"Try the key."

Eric hit the unlock button on the key.

"Where is it?"

"Dunno," Jeff said. "Try again."

This time he saw the lights flash.

"Oh, okay, there it is," he said pointing. And yes, he thought, it's Leo Vargas we're talking about here, so no surprise.

"*That's* it?" Eric said.

"Uh-huh."

"What the *fuck* is it?"

"Electric car. Two-seater. Have 'em in Europe."

Eric seemed to struggle for words.

"We can't go in *that*."

"Sure we can. Come on. I'll drive."

Eric looked at the row of black SUVs.

"You're fucking crazy. We might as well walk."

"Get in."

"No!"

Jeff grabbed the key, loped over to the car and crammed himself into the driver's seat. Noting with satisfaction that the controls were almost identical to those in the mini-truck at Rancho Colorado, he zipped up alongside Eric and opened the passenger door.

"Get in."

"It's fucking ridiculous, man!"

Two gunshots rang out from the hill behind them. All of a sudden, Eric was in the passenger seat.

"Hit the gas!"

"Battery."

"Battery!"

Jeff swung the car down the dusty ramp that led to the public road. This road, Jeff now realized, was not paved. It was composed of gravel and pot-holes. Did Vargas really use this car, he wondered? A man who could afford any car he wanted? He put his foot down. The car's velocity crept up to forty-five kilometers per hour. He tried to steer around the craters in the road but rapidly discovered that it was better simply to barrel through them. Eric started to moan quietly to himself. Not his fault, of course. He wasn't accustomed to the rigors of twenty-first century investigative *blogging*.

But a glance now in the rear-view mirror told Jeff that sang-froid could only take you so far. At least two of the black SUVs were on his tail. He glanced at Eric. Best not to say anything yet, he thought. A flashing indicator on the dashboard caught his attention. It resembled the battery-power icon on a cell phone. One bar lit up out of six — not good. Didn't Vargas bother to charge the thing? It was almost enough to make you doubt his eco-credentials.

He'd got the car up to fifty-five now. But the SUVs were probably doing — what? Seventy, eighty *miles* per hour? That meant Jeff had maybe two hundred yards in which to come up with something. Eric had curled up into a ball and was probably going to be of limited assistance.

What had this little car got, Jeff asked himself, that the big SUVs didn't have? While he mulled this question, he noticed that they were driving through a pastoral zone. On the left were cows; and on the descending slope to the right, pigs. On each side of the road was a sturdy fence of wood and wire.

And then he realized what it was that the little car had and the big SUVs didn't. Narrowness.

Coming up on the right was a flimsy-looking gate. It was roughly two pigs wide. About the same as the car. He swung to the left, then back to the right, to take the gate head-on.

Eric looked up.

"Oh shit!"

The car smashed through the gate, ripping the mirrors from its doors, and careened downhill, scattering pigs to left and right.

Jeff checked his mirror. The SUVs had piled into the fence and were stuck on it. Doors sprang open. Men in suits spilled out. Weapons were raised and lowered. The SUVs struggled to reverse out of the fence. Clouds of dust and smoke rose up. There followed much pointing, gesticulating and waving of arms. Shouting. Arguments.

"That went quite well, I thought," Jeff said.

Eric tipped his head back and closed his eyes.

*

The pig farmer had been quite taken with Jeff's high-tech, emission-free vehicle. So much so, in fact, that he had agreed to accept the car, albeit in less than showroom condition, as payment for a lift into town.

Back at Eric's place, Eric had decided he needed to lie down for a while.

"Those guys don't know who we are, right?"

"No," Jeff said. "Unless Isabel told them."

"She wouldn't tell them."

Jeff thought about that for a moment. Isabel was a tough lady, wasn't she? She was close to, and presumably enjoyed the protection of, Leo Vargas. Wherever he was.

"I think I'll take a walk," he said. "Be on guard, okay? Just in case. You got my number."

"Yup."

"All right. See you later."

He left the hostel and walked towards the center of town. Things were pretty quiet, as you'd expect in the middle of the afternoon. This was good; everything looked normal. No *Yankees*. No Texas license plates. Few people around, but he might ask a discreet question or two, if the opportunity arose.

In some private spot he would stop and check his messages. And he intended to listen to the clandestine recording he'd made, tottering on Eric's shoulders, bugging pole in hand, underneath the Pelican Room.

Speaking of which, it turned out that the incoming message responsible for terminating the bugging session, and thus precipitating a high-speed chase into pig country, was another nugget of social-media wisdom from Dolt, the idiot Brit whose ravings, Jeff remembered, Katherine had chosen to inflict on him. Now why did she have to do that? It was meant well, no doubt. But, really, what did she get out of this stuff? It was a distraction. *Things* — coups, for example — were happening in the real world.

He opened the message. It was gibberish:

> Just chatted with a butcher in Swindon. Told me he knows who the extremists are cos they boycott his shop. Will the police listen? What do you think? Political correctness gone mad!

He ground his teeth and pressed the delete key. Then he noticed something odd. He'd expected a torrent of messages from Katherine, but there was only one. And it contained a single word: *Swordfish*.

Swordfish was a pre-arranged secret codeword. He bit his lip and tried to remember what it meant. Katherine was big on secret codewords. She also favored anagrams, riddles and crossword puzzles — genetic deficiencies inherited from her egg-head parents. *Swordfish?* It was one of the more serious codewords. At the very least it meant *stop using this phone, get rid of it and get a new one.* It might also mean the forces of conservatism were on to him and danger threatened.

Seriously, though, it was time to be prudent. He removed the memory card from the phone and performed a full factory reset, thus returning it to a prelapsarian state of political innocence.

Then he headed for the gas station, which was, in his experience, a good place to ditch a compromised cell phone. One simply tossed it, turned on, into the back of a pickup truck. But as he crossed the road, something caught his attention.

At the far end of the street, a mob scene was in progress. This also appeared to be the location of the airstrip. He changed direction and set off to investigate.

As he drew closer he realized he was looking at Leo Vargas's high-paying guests — now, apparently, evicted from paradise. Free boat trip notwithstanding, they didn't look happy. A little closer, and he began to attract attention. But they weren't looking at his face; they were looking at his shirt.

"Hey, you!" someone yelled.

"Yeah, *you!* We want to talk to *you!*"

Okay, Jeff thought, talk to me. Tell me what's going on.

A wide man with a gray moustache and baggy shorts now appointed himself group spokesman and barged to the front of the crowd.

"You do *not do* that," he said.

"Do what?" Jeff asked. This set off a minor storm of vituperation.

"You do *not*... *Shut down* in the *middle* of the *week!*"

"Oh, you mean the lodge has shut down?"

This was really the wrong thing to say.

"Do you have *any* idea who I am?"

"Nope," Jeff said, scanning the crowd in search of Isabel and not finding her. "Do you know where Isabel is?"

"You have *no* idea! He has *no* idea!"

"That's what I said. So what's going on up there?"

The crowd, not particularly good-looking to begin with, now turned distinctly ugly. And it seemed unlikely that they had any useful intelligence. But it was worth one last try.

"Anybody here seen Douglas Moreland?"

The wide man stepped into Jeff's private space and stabbed him in the chest with his forefinger.

"You know what *I'm* doing, soon as I get back? I'm going on Trip Monkey and I'm leaving the *worst* review you ever saw! What's your name?"

"Leo Vargas."

"*Var*gas. Well, screw *you!*"

The wide man spun around on his heel. Before he could regain his balance and march off, Jeff lifted a flap on the man's child-sized day pack and slipped the cell phone inside.

"Safe journey..."

He turned and walked away, the half-hearted obscenities of thwarted nature-lovers ringing in his ears.

So Moreland had shut down Pelican Lodge. Why? Pique at having his breakfast meeting bugged? Displeasure at losing a high-speed chase? It would have been in character. Part of a plot to destroy Leo Vargas, or, if this had already occurred, to dance on his grave? More to the point, where was Isabel? Yet more to the point, should Eric be left alone any longer?

He began to jog, as best he could, back to Eric's hostel. When he got there, he saw fresh tire tracks in the dirt.

He found Eric's shirt in the hallway leading to Eric's private bathroom. A glistening, dark stain obscured the image of Leo Vargas's self-satisfied sea-bird.

Eric was on the bathroom floor. He had a single, large hole in his chest. He had made it from the lounge to the bathroom.

What have you done now, Jeff? For Christ's sake, what have you done?

Jeff ran to his room and recovered his belongings. Then he limped outside and collapsed on the ground under the wild plum tree, with his head in his hands.

At length, the sound of a twig snapping above his head made him look up.

The iguanas looked down on him in silence.

CHAPTER 14

John Dolt's personal assistant, or butler, had been given, or had inherited, too many names — more than a normal person could sensibly use. Dolt had unreservedly accepted the last of these, the almost middle-class *Reeves*, but had balked, with some vehemence, at the first, *Gideon*. Yet familiarity, and a weird but growing sense of brotherhood — or collegiality, as the man himself put it — had worked some kind of sentimental magic, and Dolt now reversed himself. He felt no regrets. There was *something* gnawing away there, at the back of his brain, but never mind. *Gideon* it was.

And Gideon had been by his side for almost every moment of the past five days. It had all been a bit of a whirlwind. For Dolt, to be the center of attention had been exhilarating. He'd never been the focus of so much concern before — well, not in a good way. And who would have thought that *education* would turn out to be so rewarding in its own right — when everyone said it was just a way of getting a job in a bank, if you could afford it.

He had been schooled, instructed, coached, and he was loving it. So many mysteries had been explained; so many contradictions resolved; so many paradoxes elucidated (to use a word that Gideon had recommended to him). The experts over at the Atlantic Affairs Institute had vaulted to the top of their game for him, unstinting in their solicitude (more Gideon words). All except, that is, for Eva, the vampire economist, who was off sick.

So far so good, then. And Dolt's what's-it — his *vocabulary* — had improved no end. But five days — was it enough? Dolt's first big test awaited him today.

The PM — the current one, not the one who was always hanging around on the off-chance — had convened a special session of the Policy Steering Committee of the National Government. Dolt was to be the star turn.

"They're dying to hear from you," Gideon had said. "You'll have them eating out of your hand. Just remember to look them in the eye. They're not used to it. You'll be sure to —"

"Freak them out?"

"Precisely."

This get-together was scheduled for eleven o'clock in the morning, which, Dolt gathered, was considered extremely early in Governing Circles. He might have mentioned that it was deemed quite bloody late in Minibus Circles, but didn't.

Jacqueline, Dolt's stylist, had provided him with clothes for the occasion: Jeans, a white polo shirt and a brown suede jacket. It seemed a little casual, but presumably she knew what she was doing. And Des, Dolt's ex-brickie special-forces security consultant, had laid on transport — a black Range Rover with tinted glass and too-fat tires. When he saw this, Dolt wondered what had become of the white Jobba van, and felt a pang of longing.

During the ride, Dolt asked Des if he had any information about Tamsin and Tamara, Dolt's daughters; or about Victoria, their poison-peddling mother. We'll do that later, Des replied, without turning his head.

The venue for the great event turned out to be the very room in which the PM conducted his so-called cabinet meetings. It was surprisingly poky. The principals on the Steering Committee — the blokes who did the actual steering, Dolt supposed, although one of them was a woman — were crammed in, shoulder to shoulder, at the coffin-shaped table. Why this steering business required so many of them was a question he might consider raising later. The Steerers' minions had parked themselves behind their masters on dining chairs shoved up against the walls.

Dolt whispered in his assistant's ear.

"Not much room, is there?"

"Looks good in the pictures. We're over *there*."

Gideon indicated the one empty seat at the table. It was in the middle, facing the fireplace: The Seat of Honor.

Dolt stepped into the room. Instantly, the hubbub died and all heads swiveled in his direction. What, he wondered, had they been expecting? Was he such an oddity? You'd have thought so from the looks on their faces. It reminded him of the time that Hamid, on a bet, had introduced a baby camel into the saloon bar at the Britannia Arms in Wembley. (Gideon had told him not to fret any more about Hamid, so he wasn't going to.) Except, of course, that the hard-hearted boozers at the Britannia had fallen about in delight; that didn't appear to be the case here. The committee members glared at him. Some of them had their mouths open.

Awe, perhaps? Envy? Bafflement in the face of the sturdy nobility of the common man? Well, call it whatever you liked; basically, they were gob-smacked. Calmly, he rubbed his hands and returned their gaze. The effect was gratifying. Gideon then ushered Dolt to his seat and took up his own position, nestling behind Dolt's right shoulder. Dolt surveyed the table. He recognized a few of the faces, but couldn't put names to them. Directly opposite, however, was the PM, with a fixed, brittle grin on his mug.

"Hullo," Dolt said.

"Um, hello, yes. Excellent. Very glad you're here, ah, John. Very glad."

"Me too."

The PM wafted an indifferent but well-manicured hand.

"I expect you know who everyone is, so we'll get right on, shall we? But first, the photo boys. Let them in, will you!"

The door swung open and a posse of photographers leaned in.

"Smile, everyone," the PM said, humorously.

Dolt felt Gideon's breath at his ear.

"Don't smile."

Dolt assumed a demeanor of unamused seriousness.

Cameras flashed, then an unseen hand eased the door shut.

"Now I don't want anyone to think," the PM said, a little too earnestly, Dolt felt, "that this is any kind of stunt or gimmick. John is here for a very good reason."

Dolt scanned the table and detected frowning skepticism down at the right-hand end.

"Your enemies," Gideon whispered.

"I know you've all seen it on the telly," the PM went on, "but I want to give you my first-hand version."

He started in on the tale of how fate had conspired with fortune to cause his path to cross with that of the honest, hard-working citizen you saw sitting at this table today. It had all happened down at the Big Builder DIY Warehouse — now seized by bailiffs, unfortunately — but, nevertheless...

Dolt knew this one, so he tuned out and studied his fellow Policy Steering Committee members.

Of course, he had been warned by Polly, his Political Advisor, that the PM was constantly harried by a tetchy group of *irreconcilables*, who would automatically oppose any initiative that crossed their *red lines*. Dolt, she cautioned, would find that *he* was very much the sort of thing they had in mind. Not to worry, though; Dolt should be able to tame them. Polly would supply the ammo.

Dolt sneaked a glance at the right-hand end of the table. Yes, he thought — head-bangers. Bizarre hair-styles; brightly-colored ties; blood-shot eyes that didn't blink and appeared to operate independently; raw, pink cheeks; mouths like goldfish. Yes, sir, Polly knew her stuff.

So what about the mob at the other end of the table?

According to Polly, the other main faction was that of the *utopians*. A *utopia*, she had grumpily explained, when pressed, was a really stupid idea that some simple-minded people got stuck up their arses until they couldn't think straight. Anyway, these utopians were always coming up with brilliant concepts that they never thought through. They would bang on about them until they got their way. The concept would then be tested to destruction, implementation failure blamed, the rubble brushed to one side, and the next concept lined up.

Dolt took a furtive peek at the left-hand end of the table. Polly wasn't wrong, he thought. Floppy fringes; shiny foreheads; dazzling white shirts, incorrectly buttoned; eager hands; lop-sided grins; a collective air of mania.

"...and if we are to take the country with us, as we make these momentous changes," the PM was saying, "it is imperative that we show we are on the side of... That we are listening to... That we share the same values as..."

He seemed to struggle for the right phrase — though Dolt could see that he was coming up with lots and rejecting them all.

"As…"

A seat-shuffling noise arose as the collective gaze of the entire room zoned in on Dolt.

"Yes, well, *him*, obviously," the PM concluded.

An awkward silence. Then one of the utopians piped up.

"You know, this could really work for us. We don't need to pay Roger or Peter to find out what the, ah, *populus* really thinks. He's sitting right here."

Something stirred at the right-hand end of the table.

"Who cares what the *populus* thinks? We know what we want to do."

Grunting approval from the irreconcilables.

"You see, I was thinking," the PM said, "that it wouldn't be a bad idea to have someone we could send out… Is *avatar* the word I'm looking for?"

"Human shield?"

The PM seemed cross.

"No. That's not what I mean at all. Look, I don't want to point any fingers, but our communications effort has been, well, deplorable. People don't seem to be getting it. We need *something*."

"We've got the papers."

"Yes, I know. And they're doing all they can. But they're not what they were, and it's just not enough. We need… Authenticity. That's what we need. And here he is at this very table."

It was nice that they thought he was authentic, Dolt felt. And flattering, sort of, that they thought they might need him. But did they truly understand what they were getting into?

"All right," the PM said. "I've got a list of items for this session — issues upon which I believe John here may have some exciting perspectives — but does anyone want to raise anything before we commence?"

One of the utopians did.

"A few of us were chatting last night, and we came up with this radical plan to rewire the entire national social-capital infrastructure by decentralizing planning incentives, auctioning the environmental regulation spectrum and encouraging choice and competition within families by allowing individual members to opt out and purchase their own family services. Would you like to hear it?"

"No. Anyone else?"

One of the irreconcilables had a peeve. Capital gains tax was a monstrous drain on the nation's animal spirits. Dolt studied the speaker. Pet lover? Folksy religionist? No, the problem, surprisingly, was that many people, having acquired, through no fault of their own, a not-excessive number of houses, were burdened not only with their upkeep — some of them were National Heritage! — but with extortionate taxes if they sold them. This, it was clear, was costing the country much-needed jobs.

The PM sighed and studied the plasterwork on the ceiling for a moment. Then he looked down.

"John?"

Dolt searched his memory; he knew the answer to this one, didn't he? Oh, right…

"Do we really want to penalize success in this country?" he said, "I know I don't."

A smattering of applause filled the room.

"Well played," Gideon whispered.

Dolt sensed that things were going his way, and that the irreconcilables, while still hostile, were no longer quite sure what they were dealing with. A dynamic then developed in which the PM kicked off an issue, the two factions flailed at it in their differing but equally leaden-footed styles, and then the ball got booted over to Dolt. And throughout, of course, Gideon the coach was there for him, with the encouraging word and the wet sponge.

The disturbances?

"I've been through hard times," Dolt said. "I didn't complain. I didn't riot."

Scheming foreigners?

"If I wanted to be a citizen of the world," Dolt said, "I wouldn't have been born in England."

Work-shy scroungers?

"I've never missed a day's work in my life, and I've never asked anyone for anything," Dolt said. On a technical level, these were big, fat lies. On the emotional level, they felt very right. "If anyone wants a hand-out so they can sit on their couch all day, stuffing down burgers and watching Sky Sports, they can come and ask me for it."

Interfering bishops?

"If I wanted socialist sermons, I'd go to Russia," Dolt said.

"China," Gideon whispered.

"I mean China," Dolt said.

"What about Venezuela?" one of the utopians asked. "No, wait..."

"It's why I don't go to church these days," Dolt continued. There were other reasons, of course.

Trade union wreckers?

"What do you think would happen," Dolt asked, "if all the truly productive people in this country walked out? Right to strike? My arse. Let's all have a right to hovercrafts!"

Pampered bureaucrats?

"If someone gave me a gold-plated pension for drinking tea and counting paper-clips," Dolt said, "I wouldn't be able to look at myself in the mirror. How did it all go so horribly wrong?"

Noisy feminists?

"I'm not saying they should all stay at home and do the housework. Not at all. Not by any means. But, let's face it, someone's got to, haven't they?"

Arrogant multiculturalists?

"If you come to my house," Dolt said, remembering his half-a-house just off the A40 and wondering what the *decontamination* ordered by Des might have turned up, "you play by my rules. You show some respect. Only good manners, innit?"

Subsidized artists?

"My daughter could have done better than that when she was three," Dolt said, trying to remember if either Tamsin or Tamara had ever painted anything.

Greedy single mothers?

"Yes, well," Dolt began, thinking of Victoria and her solicitor's demands, "this is a big issue because I, er..."

"Blank check," Gideon whispered.

"Because irresponsible behavior can never be rewarded with a blank check," Dolt said. "And as for claiming that I —"

He felt Gideon nudge his elbow.

"I mean, as for claiming you can't work just because you have six kids — well, whose fault is that?"

Militant greens?

"They want to come round my house and stick a dirty great windmill in my garden, they won't let me fly to Spain for a well-earned holiday, they want to force me to drive around in a death-trap electric toy car, they expect me to wash out my used baked bean tins — meanwhile, they're all sipping Beaujolais in their f—, their flippin' organic farmhouses in Tuscany? Just who do they think they are? What planet are they on?" He didn't have a garden, of course. But the principle applied.

Dangerous extremists?

"Suppose," Dolt said, simulating an emotional catch in the throat, as recommended by his tutors, "they blew up my child at her school. Suppose they kidnapped my wife and tortured her and raped her. And suppose *you knew* that they were dangerous, but you didn't put them away because, *oh well, they haven't actually done anything yet* — what would you say to me? Eh?"

This caused an outbreak of chair-shuffling and watch-checking, so he knew he'd hit the mark. But now it seemed as though the referee was about to blow his whistle. Out of the corner of his eye, Dolt could see Gideon looking very alert. The PM chucked in the final ball of the game.

The Greater Persian Question?

"We must take it very seriously," Dolt said, nodding slowly in accordance with his training. "Very seriously indeed." This occasioned some brief but impassioned applause from the utopians.

A subtle tap on the shoulder from Gideon.

"Excellent."

"Well," the PM said, "I think I speak for everyone here when I say we're all very impressed with what we've heard. And I therefore propose to appoint John as a Special Representative of the National Government. Anyone have a problem with that?"

There was a moment's uneasy silence. Then one of the irreconcilables spluttered to life, accompanied by groans from the other end of the table.

"Do we really have to play along with this pathetic charade that we give a shit about the petty concerns of the plebs? Smack of firm government, that's what they need. We're withholding our support on this one."

"Really?"

And it was at this point, it seemed to Dolt, that some unspoken communication passed between Gideon, his loyal assistant, and the PM.

"Perhaps John would like to comment on that," the PM said.

Dolt knew a hint when he heard one. He loaded up one of the zingers Polly had prepared earlier.

"It is my earnest belief," he said, "that the public is ready for plain talking. They are gagging for it, in my opinion. Look, I can't give fancy speeches, and I don't know lots of posh words but I do know two simple words very well. And so do the British people. They are *right* and *wrong*. Now, anybody and his dog will tell you that you won't find a bigger foe of job-destroying Big Government taxes than me. But I'll tell you this: I pay what I owe. I don't shovel it all in my yacht and sneak off down the Caribbean with it."

An exquisite chill seemed to descend on the table. No one spoke, so Dolt, reasoning that Polly had put in a lot of work, and it was a shame to waste it, resumed.

"What's more, I have to say I was surprised — very surprised — that the issue of migrants has not come up today. I can tell you that it is a major concern to everyone I meet. We risk being swamped. Not least by the huge number of illegal nannies coming over here and being exploited — both financially and also photographically, if you know what I mean."

A long silence.

"I take it we're all agreed then," the PM said, with bitter chirpiness.

And then it was all over. The PM stood up, reached across the table and shook Dolt's hand. It was only a single shake, it was limp, and the PM avoided eye contact — but Dolt felt that some transaction in his favor had been registered. The PM then fled the room, in the decisive manner favored by the baby camel at the Britannia pub. After that, the rest of the Committee and their hangers-on formed a scrum at the door. Dolt was pleased to note, however, that, rather like some sort of political force-field, a buffer zone of empty space had formed around him and his passage was greatly eased.

"Jolly well done," Gideon whispered as they left the room. "Knocked 'em all for six."

Dolt paused.

"You mean, back of the net every time."

"Well, yes. If you prefer. Same thing."

Power, Dolt thought. Intangible, yet you could feel it on the move. Interesting. But Gideon was looking at him strangely.

"You know, there was something you said..."

"Oh?"

"About the truly productive people..."

"What about them?"

Gideon smiled.

"I thought it was interesting, that's all."

They resumed their progress to the front hall, at the end of which, through the doorway and beyond the armed police, Dolt could see Des waiting for them by the black Range Rover. Its rear door was already open.

As he stepped outside, Dolt's new, super-secure phone bleated. A text message had arrived from his Director of Communications, whose name, Dolt was now interested to learn, was James — or, as he preferred to be known, Jaz. According to Jaz, Dolt's social media campaign was *mega-trending*, and Dolt's *follower-cohorts* were *super-scaling*. What this meant was obscure, but it sounded positive.

He acknowledged the cheers of a small but enthusiastic crowd, posed for the cameras, and then bundled himself into the back of the Range Rover. Gideon slipped in alongside.

"A very good morning's work, indeed," he said.

Work? Dolt thought. *Call that work?*

"But the real work comes this afternoon. You haven't forgotten?"

"Oh, you mean the *Faith Initiative*. Are you saying that's a bigger deal?"

"Of course."

How could that be? He'd just aced the PM and the entire Policy Steering Committee. Weird. It could only mean one thing.

"Will *he* be there?"

"He certainly will."

"Ah."

"Exactly. Now, how about lunch? I know a really super place in Knightsbridge."

"Sure. Whatever."

"Having fun?"

"Yes. Yes, I think I am."

"Glad to hear it. You finished the book, I gather?"

"What, Amber?"

"Read any other books lately?"

"No."

"Enjoy it?"

"Uh-huh."

"Thought you would. Onward!"

Des put his foot down and they powered through the traffic of the metropolis on their way, Dolt now permitted himself to imagine, to glory.

*

O ver lunch — one order of Lobster Provençal and one of Steak Frites — Dolt's personal assistant brought him up to date on developments.

Des had completed the *decontamination* process, and everything was satisfactory on that score.

"Did he, er — did he find anything?" Dolt asked.

"Should he have?"

"No. Not at all."

"That's all right, then."

Play along, Dolt thought. Play along, for now.

Gideon was squinting at him.

"Did Des mention he wanted to talk to you later?"

"About the girls? Yes."

"Good, good. Best all round if we get that out of the way."

That queasy feeling in his stomach wasn't the frites, Dolt knew. But he was afraid to follow up on it. Instead, subtly, he changed the subject.

"Did Des do anything with the Jobba?"

108

"What's a Jobba?"

"It's... Never mind."

Dolt's phone bleated again. This time it was some kind of social media blast — apparently from himself:

> Had a natter with an electrician in Luton. Says the euro red tape he has to put up with is diabolical. Can't change a plug without permission from Brussels. Next thing we'll all be driving on the right! Independence now!

He showed his phone to Gideon.

"Ha! I see young James has been busy."

"Jaz."

"Really? Wonder how his mother likes that."

Dolt put his phone away and finished his meal. Gideon ordered dessert — a confection of chocolate and meringue.

"Into rich food, I see," Dolt observed.

"Rich everything, really. Listen — more good news. You met that big chap from Freedom News — what's his name? Gunner? Well, the new media rules go into effect tomorrow, which means that FNN-UK can finally take to the air."

"What new rules?"

"Oh, it's just that you're allowed to have opinions now. Like in America. About bloody time. Right?"

"Suppose so."

"*You* are going to have your own slot. It's called *John's Jury.*"

"I'm getting my own TV show?"

Perhaps there were islands in his future, after all.

"Just a slot. You and your guests debate some case and then you pass judgment."

"The jury does."

"Not really, it's just you."

"Then the name doesn't make sense."

"It's only television, John."

Gideon's dessert arrived. Dolt took the initiative.

"Question."

"Yes?"

"Why did you tell me not to smile?"

"You'll understand when you see the pictures."

"Okay. What about these *factions*, though. Whose side are we on then, Gideon?"

"We're on our side."

"Not the PM's?"

"No. Ours."

"Right. But you and the PM... It seemed like..."

"He made you a sprong. That's a better result than we anticipated."

"A *sprong?*"

"Special Representative of the National Government. It's something they do when they're in a panic and they need to distract attention. Usually, it's some celebrity businessman or Olympic medal-winner. You're in good company."

"So what will they make me do?"

"Nothing. *They're* going to be dancing to *your* tune."

"Oh? How?"

Gideon finished his dessert and chucked a couple of fifties down on the table. "Later. It's time for some *Faith*. Come along."

*

Though its official Head Office was located in Kensington, the Global Faith Initiative had decided to house its main operations in yet another Mayfair townhouse, just a couple of streets away from the Atlantic Affairs Institute. There was obviously something about the neighborhood. But this townhouse, Dolt noted, was grander still. You had to conclude that the really serious money was in Global Faith.

The contrast with that morning's meeting was instructive: No cramped spaces; no spindly dining chairs; no dim and dusty chandeliers; no orange curtains; no choking mist of fear, hatred and suspicion. Here, all was space and light. The conference table was high-tech, pale and circular. All the fixtures and fittings were top-quality. Air-conditioning was installed and functioning. The carpet was new, the artwork tastefully modern, and the staff courteous and relaxed. Sure, there was major security on the way in, but then you'd expect that, wouldn't you?

Dolt had barely finished admiring this splendiferousness when he became aware that Gideon had been distracted by an elegant woman in a black suit, who was all too apparently a dear old friend. Finding himself off the leash for the first time in days, he wandered the room in a mood of amiable curiosity. In the far corner, a discreet door stood ajar. He peeked in and got a rear view of a man in shirt-sleeves, sitting at a desk, in front of a computer. On the screen was some kind of corporate web site. It featured a picture of a Land Rover cresting a sand dune, under the heading "Boschenkop".

He was about to tip-toe away when he spotted the man's reflection in the window beyond the desk: It was the former PM — the one who was always angling for high-paying jobs while devoting his time to unpaid diplomacy — in person. He was frowning at a sheet of paper filled with columns of numbers.

Dolt studied the reflection: Tensioned eyes; dangling jaw; crazy hair; skin creased like worn-out leather; the stench of desperation. He backed away silently with the same sense of horror he'd felt when, aged about six, he'd seen his father naked.

"There you are!" Gideon said. "What's the matter, John? Are you all right?"

"Um, yes, fine," Dolt said. "Could I have a glass of water, please?"

"Over there. Help yourself."

"Yes. Thanks, Gideon."

In order to steady his nerves, Dolt spiked his water with a sly shot of gin. Not being a gin-drinker, he could only estimate the appropriate magnitude of this courage-booster. But there wasn't any vodka and this, he felt, was an emergency. Duly fortified, he re-joined his personal assistant and told himself to get a grip.

But hang on. What had just happened here? The PM — the current one, that is — held no fears for Dolt at all. The question of who was boss had been settled, for all practical purposes, back in the bathroom department at Big Builder. Dolt could, if necessary, take him down with one hand tied behind his back. And he wasn't fazed at all by the Steering Committee and its *factions*. Yet *this* bloke...

"Feeling better?" Gideon asked.

"Think so."

"Then let's take our seats. Put this on."

"What is it?"

"It's a lanyard with your credentials."

Actually, it was just a loop of string with a card attached. Dolt inspected it: *Rand Purdo Fellow in Strategic Studies, Atlantic Affairs Institute.* Were they having a laugh?

"What's a Rand Purdo?"

"He's a very successful entrepreneur, who sponsors philanthropic enterprises."

"Yank?"

"American, yes."

"And what are —"

"Later, John, later."

"What does yours say?"

"Just 'Secretary.'"

"Should say, 'Personal assistant.'"

Gideon gave him a look. Dolt decided to shut up.

The table began to fill. Eventually, there were about twenty men and women, and what struck Dolt — apart from the ample elbow room at the table and the perfect gender balance — were the confidence, poise, elegant manners and generally sunny mood of the gathering. And they were all so *good-looking*, somehow. How did they do it? There was nothing intrinsically beautiful about any of them. It was mysterious — but much to be preferred to the carnival of ugliness that called itself the Policy Steering Committee. Dolt began to relax. These people seemed to be, for the most part, strangers to each other; yet they treated one another as old friends. It was so... *Civilized.*

But then Dolt became aware of a presence. Someone was standing behind his chair. He felt too heavy to move. The back of his neck felt cool — the air conditioning?

Someone was trying to attract his attention by jiggling his elbow.

"John?" Gideon said.

"What?"

"Stand up and say hello."

Dolt rose and instantly found himself smothered in the warmest, most all-enveloping handshake he'd ever experienced.

"John — cool! Really great that you could make it. Just wanted to say I'm a fan, actually. You know, really, I just love those text things you send out. I mean, come on, gosh — wish I had cred like that!"

It was the former PM — the scary one. Dolt was sure of it. But, then again, it wasn't — at least, it wasn't the version that, minutes earlier, Dolt had snuck away from in terror. This version, like a non-evil twin, radiated charm and bonhomie. Was *doppelgänger* the word? Gideon would know. The face was the

111

same, but some unspeakable energy had animated the eyes and the mouth, such that Dolt was immobilized in their magnetic force lines.

"Speak up, John," Gideon urged, softly.

"Um, thanks!" Dolt said. "Yeah, thanks. I, er..."

"Look, you know, we're just kicking around some ideas today. So it's like, kind of, just sit back and enjoy. No pressure. Contributions welcome, goes without saying. I mean, you know, serious issues, no one's disputing that. So, you know, let's be realistic, but, all the same, okay? Have fun!"

He gave Dolt a little buddy-punch to the shoulder, then angled away to greet some other attendees, who had been loitering, like star-struck teenage girls, just beyond Dolt's private zone. Dolt watched, unable to tear his gaze away, until Gideon yanked on his sleeve and told him to sit down.

Shortly thereafter, the proceedings got properly underway, and Dolt realized that the Global Faith Initiative wasn't at all what he'd expected. Where were the vicars, the bishops and all their foreign equivalents? Where were the nuns and the do-gooders? Everyone here represented some "corporation", "institute" or "fund".

And no one talked about God, or religion. Instead, everyone talked about investment, and money. Plus, if Dolt wasn't mistaken — and half of what they said was incomprehensible to him — the Changing Landscape of Global Power.

"Just listen," Gideon said in a low voice. "Look interested. Don't say anything."

Fair enough, Dolt thought. He didn't really speak the same language as these people. What did they mean by "leveraging institutional capital" or "underwriting liberal endogenous process factors"? At least the Steering Committee members spoke the same language as Dolt, more or less, even if, as was insultingly obvious, they considered him their social inferior. By comparison, the folk here at the GFI looked like superior beings of a higher order. Fittingly, their concerns rose above what Gideon liked to call the *parochial*.

No talk here about slashing benefits for spongers; no yelping delight at the prospect of jailing strikers or stunning protestors. Instead, you had high-minded concern for the security of the environment in Costa Rica — which sounded like a good thing — and a similar engagement with the new and rising challenges to stability in Libya. It was enough to make Dolt wonder if the life of a wealthy, globe-trotting, think-tank intellectual might not be superior to that of a semi-fake, populist attack dog like himself or Amber Pike. Well, he could see why Gideon had told him to keep his trap shut. Some things were out of reach; he shouldn't kid himself.

But a puzzle remained. Why was he here at all? And why did Gideon believe that this highbrow talk-fest counted for more than the gang that actually ran the country?

He was still pondering this conundrum when a "recess" was announced. Gideon slipped away quietly, perhaps to consort with the lady in black, and Dolt immediately felt the finger-prod of temptation. He had given up smoking; there was no *if* or *maybe* about it. It was one of Gideon's ground-rules.

On the other hand, Des, whom Dolt suspected of less than total loyalty to the cause, had slipped him a pack of ten, with the advice that Dolt should live in the now, because you never knew. And besides, he reasoned, just at this moment he could use the brain-boost everyone knew nicotine gave you. Well, all right, that was bogus, but, fuck it, he needed one.

He sidled down the GFI's grandiose staircase to the front lobby, past portraits of Winston Churchill and some French bloke — Napoleon? Then he smiled indulgently at the staff on the reception desk and strolled out on to the front steps, where the autumn sunshine warmed his face and made him feel that the universe was secretly on his side and still held marvels in reserve for him. Here he mimed his intentions for the benefit of the two machine-gun-wielding policemen at the foot of the steps, waited for the go-ahead, and proceeded to light up.

There may or may not have been a brain-boosting effect, but there was certainly a nerve-calming one. He wasn't quite over his encounter with the former PM, but he was beginning to feel a bit better about it. For a minute or so he watched the policemen, as they talked into their hidden microphones and discouraged dawdling motorists, and then he realized he had company.

"Say, you're that guy, aren't you?"

His new companion was a tall, thin American with soft, wavy, blond hair, and the whitest teeth and most perfect tan Dolt had ever seen. He was smoking a brand of cigarette unknown in Dolt's world. Cigarettes that didn't stain your teeth! How was it done?

"John Dolt."

"Yeah, I guessed it was you. Howard Hooper, Green Lake Robotics. That was a hell of a thing you did."

"I suppose it was," Dolt said, trying not to sound defensive.

"Mouthing off at the PM. Jeez. Wouldn't try that in the States."

"No, well, neither would I."

"Nice to meet you, anyhow."

"Thanks."

This Hooper bloke seemed a bit out of it, Dolt thought. Was there something in the smokes?

"So what do you make of this whole venture?" Hooper asked, with a languid gesture of bemusement.

"I'm finding it interesting."

"You are, huh?"

"I had a meeting with the Prime Minister this morning, but I think this might be more my —"

"Are they putting you to work on the Libya thing — is that it?"

"Libya? Well, no one's actually —"

"Oh, oh, wait. Maybe it's... No, forget it."

Hooper looked down at Dolt's credentials.

"Ever met Rand Purdo?"

"Not to talk to."

"Why then, I guess you haven't received the invite to the hidden valley?"

"What?"

"Hey, don't worry about it."

Hooper threw his cigarette down, extinguished it with his heel and, without giving Dolt a chance to ask him exactly what sort of robots he was into, retreated into the pristine halls of the GFI headquarters. Well, okay, Dolt thought, some things never changed. Whatever the general caliber of the crew here, there was always *one*.

He proceeded to puff away at his cigarette until he heard Gideon calling his name, like an impatient pet owner searching for a missing cat. And he would have stubbed out his dog-end and reported for duty right then, had his attention not been seized by the scene that had begun to play out at the foot of the steps.

A small girl in a thin, gray, woolen coat had been detained by the cops. They'd grabbed her by the arms and she was fighting to break free. It was a ferocious struggle — but also hopeless. As Dolt watched, she looked up, shook her short, black hair out of her eyes — and he found himself trapped in her gaze. She began to shout at him — it was in some foreign language, but there was no doubt as to what she wanted.

Dolt flashed back a quarter-century to a Turkish beach in front of a cheap hotel. He and Victoria had been in the first flush. Some local cops had harassed a girl selling trinkets. Dolt had intervened, with some success — and had won Victoria's admiration, and more. You could call him sentimental, if you liked, but he didn't see the need for police brutality where harmless girls were concerned.

He threw his cigarette away and hurried down the steps.

The cops had obviously satisfied themselves that they were dealing with a nutter, not a threat, but they weren't going to let the girl get any nearer to the GFI and its very important inmates. Close up, Dolt could see that she was about twenty years old, of Mediterranean or North African origin and quite attractive. Or rather, she would have been except for her skin, which looked dull, papery and yellowish in patches.

"Hey, hey, what's the matter, love?" Dolt said, not expecting his soothing words to have any effect and thus being quite surprised when they did. The girl stopped fighting.

"Do you know this lady, sir?" one of the cops asked.

"Actually —"

"He know me," the girl said, giving Dolt a look that chilled him more than any of Hamid's gruesome tales about his homeland. "He is old friend. Very old. We make love many a time."

The cops seemed to find this amusing, but Dolt wasn't laughing. This poor girl was at the end of her — well, something or other. If the cops weren't going to help her, who was?

"John!"

It was Gideon summoning him from the top of the steps.

"Just a mo."

The cops were waiting for his response.

"It's all right," he said, "let me talk to her. She'll be okay."

"So you *do* know her then?"

"Yes. Nothing to worry about. I'll just have a little chat with her."

The cops conferred.

"Very well, sir. If you say so, sir. We'll be right here."

"John! We're waiting for you!"

"All right, Gideon, hang on."

114

The cops released the girl. She took hold of Dolt's arm and urged him up the steps, stopping half way when she saw Gideon tapping his right foot, arms folded, at the top.

"Look, love," Dolt said. "Why don't you tell me what's the matter. Perhaps I can help."

"Yes, you can help. I know you. I see you on TV. You are a trustworthy man." She looked him in the eye. What was it about her skin?

"You don't let me down."

"Course not."

"I know *he* is here. You are his friend, yes?"

Dolt cast a wary glance at the cops, who were watching with great interest.

"Is this about... *Him?*"

The girl moved closer to him, turning her back to the police.

"What are you doing with that girl, John?"

"Nothing, Gideon."

Dolt heard Gideon take a step towards him. The girl pushed something down into Dolt's jeans. It was an envelope.

"You give it to *him*, yes?"

"All right, but you could have just —"

"I don't want police to see."

"Why not?"

The girl made a face.

"You trust *them?* You are crazy. Give it to *him*, yes?"

Gideon moved a step closer.

"I'll give it to him."

The girl gave Dolt a kiss on the cheek. Her lips were rough and oily.

"Bye."

"Hang on," Dolt said. "What's your name?"

"Aisha."

She turned and ran down the steps. The cops let her pass. Dolt watched as she strode off down the street without looking back.

"So what was that all about?"

You could tell when Gideon was being serious, Dolt had learned. He rubbed his thumb against the side of his forefinger. He was doing it now.

"Old girlfriend," Dolt said. "Having a bit of a tough time."

"Does Des know about her?"

"Des knows everything, doesn't he?"

"How did she know you were here?"

"Must have been in the papers."

Gideon looked skeptical.

"I don't like this."

He's going to check, Dolt thought. Well, let him.

"Don't worry about it. Let's go back in."

"Very well."

They ascended to the top of the steps. Dolt was about to explain that *Aisha* had always been *impulsive* and a bit of a *pain*, frankly, when the roar of a motorcycle ripped through the droning of the traffic. He turned and looked. The motorcycle mounted the pavement. Gunshots echoed along the street's stately regency facades. A passenger dismounted from the bike as it slowed. The cops began to advance but changed their minds and retreated to cover on the basement staircase. The passenger kicked at a shape on the ground then knelt down, as if searching for something. Then he was back on the bike as it screamed away into the noise of the city.

Dolt felt Gideon's hand on his shoulder.

"John, I fear something rather unpleasant has just happened to your girlfriend. Come inside. Now."

CHAPTER 15

John Dolt had never witnessed a murder before. But then he knew this wasn't a murder at all. It was an assassination. From outside came the shouts of policemen, the blaring of car horns and the mounting wail of sirens.

But in the marble foyer of the Global Faith Initiative, all remained calm. All except Gideon, that was.

"Who was that girl, John?"

"I told you."

"What's her name?"

"Samira." This was Hamid's daughter's name. Why was he lying? Well, it had to be for Aisha's sake, didn't it? Aisha, who didn't trust the British police; who'd put her faith in some hopeless git she'd seen on TV.

"Last name?"

"Never knew her last name."

"You said she was an old girlfriend."

"One of those Arabic names. Never got the hang of it."

"What were you talking about?"

"Nothing. She's being kicked out of her flat. Bit upset."

"John. This is important. You wouldn't hide anything from me, would you?"

"No! Fuck it, Gideon, the poor girl's dead, isn't she? She had no fucking chance! Didn't you see what happened?"

Gideon paused. The look on his face said *damage control*.

"We can't stay here. Come on."

"It was two blokes on a fucking motorbike! I mean, who does that? The cops'll want to talk to me."

"I think not. We'll go out the back way."

Not yet, he thought.

"No, wait. I need the toilet. Where is it?"

"Not now."

"No, really. It's urgent."

"Still not feeling well?" Gideon made an impatient gesture. "Down there on the right. Be quick about it."

As he hurried bog-wards, Dolt saw that the lofty intellects of Global Faith were taking this little disruption in their stride. The meeting had been adjourned, obviously, but there was no reason not to observe the niceties — the smiles, the handshakes, the exchange of business cards. You couldn't ruffle these people. If necessary, they would step over the poor bloody girl's remains to get into their taxis.

In the cubicle, he removed the envelope from his jeans. It wasn't sealed. He sat and emptied its contents into his lap: Some kind of letter, written in what he took to be Arabic, with one of those automatic Internet translations stapled to it; four photographs — a handsome bearded boy, some low buildings in a desert, a funny-looking plane, Aisha; a computer memory stick; a diagram or plan, perhaps of some kind of machine. He scanned the computer-English version of the letter. Either the translation was terrible or, in his panicky state, he wasn't fit to construe it; it didn't make a lot of sense. But it was addressed to the former PM, Aisha's name was at the bottom, and the word JUSTICE stood out, in capital letters, in every paragraph but one.

So what now? It was the poor girl's dying wish that he deliver this package. Mind you, she hadn't known about the *dying* bit, though, had she? She'd put her faith in Dolt and the former PM, from whom she expected nothing less than JUSTICE. On account of what? Were these photos and plans evidence of some crime? What was on the memory stick?

And as for the former PM — presumably he'd left the building by now, under heavy guard. Perhaps Dolt could run after him. *Um, excuse me, you know that girl what just got mown down in the street — she wanted you to have this.* Fuck that.

He could hand over the envelope to the cops or to Gideon. But giving it to the cops would be to betray Aisha. And as for Gideon, well... No, he decided, the most honorable course, and the one most likely to keep him out of trouble, was to seek expert advice before making any rash decisions. Problem was, he didn't know any experts. Or did he? There had to be someone. He would rack his brains later. Hamid, of course, spoke Arabic...

He put the letter, photos, plans and memory stick back in the envelope and stowed it carefully inside his suede jacket — happily, Jacqueline had selected one with a zip-up pocket. Then he took a couple of deep breaths, flushed the toilet and hastened back to the foyer.

"Better now?" Gideon asked.

"Yeah."

"We really *do* have leave the building, you see."

"Why?"

"The basement's on fire. You wouldn't know anything about that, would you?"

"No."

"Good. Come on, then. Car's waiting out the back. Des is very concerned."

"Is he?"

"See if you can allay his fears."

"Whatever."

"**W**hat the fuck are you playing at, John?" This was said softly, with the quiet menace of one who probably knew a lot about quiet menace. It was said by Des, Dolt's security consultant, who was by some distance the most aggressive and least polite of all Dolt's advisors.

They had not returned to the Atlantic Affairs Institute, because it was deemed by Des to be too close to the scene of the crime. Nor had they retired to Dolt's hotel, because Des suspected that the *jackals* — his name for the ladies and gentlemen of the national press — had learned its secret. Instead, they had adjourned to what Des called a *safe house*, in Kilburn, not too far from Dolt's old haunts — the Royal Fusilier pub in Cricklewood, for example. Gideon had declined to accompany them, declaring that he'd never been to Kilburn in his life and wasn't going there now. And it wasn't a house, either, if you wanted to argue about it — more of a *safe flat* above a halal butcher's.

"I said, what the fuck are you —"

"Nothing!"

"Do you know this girl or not?"

"No. I mean, yes. A bit."

"A bit? You said she's your girlfriend. She's not your fucking girlfriend. Do you think I haven't done any research? You've never had a fucking girlfriend."

"Victoria —"

"One quick and very unsafe fuck in the back of a Daihatsu? Not exactly a romance for the ages, was it?"

Cruel, Dolt thought. Cruel and uncalled-for; the twins, Tamsin and Tamara, had bound their parents together for far longer than had seemed likely at the outset. There had been periods of happiness, when one or both of them had been granted time off from the grind of survival. And rare moments of cut-price romance amid the long slog of climbing debts and falling expectations. Even Victoria would concede that.

"Fuck off."

Dolt flung himself into an armchair so ugly and thinly-cushioned it could only have been a liquidation special from the furniture department at Big Builder. Des took a moment to inspect the traffic crawling by below on the Kilburn High Road.

"It's my job to make sure you don't screw things up," he said, in a tone both threatening and conciliatory. "Nothing personal."

"Screw what up?"

"Everything. This girl — what country's she from?"

"Never asked her."

"It never came up?"

"No."

"Where's this flat of hers?"

"She didn't say."

"And yet you still insist she's your girlfriend? It's just some sick fantasy, isn't it?"

"No."

"She's a fucking kid, John. What's she doing with a lardy-arse old fart like you?"

"Nothing wrong with that. Bit unconventional."

"Unconventional? That's one word for it. Did she give you anything?"

"No."

"So there's nothing in that lovely jacket of yours?"

"No."

Des turned away from the window. Dolt wobbled in his armchair.

"Let's have a look, then."

Dolt took off the jacket and flung it at Des. Methodically, Des checked the pockets and felt the lining.

"All right," he said. "I apologize. I was wrong." He handed the jacket back to Dolt.

Not wrong, Dolt thought. Just stupid. You were watching the sodding number thirty-two bus and you missed it, didn't you? If the crappy Big Builder chair held up long enough, then the envelope would remain hidden in plain view between cushion and fake-teak slats until the opportunity arose to re-stow it in the jacket.

Des now seemed to take a different tack.

"Help me out, John. I don't know about you, but this job's beginning to do my head in. Some of these people... You don't know the half of it."

Half? Did he even know what *it* was?

"Getting stressed-out, are you?"

"Want answers, don't they? Whether there are any or not."

"Must be tough."

"Yeah."

Des went to the fridge in the flat's galley-style kitchen and fetched two large cans of strong lager. He handed one to Dolt.

"Here."

They drank the beer in silence. By the time they finished, Des looked as though he'd made a decision.

"This girl, though, John. It was all about *him*, wasn't it?"

Dolt decided to act as if he thought further resistance was futile.

"Yes, all right."

"Don't know why you didn't just say so. But never mind. What did she say about him?"

"She wanted me to give him a message."

"Making threats, was she?"

Dolt hesitated. The girl was dead. What did it matter if...

"So she *was* threatening him?"

"I don't know if I'd —"

But Des was on his feet, phone in hand.

"You, stay put."

He left the room, but didn't bother closing the door. Dolt could hear Des's end of the conversation.

"Yeah, she threatened him... That's right... Violent, yeah..."

A long pause.

"That could work. Run it by me again... Okay. That's official, then, is it? Sure? Fine, I'll tell him."

Des re-entered the safe flat's safe lounge, where John Dolt sat very still in his safe chair, and scratched his nose with great thoughtfulness.

"Here's the story," he said. "Listen carefully."

Dolt waited while Des appeared to gather his thoughts.

"This is what happened. The girl tricked her way past the cops. They thought she was an employee. She showed them a fake ID or something. You, on the other hand, are one smart cookie. You took one look. Your suspicions were instantly aroused."

"They were, in a way."

"Shut up and pay attention. The girl attempts to hurry past you, but you block her path. She gets closer to you. You spot a bulky object underneath her sweater. She's got wires coming out of her bra, or something. Hello, you say to yourself, this bitch is a fucking suicide bomber; I must protect the former Prime Minister, no matter what the cost to myself personally."

"For fuck's sake, Des."

"I told you to shut up. The girl realizes she's been rumbled. She calls down all the curses of Allah on you and the former PM and goes for the detonator. You stay her hand and then, not knowing for sure which is the right wire to yank out, heroically plump for the red one. The former PM and many innocent civilians are saved. The girl kicks you in the balls and runs off."

"Into the arms of the cops."

"No, she evades their grasp. Needless to say, they've already been relieved of duty."

"What about those bastards on the bike?"

"I'm coming to that. Their job was threefold. First, to finish off any survivors as they come running out of the flames. Second, to video the proceedings for upload to the top ten jihadi web sites. Third, to clean up the mess in the event of failure."

"Clean up the mess?"

"Kill the girl. Recover the bomb."

"No one's going to believe that."

"What — that she's a bomber or you're a hero?"

"Either."

Des sighed.

"Well, they *will*, John, because that's what all the papers are going to be saying tomorrow."

This, Dolt understood, was a moment of decision. He could exit now, and it would all be over. A entire safe house full of lies would crash down on his head, but he would probably survive — just. He could go back to the Jobba van and what was left of his half-a-house. Or he could stay on the bus. Look out for himself. Best them at their own game. After all, he wasn't the total idiot they thought he was — well, except for Gideon, who was beginning to catch on. And — just possibly, and perhaps for his private ease alone — he could find out precisely which bunch of bastards had gunned down a desperate girl whose only known crime was a hopeless quest for JUSTICE.

"Unless," Des was saying, "you choose to contradict them. To question the veracity of top-earning editors and award-winning journalists."

Dolt said nothing.

"Well, John — *are* you going to contradict them?"

"No."

"Well, thank fuck for that. Come on, I'm supposed to take you back to the hotel. Put your fucking jacket on."

Des lumbered out of the room and began to descend the uncarpeted stairs. Dolt retrieved the envelope from its personal safe house and restored it to the jacket's inside pocket. Then he slipped the jacket on, zipped it up tightly and trailed Des out to the car.

*

G ideon was waiting for him in his hotel suite, with a guarded but confident look on his face.

"Look at these," he said, handing Dolt a sheaf of print-outs. "Tomorrow's papers. Front pages."

Dolt scanned the headlines. DOLT FOILS SUICIDE PLOT. HERO DOLT IN BRA BOMB HORROR. DOLT DEFENDS FREEDOM.

"Bollocks," he said.

"What?"

"Nothing."

"Well, obviously, it's not exactly what we were planning. But it's worked out quite well. One has to be adaptable. To think on one's feet."

"And what, exactly, were you thinking?"

Gideon, Dolt noticed, had helped himself to a glass of sherry. There must have been a secret supply somewhere in the safari-style Swiss kitchen.

"You know, it's all right, John. I can understand if you're feeling a little, let's say, disillusioned. It's quite natural. You're not accustomed to the exigencies of news management. It must seem a little strange."

"Strange?"

"Have you ever been through the experience where you've had personal knowledge of some situation, and yet the report in the newspaper seems to get it completely wrong?"

Dolt nodded.

"Well, there's a reason for that, you see. People don't understand the random. They're not trained in statistics. Complexity confounds them. Their perspectives are understandably limited."

"So?"

"So they need a *narrative*. A story. So that things can seem to make sense."

"Even if they're not true."

"Yes, but you see — I think we've touched on this before — truth is a terribly difficult concept. Very random."

"Doesn't seem so difficult to me."

"Ah, but think about things in a wider perspective. What is the bigger truth here? We all accept that there must be Lord knows how many crazies out there who would love to tuck a bomb under our glorious former leader. It was the purest chance that it wasn't, quite, one of them out there on those steps with you today. Do we go with the extremely unlikely, or the overwhelmingly probable? There's a lot a theory on this, all to do with *noise* and *signal*, but I won't bore you with it now."

Drop it, Dolt thought. You've made your point. Now get back with the program.

"Any sherry left?" he said.

Gideon's face brightened.

"Of course. Let me fetch you a large one. You deserve it. Meanwhile, have a look at those. The inside pages."

He indicated another stack of print-outs on the zinc counter of the sun-downer-style bar.

Dolt flicked through them. DOLT TO TACKLE *THIS*, he read. DOLT TO TACKLE *THAT*. It went on and on. There seemed to be little that he hadn't been assigned to *tackle*. But the thing that really grabbed him was the photograph — it appeared in all the papers — of himself at the Policy Steering Committee meeting. As instructed by the PM, all present, except Dolt himself, were smiling. But no — not smiling; rather, they were grinning, leering, mugging, sneering, gobbing, lip-licking, eye-rolling and flat-out gurning. Only Dolt looked sane.

"Listen to this," Gideon said, handing Dolt his sherry. "It's the caption in our market-leading tabloid: A PACK FULL OF JOKERS WITH ONLY ONE KING."

"Well, well," Dolt said. "You *do* know what you're doing, don't you, eh?"

"One likes to believe one has some expertise."

Together, they browsed the papers, sipping their sherry, comparing notes, laughing at the papers' varying accounts of the Steering Committee meeting, and avoiding all contentious debate over the nature of truth and, most especially on Dolt's part, JUSTICE.

And then, when it seemed to Dolt that Gideon had judged the mood to be right, Gideon decided it was time to let John get some well-earned rest.

"What's up for tomorrow?" Dolt asked.

"Well, let's see. First off, we have another study morning. In the afternoon, you're recording *John's Jury*. And in the evening, we have the premiere."

"What premiere?"

"Didn't I mention it? You must have heard of it. *The Face of Freedom*. It's the latest blockbuster, apparently."

"I'm not really into movies."

"You'll be into this one. It's based on a story idea by Amber Pike. Some of her people will be there."

"Not Amber, though?"

"She's not overly fond of foreign travel."

"Ah."

"But all the stars will be there. I'm sure you'll enjoy it."

"You know what? I bet I will."

Gideon smiled.

"Excellent. Sleep well!"

Dolt waited for ten minutes or so after Gideon left, silent and still on his leopard-pattern couch. Then he removed the envelope from his suede jacket — which he still wore, despite the warmth imparted by the sherry. The computer rendition of Aisha's letter made little more sense than before. It had to be important, though: Here was a girl who didn't trust anyone except a computer

123

to translate her last will and testament. With a little application, he was able to deduce that the bearded youth was probably her brother, name of Abdel. It seemed that something had happened to Abdel. Something bad. And the two of them were from Libya.

Libya — didn't the robot guy say something about *the Libya thing?* And wasn't Libya a top concern for the big brains of Global Faith?

He reached for his phone, hesitated for a good thirty seconds, then dialed Hamid's mobile number from memory. But the number was no longer valid. He toyed with the phone for another minute, then dialed Hamid's home number. An answering machine kicked in.

"Um, Hamid? John. John Dolt. I meant to call before, obviously, but... Um, look, I'm going to be at the BA, okay? So, if you felt like... Well, that's where I'm going to be. Just so you know. Okay? Um, yeah, cheers, okay? See you there. If you want. Bye."

Yes, yes, it was pathetic. But, fuck it, did it matter? If you considered, as Gideon did, the wider perspective? No. What mattered was that Hamid spoke Arabic, and — who could tell? — perhaps a relationship could be repaired.

He gathered up his phone, wallet and hotel key-card and slipped the envelope back into its safe house. Then he exited his suite and took the stairs to the lobby, where, like a spy contemplating a risky rendezvous, he surveyed the scene for any tell-tale trace of Des, or of his known operatives.

Since the coast appeared clear, he sidled off, collar up, in suitably furtive style, heading by an indirect and unpredictable route for the nondescript suburb of Wembley, and its Britannia Arms pub — popularly known to its regulars as the Brit Arse.

CHAPTER 16

Compared to Cricklewood's Royal Fusilier, a dank and dreary dump, Wembley's Britannia Arms was a modern, forward-thinking, go-ahead kind of establishment.

In place of the Fusilier's dusty imperial nostalgia, glumly expressed in its fake-sepia photographs and job-lot memorabilia, the Brit Arse had 3D HD satellite sports, a commercial-grade espresso machine, and a karaoke system. Whereas the punters down at the Fusilier were aging, unhealthy and broke, the old guard dwindling as hungry developers eyed up the property for redevelopment, the clientele at the BA consisted largely of young chancers with cash to splash — despite the economic, financial and fiscal crises. Though the Fusilier might be about to sink beneath the multicultural waves, the Brit Arse stood proudly against the tide and wasn't about to give an inch — never mind the value of the pound, and never mind the performance of the England soccer team.

It was, in short, the sort of place where a down-to-earth, no-nonsense, self-made patriot like John Dolt should have felt at home. But he didn't.

Though the main reason for coming to the pub was a hoped-for meeting with Hamid, delicate undertaking as that might be, Dolt had also assumed that returning to a familiar haunt might help to *ground* him — to provide a reality-check, as it were. The events of the past few days, it was fair to say, had challenged some of his hitherto uninspected beliefs about the way the world worked. All that *populist* stuff, for example: There were things that used to seem so true that you couldn't help laughing at anyone who questioned them; now they seemed empty — mere tools or tactics to be deployed for practical advantage. It was hard to let go but, all the same, he felt he was losing his purchase on a moral universe that now seemed to have at least one dimension too many. He was a witness to a killing — an assassination. But was he also an accessory? At the very least he was complicit in a cover-up and in possession of important, perhaps dangerous, evidence.

The Britannia pub was a real place where complicated issues, after a pint or two, would always resolve themselves.

But not this time. Everyone knew his face.

He wandered the pub with his pint, acknowledging cheers, getting his back slapped, declining free drinks, secretly on edge, hoping to spy Hamid — but also hoping not to. At length, having entertained a crowd of admirers with unpublished details of his heroic adventures, he perched alone at the end of the bar, drained his glass and resolved to flee back to the safety of his hotel suite.

Then he saw Lescek the bathroom guy advancing on him, with an empty glass in one hand and a rolled up newspaper in the other.

"Lescek! What are you having?"

Lescek seemed agitated.

"Nothing from you, John."

"What?" Dolt said.

Lescek slapped his newspaper down on the bar next to Dolt's elbow.

"Why are you saying these things? I don't understand. I mean, are you always feeling like this?"

"What things? What are you talking about?"

"I hate this pub now. I'm not coming here any more."

"Why? What's the —"

Lescek waved his empty glass in front of Dolt's face.

"I always thought maybe you were one of the not-so-bad guys, John. Really, I did."

Lescek pointed angrily at his own forehead.

"But you were just messing with me. Having a laugh behind my back. Fucking with my brain."

"Fucking with your —"

Lescek glanced nervously over his shoulder, then slammed his fist down on the newspaper. The drinkers at the bar looked up.

"How can you write this, John? This is poison. Tell me how you can do it."

Dolt looked at the newspaper. MY POLISH HELL By John Dolt. WHY MIGRANTS MUST GO.

The beer began to curdle in Dolt's stomach.

"Lescek! I didn't write that! For fuck's sake..."

He scanned the article. The bile rose in his throat.

"It's not me, Lescek. I didn't write this shit. Someone —"

"So you don't think these things?"

"No!"

"Oh, really, you say? I watch the TV. I know what you are, now."

Lescek took a step back. His lips began to tremble. Oh no, Dolt thought, please don't cry, *please don't cry*.

"Lescek, Lescek — just sit down, will you?"

Lescek slumped on to the stool next to Dolt's and buried his face in his hands.

What to say? He wasn't sure he wasn't going to burst into tears himself.

"Honestly, Lescek. It wasn't me. I didn't authorize..."

Authorize? Who the fuck did he think he was now? Good question. Who the fuck *was* John Dolt these days?

"Lescek. Listen. I would never say those things. It's these people I've got involved with. They... Look, Lescek. I need your help, as it happens. Can you help me? Please?"

Lescek looked up.

"Why do you want help? You want to write more shit?"

"No, no," Dolt said gently, "I've explained that. I want you to look at something. I want your technical advice. You were a boffin of some sort, weren't you? In Poland?"

"High-energy physics."

"Right, exactly. Have a look at this, will you?"

Dolt took out Aisha's page of diagrams.

"Here. What do you think?"

Lescek looked at Dolt, screwed up his face, then snatched the page. Dolt watched as Lescek sniffed and ran his gaze over the plans.

"Where do you get this?"

"It just happened to fall into my possession."

"You stole it!"

"No, someone gave it to me."

"You bribed them."

"No, no. Nothing like that. Know what it is?"

Lescek shrugged.

"Looks like a gas boiler."

A gas boiler?

"Are you sure?"

"Fancy vacuum cleaner, maybe? Why should I know?"

"A vacuum cleaner?"

Lescek dropped the plans on the bar.

"Yes, John. Okay, so you steal the plans. You make your fancy vacuum cleaner. Now you are a millionaire. I say good luck."

Lescek tumbled from his stool and lurched towards the pub door.

"Lescek!"

But he was gone. Ironic cheers from the spectators at the bar.

A vacuum cleaner? Aisha's mission had been to deliver to the former PM the detailed manufacturing designs for a top-secret Libyan vacuum cleaner? Lescek was winding him up. Wasn't he?

Dolt returned the vacuum cleaner plans to their hiding place. What now? A glance around the pub suggested that Hamid was a definite no-show. Dolt got to his feet and made for the exit.

But before he could reach for the handle, the door swung open and he found himself face-to-face with Samira, Hamid's daughter. She didn't look happy.

"You!" she said. "You bastard. You complete and utter bastard!"

Dolt reeled.

"What?" he said. "Samira! What's the matter?"

"What's the *matter?*"

Dolt backed into the pub as Samira advanced.

"Where's your dad?"

"Where's my dad?"

"Don't just keep repeating —"

"Like you don't know where he is!"

Dolt backed into a wall, dislodging a blackboard advertising Friday's Pub Quiz Nite.

"What do you mean?"

Samira hit him across his left cheek. She must have been wearing a ring because he felt his skin rip, and a droplet of blood began to leak down his face.

"Ow! Samira!"

She hit him again — a punch to the ribcage. He grabbed her shoulders and held her back. She flailed at him. A semi-circle of spectators formed, drinks in hand.

"Fuck's sake, Samira. Calm down. What's the problem? Where's your dad?"

Samira kicked at his right knee. She was wearing pointed boots. It hurt like hell.

"Shit!"

He pushed her to the floor. She sat there, breathing heavily. The spectators, perhaps fearing exposure to more information than they required, drifted away.

Dolt crouched down beside Samira. The fight seemed to have gone out of her, for now.

"You know what you did," she said, between breaths.

"Do I? What did I do, Samira?"

"You had them slap a DPO on him."

"Did I? What's a DPO, Samira?"

She gave him a look of such bone-splitting malice that he almost toppled back on his heels.

"It's what you were writing about in the paper, yesterday. Don't you remember?"

Fuck, he thought. Who was responsible for this stuff — was it Jaz, his Director of Communications? Or Polly, his Political Advisor? Could he fire them? Not Gideon, with his *narratives*, surely?

"No," he said. "What did I say, supposedly?"

"You said, quote, that the Dangerous Persons Order was a step in the right direction, but it did not go nearly far enough."

"Uh-huh. What's a Dangerous Persons Order?"

For a moment, he thought she was going to hit him again. She struggled to get to her feet, but failed. Probably the boots.

"It's what they slapped on my dad," she said, a note of defeat in her voice.

"But what does it mean?" Dolt asked. "In practice?"

She looked at him, as if confused.

"He's gone. They took him."

"Who took him, Samira?"

"The Americans."

"The Americans? But —"

"That's what a DPO means. They can take him. You *know* that."

"Take him where?"

"The War Zones."

"But... Where in the War Zones?"

"They don't have to tell you. *That's what it means*. As you know."

Dolt's knee was killing him. He stretched out his leg and sat down alongside Samira.

"But... Why?"

"I've lost my job."

"What, because of..."

"Yes. That fucking minibus."

The minibus!

"Because..."

"Bomb-making materials."

"On the minibus?"

Samira nodded.

"Samira, I swear... I mean, I know I left the bus there, but.. Bomb-making materials? That's ridiculous."

Dolt became aware that the landlord of the Brit Arse was watching them, and not in a friendly way.

"Samira," he said. "Let's go outside. Get some air."

He helped her to her feet. She didn't resist.

Outside, they walked in the dimly-lit car park as a fine drizzle fell, and Dolt attempted to probe further into Hamid's fate. But Samira now refused to speak. Finally, in desperation, he tried one last ploy.

"Samira, I'll do anything I can to help. I mean, I know some people who might... But, look, you can help me, if you want."

"Help you?"

"Yes. I've got this thing. It's written in Arabic. I need someone to translate it. You could do that, couldn't you?"

She looked at him as if he'd invited her to help him finish the crossword.

"Arabic?"

"You could do it, couldn't you?"

She hesitated and narrowed her eyes.

"I don't know. Maybe. Let me see."

Dolt handed over the Arabic version of Aisha's letter.

"See," he said. "Arabic."

Samira studied the document for a few long moments.

"What the fuck is this?" she said.

"Well, that's what I'd like to know," Dolt said.

"What stupid shit is this?"

"Is it stupid shit? What sort of —"

But Samira had begun to rip the letter into shreds.

"No! Don't do that! Samira, please!"

But she'd thrown the fragments to the ground and begun to stride off into the night. He let her go. Frantically, he retrieved the pieces of the letter from the dirt and oily pools into which they'd fallen. He hunted around until he couldn't find any more, wrapped them in a tissue and stuffed them into his jeans pocket.

Then he retreated to the pub's Kiddie Zone — a rain-weathered slide and a happy fiberglass giraffe — to take stock. He sat on the bottom of the slide and watched the rain drip from the giraffe's nose. Someone had framed Hamid. Someone who'd had access to the minibus. Why? For fun? Because Hamid knew too much embarrassing stuff about Dolt and couldn't be bought off — part of the *decontamination* process? Just because they could? As a warning of what could happen?

So how could he be sure that, one day, he wouldn't be bundled off to the War Zones himself? To one of those black-site prisons that decent people didn't need to be concerned about because only the worst of the worst...

Fuck it, he thought. Too much for one night. Go back to the hotel.

He hobbled out of the car park to the public road. The first thing he saw was a black Range Rover. And there was Des, leaning against its grille with his arms folded.

"Shit! Des — I just came here to —"

"Shut up. It doesn't matter. Get in. And clean your face up."

They drove in silence for about ten minutes. Then Des cleared his throat and spoke.

"By the way. Your ex and the kids. It's all settled. You're off the hook. They've all been paid off. Including their greedy fucking solicitor. Relocating to Spain, I believe. Deal is, you never see them or talk to them again."

Des floored the accelerator and the Range Rover barged its way on to the North Circular, to a chorus of honking.

"Okay?"

CHAPTER 17

S urely, this was to be their last night. And the silence that filled her ears wasn't just the sound of the Sahara's empty twilight. There were things to be said; and some of them should have been said a long time ago.

But Annie wasn't present to hear an account, painstakingly constructed and revised over the years, of a mother's regrets and true intentions; of her unlimited and undying — until now — attachment to her daughter's progress, even unto true conservative bliss. Okay, Annie?

And Annie's father, Jim, hadn't shown up to be advised that, most of the time, at least, he was indeed the great guy he really tried to be, when he wasn't getting wasted with his old army buddies, or losing his daddy's money by getting in on too many hopeless, sure-fire ground floors. But that wasn't his fault, any more than falling under an uptown number two train at Wall Street was. Right, Jim?

Friends, associates and professional acquaintances would mourn her for a week and paste her picture into their blogs, or, poignantly, at the end of their monthly round-ups.

Leo, a man of too many talents and too much ambition, was responsible, but not to blame. Let God, or someone more ecologically responsible, take care of him. Of course he couldn't be here now because, like her, he was on the run. Perhaps he'd make it. He'd always been lucky. More so, now that she thought about it, than many of his partners and collaborators had been. Were he here, they might have reminisced about the little hotel by the volcano in Arenal. It would have been pleasant.

But Bonnie DiAngelo had no one to talk to in her final hours but Jay Percival, the renegade American spy and another of these can-do men, who, in his case, thanks to misjudgment of the competition and questionable flying skills, couldn't. Her throat, tongue and lips felt dry and cracked. She couldn't get the sand out of her eyes and it was painful to blink. In any event, her vision had become cloudy and dim. All the same, not to talk seemed, well, undignified.

"Well, I never had my birthday party," she said.

Jay looked up. His animal alertness remained, she thought — just. He lifted his head slowly like a cat, not wasting energy, but you could still see from the trembling of his restless fingertips that something wild and vital had yet to leak away.

"I know the water's gone, but perhaps we have something else? I mean, why not?"

He looked at her for a moment, then raised his forefinger in a gesture of triumph.

"Yes," he said. "We do."

They had been lying in the sand in the shade of the broken plane. Jay rolled on to his hands and knees and crawled inside. She listened to him shuffle the debris aside and rattle the plane's metalwork. Gently, she closed her eyes and began to drift away, until she felt his shoulder next to hers.

"Here," he said, offering her a small, brown bottle. "No, wait. Let me unscrew it. There. Scotch. Walter's favorite."

"Thanks."

She took a sip. It scoured her throat.

"Hmm. Good. Is Walter going to miss you?"

"Hell, yes. I'm unique."

She took another sip and returned the bottle.

"Pity. What do you suppose he's doing right now?"

"Oh, he's guest of honor at his daughter's show — she's a fashion designer. Or he's at some political club, having a drink with his old pals from the Liberation. Or — what day is it? — maybe he's at his beach house."

"When does he find time for spying, or whatever you call it?"

"Yeah, spying! He does that all the time. Second nature."

"Spying's a big thing now in Africa?"

"Sure. All those natural resources. All those dangerous people. Commodities. The Chinese. Modern communications. Fucking hedge funds. Place is waking up. Got to keep on top of it. So Walter says. Main thing is, no more wars. Guess I agree with him, there."

Jay passed the whisky to her and she drank. Her lungs felt as if they were burning.

"You and Walter," she said. "You're going to put a stop to it all."

"That's right. We are. Starting with those damn drones."

"Good for you."

She couldn't speak any more; her throat was raw. They drank until the bottle was empty. Then Jay tossed it into the wreckage of the plane and they lay still, listening again to the silence of the desert.

"Andy," she said. "I thought he would come."

Jay looked at her.

"Didn't you?" she said.

Slowly, Jay shook his head.

"Oh well."

In front of them, a broad, reddening sunset began to glow.

"Sandstorm," Jay said. "In the west."

"Don't have my camera," she said. "Pity."

A light breeze picked up and blew sand against the carcass of the plane. Jay sat up.

She closed her eyes again, embraced the residual warmth of the whisky in her knotted stomach, and began to drift. There she was, back in her office in Brookline, in front of her computer with a cup of coffee. What nice things people had written about her...

But Jay was shaking her by the shoulder.

"Stay awake," he said. "And stay here."

She watched him stumble to the foot of the long dune a hundred yards to the east. Then he dropped to his hands and knees and crawled to its crest.

Stay here? Sure. She wasn't going anywhere.

Ten minutes later, he was back.

"Gonna need some money," he said. "Hope we have enough left. Look over there."

She now saw what he'd seen. Emerging into view: Three ancient Land Cruisers, roofs loaded with water bottles, followed by a yet more decrepit canvas-roofed truck, heading north-west. They were attempting to scale a final dune of loose sand before entering a wide, flat zone of compacted material. The Land Cruisers made it, but the truck struggled and became stuck. The back of the truck opened up and twenty or thirty people tumbled out. Some simply lay where they fell; others stood and attempted to push the truck. A tow-rope was attached to the front. The struggle recommenced.

Jay collapsed alongside her.

"Thirty-eight hundred," he said. "Not really a lot."

No, she thought. Was that why he'd fetched his gun?

"Who are they?" she said.

"Traffickers. People smugglers. Usually Libyans and Sudanese. Pretty terrible guys, actually."

"So they're taking people —"

"They have to be desperate to do this. Eritreans, Sudanese, Ethiopians, Somalis. Military dictatorship, poverty, hunger, war. The traffickers take them into Libya, to Kufra. If they're lucky. Poor bastards."

"If they're lucky?"

"Look at that truck. No spares. Break down, you're finished. Sometimes they dump the cargo in the desert, keep the cash."

"They dump people in the desert?"

"All the time. Don't care about return business."

"Where's Kufra?"

"South-east Libya. Hell of a dump. When you get there, you bribe the police and maybe the military. Then you pay another bunch of traffickers to take you to Misrata or Benghazi, or wherever's quiet on the coast these days."

"Do these people have any money?"

"No problem. In Kufra, they have mobile phones. They do wire transfers. You call your family. If they can't help, it gets ugly."

"And from the coast?"

"Italy. The Europeans catch these people, send them back to Libya. The Europeans pay the Libyans to repatriate them. Which, as everyone knows, they don't. You end up back in Kufra. Or in the desert."

"And you think we can go with these... Traffickers?"

Jay tucked his gun into his waistband, underneath his shirt.

"If we ask politely."

He got to his feet. Then he raised his arms, took a deep breath and began to yell. She saw the doors of the first two Land Cruisers open. Then running figures and some kind of conference. Jay stopped shouting and lowered his arms.

"Here they come," he said.

The first Land Cruiser fired up and spun around in their direction. It stopped on a ridge about twenty yards away, from which point the wreck of the plane could still be seen in the dwindling light. Two men got out. One went to inspect the wreckage; the other gestured to them to approach.

"I'll do the talking," Jay said.

"I think you'd better."

They began to walk. As they got nearer, Bonnie could see that the seats had been removed from the back of the Land Cruiser. Instead there were sacks — food? — and people. The driver was a young, wiry man with a Rolex — fake? — on his wrist and a T-shirt in the livery of an English soccer team. Jay began to speak in slow, deliberate Arabic.

Then the second man returned, empty-handed, from the plane, and a three-way conversation started. What was Jay telling them? The two traffickers glanced at her from time to time, as if unable to comprehend what the hell she was doing in their desert.

"Okay," Jay said, at length. "I think we have a deal."

He counted out some money — she couldn't tell how much — and handed it over. One of the traffickers offered her a bottle of water. She took it and drank deeply. The water had an oily, chemical taste, but she couldn't help herself. She drank until she began to choke.

"They put benzene in it," Jay said. "So people don't drink too much. We need to go to the truck."

The Land Cruiser drove back to the head of the convoy. They followed on foot. The truck had overcome the final dune and its passengers had remounted. Bonnie looked up into the back: It was crammed full, mostly with young men and youths — but there were women and small children, too.

The trafficker with the Rolex reappeared and began to talk to Jay, more aggressively this time. Jay shook his head. The Rolex guy pointed to something in the interior of the truck. A commotion began inside. More head-shaking from Jay, the Rolex guy becoming agitated.

"What is it?" she said.

Jay sighed.

"He says they can't take any *more* people. If they take us, they have to leave two people behind." He paused. "He says that girl and her kid aren't going to make it, anyway."

The Rolex guy folded his arms.

"We're supposed," Jay said, "to throw them off and take their places."

She swallowed, and the foul taste of the benzene spread around her mouth.

"Which girl?" she said.

Jay pointed. The girl looked about sixteen, Bonnie thought. Her face was a blank mask of fear.

The Rolex guy was waiting. Bonnie stepped in front of him and grabbed hold of the loose material at the neck of his over-sized soccer shirt.

"No!" she said. "No! Do you understand? No!"

She felt Jay's hand on her shoulder and shook it off. The Rolex guy took hold of her wrist and squeezed it. She let go of his shirt.

"No!" she said again. "We paid. That girl paid. We're all going. You got that?"

The Rolex guy spat at her. Then he shouted something in Arabic at Jay. Jay shrugged. The Rolex guy rubbed his forehead with the back of his hand, then muttered something to himself and shuffled back towards the front of the convoy.

"All right," Jay said. "We can get on now. Well done, Mrs. DiAngelo. Though I'm guessing you don't know what you just did to that guy."

"Screw him."

"Uh-huh. Come on, these nice people want to help you up."

She saw hands reaching down to her from the gloom of the truck, and the girl with the child, blinking at her.

Up they went, and the long, blistering journey of salvation to the desert town of Kufra began.

CHAPTER 18

Jefferson Crockett and Isabel Gutierrez sat together in the manager's office of the Puerto Jiménez plantation of the Vita Tropico Palm Oil Company. Isabel had taken the manager's swivel chair; Jeff Crock perched on a wooden stool, on the other side of the manager's desk.

They were waiting for a light aircraft to land on the plantation's red-dirt airstrip, which Jeff monitored anxiously via the manager's window. They had been installed here by the plantation foreman, an old friend of Isabel's family, who had made it plain that any assistance to be provided was to be written up under the heading of familial sentiment, and not attributed to any sympathy for the elongated Yankee who'd been nothing but trouble since he'd arrived. Jeff hadn't been in the mood to demur.

He glanced again at the airstrip — nothing. He listened — no airplane engines, just the whirring of the machines in the processing plant next door and the chuffing of the manager's air conditioning. Unexpectedly, given his long-suffering and resilient nature, he felt depressed and defeated, and longed to move on.

It didn't help that necessity had obliged him to flee the scene of his greatest professional calamity in the company of that calamity's bereaved girlfriend. Conversation had been, and continued to be, difficult.

Jeff didn't care to explain to Isabel how he'd arrived at the decision to leave Eric Lapierre, the hippy hotelier, alone and unprotected in his hostel. Had he decided otherwise, it was at least possible that Eric would not have received that single, fatal, hole in the chest.

And Jeff could see that Isabel, similarly, did not wish to be invited to explain how it was that those responsible for Eric's apparently effortless murder had found out who he was and where he lived. Had she told them? After all, he and Eric had escaped from the Pelican Lodge in Leo Vargas's personal transportation, leaving Isabel behind. And no matter how tough a lady she was — well, in the end, no one's *that* tough.

Personal fortitude didn't get you very far when you were dealing with people like Douglas Moreland. But it came into its own, Jeff conceded, when, like Isabel, you rolled up and found your boyfriend dead in the bathroom, and his one and only guest in a cold funk under the wild plum tree.

And it had been Isabel, not Jeff, who'd retrieved Jeff's two hundred dollars from Eric's sticky pocket. They would need cash, she'd explained.

The cash was needed because they had to run. They had to run because the Americans, who'd ordered her to remain at the Pelican Lodge, had been on the phone to the local cops, Eric's friends, telling them to retreat to their station and stay put, on account of a US National Security Situation. Yeah, really! Whose country was this, again?

So, of course, she'd been frightened for Eric, and maybe a little for Jeff, and wasn't about to sit tight and hope for the best. She'd stolen one of the undamaged SUVs (it was now hidden, deep in, among the palm trees — they'd spent the night in it) and burned rubber. A real car, you understand? Not Leo Vargas's stupid electric buggy.

The Americans were *up to something*. They'd murdered Eric. Perhaps they'd murdered Leo, too. They wanted to steal his eco lodge. There was no question that they intended to murder Isabel, once they got around to it. How could they go about giving orders to the police? Who the hell were they, actually? And Rancho Colorado — what was *that* all about? These were all important questions, and if Jeff wanted to answer them, Isabel was listening.

"I don't exactly know," he said.

But it was clear enough that Rancho Colorado was a bolt-hole for fugitive plutocrats, a command and control center for directing rightist coups — yesterday Venezuela, tomorrow who knew? — and perhaps more besides. Who owned and operated it, and why they needed an off-campus meeting with, of all people, Douglas Moreland, the eternal happy warrior for all causes that married capital to militarism, was, as yet, unclear. So, too, was the fate of Leo Vargas — unlikely as it was that Moreland wanted to steal his lodge.

Perhaps now was a good time to listen to the audio recording. It had better be good, he thought. It had cost Eric his life.

He borrowed a notepad and pencil from the manager's stationery cupboard, plugged in his earpiece, selected the most recent file on the recorder, and pressed the play button.

The meeting had begun in a mood of raucous celebration, the participants greeting each other in hearty fashion. Jeff could pick out the sounds of back-slapping and high-fives. There was a cacophony of voices, but Moreland's, with its characteristically wide pitch-range and aggressive attack, cut through. He sounded as if he were complaining to the delegation from Rancho Colorado, not wholly in jest, about the discomfort and inconvenience he'd suffered during his journey to the meeting here today.

But would he address any of his fellow attendees by name? Jeff listened.

Judy, Moreland said. Possibly the name of the only woman present; Moreland's wife was a politician called Elizabeth.

Judy would like to buy this place.

Judy? Did Jeff know any Judys?

No. Keep listening.

Elliot, Moreland said. *How's Elliot liking the weather out here?* Probably a reference to Elliot Tucker, the healthcare fraudster, whom Jeff had photographed on the beach at Rancho Colorado.

It was all getting quite jovial, but Jeff had always found it hard to believe that Moreland really had a sense of humor. How could you, and still do the kind of shit he did?

Blabbermouth billionaires, Moreland was saying. Okay, so he didn't want to have the meeting at Rancho Colorado because the inmates couldn't be controlled and he needs to keep his connection to the place secret.

John, Moreland said. *John's doing just great, don't you think? How d'you find a guy like that? Can't be easy!* John? Come on people, Jeff thought, somebody say the guy's last name, please. Were they talking about someone in the meeting? Maybe not.

So Rand, Moreland said, *how's it going in Guayaquil?*

Rand! Not exactly a common name. How many Rands did Jeff know? One weird kid in high school. The only other Rand he'd heard of was...

Rand Purdo.

Pharmaceutical heir. Real estate mogul. Think tank philanthropist. Wingnut recluse. Liberty Club bigwig. Hedge fund investor (specialties: Africa, Latin America, places where commodities could be cornered). Big game hunter (private reserve in Wyoming, imported animals). PAC funder. Second Amendment fan. Founder of the ludicrous Club for Greed (membership by invitation only). Climate-change skeptic. VIP attendee at elite gatherings in Switzerland, Dubai and Colorado. Personal friend, allegedly, of democracy-shy foreign potentates. Show tune buff (according to a profile in Global Capitalist magazine). Amateur Civil War historian. Backer of fringe candidates. Literary manuscript collector. Owner of a golf course in Scotland, a yacht in Malta, a trophy wife in Geneva and, according to rumor, half an oil-field in Azerbaijan. Horse breeder. Compulsive litigator. Born-again Christian (not to be taken seriously). Scourge of Congressional liberals (prior to extinction of same). Supporter of States' Rights. Abortion foe. Water-colorist. Criminal.

Could it be *that* Rand?

Jeff was still taking in the enormity of this discovery when he realized he'd missed something important. He hit the rewind button.

Guayaquil?

REWIND.

How's it going in Guayaquil?

STOP.

Jeff removed his earpiece.

"Isabel?"

Isabel looked up, frowning.

"What?"

"Guayaquil. Ecuador, right?"

"In the south. On the coast. I like it there. It's nice. Maybe not for you."

"Oh, so you've been there?"

"Leo Vargas has a business office. For his coffee."

"Ah."

"Why are you asking me this?"

"No reason."

Jeff signaled the end of this exchange by plugging in his earpiece again. *Ecuador*, he thought. A poor, harmless little country, with a semi-populist government trying to protect the population from the ravages of global capital while not pillaging the oil from its rainforests. Or, looked at from the point of view of, say, Rand Purdo and Douglas Moreland, an evil, anti-American, Castro-worshipping dictatorship with development opportunities. Next in line for the treatment?

It was imperative that he contact Katherine — just as soon as he could obtain a safe phone and transmit the appropriate codeword — *crocodile*, in this case. Isabel's phone was a no-go, and the manager's landline wasn't even working.

In the meantime...

PLAY.

More babble, but no more names. Purdo assuring Moreland that things in Guayaquil were moving forward. Moreland sounding more relaxed. Something from Purdo in a snarky tone about *our distinguished friend*. A tongue-clicking response from Moreland. Two of the other guys in an argument over *mineral rights*. Moreland again, promising to explain the *marketing campaign* in *just a moment* if *you people* would just be a little *patient*.

STOP.

Marketing campaign? What were they planning that needed marketing?

PLAY.

Andrew, Purdo said. *Andrew's people are ramping up production. They got some software issues, but it's under control.* Computers? But Purdo wasn't a computer guy. What had they gotten into here?

Moreland again: *Are we dependent on these nerds? Must we be?*

Purdo: *It's not happening without them.*

Moreland: *Tell me you've got them under control now. It would make me happy to hear that.*

Purdo: *Hey, it was just one incident. It's over. We tightened the whole operation.*

Moreland: *You cleaned up afterwards, right?*

Purdo, sounding uncomfortable: *My people do what they have to do. They don't bug me with details.*

Moreland: *You're a big-picture guy.*

Purdo: *You got it.*

Moreland: *No problems with John?*

John again. The guy who was doing great and hadn't been easy to find. Mystery man.

Purdo: *He has no idea. Everything's sweet.*

Moreland, satirically: *I gotta meet this guy. You bringing him to Barbados?*

Purdo: *He's comin' with Faith Boy. I guess they're buddies now.*

Moreland: *That cracks me up. Was that my idea? Am I some kind of genius? (Laughter.)*

Isabel: *Hey, you! Move your ass. Plane's here!*

STOP.

"What?"

"We're going."

Jeff glanced out of the manager's window. A Cessna was turning around at the end of the airstrip.

"Where to?" he said.

"Wherever. I don't give a shit."

He followed Isabel outside. The heat hit him like a soft, humid wall, and he found himself squinting in the mid-morning sunlight. Then a sour, rancid smell attacked his nostrils, and he saw that to reach the end of the airstrip, they had to pass a line of open pits containing waste products from the palm oil plant.

The pilot waved at them, urging them to hurry, as if aware of some imminent danger. Isabel started to run. Jeff removed his earpiece and broke into a jog. Isabel turned to see if he were keeping up. Jeff picked up his pace, only to trip on a rogue palm tree root. As he hit the ground, he heard the audio recorder crack under his weight.

Isabel scowled.

"*What* did you just do?"

CHAPTER 19

Never mind the *who*. *What* the fuck was John Dolt? What had he become? This basic question — or *existential poser*, as Gideon might have put it — weighed upon the mind of the man himself. Which, if you thought about it, was ironic, because everybody else — Lescek and Samira, for example — had pretty clearly made their minds up.

Meanwhile, according to the midnight TV news, cars burned in Brixton and new disturbances flared in Tottenham. But events like these no longer impinged on his consciousness in the way that they once did. *The new normal* — wasn't that Gideon's phrase?

Safely installed once more in his secure hotel suite, enjoying the flowers placed there in recognition of his *sterling efforts* today by Gideon, his personal assistant, and warned not to *wander off* again or *go rogue* by Des, his security consultant, Dolt was at liberty to reflect. And, *anti-politician* as he was, he was determined to ask himself the tough ones.

Or was he?

Take the issue of Victoria and the girls, Tamsin and Tamara. How much money had they held out for? Where had it come from? What sort of pressure had been applied? Dolt didn't want to know. How could he accept that he would never see or talk to them again? The enormity of this defied reason, and humanity. It couldn't be real, could it?

And who'd authorized Des to... Oh, but what about all those papers his personal lawyer had made him sign, right here in his business den? What else had he agreed to?

Then there was the grisly business of Hamid and the minibus. The idea that Hamid was a Dangerous Person was grotesque. Something ought to be done. But Dolt's hands, surely, were tied, were they not? He could mention the affair to Gideon; that was something. And, if he ever met the former PM again — the one who was always campaigning for human rights in a *nuanced* way — perhaps he could put a word in. But Dolt couldn't be held responsible for Hamid's fate — and, not having any solid evidence or reliable information to hand, Dolt didn't want to speculate as to what, precisely, that fate might be — because whoever had planted bomb-making materials in the minibus, or had claimed to have found them, it hadn't been Dolt. Hamid's fate was unfair, grossly so. But then, as Gideon had pointed out, the world was *terribly random*. Dolt couldn't be blamed for that. And, in the end, could he be sure that he was in possession of all the facts? Was it not possible that the Authorities, whoever they might be, knew more? Could Dolt say for certain that none of Hamid's acquaintances in his homeland were Dangerous Persons?

And what about Lescek? Old Lescek had gone off the deep end a bit there, hadn't he? It wasn't just Dolt who'd thought so; the whole pub had. Now, you had to admit that what *someone* had written in Dolt's name in the paper was, well, pretty foul stuff. And that person was in line for a major ticking-off from Dolt personally, if his or her identity ever became known. But Lescek's mistake was to take it personally. When the mystery writer attacked the "innate moral deficiencies of post-communist economic migrants," and compared their habits — work, hygiene, breeding and so on — unfavorably with "native British stock," he or she couldn't have had Lescek specifically in mind. Indeed, it was highly probable that the writer had a friend very like Lescek. Which just went to show.

Wait a minute. Was there something wrong with those last observations? Dolt ran them by again, in forensic mode. No, it all made sense, didn't it? But a bollocking remained in order for the tactless scribbler in question. Gideon, no doubt, would urge *greater tact* next time, or a little *subtlety, if you can manage it*. Dolt would do likewise.

Now, then: Samira. Of course, your heart went out to a girl whose dad was banged up in a secret CIA prison in one of the War Zones. It would, wouldn't it? And if a personal assault on Dolt himself went any way towards making her feel better about things, well, he wasn't sure that he would stand in her way. But violence never really solved anything, did it? Not unless, as Dick, Dolt's Foreign Affairs tutor at the AAI argued, it was *axiomatic* that you were *virtuous*. That being the case, you could bash anyone you wanted; it was okay. (In truth, Dolt had found this a tricky concept; but a bloody useful one, all the same.) Perhaps Samira thought she was virtuous. A poll of the regulars at the Brit Arse might have disappointed her, Dolt felt. In any event, ripping up Aisha's letter was totally out of order. He wasn't even sure he could put it back together again.

Ah, yes — Aisha.

A right poser, wasn't it? On the one hand, here was a poor girl on a mission to seek JUSTICE on behalf of her brother, apparently convinced that it could only be obtained from the former PM. Why she believed *that*, was a good question. But it didn't lead anywhere.

On the other hand, what about Lescek's insinuations? If you took them seriously, Aisha had been engaged in industrial espionage, and intended to offer the former PM a once-in-a-lifetime stab at riches. And everyone knew where he stood on *that* issue.

But, really? A top-secret Libyan project to develop the killer vacuum cleaner? It didn't sound like the sort of thing that went on in Libya. If fact, it sounded ludicrous.

And then again, on another hand, why had Aisha been killed? Who were the killers? Why the cover-up story? All right, that was three hands — but it only served to show what a complicated situation this was.

What was he to do? He had failed to get anywhere with the letter, beyond establishing that the bearded youth in one of the photos was probably Aisha's brother. What about the other photos? The low buildings in the desert — the vacuum cleaner factory, if you believed Lescek's nonsense? What about the funny-looking plane?

There was also the memory stick. Surely this was key. There could be any amount of stuff on it. Documents, plans, photos, videos, you name it. Dolt's suite came equipped with a computer, but it was one of those useless, trendy things that didn't have a keyboard or any sockets. The HD LED multi-satellite system did have the right sort of socket, but when Dolt inserted the memory stick all he got was DRIVER ERROR. Fuck, he thought. He would have to carry the stick around with him tomorrow and be on the look-out for a proper computer.

But, actually, he knew he was evading the real issue here. How about some honesty, John?

He was trapped. On his own. Cut off from his old life, his family, his friends. Seduced and beguiled by Gideon. Bullied and intimidated by Des. Turned into a cartoon of himself for the amusement of the mob. Processed into a propaganda product for the mass market, pumped full of lies the way frozen chickens were pumped full of water.

But he'd understood this game all along, hadn't he? Of course. It was just that, in practice, it had proved harder than expected to keep track of what was real and what was fabricated. And he still didn't know in precisely whose service he'd been enlisted. When challenged as to whose side they were on, the PM's or one of the *factions*, Gideon had said merely *ours*. Not very helpful. Who was the real boss? The former PM? Lord Aylsham of Atlantic Affairs? This *Rand Purdo* geezer in America?

But propaganda and fabrication weren't the worst of it. Murder was. Look at the way Gideon and Des had treated Aisha's death. Ordinary people didn't behave like that; Dolt was mixed up with people for whom murder was a slide in one of those bloody PowerPoint things, or just a news management issue.

He could continue to play this game — indeed, he had little choice — but, if he were to survive, there was no point in holding back. Was there?

Next to the flowers, Gideon had left another stack of print-outs. Dolt picked them up. They were interim reports from Dolt's personal pollsters, whose names appeared to be Roger and Peter. *Small sample sizes*, Gideon had written in pencil on the top sheet, *treat with caution*.

Dolt was viewed positively by eighty-four percent of respondents, and negatively by only seven. Sixty-nine percent believed he would do a better job than the current PM, any leading member of the National Government, or the Leader of the Opposition. No mention of the former PM. Six percent thought Dolt's views on migrants were "too extreme"; eleven percent, "not tough enough"; and seventy-two percent, "about right".

He read those last figures again. Then he padded over to his sundowner bar, helped himself to a large sherry, and read the figures for a third time. *Seventy-two percent.* He sat on his leopard-print couch and flipped to the second page.

Eighty-five percent thought that Dolt understood the problems they faced in ordinary life; three percent thought he didn't. Sixty-eight percent thought he was a "natural leader"; ten percent didn't.

Comparing what the public took to be Dolt's positions on welfare, crime, the environment, foreign aid, international affairs, multiculturalism, debt and the disturbances with the policies of the National Government, Dolt was miles ahead. (There were no figures relating to the economic and financial crises, the War Zones, or the Greater Persian Question; perhaps they were to come.) Forty-nine percent would not object to their daughters marrying him.

Forty-nine percent? Dolt sipped his sherry. Well, they were only *interim* figures. He flipped to page three.

Dolt was more popular than the Archbishop of Canterbury; more popular than every adult member of the Royal Family, bar two; way more popular than any political party leader; and slightly ahead of the latest TV talent-show winner.

The remaining pages contained an analysis of the figures. Dolt skimmed them. They were full of technical waffle about *demographics, trends* and *percentiles* that he couldn't understand. But at the end, under the heading "Just for Fun', was something that caught his eye.

Fifty-five percent thought that the state of the country was so dire that only a dictator could put it right. Of those, ninety-one percent thought that dictator should be Dolt.

Dolt chucked his polling research down on the coffee table, rattling his mini fondue set. Then he took a long chug on his sherry. Had he ever thought he'd make a good dictator? Why, yes. As a matter of fact, he had.

And Roger and Peter might not take the idea seriously, but they hadn't had Dolt's experience, had they? They hadn't been touched by the soul of power.

Of course, you couldn't be what Gideon would doubtless call a *classical* dictator in a modern society with top-up mobiles and supermarket loyalty cards. But think more subtly. Think about the nature of power in a wobbly, broken-down society stressed out by *disturbances*, fearful of the future and befuddled by the in-your-face greed of the rich. Think about those rip tides of emotion; dark, ocean-floor currents of anguish. Think about all that hot blood. All that undirected *angst*, to use one of Gideon's favorite words.

What if someone could really harness it?

The papers, of course, tried to. With considerable success. And their tactics were obvious enough: Divide and rule; demonize; provoke envy; generate fear; victimize unpopular minorities; sneer and smear, bully and belittle; start fires, fan the flames and run away; always be shocked.

But the papers weren't a person. They weren't trusted. People knew they were packed full of lies, even if the lies were irresistible, like chicken nuggets.

What's more, the papers, their *black arts* notwithstanding, didn't truly understand the people. They were products created by operators like Roger and Peter, a class apart. Hadn't Gideon said something about a prince having to be *of* the people?

You couldn't be more *of* the people than Dolt. That was a given. Roger and Peter's figures merely proved it.

Think about the Policy Steering Committee meeting, and that famous photograph. Cat among the pigeons? Wolf in sheep's clothing? These animal images didn't come close. How about a kiddies' birthday party with Satan in a suede jacket?

As he pondered these things a deep, cold anger formed in his soul, taking him by surprise and giving him a bit of a fright. He wasn't sure where it had come from, but he knew what it meant.

How dare these people use him? Who had more right to rule? Who had more legitimacy?

Sure, he'd risen to his present standing though all the usual manipulations. But people recognized that he was different, didn't they? Because he was. They looked at Dolt and saw themselves — not something any normal person would ever feel about the members of the Policy Steering Committee. Dolt was genuine. He wasn't pretending. He meant it.

And what happens when you conjure up devils? Suppose you get the big guy himself. What do you do after you let Satan into your party?

Was Dolt evil? What was evil? It was what went on in the War Zones, or it might be another devious *action plan* from the Policy Steering Committee. Dolt was merely an expression of the will of the people, and you couldn't get any less evil than that, by definition.

He would be a Force for Good. He would shake things up until you couldn't breathe for the dust. But he would do it his own way. He would do it using all the tools, techniques and technology that, as he had seen, the modern world provided. And so no, you couldn't be a classical dictator. But you could be — what would Gideon call it? — a postmodern one.

There came a gentle tapping at the main door to the suite. It had to be Gideon; everyone else, including Des, was now required to phone first from Reception.

Dolt opened the door. Gideon smiled and opened his mouth to speak but then seemed to falter.

"Anything the matter?" Dolt asked.

"No," Gideon said, the smile fading. "No, I don't think so."

"Come in."

They sat on the couch in the business den.

"Ah! You've been studying the polls, I see."

"I certainly have."

"*Interim* results, of course."

"So it says."

"Mm. Encouraging, though, don't you think?"

"Definitely."

Gideon paused. Dolt waited.

"Just popped round to make sure you were... That everything's okay."

"It's all okay."

"Good."

"Yes."

"Bit of a day, wasn't it, all in all?"

Dolt straightened up the edges of his stack of poll results.

"I suppose it was."

Gideon started doing the finger-rub thing.

"Des mentioned that you, er..."

"The Britannia Arms?"

"Yes. You see, I was just a little worried that —"

"No need to worry. I'm over it."

"Oh, well that's excellent. Only..."

"What?"

"You would tell me, wouldn't you, John? If anything were the matter?"

"Of course."

"But it isn't?"

"No."

Gideon seemed to notice the mini fondue set. He picked it up.

"Curious."

"Swiss."

"I suppose so."

There was a pause. Gideon stopped rubbing his finger.

"So! Looking forward to tomorrow?"

"Yes," Dolt said. "I certainly am."

It was going to be the most glorious day yet.

CHAPTER 20

The *Face of Freedom*, that's what it was. When John Dolt examined it in the mirror, in his Afro-Swiss designer bathroom, he realized that Roberto's facial treatments had not been the girly waste of time he'd assumed.

Whatever needed to be toned up had been toned up; everything that cried out to be toned down had been toned down. It was all good.

But there was something else. Confidence? Determination? Perhaps. Call it whatever you like. It was the glint in the eye; the iron in the soul; the fire in the belly. It was whatever Amber Pike had. And maybe more.

Flicking through his complimentary morning papers, lingering briefly to enjoy *that* photograph (A PACK FULL OF JOKERS WITH ONLY ONE KING, ha-ha!) but otherwise skipping the stuff that Gideon had shown him the day before, he read that he had called for the formation of a British version of the American New Patriot Movement, and had offered his services as model, inspiration and unofficial spokesperson — all unpaid, naturally. This Movement would operate similarly to the American one, but would, of course, be entirely different, being British.

He had also written a short essay, in one of the somewhat posher papers, in praise of Amber Pike, whom he absolutely expected to be President one day. In one of the tabloids, beneath a sinister, blocky, computer-generated portrait of *Red Ron* — currently the papers' favorite subversive mastermind — Dolt had demanded that this menace to society, whose evil network bore full responsibility for the so-called *disturbances* that wracked the land, be designated forthwith a Dangerous Person. Somehow he'd also found time to expose a wicked European plot to impose a "health tax" on pork pies, and to denounce Chinese aggression. *Chinese aggression?* Well, never mind. As for the pork pies, he would have to instruct Gideon that it was time to move on from the tried-and-true to more challenging vistas.

He was satisfied, but not surprised, to note that his visit to the Britannia Arms had gone unreported.

Thus primed, and ignoring his complimentary breakfast of muesli and biltong, he launched himself into his study morning.

Dolt's new assertiveness did not go unnoticed at the Atlantic Affairs Institute.

Eva, the vampire economist, newly recovered from her tummy bug, flushed pink with pride — well, off-white, to be honest — at Dolt's determination to *break this dismal cycle of debt* once and for all, at any cost.

Norman, the basement-dwelling zombie vicar who handled domestic policy, struggled to hold himself together in the face of Dolt's insistence that, whether Society existed or not, and whatever size it might be — big, small or extra-large — it wasn't going to be sticking its hand in *his* pocket.

And Dick, the rogue walrus of foreign affairs, listened in awe, each and every particular hair of his moustache practically standing on end, as Dolt denounced *appeasement*, *pandering* and *vacillation*, and demanded an immediate and decisive resolution of the Greater Persian Question, regardless of consequence. (Sometime soon he would have to get on top of what exactly the GPQ *was*, but for now that was a side-issue.)

In between sessions, Dolt took the opportunity, variously, to upbraid his Director of Communications, Jaz, for penning the article on migrants that had so offended Lescek — mistakenly, it seemed, since Jaz all but burst into tears, pleading innocence; to return his suede jacket to Jacqueline, his stylist, demanding something more, you know, *big-shotty* — and then having to ask for it back because he'd forgotten to remove Aisha's envelope; and to congratulate Polly, his Political Advisor, for her invaluable insights into the all-too-human failings of the members of the Policy Steering Committee — and if she had more, he said, it would be appreciated.

Then it was lunchtime.

"John," Gideon said, over his Cajun bluefish, "You're on good form today."

"Am I?" Dolt said, wielding his steak knife like a pen.

"Absolutely. But you need to hold something in reserve, you know."

"Not get carried away, you mean?"

"Precisely."

Dolt put his knife down.

"Remind me why we're doing this, Gideon."

"Remind you? Well, it's as we said, right at the beginning. We're backing the New Patriot Movement, and you —"

"Ah, but it's bigger than that, though, isn't it? Eh?"

"Bigger?"

"Cause here's what I want to know, Gideon. Who's the real boss? Who pays your wages?"

"The AAI, of course."

"But who pays for that? What's his name — Aylsham?"

A sour smile from Gideon.

"Try getting *him* to pay for anything."

"It's not... *You know who*, is it?"

"Oh no."

"Then it must be... Purdo?"

Gideon sighed.

"There's a whole web of philanthropy out there, John. He's part of it, of course. Is there a point to this?"

"Just want to make sure we're on the same what's-it. Page."

"Of course we are."

"I mean, I'm looking at a long-term career here."

Gideon took another bite of bluefish and chewed slowly.

"Long term?"

"That's right. Should be possible, yeah?"

"Why not?"

"Good. Just wanted to make sure we, you know, understand each other."

"Quite."

"I'm always willing to take on more responsibility. Know what I mean?"

"Yes. I think so."

Dolt picked up his knife again.

"Good. So. *John's Jury*. You going to be there?"

Gideon looked distracted.

"Hmm?"

"*John's Jury*. You coming?"

"Alas, no. I have some appointments. I'll see you at the premiere tonight. But don't be downhearted," Gideon said, with a bit of an edge, if Dolt wasn't mistaken, "you won't be short of friends."

How true, Dolt thought. He certainly didn't intend to be short of friends.

*

N ot long after Des deposited him at the TV studios in glamorous Tooting, Dolt realized that the *friends* Gideon had alluded to were none other than Nigel Weese and his lumbering American sidekick Flint Gunner. Who said Gideon didn't have a sense of humor?

"Well, if it isn't the Man of the People," Weese said, as Dolt entered the brightly-lit room to which he'd been told he had to report if he didn't want to look like Richard Nixon.

"What are *you* doing here?" Dolt said.

"We're your guests."

"I didn't invite you."

"Your producer did."

"My producer?"

"That would be Flint here. Right, Flint?"

"You bet."

"Flint's making sure that FNN-UK gets off to a good start. He's very hands-on. Aren't you?"

"You got it."

"Wait a minute," Dolt said. "How can he be a producer *and* a guest?"

Weese smirked.

"TV's very incestuous. You'll get used to it."

"I'm not sure I want to do this."

"Oh, come on. It'll be fun. We'll have a laugh. Flint's come all the way from St. John's Wood."

"No, I think I've changed my mind."

"Nothing personal, I hope?"

Dolt hesitated.

"We're all good friends here, aren't we?" Weese said, pretending to look hurt. "I'm your chum from the popular press, and Flint's your pal from across the pond."

A thought struck Dolt like a brick through a shop window.

"You!" he said. "What's your name, Weese?"

"Nigel, please. Flint calls me Nige."

"You wrote that migrant rubbish! And all that other crap."

"Me?"

"Have you any idea —"

"I must insist," Weese said, "that if there is any suggestion that allegations might have been made, potentially implying that I could have had any knowledge of such a thing, were it to have occurred, then you would have to accept that I believe it should be considered highly inconceivable."

"What?"

"It's what I always say."

"I don't need this. I'm going," Dolt said, slipping his smart new woolen blazer back on and heading for the door.

Weese cleared his throat.

"DOLT WIMPS OUT," he said.

Dolt paused.

"DOLT IN TV TANTRUM. DOLT BOTTLES IT. DOLT —"

"Hang on," Dolt said. "You wouldn't dare."

"Me?"

"They wouldn't let you. You may not know this, but there are powerful forces that —"

"I wouldn't think of it. It's the other papers. Very competitive market. They're not *all* on your side, you know. Some of them are just waiting for you to put a foot wrong."

This contradicted what Dolt thought he knew. But, nevertheless, he felt a twinge of fear.

"We don't want that to happen, you see," Weese said. "That's why we're looking out for you. Come on. Take your jacket off and get your face done. We'll make sure that *John's Jury* gets an FNN Service to Freedom award."

"Service to Freedom?"

"On the cards, I would say. Flint here gets to hand them out."

"Damn right," Gunner said. "I'm the chooser."

Dolt studied Gunner. If he'd ever met anyone who traded in *bomb-making materials*, this had to be the bloke.

"All right, fuck it. I'll do it."

And on that note, Dolt's career as a TV host, pundit and fully-licensed loudmouth took its first, faltering steps towards stardom. They entered the studio, the lights went up and *John's Jury* began to rip its way into the public consciousness.

The Case of the Have-a-Go House-Holder.

Weese paints the scene. A dark and threatening sky. The man of the house and his wife, upstanding citizens both, retire for the night, having spent the evening assembling care packages for the troops in the War Zones. Their children, blond and cherubic, as you can see in these pictures, sleep soundly in their beds. Yet their father, privately, is troubled. Local bureaucrats have ordered the police back to their station to fill out Health and Safety forms. The streets are full of peril.

What bureaucrats? Dolt wants to know.

Doesn't matter, Weese replies, they're *bureaucrats.*

A burglar breaks in. He may or may not resemble the sinister-looking, dark-skinned young thug in this picture. Our house-holder is torn: Does he protect his wife and children or does he respect the intruder's Human Rights? What a dilemma!

Guy needs a gun, Gunner says, grimly.

In a free society, he would have one, Weese says.

I'm almost afraid to ask, Dolt says, but what happens next?

Well, you won't believe this, Weese says, but the police actually show up and who do you think they arrest?

Dolt doesn't know.

The house-holder! For not respecting the burglar's rights!

Jeez, Gunner says. If only our guy had gotten a Tech-9, and maybe also a Glock, bloodshed could have been avoided.

So is the burglar dead, then? Dolt asks.

More or less, Weese says. Verdict?

NOT GUILTY, Dolt says. Next case.

The Case of the Speeding Nun.

Get this, Gunner says. This nun is driving her humble hatchback to the hospice where a hero from the War Zones lies dying. Her only thought is to comfort him in his final moments. But guess what?

What? Dolt says, a note of expectant horror in his voice.

Wham! Speed camera. They haul her ass to court. Claim she's not a nun. Got a picture of her in Tesco's.

But she is a nun, right? Weese says.

No, Gunner says. But, hey, the camera doesn't know that!

Dolt bangs his gavel.

NOT GUILTY!

The Case of the Dangerous Person.

Weese looks grave. This is a particularly disturbing case, he says, which only goes to illustrate how serious the threat to this country is.

You're scaring me, Dolt says.

Sorry about that, Weese says, but we must face facts. We must not bury our heads in the sand.

No, Gunner says. Cause that would be stupid.

Anyway, Weese says. There's this very scary-looking, bearded bloke. He lives above the hair salon. The neighbors avoid him, but they keep an eye on him.

Very wise, Dolt says.

Smart move, Gunner says.

He gets all these letters from abroad, Weese says.

Letters? Gunner says. Who writes letters?

Good question, Weese says. Then the neighbors notice that he's having newspapers delivered. Foreign newspapers.

What, like French? Dolt says.

No, Weese says, ominously. Not *French*.

Hah! Gunner says. I think I know where you're going with this.

There's more, Weese says. He gets a satellite dish installed. But the neighbors aren't fooled. Their Sky dishes are all pointing *this* way. *His* is pointing *that* way.

I wouldn't have thought of that, Dolt says.

So the neighbors organize, Weese says, in order to watch him and see what deliveries he gets. Weeks go by. Months. Nothing. But then, their patience is rewarded. He gets a large brown box. Putting themselves in enormous danger, they snatch the box and open it up. And what do you think they find?

Dunno, Gunner says. Something bad, I guess.

Bottles, Weese says. Bottles of hydrogen peroxide. Lots of 'em. And you know what that means...

Bomb-making materials, Gunner says.

Bomb-making materials? Dolt says. But, hang on—

That's right, Weese, says. Naturally, the neighbors don't waste any time. They're dialing the Dangerous Persons Hotline before you can say *kaboom*. And guess what happens?

They slap a DPO on him? Dolt says.

No, Weese says.

What then? Dolt says.

Nothing, Weese says. They say there's nothing they can do.

Unbe-fucking-lievable, Gunner says.

You're not bleeping wrong, Flint, Weese says, with bitter humor.

Now you're gonna tell us he blew up a school, Gunner says.

Well, no, Weese says. He's a sly one. He has not acted yet. He may well be a sleeper. The point is, no action has been taken. The threat is still out there. Verdict, John?

A rare moment of silence in the broadcast.

Um, *verdict*, John? Weese says.

Oh, GUILTY, I expect, Dolt says, absently.

Commercial break, featuring burglar alarms, incontinence underwear and cat food.

On returning, the show proceeded to examine *The Case of the Patriotic Greengrocer* (NOT GUILTY) and *The Case of the Council Bin Czar* (GUILTY), and Dolt did his best, but his heart wasn't quite in it. He finished by reading a canned sign-off from a prompting device without registering a word he was saying.

Afterwards, he lingered on the set for a minute or so, deep in thought. By the time he returned to the dressing room, Weese and Gunner had vanished.

And then it was dinner time.

Well, it wasn't much of a dinner; the impending premiere of *The Face of Freedom* meant that Dolt and Des had to eat early and fast. They sat in the Range Rover, wheels up on the curb, next to a burger van in Des's home patch of Streatham.

Dolt was hungry — TV seemed to do things to your appetite — so it wasn't until he was half-way through his burger that he noticed that Des, whose own burger had so far not been touched, was studying him.

"What?" he said, with an experimental touch of the aggression he'd decided he needed to adopt when dealing with Des.

"John," Des said. "John, John, John."

"I know who I am, thanks very much."

"Do you? Old Gidders was in a panic about you. Thought you were going wobbly. Needn't have worried, need he?"

"Old Gidders?"

"That's what we call him when he's not around. Me and the lads."

So Dolt hadn't been the only one to have a problem with *Gideon*.

"What do you mean, wobbly?"

"No doubt he was asking himself, old Gidders, what kind of fearless leader gets himself beaten up in a pub by a girl."

"Why don't you shut up and eat your sodding burger?"

"Then he remembers that suicide-bomb girl, and he reads all these text messages from *Tamsin* or *Tamara* or whoever —"

"What text messages?"

"— and he probably says to himself, hello — our hard man Dolt gets pushed around a lot by girls, doesn't he?"

"I said, what text messages?"

"And he asks me what I think."

"Oh?"

"I tell him not to worry, of course. And he believes me, doesn't he? Because he hasn't met many people like you, and he still can't quite read you, can he? Lucky, that."

Was this part of some double-act designed to manipulate him, or was Des now freelancing? Either way, Dolt thought, they'd been stealing his messages, and now would be as good a time as any to tell Des what he could do to himself. But he held back.

"You see," Des went on, "your problem, John — one of your problems — is that you don't know who your real friends might be."

Not so. He'd already lost his illusions, hadn't he? He knew the difference between friendship and mere popularity. Leadership might well be lonely. He'd made his choice. Time, and events to come, would show who'd been manipulating whom. And, down the line, after he'd thrown off Des and Gideon and their schemes, after he'd won, not the hearts and minds, perhaps, but the darker affections of the people, no one would stop him ripping up any pathetic agreements he'd signed, and then summoning Tamsin and Tamara back from exile. If he felt like it.

"What I mean," Des was saying, "is, you haven't worked with these people before, have you? I have. You understand *them* even less than they understand *you*."

Dolt resumed munching on his burger, affecting not to listen.

"I'm just saying," Des said.

Dolt continued to eat.

"You ought to think about your exit strategy," Des said. "That's what I'm getting at. Have you got one? I have."

"Whatever," Dolt said, finishing his burger and chucking the debris out of the window.

Des sighed.

"Think about it," he said. Then he picked up his dinner and, joylessly, began to eat.

Dolt tipped his seat back and closed his eyes. Des was becoming tiresome. Perhaps Dolt should see about having him replaced. Well, maybe. He'd discuss it with Gideon after the glittering premiere of *The Face of Freedom*. It was bound be at least a bit *glittering*, wasn't it? Of course. And it would offer far more congenial people to talk to than Des.

Wouldn't it?

CHAPTER 21

T he *Face of Freedom* — and you could tell this from the title alone, Dolt felt — was intended to be uplifting. But, happily for Dolt, for whom every conversation with Des seemed to be a downer, the uplift began long before the opening titles were due to roll.

In a leafy square in front of the cinema, an old West End Art Deco palace newly enhanced with Premium Seating and mobile phone adverts, the scene buzzed. Lights glared. Hired security paced. Personal assistants — though not Gideon — assisted. The red carpet might have been a little on the orange side — obtained, possibly, at an advantageous price from the Big Builder liquidation — but there was plenty of it, and room enough for Dolt to parade himself for the crowd, while avoiding the squelchy bits (the result of afternoon showers).

Whether or not these film fans understood that he wasn't actually *in* the film, Dolt couldn't say. But they were clearly thrilled to see him. The noise was startling, and energizing. Cameras flashed. Mobile phones, set eagerly to video mode, tracked his movements. Hand-made banners exalted his character and proclaimed devotion. So what if the slogans were eerily similar? People had looked him up and down and had come, quite naturally, to identical conclusions. And if the crowd looked decidedly *bused-in* — well, who wanted to use the trains or the Tube these days?

He began a modern, interactive form of royal progress along the security barrier, waving and shaking hands until his arm started to ache. Were these really film fans, he began to wonder, or had they actually come to see *him*? Could it be that Dolt was the true star of the moment? Well, he didn't want to upstage the actors or the director, due to arrive shortly, having been delayed by unrest in Hammersmith, but someone had to entertain the mob, so he would do it. Guided by his publicist — he hadn't met her before and hadn't quite caught her name — he approached a gaggle of TV interviewers, to whom he offered his considered judgment on the movie he had yet to see.

Did Dolt think this movie could determine the results of the American elections?

"No doubt about it," Dolt said. "I challenge anyone to see this film and not want to rush out and vote."

Was Dolt at all concerned that professional historians had denounced the film?

"Were they there?" Dolt asked. "Have they seen what millions of movie-goers have already seen with their own eyes? Anyone can write a book. Especially one nobody wants to read. People are falling over themselves to see this film. I think that says it all."

Had Dolt felt any qualms about associating himself with the director of this movie, given the director's well-documented track record?

"None whatsoever," Dolt said. "I have absolute faith in, er, him. And I think you'll find that none of these stories about his so-called *track record* contain anything that actually stands up."

Not even the story about his teenage Thai bride?

"Er, no," Dolt said.

And did Dolt have any movie ambitions himself?

"Not at present," Dolt said. "Obviously, I'm going to have my work cut out running the — I mean pursuing our campaign for fairness, justice and common sense. Of course, if there were offers... Well, I'd have to consider them, wouldn't I?"

What did Dolt think about the *notorious torture scene?*

"Well," Dolt said. "I think it's, um, a good scene, obviously. As scenes go. And, yes, there's some torture in it. Here and there. Of course. Wouldn't deny that."

But did Dolt agree with what the film had to say about the use of torture?

"Um, I think," Dolt said, "that what the film has to say is very interesting. Obviously. And, you know, I wouldn't say I disagreed, necessarily, although —"

But Dolt's tortured answer was cut short by his publicist, who yanked at his elbow and drew him out of danger.

"Hey!" he said. "I could have answered that. Um, it's Jane, right?"

"My name's *Jenna*," Dolt's publicist told him, a little too loudly. "You're in the way. Come over here." She led him out on to the tree-lined patch of grass in the center of the square. The stars, it appeared, were shortly to step out on to the carpet. The crowd, as you would expect, became expectant.

Jenna was small, energetic and impatient, with straight-cut, black hair and a menacing fringe. With her black suit, fancy phone, metallic jewelry and heavy, expensive-looking, rectangular glasses, she had the demeanor of a short-tempered, high-tech robot. Dolt decided to humor her.

As the first limo maneuvered through the throng towards the red-carpet landing zone, Dolt took the opportunity to get himself fully briefed and/or updated.

"So, um, Jenna. What's this film about, then?"

The fringe shivered.

"You don't know? Don't you read the papers?"

Well, of course he read the papers. It was just that, lately, he'd only had time to read about himself. Supposedly, this film was based on a *story idea* by Amber Pike; and it contained a *notorious torture scene*. Probably not a romantic comedy.

"Thriller, is it?"

The glasses swiveled and locked on.

"You *have* seen the posters, haven't you?"

"No."

"Well, there's one up *there*."

158

Dolt raised his gaze to the display above the foyer entrance. *In a Land of Debt and Tyranny*, he read, *Only One Woman Can Water the Tree of Liberty*. Debt? A misprint, presumably. The poster depicted a good-looking, demographically-balanced and highly patriotic mob advancing on a White House defended by faceless, cowering storm-troopers. The general effect was of a West End musical crossed with a flying-saucer movie. But then, as Gideon had pointed out in an aside on the subject of coming up with stories for the press, originality in the arts was a rare thing. Leading the mob, and waving the largest flag, was a woman with a bloodied but valiant face, who wore perfectly-fitted blue jeans and a stained white shirt. There was no sign of the tree she was supposed to be watering. Possibly it was in the back garden of the White House, or else hidden by the storm-troopers.

"Oh, I get it," he said, even though he didn't.

"Okay, get ready. Here comes Kenworth."

"Who?"

"Kenworth."

Dolt raised his eyebrows. Jenna seemed to flip into re-compute mode.

"Kenworth Pruett? The movie star? Kenny-P? K-Pru?"

"Oh, K-Pru!" Dolt said. "Gotcha. So he's in this?"

"*She's* in it."

"Ah, right." He pointed to the poster. "Is that..."

"Yes, that's her."

Kenworth Pruett? What kind of name was that? Almost as bad as *Gideon*. Was he supposed to have heard of her? Clearly, he was going to have to think on his feet tonight, or *busk it*, as Gideon would say. Why hadn't Gideon prepared him? And where *was* Gideon?

By now, a black limo had docked in the unloading zone. Jenna snapped into celebrity-arrival mode, all systems activated. Assistants opened doors. Slowly, cautiously, in an operation that reminded Dolt of NASA astronauts exiting the Space Station for their daily Space Stroll, K-Pru emerged. She would have done better, Dolt thought, to have stuck with the jeans and white shirt, perhaps slinging a mac over the top. The autumnal London night — raw, damp and blustery — would easily penetrate the gauzy, minimal frockery she had selected. And she didn't even have the option of legging it into the foyer; the heels on her boots meant she couldn't walk unassisted.

"Doesn't she look amazing?" Jenna said.

Dolt admitted that he was amazed. K-Pru oriented herself towards the surging mass of film fans and prepared for lift-off.

The noise of the crowd cranked up to window-rattling levels. Listening carefully, though, Dolt could discern a weird stereo effect: Whereas the right channel was a symphony of joy and adoration, the left channel was more a drum-beat of anger and menace. He realized he was caught between *two* crowds, with competing agendas.

The newer of these, which was on the move, probably hadn't come to see the movie, or even K-Pru, Dolt decided. Because, if it had, it probably wouldn't have invited riot policemen to accompany it. And it wouldn't have needed all those signs, with their rude slogans about *bankers*.

159

At this point, a lot of things began to happen at the same time, and Dolt, swept up in the action, began to feel as if he'd been drafted into, well, some kind of disaster movie.

The crowd to the left, or the *banker-bashers*, as Dolt now decided to call them, though hitherto adhering to a course which would have taken them past the cinema and into the heart of political power, now slammed on the brakes. Or, at least, the ones at the front did. There followed a moderate amount of bumping-together and toe-stubbing. But, Dolt noted, this was a good-natured, if aggressive, assembly and recriminations were few. What then followed was a kind of mass double-take on the part of the banker-bashers. They looked into the square in front of the cinema. They registered the presence of what Dolt now resolved to think of as the *freedom-lovers*. They spotted the poster featuring K-Pru in her suggestively-besmirched white shirt. They read the slogans. And the net effect of all this was that the banker-bashers, almost as one and newly re-enthused, made a decisive right-turn into the square. The riot police, having underestimated the banker-bashers' ability to think on their feet, found themselves blocking the wrong street and struggled to regroup.

Almost at the same time, a second limo arrived on the opposite side of the square, bearing, according to Jenna, no less a personage than the director of *The Face of Freedom*. But Jenna, less perspicacious than Dolt for all her machine-like efficiency, hadn't spotted the advance of the banker-bashers. She launched into a potted history of the director's career — just for Dolt's information, though she could hardly believe that Dolt would be unfamiliar with the work of an *auteur* like Brandon Burrito.

Burrito? Another odd name, but what could you do?

Burrito, Jenna explained, as the banker-bashers edged forward and the first tentative missiles began to land, had first made his name in the genre sometimes dismissed, ignorantly, as *designer violence*. His *Dead Cat Poems*, about sensitive and quixotic gangsters, was a classic of its kind. There had followed nominations, awards, magazine covers, and a sequence of follow-ups that vastly expanded the language of film, while also — to the public's shame, alas — greatly contracting the takings at the box office. Burrito, naturally, had clung to his artistic vision, even as he found himself overtaken by personal tragedy — abandoned by one wife after another; enslaved by the addictions that prey on genius; traduced by jealous rivals; bankrupted by the betrayals of business partners; exiled from his homeland for a period, a victim of spite, envy, and various misunderstandings, some of a personal and—

"Um, Jenna," Dolt said. "I don't know if you've noticed, but —"

—and yet now, having discarded the political illusions of his past and having accepted his Redeemer, Burrito had fought his way back. And he had created his master-work, *The Face of Freedom*.

"Jenna," Dolt said firmly, as a beer can grazed his shoulder, "I think we should take cover behind those trees."

"Oh." It was the work of an instant for Jenna's computer brain to reassess the situation and respond.

"All right."

They took to the trees.

But, in a complex and fluid situation like this, Dolt knew, it was unreasonable to expect that other participants — the freedom-lovers, for example — would wait their turn. During Jenna's excursion into the cinematic hall of fame, the freedom-lovers had woken up to the threat posed by the banker-bashers to their putative evening of entertainment and enlightenment. Enraged at this encroachment upon their liberties, they had reoriented themselves so as to face their tormentors. In doing so, they had demolished the security barrier along which K-Pru had been tottering — and, more importantly from Dolt's point of view, had opened up a potential avenue of escape, into the foyer of the cinema. Of K-Pru herself, there was no sign. Members of her entourage, braving a now two-directional hail of bottles, beer cans, junk food and newly-liberated trash, were hunting for her.

Dolt was on the point of suggesting a dash for the safety of the foyer when fresh commotion broke out on yet another front.

"John!" someone yelled.

The voice was familiar, but the tone of alarm wasn't. It was Gideon, bearing down on them from behind, breathless and in a panic.

"John!" he said, his cheeks even pinker than usual. "There's a bit of a panic on!"

"We can see that."

"No, I mean at Number Ten. The PM —"

"Is that where you've been?"

"Yes. Listen, John. They're tearing their hair out down there." He paused to take a breath and dodge a low-flying shoe.

"What about?" Dolt said.

"It's all about IBARF."

"You what?"

"IBARF. The International Banking Activities Regulatory Forum. They're meeting just over there." He made a tremulous gesture, indicating the heart of political power. "You've got to do something, John."

"About banking activities?"

Gideon struggled for words. Dolt hadn't seen him like this before. It was serious. From the far side of the green came the sound of smashing glass, followed by a whoosh.

"Oh my gosh, what was that?"

"Petrol bomb," Dolt said. "What's all this about banking?"

"It's absolutely *essential*," Gideon said, deftly deflecting a traffic cone with his elbow, "that they reach agreement *today*. Ouch."

"What on?"

"On the new banking tax. If these hooligans disrupt —"

"A new tax on the bankers?"

"No, *for* the bankers. So that the next round of bail-outs —"

"Are you sure you've got that right?"

Gideon gave a gasp of exasperation.

"Didn't you go over this with Eva?"

He was referring, of course, to Eva, the vampire economist, recently recovered from a tummy bug and, understandably, not yet back on top form.

161

"John!"

Jenna was trying to attract his attention.

"One moment," Dolt said, as an unidentified missile crashed into the tree above and leaves fell around them. "Eva didn't mention it. What do you expect me to do?"

"*John!*"

"Jenna, *please.*"

"For pity's sake, John. Talk to the mob. Calm them. Soothe them. They'll listen to you. Tell them we're listening. We understand. We've heard their pleas."

"Pleas? What pleas?"

Gideon waved his arms, his exasperation, Dolt suspected, not yet abating.

"Whatever they are! *You* find out!"

But events, Dolt now saw, had not paused during this conversation. The two crowds, by mutual consent, had transferred their activities on to the green and hand-to-hand combat had begun. The riot policemen, keen not to be left out of the action, were roaming the periphery, seeking targets of opportunity. One approached Dolt, only to back off again when he recognized Dolt's face.

"JOHN!"

"Yes, Jenna, what's the problem?"

"It's K-Pru."

"K-Pru?"

"She's up that tree!"

Dolt looked up. Here was a vision, he thought, at once both inspiring and piteous — rather like *The Face of Freedom*, perhaps: Inspiring, because K-Pru had somehow extracted herself from the riot and ascended, in high-heeled boots, a sturdy oak that Dolt himself would have found challenging in his youth; and piteous, on account of the terrible damage inflicted by the weather, the riot and the climbing of the tree, on her attire. Plus, as anyone could see — and this explained the urgency in Jenna's manner — K-Pru was about to tumble out of the tree. One more dustbin and she was a goner.

"Who's K-Pru?" Gideon demanded to know. "What's she doing up that tree? Why isn't she wearing any —"

"Hold it a moment, Gideon," Dolt said. He had arrived, he knew, at what TV pundits such as himself liked to call a *defining moment*. Up until now, with the possible exception of his testing expedition to Heathrow with the lacrosse girls, his career as humble truth-teller and populist icon had been, to be honest, all talk. It was now time for action.

As mayhem roiled about him, he removed his smart, woolen blazer and handed it to Jenna.

"Here."

Then, with calm determination, he began to scale the tree. It quickly dawned on him that K-Pru was less than half his weight, and had benefited — rather like poor Samira, in an odd twist — from pointy toes. But he was not deterred. Gradually, he ascended, Jenna's urgings and Gideon's peevishness ringing in his ears. K-Pru herself, in a contrast to her on-screen persona, seemed frozen in fear. Well, he didn't blame her. It was her first trip to England, wasn't it? The poor girl didn't know what to expect.

"It's not always like this, you know!" Dolt said, cheerily, as he heaved himself aloft.

K-Pru stared at him, mouth open, lower lip trembling. A bicycle wheel crashed through the canopy above them. K-Pru flinched.

"Not to worry," Dolt said. "We'll soon have you down."

He'd meant this as encouragement, but K-Pru shivered, shook her head and retreated further up the branch on which she'd been crouching. It reminded him of the time he'd had to rescue next door's stupid cat.

What to do? Defining moment it might have been, but it was also a delicate situation, especially given K-Pru's state of dress. He mulled over this predicament for a moment, as petrol bombs *whumped*, the wind picked up, and Gideon urged him to *just grab her* and *hurry up about it*.

Then it came to him. And, as so often today, the answer to the problem came from TV. As an occasional viewer of the cheap and long-running TV soap *London's On Fire*, Dolt had been able to study a technique known as the *fireman's lift*. It featured on pretty much every show: A distraught young female, lightly-clad (though not nearly as lightly-clad as K-Pru) would be plucked from fiery peril by the hunk of the week. It made for great viewing, but was it feasible under the present circumstances?

He decided it was. And, moreover, it was an opportunity too good to pass up. He was about to call down to Jenna, but then he saw that his publicist was way ahead of him. She already had her phone out.

With the cameras rolling, he went for it. K-Pru, perhaps taken aback by the speed and skill of his friendly assault, did not resist. It was the work of moments for Dolt to scoop her from her branch and toss her across his left shoulder. He pinned her impressively-toned legs firmly against his chest with his left arm, leaving his right arm free to maneuver. Then, slowly and, on Dolt's part at least, painfully, they descended.

"Well, thank God for that!" Gideon said, as Dolt slid K-Pru gently to the ground. "Perhaps now we can —"

"Jenna?" Dolt said.

Jenna lowered her phone, a look of professional satisfaction on her face.

"Yes?"

"The jacket, please."

Jenna handed over Dolt's smart, woolen blazer. Dolt helped K-Pru into it.

"That's better, isn't it?" he said, doing up the buttons.

K-Pru nodded.

"John," Gideon said, lowering his voice for extra gravity. "I beg you. Now. Speak to these people. Or else we are all lost."

Dolt surveyed the scene. The riot remained in full swing. In fact, it was growing. Both sides appeared to have summoned reinforcements, and, rather as with an old-fashioned motorway rave, or a stag night with free beer, passers-by and interested parties with time on their hands had felt sufficiently emboldened to jump in with both boots.

"Speak?" he said. "How?"

Gideon seemed at a loss.

Dolt felt Jenna's hand on his shoulder. She was pointing to the balcony above the cinema foyer, just below the poster depicting K-Pru's imminent liberation of the White House from sci-fi tyranny.

"There's a PA up there," she said. "Burrito wanted to say a few words."

Dolt felt it was time to clear something up.

"That's not really his name, is it? Burrito?"

"Burrito? No, it's *Baretto*. Don't call him Burrito, that's what the critics call him. He hates it. He'll go berserk. You have no idea what he'll —"

"All right, all right. Let's go."

And so — braving Molotov cocktails, dodging discarded helmets, and swerving around the half-hearted charges of beshielded policemen — Dolt led his intrepid party across the battlefield and into the no-man's land of the cinema foyer.

His first thought was to bar the doors and erect barricades — something K-Pru had been forced to do in the movie, no doubt, before she liberated the land from debt and tyranny — but he quickly realized that the banker-bashers and the freedom-lovers were far more interested in the violent exchange of talking-points than the prospect of looting free popcorn and ice cream. So he contented himself with blocking the view into the foyer with larger-than-life cardboard cut-outs of K-Pru and her square-jawed co-star.

"Upstairs," Jenna said.

They followed her up to the mezzanine and the door that opened out on to the balcony.

"Right," Dolt said. "You lot wait in here. I'll go out and... What do you want me to say to them, Gideon?"

"Anything. Anything at all, John. It's our only hope."

"This isn't just for the bankers, is it?"

Gideon looked affronted.

"No! It's for the country. Get out there and speak for England, John!"

"Just England?"

"You know what I mean," Gideon said, the exasperation making a comeback.

Dolt gave his personal assistant a wry and superior smile, and walked out on to the balcony. Feeling the weight or burden of something or other — possibly history — on his shoulders, he stepped up to the microphone through which the great celluloid auteur, Burrito, had intended to address his acolytes. Where was Burrito, anyway? Perhaps, like K-Pru, he'd gone up a tree. It was probably something these Hollywood celebrities were trained to do in an emergency.

He tapped the microphone experimentally with his forefinger. A cavernous *clunk-clunk* echoed around the square. But nobody below seemed to notice. The riot had expanded to fill the square and neighboring streets, its energy undiminished. At its edges, you could see the wounded and the exhausted dribbling away, only to be replaced with fresh troops. Smoke rose from a nearby office block. Sirens wailed in the middle distance. One of the black limos had been turned over.

Dolt glanced over his shoulder. Behind the glass of the mezzanine, he saw Jenna, now wearing headphones, giving him the thumbs-up; and Gideon, wearing a mask of desperation, giving him the *get-on-with-it*. By contrast, K-Pru seemed a little detached from events, suffering perhaps from post-traumatic something-or-other. She was rummaging in the inside pockets of Dolt's blazer.

He turned back to face the square and took a deep breath.

"People of London," he said, "do not be afraid."

Well, yes, it sounded too much like the flying-saucer movie, but hopefully no one would notice.

"People of London," he repeated, feeling that this bit, at least, was pretty good stuff, "let us not fight one another."

It was a noble sentiment, he felt, and his voice had boomed out at car-alarm-activating levels, and yet a glance down at the green told him that the market for nobility or sentiment was currently weak-to-non-existent. Regardless, he pressed on.

"Lay down your weapons — your bricks, your paving slabs, your cones, your bicycle parts!"

A petrol bomb whizzed by the balcony, but it was okay — it was a coincidence, not a comment on his speech. All the same, he wasn't getting the attention he'd hoped for. Perhaps he was being too polite?

"Oi!" he said. "Listen, you bastards! I AM JOHN DOLT!"

That got their attention. One of the petrol-bomb chuckers, thrown off his stride, accidentally discharged his ordnance into the entrance of the underground gents' toilets, wherein its awful toll could only be guessed at.

"What the fuck do you lot think you're playing at? Eh?"

It was amazing. Apart from a handful of localized engagements — the settling of personal scores, perhaps — the mêlée had come to a halt. All right, it wasn't like a friendly soccer match was about to kick off, but hostilities had, momentarily at least, ceased. Dolt looked down upon a landscape of curious, upturned faces.

"That's better," he said. "You're a fucking disgrace. Now you listen to me, and you listen good."

It was beyond amazing, he thought. It was magical — the discreet dropping of cudgels; the foot-shuffling; the head-scratching and nose-rubbing. Weird, too: He was telling them off, and they were loving it.

"What the fuck do you think you're fighting about?" he said. "Don't you get it?" He was about to add something along the lines of *we're all in this together*, but stopped himself with a fright, realizing that this was an approved slogan of the Policy Steering Committee and thus probably the worst thing he could possibly say.

"It's bleeding simple, actually," he continued. "You lot over there," he said, pointing to the portion of the green occupied by the forces of banker-bashing. "If you think bashing a few bankers — and don't get me wrong, I'm not saying it wouldn't be bloody good fun — is going to solve anything, then you haven't been paying attention. It's all about the system, innit? The system as a whole, right? And you can't change that unless we all get on the same side. Think about it."

These remarks, he was satisfied to note, provoked what appeared to be an urgent internal debate. One skeptical dissident attempted to lob a traffic light in the direction of the freedom-lovers, but was restrained by his comrades.

"And you lot over here needn't look so smug," Dolt said, directing his attention now upon the bused-in lovers of liberty. "Watching crap films and waving a lot of flags and bigging yourselves up on how patriotic you are doesn't mean you're not just as arseholey as that bunch over there. You're not the whole country. You're just a bit of it. Get used to it."

A few freedom-lovers piped up in protest but were drowned out by their fellows.

"All right," Dolt said. "Have I made my point? You people need to stick together, whether you like it or not. Or you're all going to end up getting screwed. Got it?"

He could see a lot of nodding heads down there, and the dampness of the night air now seemed infused with shame and embarrassment.

"Oh, and one more thing," Dolt said. "If there are any riot policemen here tonight — and I think I might have spotted one or two — then I don't want any trouble from you fuckers, either. Okay?"

He stood still for a moment, legs apart, fists on his hips, defying the elements in his shirt-sleeves, glaring down at the scene below. Then, as a gust of wind ruffled his hair and rippled his shirt, and someone — probably Jenna — activated searchlights at his feet, he turned his head slowly from left to right and back again. A ragged quiet filled the square, and an air of expectation. They were waiting for their orders. It was time to wrap things up.

"I want all of you to go back to your homes, and think about what you've done," he said. He raised his right arm and made a finger-jabbing gesture that seemed to take in the entire square and all within it. "My name is John Dolt. And don't you forget it."

Had it worked? Yes, it looked as if he'd actually done it. People were beginning to drift away, heads down. He waited until he was sure, then turned his back and re-entered the mezzanine.

Gideon was instantly all over him.

"John, that was superb! I've never seen anything — just superb. I mean, of course one has studied the great orators, but this... The PM and IBARF are going to be eternally in your debt."

"I didn't do it for *them*," Dolt said.

Jenna waved a memory stick in front of Dolt's face.

"Got it," she said. "Sound and vision. Brilliant."

A thought struck Dolt like a traffic cone through a greenhouse.

"Jenna, where's K-Pru?"

"She's right... Oh."

K-Pru had vanished.

"She's got your jacket, hasn't she?" Jenna said.

"Yes," Dolt said, "that's right."

K-Pru had run off with his jacket. The very jacket that harbored Aisha's envelope and its deadly mysteries.

"Let's go and look for her."

"I'll leave that to the two of you," Gideon said. "I must report back to Number Ten. John — we'll meet later for sherry and a little chat. This might just change everything. Onward!"

166

Gideon took flight. Dolt had never seen him run before, he reflected. It looked most unnatural.

Dolt turned to Jenna.

"D'you think she went for a snack?"

"She doesn't eat."

"Burrito?"

"God, no. The calories!"

"No, no — I mean that director bloke."

"Oh. Yes, perhaps she's with him. Come on."

Back on the ground floor once more, Jenna rebooted in managerial mode and began delegating.

"I'll check the auditorium. You check the café-bar."

"Okay."

The café-bar, at first sight, seemed deserted. But tell-tale reflections in the mirrors behind the ice-cream counter alerted Dolt to the presence of a concealed intruder.

"K-Pru?" he said. "Is that you?"

No answer.

"It's okay to come out now," he continued, speaking as one would to a timid child who didn't want to come out of the wardrobe. "I stopped the riot and asked everyone very nicely to go home. And they all said *right-oh*, and they did. So it's perfectly safe —"

A figure rose up behind the ice-cream counter. It wasn't K-Pru at all. Far from it. It was a dumpy, middle-aged man in a Parka who, Dolt realized with a sense of shock, rather resembled Dolt himself — before, that is, he'd enjoyed the attentions of Roberto, Jacqueline and their top team of experts.

"I suppose you realize you've ruined my evening?" the figure said, in a sour tone.

"What?"

"We were all set to give those twats down at IBARF a bit of friendly advice, and *you* had to barge in."

This remark set the cogs whirring in Dolt's brain. Jenna, no doubt, would have got there quicker, but Dolt made it in the end. The face of this mysterious and grumpy interloper was vaguely familiar. Just add a bit of pixilation and...

"You!" Dolt said. "You're Red Ron!"

The accused made a sour face.

"Actually, my name's Barry. You know what the papers are like. Bolshy Barry doesn't really work, does it?"

"So! Red Ron, eh? Hah! At last we meet."

"You what?"

"Um, don't know why I said that, really."

Red Ron sighed.

"No. Figures."

"So what are you doing here?" Dolt asked.

Red Ron raised his right hand. He was holding a Super-Kone Triple-Deluxe, loaded up with three different flavors and topped with chocolate and sprinkles.

"Having an ice-cream, what does it look like?"

"Ah."

There was a pause.

"Do you want one?"

Dolt considered this offer. Would having an ice-cream with Red Ron compromise his political integrity? Well, there was no one else around, was there? The cinema staff had sensibly scrammed.

"All right."

"What flavor?"

"Have you got raspberry ripple?"

Red Ron inspected the contents of the freezer cabinet.

"Yes. How many scoops?"

"Just the one."

"Anything else? You can have more than one."

"That's fine, thanks."

"Take a seat."

Dolt sat down at a small, round table. Red Ron handed him his ice-cream. For a few moments they licked together in silence.

"Not bad, is it?" Red Ron said.

"Not bad at all."

Another spell of silence, broken only by the sound of slurping.

"I've got a bone to pick with you," Red Ron said, at length.

"Oh?"

"All this stuff you're putting about. Me being a Dangerous Person and all that."

"Did I say that?"

"I believe you did."

The whole DPO issue was, of course, a sensitive one for Dolt, so he sucked thoughtfully on his ice-cream for a moment.

"Must have been some mistake," he said, not taking his gaze off his raspberry ripple.

"I certainly hope so, John. I certainly hope so."

Red Ron was getting through his Triple-Deluxe at quite a pace, Dolt noticed. Perhaps he was an ice-dream junkie. In which case, how did he keep the weight off? All that rioting?

"Um, Ron," Dolt said, craftily switching the subject away from Dangerous Persons, "how did you get into this business, then?"

"What business?"

"You know, the *disturbances* and all that. Being a subversive mastermind."

Red Ron gave a derisive snort, accidentally blowing half the sprinkles off his third and final scoop.

"Mastermind? Give me a break. There's disturbances all over the place. Can't be everywhere, can I?"

"No. But, how did you get started?"

"Well, I used to work at Big Builder, didn't I?"

"Big Builder!"

"Yeah, in the fitted kitchen department. They wanted to cut our wages. Then we found out that the top bosses were giving themselves an eighty per cent rise. So we had a little strike."

"How'd that work out?"

"Not too well. Turned out it was illegal. Something in the small print. Essential services, blah-blah."

"What, fitted kitchens?"

"Apparently."

"So you were radicalized?"

Red Ron gave Dolt another of his trademark sour looks; he seemed to have quite a repertoire.

"Put it that way, if you like."

"That Big Builder bloke. He buggered off to the Caribbean."

"Costa Rica. They all seem to be going there, these days. Don't know why."

Dolt finished his ice-cream and licked his fingers.

"Think you're going to stick with it for a while, the disturbance stuff?"

"Yeah. It'll do for now, 'til I find something better."

"Got to keep your hand in."

"Suppose so."

"Must be more interesting than kitchens."

"Yes, I'll give you that. Unless someone slaps a DPO on me, of course."

"Mm."

Red Ron offered Dolt the remains of his ice-cream.

"I can't finish this. Already had one today. Do you want it?"

"No thanks."

"Oh. See a bin in here?"

"Over there."

And it was while Red Ron was disposing of his Triple-Deluxe that Dolt remembered why he'd come to the café-bar in the first place.

"Um, Ron?"

"What?"

"Have you seen K-Pru?"

"Who?"

"Kenworth Pruett, the famous Hollywood actress."

"Never heard of her."

"Small, very thin, wearing — well, not much, really. Just my jacket."

Red Ron gave Dolt another look, the sourness this time tinged with suspicion and also, perhaps, derision.

"Nope. Hope there's nothing embarrassing in the pockets."

"Oh no."

"I saw a smooth-looking bloke with chubby pink cheeks."

"Oh, that was just my personal assistant."

"You've got a personal assistant."

"Yes."

Red Ron didn't look impressed.

"Well," he said. "It's been lovely, but I have to go home now to my miserable bedsit above a horrible pub."

Dolt thought of his Afro-Swiss hotel suite and couldn't help but feel a frisson of guilt.

"Well, I hope things work out," he said.

"And you. I shall follow your career with interest."

Red Ron got up and ambled over to the ice-cream counter, where he began to rummage in his pockets.

"What are you doing?" Dolt asked.

"Didn't think I wasn't going to pay, did you?"

Red Ron withdrew a handful of coins, accidentally dropping several on the floor. He bent over, picked them up, and then counted out what Dolt was sure must have been the exact price of one Triple-Deluxe and a single.

"Oh, one last thing. That *speech* you made. All that stuff about everyone *getting on the same side*. What on Earth were you on about?"

"Dunno," Dolt said. "Just came to me."

"Right. I see. Bye, then."

"Um, do you think we'll meet again?"

"Probably not."

"Right."

"Bye."

"Er, bye."

Then, with one last look — that wasn't really sour at all — Red Ron trudged out of the café-bar and into the unquiet London night.

Dolt sat for a moment, deep in thought. Then he realized that Red Ron had left a fifty pence tip on the table. What sense did that make? Their ice-cream feast had been strictly self-service. Dolt scooped up the coin and deposited it in his trouser pocket.

Red Ron was a bit of an odd character. Not at all what you might have expected. Given the chance to get to know him, you might... Well, it wasn't going to happen. Never mind. The issue at hand was K-Pru, and the jacket.

He stood up and immediately noticed that Red Ron had dropped something by the ice-cream counter. He picked it up. It was a bar receipt from the Royal Fusilier in Cricklewood. Dolt was considering the awful implications of this discovery when he heard Jenna calling.

"John! Come quickly!"

Dolt stuffed the receipt in his trouser pocket and raced into the foyer.

"What now?"

Jenna was pointing towards the popcorn emporium, which lay on the far side of the foyer.

"We've got a hostage situation!"

"What!"

Jenna, efficient as ever, got to the point.

"It's Burrito. He's in there. He's got a gun. He's taken Gideon hostage."

It was just one thing after another, wasn't it?

"Oh no — really? You've called the cops, right?"

Jenna made the sort of face a robot would have made, were it deeply unimpressed.

"Well, yeah..."

"And?"

Calmly and methodically, Jenna put Dolt in the picture.

"You bloody well won't believe this."

She proceeded to explain how the cops had told her, firstly, that there were an awful lot of *disturbances* on tonight; secondly, that, thanks to the cuts, they really didn't have that many actual policemen any more; and thirdly, that, if she cared to take a look, she would find plenty of handy hints on their web site about how to deal effectively and responsibly with a hostage situation.

"So have you checked the web, then?" Dolt asked.

"No! They were winding me up. I think. *You've* got to do something, John. He's *your* personal assistant."

She had a point. Of course, you'd have thought that rescuing clueless starlets from trees and quelling a riot was enough work for one night. But the slog never seemed to stop when you were a leader of men and a beacon of hope.

"Well, all right. But, look — is it a real gun? Are you sure it's not a movie prop?"

"You've really never heard of him, have you?"

Dolt hesitated. Did Burrito have a history of violence? It sounded that way; even if it was *designer*, that didn't make it any less violent, did it? Moreover, could Dolt afford to do without Gideon? Probably not — and it was an unworthy thought on his part, besides. Plus, losing your personal assistant to the gun-nut director of a crappy, right-wing sci-fi movie, in — of all places — a popcorn emporium — well, it couldn't be good for Dolt's personal image, could it?

He made his mind up.

"I'm going in," he told Jenna. "See if you can get Des on the phone. And keep an eye out for K-Pru."

"Fine. Be careful in there," Jenna said, an irksome lack of conviction in her voice.

Dolt peered through the circular window of one of the doors to the popcorn emporium. Neither Gideon nor Burrito were visible. He could see the popcorn counter itself, which, thankfully, appeared unharmed. A pungent and greasy odor told him the poppers were undamaged. Above and behind the counter, attached to the wall, were large, transparent canisters containing sweets and candies in varied and enticing shapes and colors. Dolt edged the door open. Nothing happened. He cracked the door open a fraction more and peeked inside. To the right was one of those electric kiddie-rides that you stick fifty pence in for thirty seconds of jiggling and funny noises. It looked like a postman's van. To the left, he saw another cardboard cut-out of K-Pru. She was dressed all in black leather and armed to the teeth. It gave him quite a start.

Of Burrito, however, there was no trace. Nor of Gideon. Dolt stepped quietly into the emporium and eased the door shut behind him. There was only one place to hide — behind the popcorn counter. But they couldn't both be there, could they? Unless...

"Gideon!" Dolt said, in a kind of stage whisper. There was a scuffling noise behind the counter.

"John — is that you?"

The top of Gideon's head became visible above the counter — Dolt would have recognized those smoothed-back locks anywhere. But he didn't have time to respond. There was a terrific *bang*. The candy canister on the wall above Gideon's head shattered and several kilos of sherbet-filled flying saucers — a retro treat

171

that Dolt remembered from his youth — descended on him. The noise reverberated around the walls of the popcorn emporium, knocking Dolt momentarily off-balance.

"He's in the postman's van!" he heard Gideon shouting. "Look out!"

Dolt spun around. He saw the barrel of the gun emerge from side window of the postman's van. There was no time to fling open the door to the emporium and retreat. He launched himself into the air and hit the floor again by the left-hand edge of the counter. Then he curled up and rolled to safety, head-over-heels, ultimately colliding with Gideon, with the result that Dolt's white Egyptian cotton shirt became impregnated with pink and yellow sherbet.

"John, thank God!" Gideon said.

Dolt sat up and studied his personal assistant. The sherbet aside, he seemed physically unharmed. But his nerves, previously frazzled by IBARF-related panic, were now plainly shot.

"It's going to be all right, Gideon," Dolt said. "I've sent for Des. He'll be here any moment."

"I called him! I called and called. But he doesn't always answer if he knows it's me!"

"Jenna's talking to him now."

"Where's *your* phone?"

"K-Pru's got it."

Gideon seemed agitated.

"*She's* got a lot to answer for. *She's* one of the reasons he's so steamed up. And *you*, of course."

"Me?"

"Yes. But it's not as if he wasn't completely bonkers to begin with."

Dolt pondered this. Burrito was armed and dangerous. Gideon was feeble, plump and defenseless. And yet Burrito was holed up inside a kiddies' postman's van. Why? Was he acting out a scene from *Dead Cat Poems*, perhaps? Dolt, of course, hadn't seen the film.

"Gideon?"

"What?"

"Have you seen *Dead Cat Poems?*"

"No, I haven't. Is that important right now?"

"Could be," Dolt said, judiciously. "I was just wondering why he's stuffed himself inside that postman's van. Can't be comfortable."

"Because he's gone completely mental," Gideon said — a bit huffily, Dolt thought.

"Yes, but suppose, in the film —"

"Suppose what?"

"Well, suppose the killer, assuming there was one, when he was a boy — suppose he'd had a traumatic experience. And then, later in life —"

"Such as what?"

"Well, that postman's van could be a clue. When Burrito sees it, it triggers all these memories that —"

"Oh, so you think Burrito was molested by the postman. Or perhaps by his cat? For heaven's sake, John. Get a grip. He's a bloody loony!"

It was rare that Gideon used colorful language. These were trying circumstances, of course.

"I'm just trying to analyze his psychology, you see," Dolt said. "But what did you mean when you said K-Pru's got a lot to answer for?"

Gideon sighed.

"Yes, and you, too. K-Pru and Burrito were engaged."

"Really? That's nice. Probably one of these Hollywood things, though, don't you think? She's on the way up; he's a bit of a has-been, but still has a reputation, as a... What's it called? Infant something?"

"*Enfant terrible.*"

"Exactly. I can see how it would make career sense."

"She broke it off. Because of *you.*"

"Me?"

"She seems to have taken a shine to you."

It wasn't all that K-Pru had taken, of course. But that, for now, was a side-issue.

"How d'you know all this?" Dolt asked.

Gideon gestured towards the postman's van.

"He's been telling me all about it."

"Oh?"

"Hardly stopped talking until you got here. He seems particularly incensed at the circumstances in which you, as he sees it, made your move while she was up that tree without any... Well, you know."

"Talkative, was he?"

"Very."

"Hmm. Gone a bit quiet now, though, hasn't he?"

"Apparently."

There was a pause, in which they strained their ears.

"What d'you think?" Dolt asked.

"Can't be good."

"No. What shall we do?"

"I don't know. What if Des doesn't come soon?"

Dolt tried to think. It had been an exhausting day and his brain was tired.

"How many shots has he fired?"

"One. Just now."

"Right. So that means he has how many left?"

"I don't know anything about guns, John! That bloody postman's van could be stuffed to the rafters with ammo for all I know!"

A postman's van wouldn't have rafters, but it was a good point.

"Good point."

Their predicament remained daunting. But, if Dolt had learned one thing from his recent experience it was that spur-of-the-moment ideas were often surprisingly effective.

"What if," he said, "you were to make a sudden lunge?"

"A sudden lunge?"

"Yes. *You* creep down to *that* end of the counter. *I* creep up to *this* end. Then you make a sudden lunge. This distracts his attention. I then make a lightning dash —"

"A lightning dash?"

"— a lightning dash and grab him from behind. You then rush forward —"

"Rush forward?"

"— rush forward and disarm him. That then permits me to incapacitate or otherwise neutralize him. What d'you think?"

Gideon took a deep breath and outlined his thoughts in moderate detail, giving it as his considered opinion that Dolt's proposal was, at best, poorly thought-out; and arguing with some passion that that the preponderance of risk fell all too heavily on one side. He also recommended that Dolt take fully into account all the known facts about their adversary and his history, drawing Dolt's attention particularly to the extreme flakiness of the aforementioned and the oeuvre for which he was renowned.

"So... *Are* you going to make a sudden lunge?" Dolt asked.

"No, John."

And that was where things seemed to rest for a while. Gideon turned to picking flying saucers out of his pockets, while Dolt racked his brains in search of an alternative scheme. In the end, he resorted to the obvious.

"Shall I talk to him, then?"

"Do you think that's wise?"

"You know, reason with him, as it were."

"I don't know, John. Why take the risk?"

"Well, it's just that he's sitting over there, in that postman's van of his... Who knows what he's thinking? He could tip over the edge at any moment. If we engage with him —"

"Engage?"

"— and try to take his mind off things..."

Gideon removed the last sugary saucer from his pocket and, glancing up, shifted his position so that he was directly underneath the shattered candy silo.

"Very well. Give it a go, if you want."

Dolt maneuvered himself into a crouch and, very slowly, raised his head above the parapet.

"Um, Mr. Burrito?" he said.

Burrito snapped to attention and squinted through his glasses in Dolt's approximate direction. Well, this was a bit of luck, Dolt thought: Burrito obviously hadn't bothered to update his prescription; he didn't look like he could see straight, let alone shoot straight.

"Mr. Burrito? It's John Dolt here."

"Dolt? Dolt? You fat bastard! Where are you? Let me see you!"

"I'm over by the hot butter thing," Dolt said. It wasn't true, of course. It was a ruse.

"Oh, there you are! Well get this, motherfucker!"

Burrito let loose a fusillade in the direction of the hot butter dispenser. A spray of foamy, yellow liquid erupted, much of it raining down on the sherbetty patch where Gideon sat.

"How'd you like *that?*" Burrito demanded. "That's what you get for turning all those folks away from my *crap* movie."

So K-Pru wasn't the only grudge he had against Dolt. Tact might be necessary.

"Look, Mr. Burrito," Dolt said, keeping his head down this time, "I'm a great admirer of your work, as it happens."

"Stop calling me *Burrito*, you cocksucker! It's *Baretto*!"

"Pardon me. My mistake."

"You don't realize what this movie means to me."

Dolt recognized a hint of vulnerability in Burrito's voice and moved quickly to capitalize on it.

"What *does* it mean, Mr. — I mean, Brandon?"

"If they pull this movie from Europe, I don't get to make the Big One."

"The Big One?"

"The Amber Pike Story."

"Oh, I get it," Dolt said, sympathetically. "This was just a try-out. For the Big One."

"Yeah. Purdo says I'm finished if this movie doesn't play."

Purdo! How many Purdos could there be? Dolt decided to probe gently.

"Do you mean *Rand* Purdo, Brandon?"

"Yeah, that tight-ass."

Resentment? Possibly. Dolt probed further.

"Must be tough, working for someone like that."

"No kidding! He wants script approval, he wants a writing credit. I mean, Jesus — the creep's barely literate!"

"But he's paying for the film, is he?"

"Yeah, but the budget's shit, man. I told him, you'll see the money on the screen. He says, if I want to see money, I'll look in my wallet. Dipshit. How much is he pumping into that *Magic Kingdom* of his in Costa Rica? Fucking billions!"

Costa Rica? Like an annoyingly-syncopated salsa riff, the name of this Central American get-away kept on dancing its way back into Dolt's consciousness. What was going on down there?

"Magic Kingdom?" Dolt said, subtly. "What's that all about, then?"

"It's, like, total bullshit, man. All the fat-cats are going down there. It's gonna be like the apocalypse or the rapture, or something. Have you seen *Dead Cat Poems?*"

The only option, Dolt felt, was to dissemble.

"It's one of my favorites."

"Director's cut, right?"

"Naturally."

"You remember the scene where Beach Boy and Bad-Ass Sue shoot the waitress in the waffle house 'cause they can't remember where they stashed the drugs?"

"Uh-huh," Dolt said. "Go on."

"I thought that was a good scene."

"One of the best. Getting back to Costa Rica..."

"That's where I'm going, man! Pay attention, okay?"

"Okay."

"Well, Beach Boy and Bad-Ass Sue knew they would have to run one day."

"Because they shot the waitress."

"Right, and the other people. And they knew that the world would never accept them the way they were —"

Not surprisingly, Dolt thought.

"— so they planned ahead. This is kind of neat. Remember? They found this island — I forget where it was — and they were going to take it over by force, using all the money they stole. And they were going to run their whole operation from there. Pretty cool, huh? Anyhow, that's what Purdo's doing."

Gideon tapped Dolt on the shoulder.

"Rambling," he said. "Utter gibberish. Completely gone. John, I've been thinking about that sudden lunge —"

"Just a moment, Gideon. Um, Brandon — are you saying that Purdo is planning to take over Costa Rica?"

There was a pause, filled only by the sound of Burrito rearranging himself inside the postman's van.

"Hey, dude — did I say that?"

"I think so."

"Nah, I couldn't have said that. No way."

"But you said Beach Boy and —"

"Mr. Baretto!" Gideon said, interrupting in unusually high-pitched tones, "John here thinks you had a nasty experience with the mailman!"

Silence from Burrito.

Dolt scowled at his assistant. Gideon assumed the demeanor of a stuffed frog.

"What d'you think you're doing?" Dolt demanded, in a savage undertone.

"Well, *you* weren't getting anywhere!"

"Oh? Wasn't I?"

"No. All that nonsense about Magic Kingdoms!"

"You've upset him now."

Gideon flicked a sticky lock of hair behind his ear.

"No, I haven't."

Two gunshots rang out in quick succession. Jelly beans and sugar-dusted chocolate coconut balls rained down on Gideon's head.

"Yes, you have."

There was a short moment of quiet as they waited for the icing sugar to settle.

"Hey, Dolt!" Burrito said.

"What?"

"What kind of coins do you have to put in this thing?"

"Um, it's usually a fifty pence."

"Fifty *pence*? Shit. All I got is quarters."

Dolt looked at Gideon. Gideon had morphed from stuffed frog to smug frog.

"Give me a fifty pence," Dolt said.

Gideon delved in his pockets.

"Here."

Dolt attempted to remove the butter and sugar from the coin by rubbing it against his Egyptian cotton shirt. It was hopeless.

"This'll just get stuck! Got another one?"

"No."

"Shit. No, wait — I've got one."

Dolt pulled out Red Ron's redundant tip.

"You'll never guess where this came from!"

"Where?"

"Er, actually that's not important right now. Brandon? Here you go, mate!"

Dolt tossed the coin in the direction of the postman's van. He heard it land on the roof and roll to a stop. Then came the sound of Burrito snatching at the coin. There followed an interlude filled with metallic rattling and curses. And then, accompanied by whoops of delight from Burrito, the postman's van whirred into creaky action.

"Now's our chance, if I'm not mistaken," Gideon said, sounding like the plucky major in some ancient British war movie. "You first."

Dolt sprang to his feet and made for the exit, only to switch direction and make a sudden lunge towards the postman's van. The gyrations of the van had proved too much for Burrito; he had dropped his weapon. Dolt made a dive for the gun, but Burrito snatched it away. As he looked up, Dolt found himself staring, quite literally, down its barrel. Behind him, he heard Gideon retreat once more behind the counter.

Shit, he thought. So near, and yet...

But then, before Burrito could steady his aim — the fifty pence hadn't run out yet — Dolt heard someone fling open the doors to the popcorn emporium.

"Oh, Brandy! Quit bein' such an a-hole! Give me the gun, honey!"

It was K-Pru. And the effect she had on the matter in hand was astonishing. Burrito dropped his gun. Just after that, the postman's van ran out of juice.

"Brandy, that thing's just for little kids. Now, you come on out of there right now, y'hear?"

Burrito exited the van. He looked sheepish.

"That's right," K-Pru said. "Now, cross your heart and swear to tell the truth. Do you have any more guns?"

Burrito shook his head.

"Well then, you run along now, and don't you be causing any more trouble to these nice gentlemen."

Burrito gave Dolt a rueful look and a little wave. Then he scuttled from the emporium. Dolt rolled over on his back and looked up at K-Pru. Jenna stood alongside, arms folded.

"Des should be here *any minute*," she said.

"Thanks, ladies," Dolt said.

K-Pru waggled her hips in his direction and made a little pout.

"You're welcome, John."

Inwardly, Dolt groaned. Was it the power thing? It certainly wasn't his waistline. But then he noticed something. K-Pru had clothes.

"You've got clothes," he said.

"I went shopping," K-Pru said. "I *had* to. *You* know why."

She gave him a wink.

Don't do that, he wanted to say. What he actually said was "Have you seen my jacket?"

"Oh. You mean you want it back?"

"Yes, please."

K-Pru bit her lip.

"I hope y'all are not gonna be mad at me, John. Only I saw this poor, sweet homeless guy, and I —"

"Okay," Dolt said. "Homeless guy, homeless guy. Right. And where, exactly, did you find him?"

"There's like a wide street with stores and theaters —"

"Okay, got it."

He paused to watch Gideon emerge from the popcorn counter and dust himself down.

"Gideon, I've just got to nip out for a moment. Maybe someone should go after Burrito?"

There didn't appear to be any volunteers.

"Never mind. I'll be right back."

Still pumped from his ordeal at the hands of the crazed — and, to be fair, perhaps also emotionally-damaged — auteur known as Burrito, and refreshed by the night air, it didn't take Dolt long to locate his missing blazer. But when he saw its new owner, he decided he didn't need it back.

"It's all right, mate — I just want to have a look in the pockets, okay?"

He retrieved his phone and wallet. But Aisha's envelope wasn't there.

"Did you see an envelope, mate? An *envelope?* No?"

The jacket's new occupant was all at once animated and voluble — but also incoherent.

"All right, mate. Never mind. Take it easy, okay?"

Dolt jogged back towards the cinema. Parked in front of the foyer, next to the overturned and now smoldering limo, was the black Range Rover, with Des leaning against the driver's door. Somehow, Dolt wasn't surprised.

"Des!" He said. "Nice of you to drop in."

He headed towards the foyer door, but Des barred his way.

"What the fuck?"

Des held up a tattered brown envelope.

"Know anything about this?" he said.

CHAPTER 22

It was Aisha's envelope all right — and, like Dolt himself, it looked as though it had endured an eventful evening. Dolt didn't know what to say, except for "Where did you get that?"

Which hardly seemed adequate, somehow.

"Get in the car," Des said. "We need to talk."

These words reminded Dolt of the wife he had once had, whose name was Victoria. *Ominous*, he thought, borrowing another of Gideon's words, and bracing himself for what was coming.

Des drove the Range Rover into a darkened alley by the rear of the cinema, where commercial waste skips had been tipped over and garbage spread across the road — almost certainly by the banker-bashers, to judge by the slogans sprayed across the cinema walls. The Range Rover's hefty tires crunched over cardboard boxes and paper cups. Once they were adequately hidden from public view, Des stopped the car.

"Here," he said, offering Dolt a cigarette, "you're going to want one of these."

"I've given up."

"No, you haven't."

Dolt took the cigarette and rolled his window down.

"I want Gideon here."

"No you don't. Trust me."

"Where is he, anyway?"

"Gone to clean up. I'm not having him in the car like that."

Dolt puffed on his cigarette.

"You're in an interesting situation, aren't you?" Des said.

Dolt didn't reply.

"Have you had this all the time, then?" Des said, tapping the envelope, which now lay in his lap. "Shame, isn't it? You keep it hidden for so long, and then you give it to that dozy Hollywood bird, and — oops!"

"Fuck off."

"Don't be like that. I'm trying to help you. Yet again. Have you looked at this?"

"Course I have."

179

"What d'you make of it?"

Dolt shrugged.

"Dunno."

"I'm taking it that you're not an expert in Middle Eastern languages? Assuming, that is, you could stick all these pieces back together."

Dolt said nothing. Des tipped the contents of the envelope into his lap.

"Well, let's see what we've got. We've got photos. That's *her*. Know her name, by any chance?"

"No."

"Let's call her Aisha, then. This must be her brother — pretty obvious family resemblance, don't you think?"

"If you say so."

"What else have we got? Picture of some kind of building. Wonder what that could be. Technical diagrams of a curious nature. And then this. Have a look at this one, John."

Des dropped the picture of the funny-looking plane in Dolt's lap.

"What's that, then?"

"Fuck should I know?"

"Did I mention that I used to be in the Special Forces?"

"Yeah, right."

"It's true, actually, John. Obviously, I was in better shape then. But that's life, isn't it?"

Dolt's cigarette was starting to make him feel sick. He stubbed it roughly against the side of the Range Rover and dropped it on the road.

"Don't do that, you'll ruin the paint. Now *this*," Des said, holding up the photograph in front of Dolt's face, "is a drone. You know what a drone is, don't you?"

Dolt nodded.

"One of those remote-controlled what's-its."

"That's right. One of those remote-controlled what's-its that are changing the face of modern warfare. Did you know that? They're revolutionizing military strategy."

"So?"

"Have another look at the picture, John. How big do you think that thing is?"

"I dunno. Can't be that big. Otherwise it would have a pilot, wouldn't it?"

"Not any more. Look *there*, underneath the wing. It's a bit fuzzy, but what do you see?"

Dolt studied the photo. He hadn't noticed it before but, in the shade under the wing, a small animal had taken refuge from the sun.

"Is it a cat?"

"No. It's a camel."

"Oh."

"Get the idea?"

Dolt began to feel as if the Range Rover were spinning on ice, rather than squatting on rubbish. Where was Des going with all this? Why the sudden interest in camels?

"John," Des said, a new tension in his voice, "isn't it enough to be a fucking populist demagogue? Why do you have to be a sodding spy as well?"

Well, now he was raving. Almost as bad as Burrito.

"Spy? What are you talking about?"

"Don't you realize that professionals are employed to do this stuff?"

"What?"

"Do you have any idea how long they've been working on this? And here you come waltzing in, and you hand over what is quite possibly the hottest intelligence *in the world* to that lame-brain hillbilly tart, who then dumps it on the first wino she trips over on her way to Top Shop! It makes me want to cry. Honestly, it does."

Des seemed emotionally overwrought. Dolt gave him time to calm down.

"Um, Des... I don't really understand —"

"Look. I'm going to help you out. We're going to make a deal, you and I."

"We are?"

"Yes. I am going to cover for you. I've got enough to do, God knows, but there it is."

"Cover for me?"

"Yeah. Are you stupid? Do you realize what could happen to you?"

Of course he wasn't stupid. And yet...

"You mean, if Gideon —"

"Jesus! It's not him you have to worry about."

"No? Then who..."

Des slapped the photo down on the dashboard and stabbed at it with his forefinger.

"The people who made *this!*"

That seemed to put things in a fresh, albeit stomach-turning, perspective. People who could make camels look like cats were probably people to be afraid of.

"Now listen very carefully," Des said. "Time is short, and I'm only saying this fucking once, as we like to say. In a few minutes, we shall be tearing up the M1 to Luton. Once there, you will embark on a private jet. The schedule's been moved up, it's chaos as usual, but don't get me started. You will fly to New York, where you will refuel and special immigration arrangements have been made. You will then fly on to Greenwich, Connecticut, where you will attend various functions. You will be doing all this in the company of a certain Very Important Person."

Dolt was sure he knew what was coming, but he asked anyway.

"Who?"

"You met him the other day. You were supposed to give him *this*."

"Ah. *Him*."

"Yup."

There was a pause, in which they both shifted in their seats.

"Now here comes the tricky bit," Des said. "Pay attention. We — that's to say I — want you to give him this envelope, like you were supposed to."

"But —"

"Shut up and listen. Except for the ripped-up letter. Don't know how you'd explain that. It's all right, though — there's a video on the memory stick, she's probably saying the same stuff."

"So you've —"

"Just a quick look. Haven't been able to make a copy, the fucking laptop's broken. You'll have to make one. You can do it on the plane, when no one's looking. Here."

Des handed Dolt a new memory stick.

"Now, then. This is what you have to do. I can't believe I'm giving you these instructions, but I'm not the one with the Oxbridge education and the knighthood pending, and I have to do as I'm told."

Des muttered something under his breath, then shifted in his seat so that his face was close to Dolt's.

"Here goes. You get on the right side of him. He likes you, he thinks you're *authentic*. You butter him up. Talk a lot about the Greater Persian Question. Got that? That's important. The Greater Persian Question. You're all in favor of military action. Start talking about drones. Keep it simple, or you're going to sound ridiculous. Try to make him think that all that populist shit you do is really an act. The GPQ is what you're really all about. Which is ironic, really — being as that's why they plucked you from well-deserved obscurity in the first place, in case you hadn't worked it out yet. Following me?"

"Um..."

"You better be. Aisha was a smart girl. Look what happened to her."

Dolt flashed back to the steps outside the Global Faith Initiative. Aisha striding off down the street, her quest for JUSTICE in Dolt's hands, the motorcycle...

"You let him believe," Des was saying, "you give him to understand — without saying anything explicit at all — that you are... That you are, in fact..."

Des seem to struggle. What was he trying to say?

"That you are the fucking James Bond *de nos jours*. Understand? You're a spy. On his side. If he asks you any direct questions, don't answer. Let him assume. He will. And once he sees what's in the envelope, he'll be hugging you close, believe me."

Dolt swallowed, hard.

"I can't do any of that."

"You haven't got a choice, John."

"Look, Des —"

"And you report back to me. I call you, you don't call me, okay? Not a word to your pal Gideon."

Dolt felt he needed another cigarette. But he couldn't face one, because a rising nausea was cutting off his oxygen.

"Now, as I said," Des went on, "I'm going to do everything I can to protect you. But *you* have to give *me* something. Now. I have people to keep happy. I have to *produce*. That's all we hear about these days, *productivity*."

"I can't do it."

"The spying or the giving?"

"Both."

Des reached across Dolt's lap and pushed his door open.

"You can get out now, if you want. And spend the rest of your days, however few they might be, looking out for motorcycles."

Dolt took in a lungful of cool night air. Then another. And another. Close nearby, something was burning; he began to cough, and slammed the door shut.

"I want you to give me Red Ron," Des said.

"What? No, come on — he's about as dangerous as —"

"I know. Just give me him. Whatever you've got."

Dolt hesitated. Then he reached into his trouser pocket, pulled out the bar receipt, and offered it to Des. Des took it and inspected it.

"Jesus. Poor old Ron must be desperate."

"He is."

Des sighed.

"Thanks, John," he said. "Deal."

*

T he ride to Luton Airport was not a comfortable one for Dolt. And it wasn't just because of Des's driving. There was an *atmosphere* in the Range Rover, and Dolt struggled to decode it.

Gideon, in fresh clothes that most certainly were not from Top Shop, sat tight-lipped in the back of the car. There were furrows on his shiny brow that Dolt hadn't seen before. And Des, whose everyday mood was rarely less than grim, looked grimmer than ever. But also determined.

The only moment of lightness came when Gideon, having received the news on his mobile, informed those present that the cinema that was to have hosted the premiere of *The Face of Freedom* had canceled the event, owing to an unexplained blaze. Cinema chains across Europe were following suit, citing "health and safety" concerns. The film's director was said to be "disappointed."

As for that *atmosphere*...

Did Gideon suspect Des of having his own agenda? And did he further suspect Des of imposing that agenda on Dolt? Meanwhile, was Gideon's original agenda for Dolt — all that honest-to-God, freedom-loving, populist stuff — not, as Des had insinuated, Gideon's real agenda at all? If not, what was? And if Gideon's real agenda was the Greater Persian Question then, well, what did that mean? And why hadn't he been upfront about it? Were Gideon, Des and the former PM all playing different angles on the GPQ? What should Dolt's angle be?

But this swamp of mistrust didn't stop there. Dolt suspected both Gideon and Des of hiding their true allegiances. (As for the former PM, that was probably a given.) Gideon was holding back on Purdo; and Des seemed to want Dolt to believe he was still on the Special Forces payroll, or moonlighting for MI5. And, to add insult to injury, neither of them gave any impression of suspecting that Dolt had been capable of formulating his own secret agenda. Which he had, hadn't he?

And the more Dolt pondered, the worse it all seemed.

He regretted not binning Aisha's envelope at the Brit Arse, right after his painful encounters with Lescek and Samira. Of course, he still felt for the poor girl, in her deluded quest for JUSTICE. But he had been naive. There was nothing

183

he could have done for her. And the contents of her envelope had now to be regarded, if Des were right, as radioactive. Which led in turn to...

The former PM. The one who, though far above mere domestic politics these days, never stopped giving his successors advice. Des actually wanted Dolt to spy on him. To engage in subterfuge, bluff and misinformation. To go one-one-on with him, without backup. To match wits. To get to grips with perhaps the slipperiest operator known to modern statecraft. To pass on to him the *hottest intelligence in the world*. And assess how he reacted!

It made his head spin.

And it was, perhaps, this spinning process that helped to jog Dolt's febrile brain into making the big connections. What, he asked himself, was the common thread in all of this? And how come he found himself at the center of the spider's web? Actually, it was blindingly obvious. It was Big Builder. Ludicrous? Only at first sight.

Consider the following.

The boss of Big Builder, shrewdly cashing in before the auditors arrived, had decamped to Costa Rica. According to Burrito, Purdo was constructing a Magic Kingdom there. Coincidence? Red Ron had asserted that *they* were *all going* to Costa Rica, and had claimed not to know why. A lie? Perhaps. The Policy Steering Committee, and Des's over-educated yet shadowy masters, were much exercised by Red Ron. Yet this poorly-housed and jaundiced ice-cream junkie, as far as Dolt could see, posed little threat to anything but the over-inflated self-esteem of a few fat-cat bankers. *This* was a Dangerous Person? Ah, but Red Ron had worked at Big Builder. Did he know too much?

And Lescek, whose reaction when presented with Aisha's diagrams had been quite extreme — he'd been one of Big Builder's best customers. Okay, that was a stretch. For now, at least.

What about Purdo? Purdo, the moneybags magician behind the Magic Kingdom, had also backed *The Face of Freedom* and The Atlantic Affairs Institute. Dolt himself was a Rand Purdo Fellow of something-or-other. And it was in this capacity that he had attended a session of the Global Faith Initiative, where he'd had his first alarming encounter with the former PM. Gideon had said that the GFI talk-fest was more important than the Policy Steering Committee meeting. But he hadn't permitted Dolt to speak. And Howard Hooper, the robot guy, had alluded to a *Libyan thing*, but had backed off the subject when he realized that Dolt wasn't exactly in the loop. There was unfinished business there, Dolt suspected.

Libya. Deserts. Camels. A building in a desert. A camel beneath the wing of an enormous robotic plane. Hooper, the robot guy, doing the Global Faith thing with the former PM. Somehow it all had to tie back to Big Builder. Didn't it?

And, of course, Dolt and the PM — the current one, with the *faction* issues — had first met at Big Builder. But that could have been a coincidence.

All in all, it was enough to baffle the shrewdest brain. But Dolt was certain of one thing. It was vital that he stay out of the sights of the Drone People and their motorcyclists.

He tipped his seat back and, ignoring Gideon's protests, closed his eyes and attempted to clear his mind for the challenges ahead.

J ohn Dolt had never flown in a private plane before, let alone a fancy corporate jet. Thus he was interested to learn that, even in such exalted circumstances, you still had the posh end and the cheap seats.

Gideon had been banished to the latter, while Dolt, his nerves tingling like those of the newly-qualified spy dropped in at the deep end on his maiden mission, disported himself in the Senior Cabin.

The plane, he figured out from the corporate branding on the linen napkins, belonged to Fair Meadow Solutions, Inc. It must have been recently acquired; they hadn't got around to painting the name on the outside.

Dolt was alone in the Senior Cabin. His sole companion, he'd been informed, had been delayed by an incident near Whipsnade. His motorcade was expected shortly. This hold-up, he realized, once he'd completed his inspection of the Senior Cabin's private bathroom and galley kitchen, gave him a window of opportunity.

The Senior Cabin contained a desk. On the desk was a computer — a proper laptop, not one of those things you used for wiping your fingers. He whipped out his memory sticks — Aisha's original and Des's Special Forces-approved duplicate — and set to work copying. For a tense six or seven minutes he watched the drive light flicker as the machine copied Aisha's data to its hard disk. She'd obviously collected quite a lot. Then, of course, he realized that it would have been better to copy directly from one stick to the other. Well, never mind — no harm done, and it was his maiden mission, after all. He plugged in Des's stick and kicked off another copy. When it finished, he returned both sticks to Aisha's envelope, rotated a couple of times in his Senior swivel chair, and wondered what to do next.

Well, what would any normal person have done, let alone a newbie spy on probation? There were no motorcades to be seen from his Senior window. The news web sites that he consulted made no mention of an incident at Whipsnade — but then they wouldn't, would they? He clicked his way down to Aisha's data and began to explore.

First to grab his attention were some video files. And Des had been right: One of them featured Aisha, alone in what might have been her bedroom, speaking to camera in calm but passionate tones. She spoke in Arabic, of course, but Dolt fast-forwarded through the video in the hope of chancing on something in English.

At the very end, he found it.

"You must know this is wrong. You have said it. You have said it is a War Crime. I know you believe this. I think you do not know what they are doing. So I tell you. Now you must act. You must bring JUSTICE for Abdel and many other people." Aisha hesitated for a moment, her face blank, then reached forward to the camera. The video ended.

Dolt sat rigid in his Senior chair, immobile but for his toes, which were curling up on their own. Abdel was the brother. Who were the *many other people?* What *War Crime?*

A glance out of the window told him the motorcade had still not arrived. Frantically, he sampled a few of the other video files: Jerky, zoomed-in footage of the drone circling above the desert; Abdel, looking uncomfortable, at a picnic under palm trees; a line of black, American-style SUV's arriving at a camouflaged hangar, and a blurry zoom-in on the passengers as they alighted; a village full of empty houses; a pen full of dead goats.

Dolt froze the video. He felt himself in the grip of a novel sentiment — a hot-under-the-collar desire that Des were here at his side in the Senior Cabin, now. But he wasn't, and Dolt was under instructions not to call. He closed the video files and drilled down deeper into Aisha's deadly world of data.

He found a spreadsheet full of bank names, account numbers, passwords and large money amounts, in various currencies. In another file, he found a list of what appeared to be company names, sorted in alphabetical order, alongside contact names and phone numbers. The first name was BBG International Construction. He switched to his web browser and searched. BBG was Big Builder Group. Not so ludicrous now, huh? Clearly, they'd diversified away from tiles and fitted kitchens. But the contact name wasn't Ron or Barry.

He scrolled down. Boschenkop Logistics, contact name Andreas Braag. Fair Meadow Solutions, contact name Andrew Willoughby-St. John. Green Lake Robotics, contact name Howard Hooper.

Other files contained email dumps or scanned images of commercial documents. He found letters from *funds* that bragged about *innovative capital structures*. There were *apps* that didn't seem to do anything when he activated them. In all, there were hundreds, perhaps thousands, of files. Where to look? Feeling flustered and panicky now, and resentful that his spy training at Des's knee had not even touched on data mining, he focused in on the one file that absolutely screamed out for attention: *friends and enemies.doc*.

He opened it up. It was a simple document file with embedded photos. Under the heading "enemies' were seven names:

Françoise Cécile Clément

Jefferson Crockett

Katherine Jane McPherson

Walter Gabo

Jay Harrison Percival

Leo Vargas

Henry Wong

Dolt had heard of none of these people. All of them resembled the dull, worthy, technocratic types you saw on the boring foreign news channels as you flipped through to the sport. Except, that is, for Crockett, who looked like an angry, aging hippy, and Percival, who didn't have a picture.

But Dolt didn't care about these people. Under the heading "friends???" there was only one name:

John Dolt

186

And it was accompanied by one of those hideous smiley graphics that the kids put in their instant messages. Was it some kind of sick joke?

He was trying to figure out who the sick joker might be when he heard someone tapping on the door to the Senior Cabin. Before he could say anything, the door opened and Gideon's face appeared. He looked anxious.

"May I come in?" he asked, not waiting for a reply but sliding in and installing himself in a corner of the Senior Cabin's two-seater leather couch. "*He's* nearly here. Ten minutes."

With supreme nonchalance, Dolt powered off the laptop and clicked the lid shut. Des would have been impressed.

"Just thought we should have a little chat," Gideon said, like the soccer coach whose pricey protégé had been taking a few too many risks on an icy pitch.

"Um, yes," Dolt said. "Good idea. Compare notes and all that."

"Exactly."

"Makes sense."

"Quite."

"Get all caught up with everything."

"Precisely."

There was a pause. Dolt saw Gideon's gaze fall on the laptop.

"Catching up on the headlines?" Gideon said.

"That's right."

"Did you see the video of you rescuing that Pruett girl?"

"No, actually, I —"

"Had to be edited, of course."

Gideon permitted himself a superior snicker.

"But the pictures of you dominating that mob, searchlights and all... You're on a new level now, John. Believe me."

New level was right, Dolt thought.

"But I'm getting ahead of myself. What I really wanted to do, John, first of all, is thank you. Thank you for saving me from that maniac of a film director. I shall be forever in your debt."

Actually, Dolt thought, it was mainly down to K-Pru and the weird power she held over Burrito, but he wasn't going to argue about it.

"No problem."

"That you were willing to sacrifice yourself... Well, naturally, one doesn't wish to seem over-emotional, but I do feel — I do believe that this has brought us, ah, closer together. Wouldn't you say?"

"Definitely," Dolt said, playing along and recalling that Gideon had seemed fairly *over-emotional* at the time.

"We have a bond, do we not?"

"That's right."

"A unique bond?"

"Yeah, very."

Gideon's face seemed to brighten. Here we go, Dolt thought.

"And if," Gideon said, "you became at all uncomfortable with any member of your team, or you were *miffed* about anything, you would let me know, wouldn't you?"

"Well," Dolt said, "now that you mention it..."

"Yes?"

"Now that you've raised the subject..."

"Mm?"

"I think Roberto cut my hair a bit short. What do you think?"

Gideon looked deflated.

"I think your hair looks immaculate, John."

These triangular relationships were always unstable, Dolt reflected, but he would attempt to play one corner off against the other for a while yet.

Gideon was now all business, briefing Dolt on the people and events likely to fill his schedule over the coming days. The names were all new to him. Purdo wasn't mentioned, never mind Clément, Crockett and the gang.

"What about Amber?" Dolt asked, after Gideon concluded.

"Ambition is admirable," Gideon said. "Patience is necessary."

At that point Dolt saw the motorcade draw up alongside the plane.

"He's here."

Gideon checked his watch.

"Excellent. We remain on schedule."

They sat in silence for several moments, waiting. Then Dolt nodded towards the rear of the plane.

"Shouldn't you, um..?"

"Excuse me?"

Dolt nodded again.

"Shouldn't you be back there?"

"Oh."

Gideon got to his feet.

"Of course. If you need me, I'll be —"

"Back there."

"Right."

Gideon exited the Senior Cabin. And if he'd felt *miffed*, Dolt noted, he'd hidden it well.

But putting down personal assistants was one thing. Pumping well-connected former Prime Ministers was another. Talk about a *new level*.

CHAPTER 23

Crockodile. *That* was the code word. It had taken a few iterations to get it right, and Katherine had had to prompt him ("If that's you, Jeff, it's *Crockodile...*"), but contact between the fugitive leftist *blogger*, Jeff Crock, and his indulgent boss had, at length, been successfully re-established.

So everything was good.

Actually, it wasn't.

Jeff and Isabel sat at a white, plastic garden table in an open-to-the-street sidewalk restaurant in a sticky, smoggy suburb of San José. All about was noise and motion: Clattering and shouting from the kitchen behind them; electric fans rattling on their bearings; cars and trucks jamming their way down the street; happy school-kids on the rampage; shoppers shopping with a shrewd eye, businessmen lunching, workers sweating; everywhere loading and unloading; darting, opportunistic dogs; refrigerators buzzing; gusts of diesel fumes; a chattering TV on the wall. It was the tropical economy in all its vitality; everyone on the go.

All except for the guy in the white Honda. He'd been sitting in his parked car, window open to the clamor and the smog, reading the same page in his newspaper for — how long now? Long enough for Jeff and Isabel to visit the *Cabinas* next door to acquire Jeff's new phone, paid for with the blood-stained bills from Eric's pocket; to order, consume and pay for a meal of rice and black beans, with papaya on the side; and to get through the whole *Crockodile* mess. Had this guy followed them all the way from the headquarters of the Vita Tropico palm oil company, dogging their footsteps during the five-mile slog to the highway, then tailing their bus all the way into the city?

Jeff had no idea. There were other problems.

Katherine had a new phone, too. She wasn't calling from the office.

"Where are you?"

"I can't tell you, Jeff."

"Huh?"

"I'm in an undisclosed location."

Well, obviously.

"It really is *me*, Katherine. I knew it was *Crockodile*, I just —"

"No, Jeff. It's better if I don't."

Jeff felt Isabel's elbow in his ribs.

"Tell her we need money."

It wasn't the elbow action that surprised Jeff; it was more the fact that Isabel hadn't, as he'd expected, ditched him as soon as their escape from Puerto Jiménez had been made good. Instead, she seemed to have formed an attachment to him — more in the physical than the sentimental sense, however.

"Sure. Uh, Katherine — we kind of need some money, so I can fly back to New York, and Isabel here —"

"Jeff..."

Katherine paused, and it was almost, he felt, as if she were backing away from him — to a safe distance, as it might be.

"What?" he said.

"Jeff. You can't come back."

Jeff looked at Isabel. Isabel narrowed her eyes, in an ostentatious display of suspicion.

"Can't come back? But surely there's enough money —"

"It's not that. You see, Jeff, if you come back now, well... Look, I just need to ask you a simple question. Okay?"

"Yeah, sure. What?"

"It's just a very simple question."

"So you said."

"Jeff?"

"Yes?"

"Did you kill someone?"

He rubbed his eyes. As so often, she'd gotten the wrong end of the stick. But wait — how did she know about Eric?

"You mean Eric?"

"I don't know the victim's name, Jeff. Only that the victim was Canadian."

"Right. Eric's a Canuck. Was."

"Jeff. Please tell me the truth. Have you murdered any Canadians?"

Jeff pushed aside his plate of rice and beans and slammed his forehead against the table. Isabel scowled. Jeff lifted his head and cleared his throat.

"No," he said. "I have not."

"Well, the thing is this, Jeff. I had two gentlemen from the FBI —"

"Huh?"

"— in my office, and two other gentlemen. I really don't know who *they* were. And —"

"Wait, wait. They said I killed Eric?"

"So Eric *is* dead?"

"Of course he is."

"Oh, Jeff!"

Jeff looked at Isabel again. Isabel folded her arms.

"No, listen, Katherine. Eric was my *friend*. Yes, I only knew him for a couple of days, but — like, if you'd been there... I mean there were these iguanas, and..."

"Iguanas, Jeff? Are you saying that the iguanas killed —"

190

"It was Purdo and Moreland, Katherine. *They* killed him."

Down at the undisclosed location, everything went quiet. He wasn't surprised. Isabel sniffed and scratched her nose. Jeff waited. In due course the undisclosed location came back on line.

"*Rand* Purdo?"

"That's right."

How many *Rands* did *she* know?

"And *Douglas* Moreland?"

"Uh-huh. You got it."

"You're accusing them of murder?"

Sometimes you really had to wonder about Katherine. Sure, she was one of the good guys — or *gals*, if you preferred — and you had to admire her dedication to The Liberal and so on, and she really did think the right thing *nearly all the time*. But, now and then, he found himself forced to ask: Did she really *get it?*

Was Moreland a murderer? Why, no! He may have been an A-list enabler and top-security sidekick to War Criminal Number One, but *homicide* — no way!

And Purdo might have poisoned the air and water of three continents, as well as the minds of war-mongering politicians, but *bloodshed* — impossible!

All the same, they had arranged for a hole of fatal proportions to be created in Eric's chest and it was almost a pity that Katherine had not been on hand to witness it for herself.

"I'm afraid I am," he said. "And there's more. Would you like to hear my report?"

She said she would.

While Isabel kept watch on the white Honda, he let her have it. Upon finishing, he was rewarded with a long, thoughtful silence down at the undisclosed location and a shrug of grudging respect from Isabel. But then Katherine — and it seemed more like the Katherine of old this time, not the simpering FBI dupe — came back strongly with a series of questions. Maybe she did get it, after all.

"So Purdo and Moreland are running coups out of Rancho Colorado."

"That's right."

"And you think Ecuador's next?"

"I do."

"Why do they care about Ecuador?"

"I'll give you three reasons. One, down in Quito the government bought into this whole New Latin American Economic Model thing. You know, the Leo Vargas stuff. Right, Isabel?"

Isabel made a face.

"Isabel says that's correct. Two, they just kicked out the US ambassador *again*."

"She's a friend of Elizabeth Moreland."

"There you go. And, three — and this is obviously the big one — the oil under the Amazon. Everybody there's against digging it up. The indigenous tribes, the middle class, everyone. Except the business elite. So..."

"Well, how many coups are they planning?"

"How many countries are there?"

"Okay. Look, you said you saw a bunch of corporate crooks hanging out on the beach. Did you get pictures?"

"I certainly did."

"Can you find a way to send them to me?"

"Not really."

"Why not?"

"I dropped the camera in a pond."

"Mm-hmm. What about this audio recording?"

"No can do."

"What happened?"

"Broke the recorder."

Isabel rolled her eyes, meaningfully.

"All right, Jeff," Katherine said, "let's think what we do next."

There was a pause. Outside, the commotion in the street continued, the heat built and the humidity thickened. The white Honda hadn't gone anywhere.

"By the way," Katherine said, "those guys from the FBI, or wherever — they wanted to know if you'd been in contact with your wife. Or your mother-in-law."

Shit! He'd had a message from Annie — with the subject line *stuff*. But he'd deleted it before reading it, because — thanks to Katherine's coded warning — he'd been in a panic to dump his compromised phone on that annoying tourist from the Pelican Lodge. What had she wanted? And why did the FBI — or whoever they were — think he'd be chatting with Bonnie DiAngelo? Not that he had anything against her, of course; she was a sharp-minded and obstreperously impressive lady, and had shown herself to be as confounded by Annie's road-trip into cultish ideology as he was.

"Huh?" he said.

"So you haven't been in touch?"

"Annie sent me a message."

"What did she say?"

"Don't know. I deleted it."

Isabel yawned with excessive weariness.

"Pity. I tried to contact Mrs. DiAngelo. She's gone missing in Africa. Ethiopia."

Jeff paused to give his brain time to catch up. Was it encroaching age, or was he just tired? Isabel seemed to have her own opinion.

"Okay. So Bonnie was with Vargas? What's that all about?"

"I don't know."

"Where's Annie?"

"I don't know that either," Katherine said. "But I know this. She works for Fair Meadow Solutions."

Fair Meadow Solutions. The Drone People. With their cook-outs and bouncy castles. Drones flying over a desert, in a big empty country. An app on your phone. War criminals on the lawn. Well, sure, Jeff might be getting on a bit, but the old instincts were still there. You could take away his pride and his dignity, cut his expenses, hand him a cheap laptop and tell him to start *blogging*, but you couldn't erase from his analogue brain the switches that flipped and the circuits that sparked when the connections started connecting and the circles of conspiracy began to chime.

"I think there's a conspiracy," he said.

"You could be right."

Isabel poked Jeff on the shoulder and pointed to the street. The white Honda had gone. Great, he thought; false alarm. Back to business — conspiracy-busting business.

"Katherine," he said, "I need to follow Purdo and Moreland to Ecuador. Isabel here knows Vargas's people in Guayaquil, so if we could just have some money to —"

"No."

"No?"

"They're not going to Ecuador. Not yet, anyway. They're going someplace in the Caribbean. Some big celebration, in a mansion on the beach, with a bunch of hedge funds and people like that. Supposedly, it's all to do with charity, but I don't know. The Global Faith Initiative —"

"Wait, wait. The Global Faith thing? But that's — that's that fucking war criminal! Number Two!"

From the undisclosed location came the sound of breath being drawn.

"Oh, Jeff. I thought we'd worked our way through these issues. Don't you remember what we —"

"No, but don't you see what this means? It means he's still at it! He's going to do it again!"

"Do what again, Jeff?"

"Start another fucking war!"

"No, no, no. We don't know that. Let's keep focused on the things we *do* know. And one of those things, Jeff — and I think I need to *remind* you, at this point — is that you are now officially wanted by the law enforcement agencies of half a continent. Do you understand?"

Well, sure — *that* was a bummer. But it would have to wait. The sparks were flying again across the circuit-breakers in Jeff's brain.

"It's Barbados," he said. "That's where they're going. Shit! How do we get there?"

"You need to lie low somewhere, Jeff. And Isabel. Until —"

"Who's *John?*"

"John?"

"Yeah, *John.* Purdo said *Faith Boy's* bringing him to Barbados. They're *buddies.* Moreland said it was all *his idea* and it *cracks him up.* So who's John?"

This question seemed to put Katherine off-balance for a moment. But then, with what Jeff recognized as Katherine's good-taste version of a regular person's derisive snort, she came back with the answer.

"Oh, it must be that populist idiot from England."

"What populist idiot?"

"John Dolt."

Oh. *Him.*

"He's quite the thing in London, these days," Katherine went on. "You might not be up to date on this, but things are falling apart over there and he's going to be their savior. He makes speeches by searchlight."

"No kidding."

"Exactly. They can't get enough of him on Freedom News."

Well, Jeff reasoned, if England wanted to fuck itself over yet again, let it. There were more important things at stake — such as how to get to Barbados. And how to infiltrate a beach-side mansion under the protection, no doubt, of the finest private security that hedge-fund billions could purchase. His brain must have been fully warmed up by now, because the answer came quickly, and his mind focused in on the logistics of an amphibious landing.

He gave Isabel a look of shrewd intent. Isabel picked up a piece of papaya and began to chew.

"Katherine?"

"Yes?"

"When's this frat party scheduled?"

"Two days from now."

"Uh-huh. Okay. Uh, Katherine?"

"What, Jeff?"

"Roy and Peggy. They have a boat, don't they?"

Roy and Peggy were Katherine's parents. They lived on Saint Vincent. They owned a motor yacht.

"Oh no, Jeff. Don't even think about it."

"Come on — they'd love it. They're always looking for excitement. And they're on our side."

This was true. Roy and Peggy were practically Marxists. How they squared their political outlook with their unearned riches and ritzy lifestyle was a puzzle. But then again, they *were* trained academics.

"No," Katherine said. "You can't possibly involve them. They're too old. Don't get me wrong — I love them dearly, but they don't know what they're doing. You know, they really shouldn't have that boat. They're crazy people, Jeff."

"Don't worry, I can handle them. Just send us some money so we can get to Saint Vincent. We're sitting next to a place that does wire transfers. Five thousand okay?"

The undisclosed location went quiet again. Jeff waited. Isabel finished her papaya and licked her lips, expectant.

"Katherine?"

Another pause.

"Two thousand, Jeff. But you've got to promise me two things."

"Sure. What?"

"Keep mom and dad out of trouble."

"No problem."

"Then, when you're done, hole up somewhere until this, uh, *Eric* issue is resolved."

"Will do."

"Oh, and actually there's a third thing."

"Mm?"

"Try and do some *blogging*, will you? I mean, it's your job after all."

Blogging!

"If you say so."

"On unrelated matters, for now, obviously."

"Obviously."

"Go get the wire transfer details."

Luckily, Jeff had them to hand.

"Fine. Go wait for your money."

"Okay."

"And Jeff…"

"Yes?"

Was there a catch in her voice? No, there wasn't. But only because she'd suppressed it.

"Don't end up like Eric, okay?"

"I won't."

"That wouldn't be good."

"No, it wouldn't."

"Call me from Saint Vincent."

"Yup."

Then she was gone.

"Two thousand?" Isabel said. "That's all?"

"That's pretty good, let me tell you. You have no idea —"

"Whatever. Let's go."

"Let's go? *Us?* Hey, you don't think you're coming —"

"Oh, so here we go. Why should I be surprised? You come here, you use, you exploit, you destroy, you abandon —"

"Now, now —"

He wasn't opposed to a reasoned critique of Yankee imperialism. Now just wasn't the time.

"You rape our —"

"All right, all right. Come on."

They went next door and collected Katherine's cash without difficulty — although Jeff noticed that he'd been given back Eric's blood-stained bills.

But when he stepped back out into the street, something seemed wrong. It was too quiet. The rambunctious kids and the discriminating shoppers had gone. Nothing was being loaded or unloaded. The white Honda was back.

And each end of the street was blocked by a large, black SUV.

Isabel summed up the situation quite neatly, he thought.

"Fuck."

CHAPTER 24

From the vantage point of the Senior Cabin — a privileged zone in which, the stresses of espionage notwithstanding, he felt calm, cool, comfortable and collected — John Dolt could readily understand the advantages of being a *former* Prime Minister, as opposed to still being stuck in the job.

You could travel in ultra-style, without anyone moaning, or even knowing; and you could have your friends pick up the bill without a thought for potential future embarrassment, or the hassle of declarations and form-filling. Your circle of chums could be extended, well beyond the pale, into a wonderland of back-scratching, bogus jobs, crony deals and juicy under-the-counter stuff that your average wage-slave public servant could only dream about. Economic opportunity knocked at your door, in a way that it never did when nosey newspapers were picking through your expenses.

You didn't have to worry about your public reputation because you got private respect — not from the voters, but the from the people who really mattered. And you got to swan about in an almost perfect world of leg-ups, words-put-in, favors returned, recommendations picked up, cards marked, quiet advice on the side and off-the-books luxury.

And then, gazing down from this lofty, diamond-class nirvana, you could piss away a portion of your healing magic onto the poor sods below and bask in the applause of your god-like mates.

Nice, eh?

In short, Dolt decided, you were on to a nice little earner. Would the current PM — the one running out of ideas on how to *get tough* on the *disturbances* — ever ascend to this state of perfect being? Dolt wasn't sure. But it looked like he'd arrived in the job loaded, so not to worry.

Meanwhile, the former PM — the one who'd paid his dues and discharged his duty to The People; who'd subsequently risen to his proper station in the society of plutocrats, oligarchs and dictators; and who sat now at Dolt's side in the Senior Cabin's leather love-seat — beamed at Dolt in a leery sort of way as he listened to Dolt's highly amusing account of his summit meeting with the Policy Steering

Committee and subsequent adventures with K-Pru and Burrito at the ill-fated premiere of *The Face of Freedom*.

Of course, Dolt omitted certain details that were not relevant — Gideon's scheming; the true story of Dolt's strange encounter with Red Ron; and anything to do with Des. One thing you learned pretty sharp when you became, like Dolt, a top political figure, was the importance of *shaping the narrative*.

Thus, it had all been a bit of a love-in, so far, actually. The former PM loved what Dolt was doing for the country. Dolt, in return, was full of admiration for the work of the Global Faith Initiative.

And, together in their bubble of mutual esteem, they were but a short way into their progress along the mile-high VIP lane to America when the conversation began to circle around subjects of mutual interest.

"So, gosh, you're actually a Rand Purdo Fellow in — what was it? International Affairs?"

Dolt couldn't remember what he was a Fellow in.

"Pretty much. That sort of thing. Rand gave me a pretty wide brief. I said I wanted to take a very high-level view of things, and he said, 'Good on yer, get stuck in.' Know what I mean?"

"Absolutely. I mean, Rand has, you know, a very holistic approach. I've always found that."

"He's a very holistic bloke."

"Right, right."

"I knew that as soon as I saw him."

"Oh, so you *have* already met?"

"Er, no. Gideon showed me a picture."

"Oh, right. Okay. So I guess you must be looking forward to meeting him?"

"I can hardly wait."

"Can you wait until Tuesday?"

Dolt tried to remember what Gideon had slotted in for Tuesday.

"Tuesday?"

"We're popping down to Barbados for a little celebration — you know, various projects coming to fruition, the GFI's involved, a lot of good friends, interesting people — and, um, I was hoping you'd agree to come along?"

Barbados? Dolt hadn't seen that coming. What would Des advise?

"Well, er..."

"Rand'll be there of course. It's at Kenny Pruett's sister's house on the beach. I believe she paid eleven million for it. Eleven point two. US. Beautiful place."

K-Pru had a sister? Surely one Pruett girl would have been enough.

"Um, don't see why not, really."

Des would no doubt approve if Dolt mingled and eaves-dropped. At least there wouldn't be any *disturbances* or mysterious fires.

"I didn't know K-Pru had a sister."

"Gosh, there's lots of them. This one's called Reagan..."

R-Pru?

"...she's a country music singer. Nashville and all that. I'm, you know, more of a rock fan, actually. Don't tell her, will you! Ha-ha!"

"It'll be our secret."

"Funnily enough, that house used to belong to a rock star. Forget his name. Bit of a scandal. Never bought his records myself. Then some other guy — English guy — had it. Don't recall what happened to him."

"Why there? Any particular reason?"

"Well, Rand's doing a refurb on his island. Think he's spending about fourteen million on it. US. Paid twenty-three point seven for it. But that was a few years ago, obviously."

"Obviously."

There was a pause while they reflected on trends in the international real estate market. Then Dolt, jolted from his sense of ease by a sudden flashback to Des's rant on the subject of drones and motorcycles, decided it was time to get serious about the spying thing.

"I suppose," he said, judiciously, "the international property market is influenced by many things."

"Well, that's right. I mean, look at America. Some places, it's terrible. It's the economic crisis. Until people get real and start pulling in their belts... Then again, look at Zurich! Look at London!"

It was a strange, but irrelevant, fact that the disturbances had not — so far — affected the notional value of Dolt's half-a-house just off the A40. Of course, once Dolt's career in the public sphere had been concluded, he too, like the former PM, would be lusting after private islands in the Caribbean. In the meantime...

"Exactly," Dolt said. "And I think you would agree with me if I said that uncertainty is a major factor."

He'd pinched this line from Eva, the vampire economist at the AAI, who'd explained that everyone who mattered hated uncertainty; it was a terrible evil and it put the willies up the markets.

"Oh, without a doubt."

"Uncertainty," Dolt went on, "such as, for example, the kind caused by — shall we say? — the Greater Persian Question?"

This remark had an effect on the former PM rather like that to be expected had a rogue spring erupted from the love-seat in just the right place. But the expression of suppressed panic that suffused his face quickly morphed into something else — a glow of ambition and — could it be? — greed?

"Jolly interesting you should mention that. I mean, naturally, I read your piece in Global Capitalist. Spot on, if you ask me, but... Well, kind of a brutal analysis, you know. Using that sort of language..."

Who was it this time, Dolt wondered. How many ghost-writers did he have? *Global Capitalist* sounded way too classy for a bottom-feeder like Weese. Gideon himself, perhaps? But the former PM had more to say.

"I mean, when you talk about economic opportunities — jolly hard to disagree with that! Ha-ha! But, you know, when you've been in this business as long as me... Well, sometimes you have to express yourself... I always say to people, don't forget that the critics are always there, those people off on the far left, they never grow up and —"

"I'm not worried about *them*."

"No, I mean, I don't suppose *you* are. But there are always low-information voters out there, and you have to find a way to explain things."

Low-information voters?

"But," Dolt said, narrowing his eyes for extra shrewdness, "you *are* in favor of military action?"

It was as if a second spring, spurred into action by the first, had made a mad leap for freedom.

"I mean, come on. I always say it's crazy not to have all the options on the table."

Des might not have approved, but Dolt couldn't resist pressing his advantage.

"But... Isn't it a bit funny how the same option always ends up being the last one on the table?"

The former PM shrugged and blinked.

"Just worked out that way, I guess. When you're dealing with people who refuse to cooperate..." He shifted in his seat. "Sometimes your hands are tied. And you always have to respect the views of your allies."

"Where would you be without them?"

"Exactly."

Dolt fingered the envelope in the inside pocket of his jacket — a natty navy-blue number selected for him by Jacqueline at Gideon's urgent request and ferried to Luton Airport by special messenger. *Shape the narrative*, he thought. Get the *timing* right. Learning fast, wasn't he?

The former PM was studying him keenly, the ghost of a smile on his lips.

"I get through to people," Dolt said, pointedly. "They get my message."

"They certainly do."

"But I am not a professional politician. I am not a... A what's-it. Careerist."

"No, ha-ha! Not like... Got to laugh, really. We get on, of course."

He seemed to be referring to the current PM.

"Military action," Dolt said. "Not always popular, is it?"

"It's like I was saying, you have to explain —"

"*Someone* has to explain. Someone with some cred, right? So not *you* and not *him*."

"Er..."

"You need me, in a manner of speaking, to deliver the *low-information* vote. Don't you?"

A flash of irritation wrinkled the former PM's nose before he could suppress it.

"If you want to put it that way."

"I am sorry if my analysis seems *brutal*. But such are the times in which we live. Am I right?"

"Well, yes, up to a point... But the case has really been made already."

"You think so?"

"Oh yes. No one seriously argues against it any more. It's just a question of the, ah, let's call it the *trigger*."

The trigger? What did he mean? Best to press on.

"Be that as it may," Dolt said, sternly, "I am aware of concerns. Concerns in certain circles."

"Circles? What circles?"

"These particular circles wish to remain nameless," Dolt said. "But they are concerned. Very concerned."

"Yes, but... What about?"

"Information has come to light."

"Information?"

"Information of a certain nature."

"Nature? What nature?"

Dolt held back, fixing his gaze on the former PM the way you might stare at an over-eager puppy in order to intimidate it back into its basket.

Then he reached inside his jacket and withdrew the envelope. It was only after he'd handed it, silently, to the former PM that he realized he'd forgotten to remove Des's copy of the memory stick. Shit! He'd have to think of a way of retrieving it. In the meantime, the main thing was to stay calm, not panic and observe his prey.

The former PM, his face now a mask of insouciance, peeked inside the envelope. The first thing he took out — and Dolt could tell because, in a master-stroke of spy-craft, he'd dog-eared the corner — was the photo of Abdel, Aisha's unlucky brother.

It was like watching a large, black cloud pass briefly in front of the sun. Once this partial eclipse had vanished, Dolt found himself bathed in the frosty sunlight of the former PM's icy glare.

"In case you're wondering whose side I'm on, it's yours," Dolt said.

Out came the picture of the building in the desert, to be accompanied by the sucking, and then biting, of the upper lip. Then the image of the drone itself, which occasioned a concerted clearing of the throat. After which, the "vacuum cleaner" diagrams that had so offended Lescek at the Brit Arse. A firm pursing of the lips.

"Could be worth a fortune," Dolt said. "Or so I'm told."

"Eh?"

"The high-tech vacuum cleaner market. The sort of people who buy 'em, but pay other people to use 'em. Whether they actually work or not. Very lucrative."

The former PM was looking at him strangely.

"That's a joke," Dolt said.

"Oh. Yes, ha-ha! Had me going there for a moment. So, um, just hang on a moment..."

"I actually have no idea what it is."

"No? But — oh, I get it! Bit slow on the uptake, sorry! So, am I correct in assuming that, in fact, you work —"

Dolt raised an imperious finger.

"Uh-uh-uh!" he said. "Need to know and all that." He reached for a phrase he'd heard Des use. "Plausible deniability."

"Oh, absolutely. I didn't mean to... But, how did you, um, *intercept* this?"

"Remember that morning at the GFI?"

"Oh!"

"That's right."

The former PM scratched the top of his head — it seemed to be a nervous habit.

"Awful business. Well, I guess I'm in your debt."

"Don't mention it. All part of the job."

"I mean, you guys — really impressed, that's all I can say. That whole Libyan liberation thing — brilliant. That was originally my idea, by the way. Obviously, you guys deserve the credit, not that, you know, you or I can stand up and take it, like some people..."

A poke at his successor? Perhaps. But Dolt, in full-on Smiley mode now, fastened on to each nugget of intelligence as it came to light, probing ruthlessly, but subtly.

"Libya, eh?"

"I always tell people you've got to expect *birth pangs*, but the work you guys have done with the new régime there, you know, it just blows me away. I always say you guys are the professionals. I mean, you've got to admire the Americans, they've got all the kit and whatever, but... Anyway, it's all gone perfectly."

"Except for Aisha."

"Was that her name?"

"Yup."

"Well, okay. But, I mean, you always have to look at the greater good, don't you?"

"I expect so."

It was important, Dolt realized, to keep his target on the defensive; only by doing so would he be likely to dig up the sort of intelligence he needed to keep Des off the boil and thus hold the motorcyclists at bay.

"All the same," he said, "there are concerns. As I said."

The former PM put the envelope in his lap and shook his head.

"What can I say? Andy tells me everything's fine. They had a problem — he said it was just a bug in the system — and now it's fixed."

Andy. A name for Des.

"Is Andy — what's his last name, again? — is he *sure* it's fixed?"

"Yes, yes. He was categoric. Quite categoric."

"So Andy... Andy Smith..."

"Andy Willoughby-St. John."

"Right, old Willers — he's categorical?"

"Absolutely."

"What about the other guys? You know, the rest of the gang. Do they agree with Andy?"

"Well, I was just over at FMS in South Carolina, and it was, like, everything's full-speed ahead."

FMS in *South Carolina*. More nuggets for Des.

"No problems in South Carolina?"

"No. Well, there was a bit of a kerfuffle over an intruder."

Dolt put on a grave face.

"An intruder? Did anyone report this?"

"What? No, it was just that loony guy who's always on my case."

The former PM made a face and waggled his hand by his ear. "Total nut-job."

"In *our* job," Dolt said, coldly, "we take *nut*-jobs seriously."

"Oh, well, I didn't mean —"

"Name?"

"Whose name?"

"This alleged nut-job of yours."

This seemed to provoke the former PM.

"There's nothing *alleged* about it, let me tell you. Totally whacked-out. It's the vindictiveness I don't understand. American, too. You'd think they'd get him off the streets, but they're stuck with this *First Amendment* thing. He can go round saying what he likes! Well, almost."

"And what *does* he say?"

"Oh, come on, you know what these people say."

"What do they say?"

The former PM rocked to and fro in his half of the love-seat. Then he made a pair of air-quotes.

"Oh, *war criminal*. Rubbish like that. Total garbage."

Dolt affected a look of severity.

"He may be a terrorist sympathizer. Or an anti-war protestor. I shall need to know his name."

The former PM screwed up his face. *Spit it out*, Dolt thought.

"Crockett."

Dolt held up an imperious hand.

"Wait. Not *Jefferson* Crockett?"

The name from the *enemies* list on the memory stick.

"Yes! What do you know about him?"

"I am not at liberty to say."

"But —"

"The question is, what does *he* know about *you?*"

There was an interlude of silence in which the former PM appeared to be thinking very hard.

"Nothing! He can't possibly know anything."

"Nothing that could endanger the..."

"We're trying to sort out all these problems, right? You know, like the Greater Persian Question. And things that could be of great benefit to the world, yes? And you've got people like that running around. And, okay, maybe, technically, it's not against the law or anything, but then what happens is, people get the idea that they can just protest and expect to —"

"Wait. How did he know you were going to be in South Carolina. At..."

"Fair Meadow Solutions."

Fair Meadow Solutions — the very owners, if the napkins were to be believed, of the plane on which they presently rode. More *intel* for Des.

The former PM seemed troubled.

"I don't know."

Dolt waited, milking the pause that followed — a pause pregnant, of course, with meaning — for all it was worth.

"Can't you do something?" the former PM asked, softly.

"About this Crockett?"

"Yes."

"That depends. I'll see what I can do. My boss's bosses — Oxbridge. Know what I mean?"

Actually, it looked like he didn't. Swiftly, Dolt moved on.

"What was the purpose of your visit to Fair Meadow Solutions on the day in question?"

He was sounding too much like a policeman investigating a mysterious blaze on *London's On Fire*, but he doubted that the former PM would know the difference; real spies talked like Des, of course.

"It was the fourteenth. They were doing a presentation. On the drone."

"The big one?"

"Yes."

"Did anything strike you as unusual?"

"Well, it's bloody enormous."

"Apart from that."

"No."

"And in what capacity were you visiting?"

"Capacity? Well, as I'm sure you guys know, our sponsors — I mean, our clients — um, our *partners* have placed significant funds with us, our companies, in order that we can invest in FMS. So, obviously, we need to make sure that the returns... Well, you know."

Who were these *partners* and why couldn't they invest directly, if they wanted a piece of mega-drone action? Perhaps Des could figure it out. Meanwhile, Dolt decided to make a play for his advanced-level badge in conversation-as-interrogation.

"Tricky business, though, all in all, wouldn't you say?"

"You're telling me. I mean, crikey."

"Worth it though, I suppose."

"Oh, undoubtedly. No question."

"You must be exhausted."

"Bearing up, you know."

"Not long to go...?"

"No, thank God. It's just the *trigger*. The hardware's ready. Andy swears the software's fixed now. The PNC, well they're champing at the bit, as you can imagine."

The *PNC?*

"I'm sure they are," Dolt said. "What's the first thing they're going to do, then?"

The former PM sat up in his half of the love-seat, newly enthused.

"Well, first off, we get UN recognition. The Persian National Congress is the legitimate government."

"Uh-huh."

"Then we move to stabilize the economy — you know, the banks and the oil. Get the frozen funds back."

"Right."

"Then we tackle the clean-up."

"Clean-up?"

The former PM gave Dolt a shifty glance.

"Andy says it's not a problem. It's been thoroughly tested."

"Glad to hear it."

"Then you've got the new constitution, new police, new army, deregulation and privatization, obviously, and er…"

"Bob's your uncle."

"Right."

"And this is all thanks to…"

"Well, Andy's drones, basically. It was the only method that really worked. We war-gamed it with the PNC guys, and everybody said, that's it. That's the one."

"War-games?"

"Figure of speech. It's totally surgical. No boots on the ground. That's the whole point."

"Gotcha. It's useful for me to know this stuff, you see. For my other role."

"Right, of course."

"This PNC lot, for example. Good blokes, are they?"

"The best. Great guys. They've got it all. Free markets, liberal democracy, you name it."

"Full rights for women?"

"Absolutely. In due course."

"Religious tolerance?"

"Mad for it. Except the extremists, obviously."

"Freedom of speech?"

"Totally. Within the parameters of traditional culture, naturally."

"You're giving me the warm and fuzzies. No blips on the horizon?"

"Not really. Not to speak of."

Dolt aimed a reassuring beam at the former PM.

"So, going back to those *concerns*. Is there a message I can pass on to the, er, the *circles?*"

"I would just say, look, don't go wobbly. We know what we're doing and the world is going to be a better place."

Dolt maintained his beam on high.

"Well, then. That's exactly what I'll tell 'em."

The former PM, cautiously chipper now, delved into Aisha's envelope and withdrew the two memory sticks.

"What are these?"

"Memory sticks," Dolt said.

"Gosh, technology today! What's, um, what's on them?"

"Actually, that one's mine," Dolt said, snatching back Des's copy and noting that it was a dodgy make he'd never heard of — defense cuts, presumably.

"Quite a lot, actually."

The former PM glanced at the laptop on his Senior desk.

"Do you know how to, um…"

The prospect of observing the former PM as he watched Aisha read her last will and testament was horribly appealing, yet Dolt now felt himself teetering at the edge of his spying competence; he had little idea of what most of the data on the stick meant, and wasn't sure he could sustain his cunning smokescreen of all-knowing spy cool.

"Is that laptop secure?" he said.

"I've no idea. I just use it for, you know, research. My staff handle anything sensitive."

"Then I recommend you find one that is," Dolt said, sternly.

"Oh, well, if you say so."

"I can tell you that some of the material is highly sensitive," Dolt said, improvising now, "and, in some cases, highly technical. If it were to leak out..."

"Crumbs! What can I say? If you hadn't... Thanks!"

"Too right. Imagine technology like that in the wrong hands."

"Gosh. Doesn't bear thinking about. Andy says you could..."

"Could what?"

The former PM gave Dolt a cagey grin.

"Not that you would, of course. It's like I constantly tell people, proliferation is always an issue, whether you like it or not, and you have to face up to it. I would say we've been pretty successful."

Dolt had always considered himself a man of refined instincts, someone whose judgment, reliable and sound, was seated firmly in the gut. Right now, something was giving his innards a kicking — but he couldn't quite grasp its import. It seemed to lead him back to the "vacuum cleaner" plans. He didn't know what they really were, and Des hadn't told him. But when Dolt had said as much, the former PM had read it as a bit of pre-emptive ignorance — or *plausible deniability*. And he had conspired in it. What kind of vacuum cleaner would you want to be able to plausibly deny? And why would you worry about it *proliferating?* The tug in his gut was turning queasy.

But the former PM had changed the subject. Relaxed now, he had become eager to natter. Dolt, his confidence waning, let him talk.

Drones, it turned out, were the future of peace — and not, apparently, of warfare, as Des had claimed. The former PM seemed knowledgeable. He waffled happily about *shadow coverage, signature strikes* and the *Joint Priority Affects List.* There seemed to be little he didn't know about *autonomous targeting* and *heuristic threat encapsulation.* For someone who didn't know how to plug a memory stick into his computer, it was impressive.

Next up — human rights, which the former PM very much favored and worked tirelessly to promote, if he said so himself. Dolt was interested to learn that many of these were, however, *phony*, and only led to dependency. He said it sounded like something he could use in one of his speeches, and the former PM agreed.

The global economic crisis had inflicted terrible suffering on people all across the world, but no one had seen it coming and it was thus unfair to blame the people who'd caused it. Except, obviously, for those irresponsible *sub-prime* people, who'd fibbed about their incomes. What was needed was a new culture of responsibility and self-reliance, especially at the lower end of society. And, on the bright side, donations to the GFI had never been better.

Then it was back to the international real estate market, which appeared to hold a particular fascination for the former PM. He seemed to be extremely knowledgeable about who had paid how much for what. Dolt's mind began to wander; did they have motorcycles in America?

After that, the former PM took a short detour into domestic policy, principally the *disturbances*, stressing his full backing for the current PM on *pure criminality*, but begging to differ somewhat on *moral decline* over the preceding decade. The real answer, as everyone knew, came back to Dolt's point about confidence. Business would only invest if wealth-creators felt confident. And the only path to what Dolt had called the warm and fuzzies lay in reducing the burdensome weight of taxes and regulation. This, unfortunately, was something that low-information voters failed to understand. Something was needed to get their attention. And — this was quite funny, actually — the former PM, in one of his regular phone calls to Rand Purdo, had mentioned Dolt's joke about all the truly productive people going on strike, and Purdo had been very taken with it.

And so, in this manner, with breaks only for meals and trips to the Senior Toilet, the larger part of the flight passed, until Dolt noticed that the former PM had nodded off, and permitted himself a fitful drowse.

When he awoke, startled back into fearful consciousness by a re-run of his nightmare concerning Amber's cabin, the plane was descending and a Senior Attendant was telling him he might like to consider fastening his Senior Seat Belt.

The former PM looked upbeat — happy, in fact.

"In a funny way, it always feels like coming home," he said.

"Uh-huh," Dolt said, dozily.

Then the former PM popped a question that Dolt felt he must have been saving up for this moment.

"So, John — this whole populist thing of yours... It is really just a..."

"It's the GPQ, innit?" Dolt said.

The former PM grinned his famous tabloid grin.

"Brilliant. Bloody brilliant."

The plane banked and Dolt glanced down through his Senior Window.

There it was. The land of Amber Pike. Gideon seemed to think that Dolt wasn't in her league.

He'd show them.

CHAPTER 25

Bonnie DiAngelo, the professional travel agent from Brookline, Massachusetts, knew from long experience that there were journeys — those that tested both body and soul and hurt like hell at the time — that could nonetheless be re-experienced, from subsequent repose, as life affirming and, hey, if you were lucky, character building.

This would never be one of those journeys. And you could read this fact in the face of Jay Percival, the resourceful spy-at-large whose resources were plainly at an end. He looked defeated. And, in an exhausted way, embarrassed — like a cat who'd just done a random inventory on its remaining lives and come up short.

It was dawn in the desert for the third or fourth time and their squalid little convoy cast long shadows across the dunes. She could feel the warmth of the sun begin to feel its way into the back of the truck; it was not so necessary to huddle now.

The indifferent promise of their guides from the night before was that this morning they would reach the town of Kufra. Jay had told her that their GPS had broken and they were plucking the route from memory. This seemed impossible; but so did the entire journey.

Most of her fellow passengers were sick or ailing in some way. She feared most for the small children; they were terrifyingly quiet. The young men seemed anxious; the women, resigned. Everyone had a bad taste in their mouth; everyone was thirsty; everyone stank.

For some reason other than the usual — that the truck had dug itself into the sand — the convoy halted. She couldn't tell why, but she could see that Jay was listening — just as he did when they were lying by the crashed plane. Then he slid himself off the back of the truck, collapsed into the sand, picked himself up and limped out of view.

The interior of the truck was silent, but for the coughing of one of the children, so she listened. Way off to the north, something was happening; the sound was a kind of low pounding. Then she heard Jay calling her name. He must be joking, right? He wanted her to move?

But she did; she hadn't quite given up on him yet. She crawled carefully over two listless little girls and fell out of the truck, landing on her back. The sand was soft and warm, so she lay there for several moments, stretching her limbs and wondering if she had the strength to stand.

Before she could decide, Jay was beside her, helping her up.

"Come see this."

"There's something to see?"

"Yes. Come on."

"Okay, let's see the sights. Get our money's worth."

"That's right."

They crawled to the edge of the dune ridge that crossed their path to the north. Their hosts, she saw, were already there, including the kid with the Rolex and the soccer shirt; an argument was in progress. She peeked over the rim and looked across a flat, gravelly plain. The air was still cool enough to see clearly for some distance. What she saw was a thin black line that ran for maybe a mile or more. At one end of the line were three large constructions that seemed to merge into the plain, being the same color. A short distance from these were six or seven smaller boxes, and four bulky cylinders, all in the same modest hue. And in the distance, the pounding noise again.

"Those guys," Jay said, indicating the traffickers, "knew it was here. They knew to avoid it. Now there's a problem."

"What am I looking at?" she said.

"You're looking at Andy's drone base."

Andy? Oh, of course she remembered Andy; he'd been rather rude to her. And there was something else, wasn't there? Oh yes...

"Oh, but this is what you were looking for, Jay! Mission accomplished!"

He looked at her, began to laugh, and then stopped himself.

"You hear that noise?"

"Yes."

"Andy's toys. The little ones. But what the hell are they doing? That's Kufra over there."

She listened, and looked again at the base. Nothing seemed to be happening.

"Does this belong to the Libyan government?"

"Libyan government, what's that?"

"Is it ours?"

"It's Andy's. Private. Off the books. Nothing to do with anyone. Nobody knows it's here."

"Nobody?"

"That's not true, obviously. Can't hide a thing like this."

"Sky full of spies."

"You got it. But not knowing it's here is convenient."

Jay clambered higher up the dune and turned around in a circle, shielding his eyes from the sun. Three quarters of the way around he stopped.

"Over there."

She looked but couldn't see anything — just the dunes rolling away to the southwest.

"It's been cleaned up, but something big crashed over there. That's really interesting. Why are the big guys crashing? What's their problem?"

"Was that the one that chased us?"

"Maybe. Don't rightly know. How many of those suckers have they got? Look at those hangars. Maybe six or seven — what do you think?"

"I wouldn't trust Andy with one."

"Nor me. But someone does."

Jay sat in the shade of the dune. She slid down alongside.

"What happens now?" she said.

Jay looked at the traffickers; they were still arguing.

"I don't know. Those guys are scared."

"Of Andy?"

"Yeah."

"Can we walk to Kufra from here?"

"No. Besides, they're bombing it."

She looked at the truck. No one else had made the effort to dismount.

"What's going to happen to them?"

Jay shook his head.

Their situation, she thought, was hopeless — but also absurd. They sat practically on the edge of the runway of a state-of-the-art airbase. They had a truck full of desperate, helpless people — children, for God's sake. Could they not simply roll up and ask for assistance? What did Jay think?

"*You* could try it. They'll turn these people away. That's how it works around here. Not an option for me."

"What could Andy do to me?"

"Well, that's a good question, right there. Couldn't let you go, though. Not until it's over. Maybe not then."

"Until what's over?"

"Whatever they're planning." He seemed to gather his thoughts. "See, this facility here is mainly a long-term strategic thing. That's what I think. This is the perfect place for it. Not surprised that Andy jumped at it. From here, they cover the Horn, Maghreb, Sahel. All the hot spots."

"But you said it's *private*."

"That's the new way of doing things. Sure, there's probably a piece of paper out there somewhere, says it belongs to the Libyan Air Defense Agency, or some such. But it doesn't."

"And you said *mainly*."

"Something big is coming up. A one-off."

"What would that be?"

"Seen Freedom News lately?"

"The Greater Persian Question."

"That's the one."

She glanced again at the traffickers. They were all looking in the same direction, silent now. Then she heard the sound of engines. Two pickups roared up the slope to the rear of the truck and came to a halt by its side. These she recognized as the very vehicles of democracy, as offered by the nightly news: The heavy machine gun, tipped aloft; the cracked windshields; the excitable young men, red and green scarves wrapped around their faces. The traffickers didn't move. She saw Jay's hand slip down to his gun.

"No sudden movements," he said.

Whatever this group was, it had organization and discipline, she saw. A leader — short and stocky, in sunglasses and bulging military fatigues, rather than the branded sports clothing worn by the skinny young guys in the back — climbed out of the cab of the first truck and approached the traffickers. If he'd had a proper army instead of these kids, she thought, he might have been a Colonel. A negotiation ensued, the traffickers clearly on the weaker side. It didn't last long. She could tell it was over when the traffickers turned in unison and pointed to Jay.

The Colonel signaled to his men. Two of them jumped down from the second truck and advanced on Jay. Jay got to his feet and held his hands, open, at waist height, away from his body. She started to get up.

"Stay there," he said.

The Colonel's men kicked Jay to the ground, pointed their rifles at him, and waited for the boss to amble up. Jay said nothing. They hadn't noticed his gun, which was partly hidden by his shirt. Not professionals, she thought.

The soldiers had ignored her, but the boss didn't. He gave her a long, curious examination; seemed to decide that here was one of those famous desert anomalies that defied explanation; dismissed her a with curt nod of acknowledgement; and then glared down at Jay.

"American?"

Jay nodded.

"NATO?"

Jay shook his head. The Colonel paused to give his troops a skeptical glance.

"OK, CIA?"

"Quit that gig a long time ago. Musical differences."

She wasn't surprised at the confusion this remark caused; Jay had some nerve.

"NATO! Special forces!"

"No."

Jay began to talk, quietly but forcefully, in Arabic. The Colonel's mouth fell open. Shortly afterwards, he took his glasses off. Jay gestured with his left hand but kept his right hand still, covering the lump in his shirt.

Then Jay stopped speaking. The Colonel looked distracted for a moment, then waved at his troops to lower their rifles. An urgent conversation began; this time Jay did most of the listening. When it was over, the Colonel and his men retreated to their vehicle, an informal parade was convened, and the Colonel got busy — issuing new orders, she thought.

"Well," Jay said. "That was kind of interesting."

"Who are they?"

"Local militia. Call themselves the Kufra Regional Citizens' Defense Council, or something. I guess Andy would call them *insurgents*."

"Do they have a cause?"

"I wouldn't say that. But they are kind of pissed. They don't like what they call the *NATO régime* in Tripoli. They don't care for Andy and his base. There's been a clampdown on the migrant trade, and they're sore because this has affected their income. All politics is local, right? They're angry at the British and the Italians for pressuring Tripoli on migrants. They're cross with *us* for making Tripoli send northern troops down here to the south to protect Andy's base and his convoys — Andy needs a shit load of fuel and ordnance, obviously."

He paused to let her absorb this.

"I suppose he does," she said.

"So, to make up for their lost income, the chief says, they've been forced to raid or hijack Andy's convoys. The fuel's very valuable and the ordnance is highly desirable. There's been some violence. Not their fault. They say they've been designated a terrorist group, even though, as we must surely be able to see, they're only trying to protect their way of life."

"What are they doing here now?"

"Their plan was to spin by Andy's HQ while he was having his breakfast, and rattle his windows. I attempted to propose more sophisticated tactics."

"What about Kufra? Is it a war zone?"

"Doesn't sound too safe."

"And what about *them?*" She was pointing at the truck.

Jay sighed.

"The chief here says their best option is to turn around and go back."

"What? How can they?"

"They've got no chance of getting to the coast. Even if they did, they'd probably sink in the Med. The Med's still full of NATO ships and planes, but they're kind of busy, you know — and they tend not to notice when that happens. The Italians used to rescue as many as they could. There was an EU program. But then the Brits pulled their money out."

"But they can't go back, can they? Look at the state they're in."

Since she'd known him, Bonnie had heard a lot of attitude in Jay's voice. Now, for the first time, she heard anger.

"In Kufra, they have these filthy, disgusting prisons. The deal used to be, if you had money, or your family could send it, you bought your way out, paid the traffickers again, and made another run for the coast. Thanks to the Brits and the Italians, that option's gone. So it's standing room only, for as long as you can take it."

She looked at the truck. Still, no one else had tried to get out. Perhaps they knew?

The Colonel and his men were leaning against their pickups. It looked like they weren't sure what to do. Back up on the dune, the Rolex guy and his crew seemed to be waiting, too. Off in the distance, the pounding resumed.

The shade was retreating; the temperature, rising. Her mouth was dry, her throat felt like a knotted rope and there were cramps in her stomach. She could not focus her eyes properly. Holding tight against light-headedness and nausea sapped what little energy she had left. Simply to lie down in the warm sand and sleep — a temptation, to be sure.

But there was something just so *damned annoying* about this whole shitty setup. There were men here, with guns — quite big guns, actually — and Andy's HQ had no obvious defenses that she could see. They could capture it. She would give Andy a dirty look, then march into his office and use his phone. She would call Leo Vargas. Leo would send a plane. Leo's plane would land on that *very long* runway, and everyone would get on — including that sixteen-year-old and her sickly kid. They would fly to... Well, to Costa Rica, presumably.

Well, it was a fine plan. Assuming, of course, that Leo, unlike Bonnie, had made it home. Failing that, perhaps this flying saucer could beam them all up and—

"What are you looking at?" Jay asked.

"It's my eyes," she said. "I thought I saw... Oh, there it is!"

She could hear it now, too. A sharp buzzing sound, varying in pitch. Oh, but it was far too small to be a UFO; it was a skeletal gray Frisbee with stubby wings. It hovered and zipped, bouncing and flitting on the morning thermals.

As she tried to follow its movements, she heard Jay calling out to the Colonel. Then, the voices of the Colonel's men, half a dozen rifle shots, and all the engines starting up. Looking down, she saw the Rolex guy jump into the passenger seat of the third Land Cruiser; the other two were already on the move.

"Andy's found us," Jay said.

"Oh, of course. So that was —"

"Spotter drone."

"It's really the cutest one so far."

He looked at her with what she felt sure was his most agonized expression of embarrassment yet. Had those cold, feline eyes ever seemed closer to tears?

"I hate to do this," he said. "It's real impolite of me. I know that."

"They've all gone," she said. "Who's going to drive the truck?"

"The truck's stuck in the sand, Bonnie. Look at the wheels. Those guys are gone. They're not coming back."

"The Colonel and his men —"

"He's not a Colonel, he's the local rep for a building contractor. Specializes in concrete."

"Oh."

"They don't know what they're doing. I can help them."

"Yes. Of course you can."

"I have to go right now."

"Because if Andy..."

"Right."

"But you'll be back."

"I will."

"When have you ever let me down?"

He glanced over his shoulder at the two *technicals* — that was what they called them, wasn't it? Could she see herself riding shotgun with those kids? No, she couldn't.

"By tonight?" she said.

"Yes."

"There's no water."

"The chief's got some. I'll get it."

He seemed to be waiting for her permission.

"Well, you'd better go, then," she said. "And thanks. Thanks for everything. I guess we did as well as we could."

"Keep out of the sun," he said.

"Help me up."

He helped her to her feet. They walked back down to the truck. Then she watched as, under the Colonel's stony glare, Jay took two twenty-liter water bottles from the second technical and stowed them in the shade of the truck. The Colonel ordered his men to remount and directed Jay to join him in the lead vehicle. They drove off slowly up the dune, accelerating away in a cloud of dust once they had ascended to the plain.

She felt someone touch her arm. It was the sixteen-year-old with the sickly child. She'd gotten down from the truck unaided. She looked scared to death. Say something, Bonnie.

"Oh, no need to be alarmed," she said, smiling, even though she knew the girl spoke little English. "He promised to come back. For as long as I've known him, he's never broken a promise. He used to be a spy, you know."

"Water," the girl said. She was looking at the bottles.

"Yes. And it'll taste good."

But it took the two of them a good ten minutes to get the top off the first bottle. Men didn't think of these things. Not in the heat of battle, anyway.

She did as she'd been told and sat in the shade of the truck. Most of her fellow abandonees did the same, eventually. Half of the water was gone within thirty minutes.

After about an hour, the pounding in the distanced stopped.

And it was then that Andy's armored vehicles arrived.

CHAPTER 26

Katherine Jane McPherson, Jeff Crock's wise but word-obsessed and unworldly boss at The Liberal — which used to be a heavy-weight magazine that you could throw at people, but was now weightless digital noise — had made a habit of impressing on him, at the point of his venturing forth from her office into the hostile maw of Capital, War, Oppression or Republicanism — as the case may have been — her strongly-held view of what he should do if — *are you following me here, Jeff?* — the worst came to the worst.

If he really found himself up against it.

If he felt certain he was about to go down for the last time.

If not even a front-page editorial in the New York Times could save him.

If it was life or death.

There were two things he was supposed to do. The first of these — *don't shake your head like that, Jeff* — was to not resist. Well, as far as *he* was concerned, Jeff felt, he hadn't. But you had to kind of admit that these things were matters of interpretation, and he'd never been much surprised by the alacrity with which Faceless Authority detected resistance in the most abject demonstrations of surrender. This explained the bruise on his cheek, the cut above his eye and the sprain in his ankle.

The second — and far more important — thing was the *code-word*. Of course Katherine had a code-word. She had one for every occasion. This one, self-evidently, was the code-word of code-words. The mother of them all. Katherine had given him to understand that it could only ever be used once, and had refused to explain why. Was it a get-out-of-jail-free? How did it work? He had no idea. Perhaps it had something to do with those high-society connections Katherine was so cagey about. Most likely, it didn't work at all.

It was *stovepipe*. And he'd used it. There'd been just enough time to send the message, delete Katherine's number, reset his new phone, and drop it down a drain before the occupants of the black SUVs had grabbed him. After that, he'd been fully occupied with not resisting. The same could not be said for Isabel.

Now, he was at the airport, waiting for his connection. Where they had put Isabel, he could only guess; she was probably in an adjacent room. Not having had the benefit of Katherine's advice, she had been noisy. For a while.

Of course, he wasn't in the official departure lounge. He was in a commercial office suite that simply screamed *Front Company*. This particular firm had never exported a banana in its life, he felt sure. And so that huge calendar on the wall, with its color-enhanced pictures of happy fruit-pickers — well, that was just an insult. And he hadn't needed to check in. Indeed, he couldn't have, because he was anchored to an office chair with military-grade plastic. And he wasn't waiting for a scheduled flight, either. No, there was a corporate jet on its way from Miami. They'd been quite happy to let him know this. Because, of course, they knew what he'd infer from it. In fact, they were pretty relaxed — not quite relaxed enough to take off their shades, but otherwise gig-happy, like a bunch of college kids anticipating Spring Break madness. Well, they *had* accomplished their mission and they *did* look young. For a year or two yet, that ideal-for-remodeling colonial in the outer burbs lurked over the horizon, along with the first stroller purchase. Cool cats. Slick dudes. Smart boys. Rendition kiddies.

He looked again at the banana calendar. Someone had circled October 28 and drawn a smiley-face alongside. What was that about? It certainly wasn't the banana harvest.

Not having a boarding card, ticket or itinerary, Jeff could only speculate as to his destination. It was certainly not Miami. A refueling stop in the Azores seemed likely. And possibly a second one on Diego Garcia. It all depended on which War Zone had been selected. How were such decisions arrived at? Was it like a cheap package holiday, where you didn't know which hotel you were in until you arrived? Did someone in Maryland or Virginia have to consult an Excel spread sheet? Some of the War Zones were very cold in winter. His ancestry notwith-standing, Jeff was a creature of warmth. And so he hoped, despite his proven disposition, that he would be lucky this time.

What a way to end a career. From Honduras to Uzbekistan; from Nigeria to Iraq; from Belarus to Bahrain — nobody had been angrier, wittier or more trenchant, on behalf of the disappeared, than Jefferson Crockett, Special Reporter. Or, he had to admit, more righteous, on occasion. But who would fulminate for him?

Katherine would. Forget those silly code-words. She would hire a cut-price civil liberties lawyer — there were a few of those left, Jeff knew — and start filing. Complaints, petitions, denials, appeals, reviews, more filings, missed deadlines, lost paperwork, technical violations, clarified opinions, changes of personnel at the DOJ, canceled appointments with congressmen — so it would go and the years would pass. He was not young; he was twice the age of these young defenders of freedom. Ultimately, in the unlikely event of his becoming a *cause celêbre*, the Supreme Court — citing precedent, executive privilege, the Non-State Actors War Powers Act and evolving legal opinion in respect of the threat posed to national security by hackers, cyber-criminals and *bloggers* — would decline to accept his case.

The most shocking thing was how quickly it had happened: A translation so rapid, like whiplash in a car wreck, that it gave you cognitive dissonance. You're a free citizen of the First World, checking out some funny business in the safest country in central America? Why, no — you're a non-state actor en route to an underground cell in Sana'a or Tashkent. Due process? Outmoded. A luxury of the past, like clean air. Forget about it.

If only he could talk to Isabel. She might have a thing or two to say about her treatment at the hands of the *Yankees*. It would keep his spirits up. So long as she didn't mention Eric.

As his body succumbed to numbness, he struggled to keep his mind focused. But there was little visual stimulus in this desolate, fake office but for the banana calendar. What was so special about October 28? Was it the date for the coup in Ecuador, or was it something else?

"It's going to be a glorious day."

Was this voice in his head? Would it accompany him into perdition? If so, something would have to be done. It was a rich, modulated, hateful, familiar voice.

"And if you think it's Ecuador, you're wrong. That's what you heard on your little tape recorder, am I right?"

Douglas Moreland walked into Jeff's field of vision, brushed some dust from the sleeve of his suit and perched on the edge of the never-used desk that stood against the wall underneath the calendar.

"Once in a while you have to tidy the backyard. You can't neglect it forever. If you neglect it, stuff starts growing. You can fix it yourself. But these days it makes sense to call in contractors."

Jeff stared at the man; he'd never seen him in the flesh before. Must have been handsome in his youth, he thought. But now you could see the gaps beginning to open, the latticework starting to collapse. He was like a brick building abandoned in a desert, mortar scoured out by the blown sand, foundations subsiding. The energy of youth remained — that was the scary thing — but the frame that it suffused was brittle. An old-timer with battles still to fight, and the will to do it.

"Nobody cares about Ecuador."

Jeff opened his mouth to speak, but no words came. He found himself coughing.

"Oh, well I expect *you* do, but it's too late now."

"Well, fuck you."

Moreland tugged at the knee of his dark gray suit pants; here was a man made of sharp creases, hard angles, blunt objects, razor wire and brute force.

"That's disappointing. You used to be so articulate. What's that? Why, of course I used to read you. We don't have closed minds, on our side. We're interested in what the opposition has to say. Right up until you started going downhill. You let it get personal. That's a mistake. You start harassing our distinguished friend. It looks so petty. You make yourself look small. What have *you* ever done for your country?"

"*He* wasn't doing anything for *his* country."

"Well, that's debatable. Very debatable."

"Where's Isabel?"

"Your *Latina* friend?" Moreland made a show of peering out into the hallway. "I'm sure she's around here someplace. You'll be traveling together."

219

"If those kids of yours have hurt her..."

"Why would they? Plenty of time for that later. Though I wish it to be said, for myself, that I can't see that there should be a need."

Moreland removed his heavy, steel-rimmed glasses. Then he took a cloth from his breast pocket and began to polish the lenses. As he did so, his head moved in rhythm and Jeff saw that his hair, though loaded with old-geezer grease, remained lush and dark; and the strands that fell over his temples flicked to and fro with the vigor of unnatural youth.

"What's happening in October?" Jeff said.

Moreland stopped polishing and looked up.

"So what are you now, James Bond? I'm your super-villain? You want to know my plans? Good gracious. Where's my cat?"

"I know what you're doing down in Rancho Colorado."

"No, you don't. Not really."

"You and that Purdo creep."

"You see, there you go again. He's not a creep, he's a patriot. A concerned citizen. He steps up when he hears the call of duty. He devotes his own time. He spends his *own money*. Is that selfless? I would characterize that as selfless."

"Nobody voted for him."

Moreland put his glasses back on.

"You're one of those people who put their faith in our elected representatives. One of the few. Good luck with that."

"It's called democracy."

"You know, darn it, you're absolutely right. And that's what we're fighting for. It's our entire policy. And you know what? I don't think we're so far apart, you and I. I'm betting you come around in the end. Let's just see if you don't. But, you see, you forgot the other thing. Freedom. Can't have one without the other. No, sir. That's why we have to go to Ecuador. That's why we have to go to Venezuela."

"Freedom? What a crock. You mean empire."

Moreland clicked his tongue.

"Now, that, if I may say, is kind of insulting. Hurtful and insulting. If you only knew —"

Something was bleeping inside Moreland's suit coat. He pulled out a cell phone.

"Do you have one of these? This is the latest model, they tell me. Darn clever."

He lifted his glasses and peered at the screen.

"Golly. It's another one of those — what are they called? I forget. It's like a little snippet of wisdom. Listen to this, it's from that opinionated gentleman in England."

> Had chin-wag with ex-squaddie in Dartford. Says Persians could
> crater Bluewater in mins but UN vetoes action! Daft!

"Do you understand any of that? Not sure I do. Sometimes you have to think about them for a while."

Gentleman in England? Jeff's heart sank and he gave in to a small shudder of surrender. If Moreland and Purdo were truly in league with John Dolt, the foaming, demented populist who'd bitten England in the ass, then there was no stopping them. But wait — was this the *John* they'd been talking about on the recording, the one who was accompanying *Faith Boy* to Barbados? Shit!

"Are you trying to use that idiot?"

Moreland made a sarcastic face.

"You know what the trouble with you people is? I'll tell you. You lost the battle thirty years ago. But you don't know when to stop fighting. You had your chance, back in the sixties and seventies. You blew it. It was one-time only, my friend. It's over. We're never going back. For you, there is no road back. Your generation is over. And, you know, there's a certain satisfaction in that, for an old guy like me. Think back. You had some fun at the time, didn't you? Well, gosh — you know what they say about payback. You don't even have a new generation coming up behind you."

Moreland pointed a steady but bony finger at the door to the hallway.

"See how the kids are these days?"

He held up his cell phone, holding it between thumb and forefinger like a piece of evidence from a crime scene.

"Think this is your weapon for democracy? Your Saudi spring? Think again. Who controls the networks? Who owns the computers? This doesn't belong to you. This belongs to Mr. John Dolt of England. For now."

Moreland slipped his phone back into his jacket. If Jeff had been sitting at his typewriter in 1979, or in front of his Macintosh in 1984, or his PowerBook in 1992, he would have had something pretty forthright to say, right here. But this old man, with his cadre of well-fed kids and his private planes on call, had sapped the anger from his soul. All that remained was scorn.

"You're full of it."

Moreland looked at his watch, a heavy, gun-metal antique.

"Are they late? I think they're a tad late. Never mind. Well, I have to leave you now. I have a flight of my own to catch. Don't you just hate airports?"

Moreland clicked his fingers and pointed at Jeff, holding the gesture momentarily, then brushed some invisible fleck from his lapel and walked out.

Jeff closed his eyes. He heard the blood pumping in his ears and felt his finger nails pressing into his palms. This, presumably, was just the beginning; it was the physicality of defeat. It was his future; it would define him. How much future could he take? Wouldn't it be better to depart now, and let those kids take it all? Moreland was right, wasn't he? A once-only chance, gone and not coming back. Whose fault was that? Perhaps it was Jeff's.

As he concentrated on easing the tension in his limbs — a challenge for a tall guy strapped to a small chair — his mind wandered. Defeat? Yup. But not total, surely. A difference had been made, had it not?

Well, not for those Chinese smallholders whose plots were needed for a cell phone assembly plant. Nor for those Nigerians in the delta whose poisoned water had been proven safe by top-dollar scientists. And not for the Amazonians whose homes had been razed, and whose leading advocate had been dismembered, after the latter appeared, alongside development issues expert Jefferson Crockett, on a cable news special devoted to Our Fragile World.

No difference? Well, not much to Jeff's parents, who had succumbed slowly, in turn, after their insurance ran out. But the prize money from that photo-essay thing on Global Problems, Local Solutions had bought some time, hadn't it?

And then, Annie. Epic failure, Jeff. It was as if Moreland had personally stolen her from him. Someone should have made a movie.

He was drifting into mental incoherence, his mind filled with a collage of images and sounds — not random, either, but a slideshow of desuetude. Then he noticed that he was being transported, somehow, still attached to his chair. A stab of daylight, a glimpse of metal steps, a blindfold, something tight around his face, the sound of the chair rolling away, feet leaving the ground, the smell of aviation fuel, a clammy atmosphere, the softness of the seat and some new tightness around his wrists.

And then the engines starting. Helpless, he thought. Now you're *really* starting to understand how all those people felt.

A door closed, all sounds muffled now. Then something clamped over his ears and no sound at all. Forward motion, a pause, then acceleration and his head pushed back.

All right, Jeff. It's time to let go, now.

*

How long had he been asleep? Had he slept at all, or merely gone absent from himself? Yes, that was it. He was gone, for sure — way out there, somewhere. Nobody had restored his sight; that voice was imaginary; he couldn't really move his limbs.

"Mr. Crockett?"

"Huh?"

"It's Mr. Crockett, isn't it?"

This movie dream-pilot in his short-sleeved white shirt, epaulettes and aviator shades was mocking him. What a total figment. Why was he doing this to himself? This fake flyer resembled an actor too old for the part; way too corny. Really losing it now, Jeff?

"Speak to me, Mr. Crockett. Are you in any distress?"

Yes, he thought — distress. You got it in one.

"Have some water, Mr. Crockett."

The water did the trick.

"What the fuck?"

"Just relax, Mr. Crockett. Everything's fine. Nothing to worry about, now. Well, okay — not as much as before."

"Who are you?"

"Aw, you don't want to know that. Just be happy that my partner and I are not who we were supposed to have been."

"Your partner —"

"Is flying the plane. Someone has to."

"But —"

"We're not going to Djibouti."

"Djibouti?"

"No. Not unless you want to. But we wouldn't advise it."

"So you're not..."

"No, we're not."

"And you actually..."

"Yes, we did."

He finished his water, slowly.

"Does, er, does Mr. Douglas Moreland know what you're doing?"

"Not yet."

"Huh. Well, this is quite... I never heard of anything like this before."

"It *is* pretty unique."

"Oh no, wait. You guys must be part of that —"

"You want more water?"

"Uh, yeah. Hit me with another one. Thanks."

Where did they get this water? Such a fine taste!

"So where would you like to go, Mr. Crockett?"

"Where?"

"Yes. Pretty much anywhere you like, with obvious exceptions."

Where *did* he want to go?

"Free transportation, huh? Choice of destination?"

"That's right."

For a moment or two, he actually thought about this question. It was excusable, under the circumstances.

"Saint Vincent."

"*Saint Vincent?* Interesting choice."

"Is that do-able?"

"We'll look into it. Do they have a suitable runway?"

"No idea."

"We'll check it out. You're sure about this? We couldn't interest you in Brazil? Canada? South Africa?"

"No thanks."

"Saint Vincent it probably is, then."

"Thanks."

"Before I consult my partner, though... One thing."

"Uh-huh?"

"You need to pass on a message to Ms. Katherine McPherson. Understand? Do it in person."

"Katherine? Sure. What?"

"She has no credit left at the bank, okay? Her account has been closed. Permanently."

"All right, I read you."

"Make sure she gets the message."

"Oh, I will."

"Good."

The movie pilot gave Jeff a broad, stiff smile and retreated to his cockpit.

Katherine. *Stovepipe*. Jesus. Talk about the power of words. You couldn't beat it. He noticed that his hands were trembling. But that was a good thing; it meant you were human.

223

There came a rustling sound from the back of the plane. Twisting around, he saw that Isabel was struggling to take off her high-tech, patented gagging device — which the movie pilot, for some reason, must have neglected. He limped down the aisle and helped her remove it.

"Bastard *Yankees*," she said, softly, a tear in her eye.

CHAPTER 27

J
ohn Dolt, stepping on to American soil for the very first time, at the right hand of America's favorite adopted son, felt he could taste Liberty in the very air.

Well, all right, that might be putting it a bit too poetically, but there was a whiff of *something* abroad. A kind of energy, perhaps; pure and primeval. He had been prepared for the bigness of America, and had discounted it in advance. But now he saw that there was more to it than mere physical scale. Written into the very fabric of the city before him were ambition, confidence, ego, extravagance, guts, wastefulness, nerve, brashness, longing, authority, power, restlessness, muscle, weight, intelligence, loudness, brightness, color, big ideas, and commotion.

On the other hand, this same fabric seemed to suffer a lot from flaky paint and potholes. He put this to Gideon, as they rode together in the unarmored limo at the tail-end of the former PM's motorcade. The War Zones, Gideon said, were costing forty billion a month. The on-going economic crisis continued to demand budget cuts. You had to prioritize. In the end, any rottenness would be purged from the system, and all would be shiny and new once more.

Gideon declined to elaborate on the nature of this rottenness, arguing that he had *absolutely stacks and oodles* of email to respond to on Dolt's behalf. So Dolt divided his time between peering out of the window and glancing at the limo's built-in TV screen, which happened to be tuned to Freedom News.

Out of the window, he saw the great city of his imagination; it was a bit grayer and grubbier than his mental image, but wasn't far off. The checkpoints were a bit unexpected, though.

Dolt turned to Gideon and raised his eyebrows. Gideon gave him a twisted frown.

"Freedom's messy, John."

It was a wise comment — and one, Dolt felt, that he could profitably use in his speeches, were he ever to write one on his own. So far, his only unscripted address had been the one he'd given at the premiere of *The Face Of Freedom*. On that occasion, he'd been inspired and eloquent. But, as Gideon had pointed out, you couldn't count on the muse descending on cue. You needed professional backup.

Thus it was that Gideon had, personally, crafted for Dolt a *corker* of a speech, as the man himself put it, adding that Nigel Weese was all very fine in the British tabloids, but didn't know how to write for a sophisticated American audience that might think a *plonker* was a new type of credit default instrument. Dolt was to deliver this speech, that very evening, to a gathering of the Club for Greed.

This body, Dolt wasn't surprised to learn, was another of Rand Purdo's philanthropic endeavors. And tonight's convocation — unannounced for security reasons — was the explanation for this detour into Manhattan on the way to Greenwich, wherever that was. Dolt was scheduled to speak immediately before the former PM, and was under strict instructions not to digress or dawdle.

The Club for Greed held few fears for Dolt. Regardless of the contents of Gideon's speech, Dolt felt confident that he would be able to speak to his listeners' concerns, ad-libbing wittily and against instructions, if necessary. The clue, after all, was in the name.

No, what weighed on his mind was the intelligence he had gained, high above the Atlantic, as Dolt had matched his wits — quite successfully, as it turned out — against those of the former PM. Certain things were clear: The former PM was fully engaged with the Greater Persian Question, and this meant that, even if there was not yet an out-and-out March to War, there was at the very least a pronounced foxtrot in that direction. There was the question of the *trigger*. And it was also blindingly obvious that the former PM knew more than he had shared on the subject of Aisha and her brother. Dolt had not pressed the issue at the time, fearing that his ignorance of the contents of the memory stick would expose him; should he have? Des would know.

But other things were far from clear. What, precisely, was the significance of the huge drone? How was it connected to the "vacuum cleaner" plans? Or what the former PM had referred to as the "clean-up"? Who the hell was Andy Willoughby-St. John? And the very moniker "Persian National Congress" had a ring both familiar and ominous. Who were they? Who was funneling money to them via the Global Faith Initiative? It was imperative that Dolt speak to Des as soon as possible.

But Dolt, as latterly with Victoria, was under orders not to call. Instead, and when circumstances allowed, he was to insert the special SIM that Des had given him into his phone. And then wait for instructions. Well, it might have been special, or even Special Forces-approved, but this SIM looked just as crap as Des's memory stick. Would it work? When they got to the hotel where the Greed-Clubbers planned to assemble, Dolt would slope off to the gents' and find out.

*

The only problem with the gents' at the rear of the gaudy and glittering lobby of the Sheffield Park Hotel (Central Park) was that it harbored a uniformed bouncer whose attentions Dolt immediately found intrusive and creepy. Stymied for a moment, he then recalled Gideon's advice on how to behave in American Society. He dipped into his jacket pocket, withdrew a portion of the *pocket money* he'd been given, and slipped it to the bouncer. A hundred dollars. How much was that, these days? Well, it didn't matter. The commissar instantly got the message; it wasn't even necessary to nod towards the door. Gideon knew his stuff.

Safely installed in the remotest cubicle (why such a big gap under the door?) Dolt listened for a minute or so to be sure that he was alone, then activated his spy-phone. It didn't work. *System error*, it said. He cursed Des silently, then set about removing and reinserting both battery and SIM in various permutations. Eventually, the phone succumbed to his persistence: *spy-fi 1.0 beta*, he read, *loading...* He rolled his eyes — not that there was anyone present to see him do it, of course. Was this the best that Des's employers, whoever they truly were, could come up with? What chance a fountain pen with a laser beam, or a pair of X-ray specs?

After the phone finished booting in *spy-fi* mode, he placed it in his lap, leaned back against the cistern, and waited, clicking his heels with impatience. Nothing happened. How much time, he wondered, had he bought with his hundred dollars? How long before a Greed-Clubber felt the need? Not long at all, surely, if they lived up to their ideals. Had Des's bosses remembered to pay the phone bill? It was the very sort of niggly detail that *Oxbridge* types would be likely to neglect, wasn't it?

But after a minute or so the phone rang. *Desmond Crabtree*, Dolt read. Bit of a security lapse there, he thought. No doubt it would be fixed in version 2.0.

"Des?"

"Yeah. John?"

"Yes."

"Where are you?"

Dolt told him.

"Anyone in there with you?"

"What, in the cubicle?" Dolt said, satirically.

"Don't get funny with *me*, John."

"No, all right. Just me, on me tod."

"Any surveillance?"

Surveillance? In the gents? Was that normal in America? Gideon hadn't mentioned it.

"How would I know?"

Here was another painful gap in his spy training. There was a pause at the other end of the line.

"Never mind. Tell me what you've got."

Dolt gave Des a terse but exhaustive account of his stealth interrogation of the former PM. Des was impressed.

"Oh, shit!" he said.

Dolt adopted a sympathetic tone.

"Problem?"

He could hear Des coughing and spluttering at the other end of the line.

"Do you know," Des asked, a note of petulance in his tone, "what our current leader is going round saying, in private?"

"Is he going to get tough on something?"

"No. He says he doesn't object in principle to participating in another American war — he'd just like to join in a *successful* American war."

"Oh. So it *is* the old March to War, then?"

"Not if *we* have any say, it isn't. Listen, John. You've got to find out what this *trigger* is. That's key. And this Andy bastard. We've had run-ins with him before. Find out where he keeps his drones. It's probably in Africa. Got that? Africa. Plus who's really paying for 'em. That's key as well. Everything depends on you."

Dolt hesitated.

"Um, look, Des. I sort of thought... I mean, love to help and all that. But... Well, I've already done my bit, haven't I?"

The silence that ensued was long and ominous.

"John..." Des's voice oozed down the line — soft now, and menacing.

"...you haven't forgotten about the motorcycles, have you?"

"Well, no. But —"

"We have our own motorcycles, you know."

Right, Dolt thought. Scooters. Mopeds with flat batteries.

"Do you?"

"Yes. So stop fucking around and do your sodding patriotic duty."

"I don't know..."

"You understand what they're going to do with that drone, don't you? And that *apparatus?* Don't pretend you don't. Can you live with that? What about Aisha? I thought you felt sorry for the poor cow?"

Apparatus? Dolt swallowed slowly and clicked his heels again. Aisha? He flashed back once more to the steps outside the GFI. Did John Dolt stand for JUSTICE or not? If not, what? How about Greed?

"All right, Des. Call the fucking mopeds off."

"What did you say?"

"Nothing."

"Right. Find out about the trigger. Do whatever you have to do."

"Like what?"

"Improvise. Get him drunk — you're going to that piss-up in Barbados. He likes a glass of wine. Blackmail him. Anything."

Blackmail? Dolt performed a quick mental review of the former PM's career — the catastrophes, the embarrassing friends, the revelations, the deceptions, the bad smells, the jiggery-pokery, the fall from grace and the present prosperity. Blackmail wasn't an option, he concluded.

"Maybe I'll try the booze."

"You'll think of something. One more thing. Did you copy that memory stick?"

"Yes."

"Good. Well done. Here's what I want you to do. Go out into the lobby — not now, when we're finished. Look for a bloke reading Global Capitalist. The issue with your ugly mug on the cover. Go up to him. Say 'Are you reading about new oil prospects in Ecuador, by any chance?'"

Dolt found himself rolling his eyes again. He couldn't help it.

"If he says, 'But surely the Amazon is off-limits, is it not?' bung him the stick. Then bugger off and do your speech, okay?"

"All right. But..."

"But what?"

"How did you know we were at this hotel? It's supposed to be top secret."

"We're not totally useless, you know."

Perhaps he had a point.

"Never said you were."

There was an awkward pause. Not wanting to end on this note, Dolt brought up a non-related issue.

"Um, Des?"

"Yeah?"

"This populist thing. I was thinking I might just go for it."

"Knock yourself out."

"I think I'm really getting the hang of it. And, you know, what with being in America..."

"Have a blast. Embrace the dark side. Take 'em for whatever you can get."

"You don't mind?"

"Couldn't care less."

"Good."

"Yes."

"That it, then?"

"Yeah. Get on with it. Oh, and..."

"Yes?"

"Just... Mind yourself, okay? It's not just motorcycles. Know what I mean?"

"I think so."

"Good. Don't forget to report back."

"No."

"Bye, then."

"Bye."

Dolt ended the call. So then, his spying career wasn't over yet. Well, to be honest, he wasn't surprised. Such was his life story. Just when you thought you were finished, they wanted more. Hamid was the same. And Lescek. Victoria too, though it pained him to admit it. Take, take, take. When would it be his turn? Had a single penny yet been deposited in his secret account in the Cayman Islands? As for *embracing* the *dark side* — well, it was what he'd been contemplating ever since that night in his Afro-Swiss hotel suite when he'd looked at his poll numbers and recognized populist gold. Had Amber Pike got where she was without embracing her dark side? Hardly.

He stowed his phone and made for the lobby, brushing past the commissar and a lithe young man in tight trousers on his way out. It was the work of moments for him to locate Des's stooge (no doubt there was a colorful name for such an operative, but he didn't care) and perform the required pantomime.

And he'd just made it to the bar and ordered a large vodka and orange when he felt a tap on his shoulder. It was the stooge.

"That stick's fucked," the stooge said, in a panicky stage whisper. "It's fried! It's useless!"

Dolt took a deep breath.

"And are we surprised?" he said. "What did you expect? You have to pay for quality." This wasn't what Lescek claimed in the ads he shoved through people's doors, but it was true, nonetheless.

"What are we going to do?" the stooge asked.

"For a start," Dolt said, "we are not going to panic, okay?"

Dolt's vodka arrived.

"But Des —"

"Tell Des I'll get another one," Dolt said. "Do I have to do everything around here?" And at his own expense too, he thought, bitterly. "All right? Now sod off."

The stooge, calmer now, shrugged and duly sodded off. It had not been, Dolt reflected, a very convincing display of professional spy-craft. But then spy-craft interested him far less at this point than vodka did.

And then, moments later, as the booze worked its magic, he realized what he had to do. He had to get hold of the former PM's laptop. Because he'd accidentally left a copy of Aisha's data on it. Problem solved! Back to the vodka.

But there came a new, more rhythmic tap on his shoulder. It was Gideon. And it was speech time.

CHAPTER 28

Geneal Kadiya — he had many other names, but this was his current preference — told Bonnie DiAngelo that he had great respect for Mr. Andrew Willoughby-St. John, and for his American sponsors, but they should have sought his services sooner. The base was poorly protected from local insurgents. Given the length of the runway, the facility as a whole was too spacious to be fenced, and this was impracticable in any case. Only the hangars and the special storage facility had proper defenses. The insurgents were, for now, merely an annoyance. But General Kadiya expected that to change. And he was prepared.

He was a tall, stringy man with sunken eyes, a wide forehead, and tangled, graying hair that looked as if it had been in a fight all of its own, without indisposing its owner. His hands were large, thin-fleshed and calloused, and he gave off a brutal and casual confidence to match them, Bonnie thought. But the swagger of the bully — something she'd seen in *Mr. Andrew* — was absent, and there was something quieter and more dangerous in its place. And she'd tagged him as Somali even before he'd begun his tales from Mogadishu. Here was an aging desert lion that made Jay Percival look like a house-cat from a nice neighborhood.

It had been General Kadiya and his *advance guard* who'd brought her here to Andy's castle in the desert. Her companions had been menaced at rifle-point and then left behind with the disabled truck and its empty water bottles. They weren't insurgents, the General said, so they weren't worth the ammunition.

Andy's castle resembled a mediaeval Italian fortress or a modern-day US embassy, without the moat. It was designed to repel. She wondered how much of the Colonel's concrete had gone into its construction. (Could he have neglected such a business opportunity?)

While they waited for *Mr. Andrew* to conclude his *transatlantic teleconference* — which he was conducting in his *media suite* — General Kadiya, whose uniform, she suspected, had been tailored to the General's own design, was happy to entertain his guest with an account of his achievements. Well, they were boasts, really. She was a sixty-something white woman from Massachusetts. Would he have spoken like this to the sixteen-year-old with the sickly child?

He had fought for stability and peace in Somalia since the early nineties. Many times, he had been an ally of the United States and the CIA. His forces had captured or disposed of more militants and extremists than those of any other leader. He was respected by the government in Mogadishu and was pleased to offer his protection to large parts of the city — a city in which he, personally, maintained several residences. The African Union's AMISOM valued his services — the Americans and the Ugandans particularly, and a new joint-venture in Kampala, to counter Sudanese proxies, promised much. His business interests extended to Nairobi, where he had been successful in the real estate business. And he had valuable commercial contacts in South Africa, which was only to be expected of a person of his standing. Now, he felt privileged to be able to play such an important role in Mr. Andrew's Strategic Stabilization Operations.

Warlord, she thought.

They sat in a space that resembled the conference room of a regular office — except that the windows were dressed with blast shielding. Andy's castle had towers and battlements; did it have dungeons, too? Surely, the General would have demanded them. And the Colonel would have dug them, wouldn't he? What a wonderful new kind of war this was, where combat and commerce bloomed side by side; in which entrepreneurialism flourished and talent was rewarded; and where enemies were not enemies forever, but merely business rivals, and the occasion was rare upon which a coalition of the interested could not be formed.

The General was a thug; he was also a networker.

But there wasn't much to be gained from networking with a doomed travel agent afflicted by cash-flow problems, so when Mr. Andrew Willoughby-St. John made his entrance, in desert boots, camouflage pants and a clean white shirt, the General ambled from the room without a word or a glance. Andy muttered something as they passed one another, but she couldn't hear what it was and the General didn't reply.

"Hello, Andy," she said.

Andy scowled and flung himself on to a couch by one of the bomb-proof windows. He didn't wish to be close to her, it seemed. Okay, she didn't smell great.

"This is not awfully convenient," he said.

Well, not for him, perhaps. But her recent failure to die of desiccation in the desert was something she was prepared to live with, if she could.

"Have they checked you out? Heath-wise, I mean? Any problems?"

"I'm a little tired," she said. "I wouldn't mind a shower."

He stared at her.

"But I don't want to inconvenience you."

For a moment, she thought he was going to get up and march out. But it was only a passing fit of irritation.

"This is not some kind of family therapy institute."

The absurdness of this remark demanded a reality check of uncommon severity. Was she, as her senses claimed, an unwelcome guest at Drone Central; or — more likely, surely? — was she dried out in the desert, drifting off in some final self-mocking dream? She decided to play the unwelcome guest for all it was worth.

"Well, I didn't think it was. It's far too ugly."

"Do you understand me?"

"Not really. Do you normally make sense?"

He sat still for a moment, watching her, then began to shake the sand from his boots.

"Where's your companion?"

"Jay? He went off with some friends."

"*Friends*. Was it his idea to come here?"

"Yes and no."

More boot-shaking.

"Don't you know what he is?"

"I've got a pretty good idea."

"Do you?"

The building began to vibrate. From outside came the growl of jet engines; a large airplane was maneuvering. Andy glanced at the reinforced window, distracted for a moment.

"Got them working yet?" she said.

This seemed to provoke him, as she had intended.

"He's a turncoat. A bloody traitor. He's on his own government's wanted list. Half his chums are terrorists. You're in a lot of trouble."

"Am I? More than when that thing of yours —"

"Did you retrieve anything?"

"Retrieve?"

"From the crash site?"

"Oh. Well, I'm not going to tell *you*."

Outside, the noise of the drone mounted. It was preparing for take-off. But where, she wondered, was the pilot? Was he here at the castle? Or was he — she? — in an office park in Nevada or Tampa or South Carolina?

Andy had gotten to his feet. He put his hands in his pockets, then took a step towards her.

"*Vargas* told us," he said, softly.

She felt a movement in her chest. But — the smallest of mercies, no? — no sound came; the roar of the drone drowned all. She held her breath. He waited, watching. Wasn't there, she thought, really something to be said for General Kadiya after all?

"Where is he?" she said.

Andy shook his head.

"I'm not dealing with this any more. *She* can do it."

He turned and marched out of the room, boots clumping on the cement floor.

She? Never mind *she*. What had happened to Leo? Had he gotten any further than she and Jay had? How could these idiots be so powerful, so capable? Wayward drones notwithstanding. There was nothing remotely *fair* about that. Oh, but fair wasn't fair any more. You did what you could get away with. Power was justice. Ask General Kadiya. And you could get away with anything if you had enough money and you did it in Africa. Leo, rich as he was, had nothing on these people.

She sat still, as still as she could, and stared at the Colonel's cement floor. And she wondered — might it be so? — if the worst crime the General had ever committed was to *not* shoot that girl and her child.

When she looked up, her daughter was standing in front of her.

Annie? Of course. Annie. Her daughter who *worked in the defense industry*. Why wouldn't she show up? But was it *family therapy* time again? Oh, no. Not that. Not in Andy's castle, in an African War Zone, under the shadow of the drones of mass destruction.

"What are you doing here, Mom?"

Sensible question, right? Implied answer, as ever: Embarrassing the kids.

"Mom?"

"Is it really you? Your hair looks funny. You look older."

"This isn't a joke."

"No kidding."

"Why are you here?"

That should have been *her* question, but these conversations were forever pulled off-balance by unspoken resentment.

"Well, it's really all down to your pal, Andy. Or is he your boss? What is he?"

"What were you doing in the Danakil?"

"I was minding my own business. Literally."

Annie looked at her as if she'd done something sad and painful, but just about forgivable, like a dementia-sufferer who'd put the cat out in the garbage.

"But why were you with Leo Vargas?"

"Why not? He offered to come with me."

"He had a reason."

"Oh, well. He *did* have one of his *agendas*, as it turned out."

"He's a communist."

"Is he? Well, he's done very well for himself in business, considering."

Annie didn't reply. Her face looked frozen, but her eyes were busy. She was looking over her mother as if taking some kind of inventory.

"They're going to search you."

"Search?"

"Search you properly."

"What on Earth for?"

"Data."

Her daughter had run off to join the neo-con circus and now she was demanding *data?* Too much, really.

"I haven't got any data! Really, it's all *data* now. Everyone's mad for machines and *data*. It's like these ridiculous drones. They crash all the time. They've got the wrong data!"

Annie leaned forward and put her hand on her mother's shoulder.

"What do you know about that?"

"About what?"

Annie shook her — the way you might rattle an old radio that wasn't working properly.

"About the drones."

"I don't know anything about them."

"You do! You *know* about it. You and Vargas and Percival and the rest of them!"

"Annie. Let go of me, please."

"How can you be involved in this?"

"How can *you?*"

The shaking stopped. Annie let go and stepped back.

"You know about Abdel."

"Who's Abdel?"

"You know what they made him do."

"Annie —"

"And that stupid sister of his. They used her. To get to him. But he was..."

Annie stopped speaking and turned her back. Bonnie took a deep breath, rubbed her shoulder and waited.

"I mean, they killed him, you know. They had to. But they got that bitch Aisha in the end."

A long pause. Then Annie turned around. Her eyes were red.

"Why did they kill him, Annie?"

No answer.

"What did he do?"

"He put something in the code. You know it. He changed all the backups. They can't find what he did. It was so stupid. He was the only who knew."

Code? This man, Abdel, had *programmed* the drones to crash. No wonder Andy was so grouchy.

"I really don't know anything about this, Annie."

"Andrew says Abdel gave it to someone. The original code. He needs to find it. You understand?"

"I don't have it. I don't think Jay does."

"You don't *think?*"

Unless the cell phone that she and Leo found in the crashed drone...

"No."

Annie said nothing. Overhead, the drone seemed to be circling. But its engines, by turns, were screaming and choking, as if it could barely control itself.

"Why are you like this, Annie? Why did you change? I don't understand. Jeff doesn't —"

"Jeff?"

"He doesn't get it either."

The frown on Annie's forehead disappeared. Her features relaxed. Then the corners of her eyes, and her mouth, configured themselves into an expression — not quite a smile — that spoke to some invisible passion, exalted and almost beatific.

"But it's *such* a good thing that we're doing for you. Oh, you don't understand! Well, don't worry. Just stand back. Keep out of harm's way. There'll still be room for you. We'll let you live in the world we're creating."

She held the look on her face, unblinking, for several moments, then turned and walked towards the door.

"You can't spray the whole world with your chemicals."

Annie stopped and turned around. Outside, the drone sounded as though it were attempting land in a hurry.

"What?"

"You just can't. I'm sure it's not legal. Isn't there a convention? I guess Andy didn't sign it."

"*Chemicals?* We're not using *chemicals.*"

Sirens sounded outside.

"You didn't *know* that?"

"You're full of shit."

"I've seen the evidence. Why are those things so big?"

"It's just for the range. And the capabilities."

"Capabilities?"

"There aren't any *chemicals.*"

The drone had reached the end of the runway. Its engines shut off abruptly. She heard shouts and the tire squeals of vehicles.

Annie gave her a look of hatred and walked out. Moments later, the General returned. He looked weary.

"Please. You must come with me now."

"No."

Slowly, the General approached.

"You have to come now."

"No."

The General began to reach for her arm.

"Don't touch me!"

He stopped, arm aloft. She met his stare.

"Get out."

The General lowered his arm and sighed. Then he ran a hand though his rebellious hair, shook his head and retreated from the room, closing the door.

After that, she was left alone. Darkness fell. There were no further drone maneuvers. The conference room door turned out to be locked. Fortunately, there was a bathroom. She was able to clean herself up somewhat.

For three or four hours she was unsupervised, and able to think.

Some of the things Jeff had said about Annie no longer seemed so far-fetched. He had blamed himself, in his own, goofy, indirect way. But it wasn't his fault. Ideology got into people; how did you get it out again? They looked for things, or people, to hate. And they always found them. You could switch if necessary; paranoia never lacked for enemies. And the more you insisted you were living in the real world — mugged by reality! — the less likely it was.

For some reason, the lights in the conference room did not work. And so, when Annie eventually returned, their reunion was conducted by flashlight.

"We're going out."

"What for?"

"We're going to look. We're going to look wherever we can. You're going to show me."

"Show you what?"

"The chemicals."

Annie grasped her hand and pulled her to her feet. They left the conference room and descended to ground level. All was dark.

"Why are there no lights?"

"The insurgents."

At the end of a corridor, Annie punched a code into a mechanical keypad and pushed open a heavy door. Then they were outside, under a clear desert sky and a new moon.

"Where is everyone?"

"On patrol."

"Even Andy?"

"Eating his dinner."

She hadn't eaten for at least a day, but she felt no hunger. Annie led her to what looked like a warehouse. Again, she entered a code. Inside, they roamed the aisles, Annie's flashlight bouncing from floor to ceiling. It could have been a Home Depot.

"See? Nothing."

"But this is just ordinary... Wouldn't it need some kind of..."

What had the General said? Something about special storage facilities with proper defenses?

"A bunker, maybe?"

"You want to look for a bunker?"

"Yes, let's look."

They exited the warehouse.

"Go find your bunker."

She chose a direction at random and they began to walk.

"Annie, what do you actually do here?"

"PR. Media relations."

PR for chemical warfare?

"What does that *mean?*"

"It just means we'll be explaining what we're doing."

"After you've done it?"

"Yes."

A bunker would be underground, by definition. How would you spot it? They walked on.

"Is Leo here?" she said.

"Yes."

She stopped. Annie kept going.

"Where?"

"In the cells. Under the command block."

"Is he okay?"

"I guess."

She ran to catch up with her daughter.

"What did Andy do to him?"

"Kadiya."

"Andy let that thug —"

"Shut up. Show me your chemicals."

They reached the hangars. Annie's flashlight revealed an outer steel fence and an inner concrete wall.

"I can't get inside there."

"I think it must be hidden. Probably underground."

"Where?"

If Jay were here, he'd know where to look. Tonight, she'd have to do his job for him. She shivered; the air was cooling rapidly. At least she wouldn't be sleeping in the truck tonight. Or on the ground. She looked down. There were tire tracks in the sand — like those of a small tractor, perhaps; not wide enough for a truck and too fat for a car. Well, why not?

"This way."

They walked in silence for ten or fifteen minutes, following the tracks. But then, in the middle of nothing, the tracks stopped: It looked as though whatever had made them had paused, reversed and then taken off in a new direction.

"Here," she said. "I think it's under here."

"I don't see anything."

She began to kick away the sand with her feet. Nothing. She got down on her knees and dug with her hands. Annie held the flashlight steady, but didn't help.

It was about eight inches under the sand: A steel box with a lid. She lifted the lid. Inside was another keypad.

"Annie?"

Annie didn't move or reply. She directed the flashlight at the steel box.

"It must be here. Do you see? We need a number."

Silently, Annie reached into a pocket and pulled out a scrap of paper. Then she knelt alongside her mother. On the paper was a list of eight-digit numbers, six in all. The third number did it. The sand whirred and parted.

It was like some movie about tomb-robbers in Egypt, Bonnie thought — curse and all.

A deep stairwell opened up before them. At the bottom, a door and another keypad. Annie's fifth number opened it.

They entered a spacious antechamber. It was dimly lit but well-equipped: Heavy-duty ventilation and a non-slip floor; suits, gloves, boots, masks, oxygen tanks and breathing gear; fire extinguishers; metal cabinets; shower cubicles; blue lights blinking on the ceiling; a desk with a red telephone and a green folder labeled *Boschenkop*; computer screens with graphs that ticked along in real time; a sickly, oily smell; security cameras.

Crossing to the far side, they found a door — like something from a submarine — with a porthole window. They peered through. Inside, stacked in rows on steel shelving, going back as far as they could see, were small, gray, steel drums. Just so that there could be no doubt, someone had taken the trouble to stencil each one with a skull and cross-bones in vivid burnt orange.

She waited for her daughter to speak. But Annie continued to stare through the porthole. Then the antechamber behind them lit up in bright yellow. A distant boom followed, then a closer explosion and the faint chatter of machine guns.

"What's happening?" she said.

Annie turned away from the porthole and listened, a child-like look of puzzlement on her face.

"They're different tonight. New tactics."

"Who?"

"The insurgents."

CHAPTER 29

J ohn Dolt's speech to the august yet secretive body known as the Club for Greed did indeed turn out to be a corker. Primed with a stiff vodka and orange, he'd been on top form. Had his listeners not already stuffed themselves at the pre-speech fund-raiser banquet (in aid of a poorly-named, grass-roots outfit called Americans for Religion, Security and Enterprise), they would have been eating out of his hand.

And it had been a pretty smart move, Dolt felt, to have equipped himself with a second large vodka and orange, concealed in an opaque paper cup and camouflaged as New Hampshire Pure Mountain Spring Water. This sustained him as he fought off jet-lag and threaded his way through Gideon's sinuous prose.

After a while, though, he couldn't resist going off-script. Gideon's assertion that environmental regulation was choking small business reminded Dolt of the time that the Jobba van had failed its yearly inspection and he'd been forced to strike a blow against bureaucracy by switching its number plates. And Gideon's attack on the evils of inheritance tax moved Dolt to imagine a time in which he would be able to bequeath to his children — Tamsin and Tamara, by the way; nice girls but don't talk to him about their boyfriends, ha-ha! — not merely a half-a-house but a (pause for emotional effect) *whole* house!

These anecdotes and asides left Gideon frowning in the front row, but the former PM was urging Dolt on, and the Greed-Clubbers — a very sleek and well-upholstered bunch, as far as Dolt could tell — seemed to be enjoying themselves mightily. Much as they obviously appreciated all the stuff about supply-side reforms, sound money and capital investment relief, it was Dolt's tales of entrepreneurial life on the gritty streets of northwest London that really gripped them. It was as if he were painting for them a picture of a world that they never knew existed. Subtly, of course, Dolt tweaked his stories to conform to the Club's guiding philosophy. It wasn't actually true, for example, that Hamid had boosted the profits of the Super Westway Limousine Company by fitting smaller wheels to his vehicles in order to inflate their recorded mileage. Nor was it the case that Lescek had once stashed a consignment of Big Builder reject tiles in a smoky pub for three months before passing them off as reclaimed Victorian originals. After about twenty minutes of this sort of stuff, Gideon folded his arms and assumed an expression of bemused tolerance.

When it was all over, Dolt got a standing ovation and a tribute from the former PM, who was next up to speak: *Gosh, how do I follow that?*

He did, though — largely in an anecdotal style that Dolt felt sure he had himself inspired. Of course, whereas Dolt's fables revolved around dodgy tradesmen, petty hustlers and other denizens of the black economy, the former PM's featured Kings, Presidents, Prince Regents, Glorious Leaders, and a surprising number of their close relatives. Spivs, Dolt mused, of an entirely different order.

After the final curtain came down, and Dolt had graciously accepted Gideon's lukewarm congratulations, he somehow found himself back at the bar again. But this time he had a friend.

"What's your poison?"

The speaker pronounced the last word as *poisson*, but didn't look or sound French. Dolt concluded he was drunk and trying to be funny.

"Vodka and orange. Ta very much," he said.

"Nice speech."

"Thanks."

"Name's Prickler. Fake Prickler."

Dolt had grown inured, mostly, to weird names by now, but this was something else. Then he realized that what his new companion was trying to say was *Drake Strickland*. This was a name that Gideon had dropped a few times; the man was some kind of private aviation tycoon. He was a large, thin, oblong man with an over-engineered frame and fluffy white hair, aged about seventy. Basically, he resembled a crusty, vintage skyscraper with snow on top.

Their drinks arrived. Dolt noticed that Strickland — or *Prickler*, as he decided to dub him — was drinking some sort of whisky — bourbon, possibly.

"You're one of the guys who get it," Prickler said, approvingly.

"I am," Dolt admitted.

"Not everybody gets it."

"They don't, do they? Don't know why."

"I would have thought it was ov-, obvious."

"Me too."

"But you... *You...*"

"Yes? What about me?"

Prickler made a reckless gesture in the rough direction of the ballroom where Dolt had given his speech.

"You're not like them. You're different."

"I suppose I am."

Prickler leaned in towards Dolt and examined him closely, like a train-spotter who'd chanced on a hitherto unknown species of goods wagon.

"You a millionaire?"

This question took Dolt by surprise, but it shouldn't have; Gideon had said that Americans liked to talk a lot about money.

"No," he said. "Well, I might be by now. I haven't checked the account, you see."

Prickler shook his head.

"You gotta check every dime. Otherwise, those bastards, they'll... You sure you're not a millionaire?"

"As of now, probably not."

"Boy. Never heard of that before."

"But, surely —"

"Someone like you should be a millionaire. Must be true what they say about England."

"I expect so, but —"

"See, we got people in this country. I don't know about England. They're not millionaires, but they think they should be. What do you make of that? Pretty bizarre, huh?"

"Weird."

"They're not like us. You know what they do?"

"Why don't you tell me?"

Prickler began to gesture wildly. Dolt moved his vodka to safety.

"They go downtown and they protest. They have these shitty little signs. They have sex in the street, it's on video. They think the government should make them millionaires. I'm not making this up."

"Unbelievable."

"And you know what? We're under socialism, now. So the government will start *spreadin' the wealth*, if we don't stop 'em."

Dolt knew, deep down, that this was the moment to make his excuses and retreat to his suite on the thirty-second floor, but the vodka had sapped his instinct for self-preservation.

"That's why we gotta get rid of the government," Prickler said.

"What, all of it?"

Prickler shrugged.

"Heck, eventually, sure. But we got to start somewhere."

A conspiratorial pall fell over his face.

"We need to start where they make the money. But you know what?"

"What?"

"It's not real money. There's no gold. If there's no gold, it ain't real."

Dolt recalled a TV ad that seemed to run every time Freedom News took a break.

"Are you talking about guaranteed mortgage-backed convertible gold bonds?"

"Jeez, who's trying to sell you that shit? Don't even think about it."

"Oh, I won't."

"Good. You see, those guys — they're traitors. They're debasing the very coin of the United States."

"Why would they do that?"

Prickler leaned back from the bar, arms folded, and would have toppled from his stool if Dolt hadn't steadied him.

"*Now* you're asking."

Dolt slid back his sleeve and made a show of consulting his watch — a German model selected by Jacqueline to convey reliability and efficiency.

"Oh, look at the time!" he said, aware that the vodka had degraded his acting skills but reckoning on Prickler being even worse off.

"Time?" Prickler said. "It's time all right. That's what I've been thinking. That's why I needed to talk to someone. Someone like you. Dis... dispassionate, that's it."

Dolt dismounted from his stool.

"Well, it was nice to —"

"Wait."

Prickler had grasped him by the upper arm.

"You mind if I get something off my chest?"

"Um, no. I suppose not."

"If I'm gonna to go through with this, I need to know I'm doing the right thing."

"Uh-huh."

"D'you think I should go through with it?"

"With what?"

Prickler glanced to one side, then the other, with woozy furtiveness. Then he released Dolt's arm.

"The Fed. In DC."

"The Fed. Right. And your plan is to..."

"My plan is to take a ride down there and give them a piece of my mind. Whaddya say?"

"Sure, why not? Think they'll listen?"

"Oh, they'll hear me, all right."

"Bombs away, then. In a manner of speaking."

Prickler shook his head.

"*You*... You're amazing! You read my mind."

"If you say so. Anyway, it's been an awfully long day, and —"

"Before you go. You've done something for me. I want to do something for you."

"Very generous, I'm sure."

"I'm going to make you a millionaire."

Prickler leaned towards Dolt and widened his eyes. Dolt could smell the liquor.

"A *multi*-millionaire."

Prickler grabbed a cocktail napkin, whipped out a pen and began scribbling. When he'd finished, Dolt could see that he'd scrawled two lists of names.

"First thing you do," Prickler said, "on the morning of October twenty-eight, soon as the markets open, you short *these* and you buy *those*."

He handed Dolt the napkin.

"You can't buy Green Lake or Fair Meadow directly, they're not public. But these'll do just fine."

"Um, thanks."

"Don't mention it."

"What's happening on the twenty-eighth?"

Prickler hesitated.

"Well, I guess I can tell *you*."

"Go on, then."

Prickler leaned in again.

"You know that whole Persian thing?"

"Uh-huh."

"Well, that's when it all goes down."

"How?"

"That, my friend, I don't know. Just make sure you're on the phone to your broker, pronto. Maximum leverage."

So the trigger was scheduled for the twenty-eighth. But what *was* it?

"Do you know *where* it's going down?"

Prickler shook his head.

"No. I heard a rumor, though. Something to do with a memorial."

"Whose memorial?"

"No idea. Not mine."

"I should hope not. Memorial, eh? Wonder what that means?"

"For you, buddy, it means riches. Be thankful."

Dolt wondered for a moment where he could find the cash to profit from this tempting insider-trading starter offer, or, indeed, where he could find a *broker* or some *leverage*. But then nobler sentiments reasserted themselves.

"Wonder if Rand knows."

"He might. He loves that idea of yours, by the way."

"What idea?"

"The strike. Talks about it all the time."

"Really?"

But Prickler didn't answer. He signaled the barman for a refill, turned away from Dolt and gazed into space, apparently lost in contemplation. The prospect of extracting further intelligence looked slight. It was bed-time, Dolt decided.

"See you in Barbados, then?" Dolt said.

No response from Prickler. Dolt began to tip-toe away. As he was about to exit the bar, he heard Prickler call out after him.

"It was nice knowing you."

*

T hanks to the vodka, Dolt had fallen instantly into a deep, enveloping sleep. But it had not been the gentle, refreshing slumber he'd hoped for. Night terrors assailed him: The former PM dragging him through a chamber of War Zone horrors; a posse of deadly mopeds pursuing him through the streets of London, with Des cheering them on; and, of course, the inevitable return to Amber's cabin. And whether it was Amber's choice of costume on this occasion, or Gideon shaking him vigorously by the shoulder, that brought Dolt shuddering back into consciousness, he had the distinct feeling that something awful had happened.

"John, wake up!"

Gideon was standing at Dolt's bedside. Dolt had never seen him like this before. He was agitated. He was disheveled. He wasn't wearing a tie.

"What? What's the matter?"

"Look!"

Gideon pointed to the TV on the wall. The Freedom News TerrorCopter was reporting from Washington, DC, hovering above a cloud of smoke. It looked like a whole city block was on fire.

"The Drakester," Gideon said, grimly. "He actually went and did it. Get dressed."

"Who?" Dolt said. "What?"

"I said, get dressed. No, wait. You were in the bar with him, weren't you? Last night?"

Dolt tried to remember. Oh, right, *Prickler*. Wait a minute...

"*Who* did you say?"

"Drake Strickland. Flew his plane into a building. After loading it up with explosives. What a mess! Get out of bed, John, we need to leave right now."

"*Flew his plane...* What building?"

"The Bureau of Land Management. Don't know what he had against land management."

"Not the Fed?"

Gideon turned and fixed Dolt with a stare — it might have been withering, or it might have been penetrating; Dolt wasn't sure.

"Did you say something to him, last night?"

"No!"

"What were you talking about? I warned you he was unstable, didn't I?"

"Did you?"

Gideon indicated the TV.

"The Federal Reserve building is on C Street, just the other side of 20th Street. What did he say to you last night? Did he say anything about the Fed?"

Dolt pulled the bedclothes up around his knees.

"Um, let me think. Oh, right. He said he was going to take a ride down there and... Oh."

"What did *you* say?"

"Nothing!"

Had he, in fact, said *bombs away?* No, surely not. Best not to mention it.

"This could de-rail everything," Gideon said. "Come on, get out of bed. Greenwich is canceled. Everyone's going to Barbados. We'll sit it out there and see how things develop. *You* need to get out of the country until things are smoothed over. The FBI could be here any minute. Hurry up!"

It was a shame, Dolt thought, that he'd barely had time to introduce himself to America before finding himself obliged to scram under a cloud of suspicion. Had Amber Pike ever been forced to scram under a cloud of suspicion? Almost certainly not. It was a setback. In future, Dolt would have to go steady on the vodka and be on the lookout for further Pricklers.

As he tumbled out of bed, he glanced again at the TV and then froze in mid-stumble. Smoke, fire, devastation. One Prickler in a Cessna. How many people had there been in that building? Had Prickler even thought about them? After all, they probably weren't millionaires. He'd taken it upon himself to create his own private War Zone.

"John!"

"Yes, all right."

After that, things moved fast. Almost before he knew it, Dolt was back in the motorcade, heading for the airport under a lowering and frosty sky.

Neither he nor Gideon spoke. As he pondered the horror of Prickler's last stand against Big Government, Dolt began to ask himself if he could actually go through with his plan to *embrace the dark side*, as Des put it. If he did, there would have to be a point, wouldn't there? It couldn't be a fiery ego-trip on the Prickler model. Nor could it be mere self-gratification, or a contest with Amber Pike. He felt that the answer was close; it just hadn't come to him yet.

But this kind of self-analysis quickly became irksome. Instead, he turned to wondering what the beaches on Barbados were like.

Nothing could go wrong there, surely?

CHAPTER 30

The McPhersons, Jeff Crock was ready to admit, were quite a family. Where would he be without them, he asked himself, as he swayed in a hammock and sipped a Red Stripe, and the pimped-up and indecorous beachfronts of western Barbados slipped by, and the balmy, late-afternoon Caribbean breeze caressed his pale and elongated limbs.

Take Katherine, the daughter. Which other boss of an imperiled, progressive journal of reportage and opinion could have plucked Isabel and himself from the grinding wheels of the rendition mill, at the very last moment, without breaking a sweat? And all thanks to *stovepipe* and a movie pilot with a smooth and sardonic manner.

She'd been very cool about the whole thing, after Jeff had obtained yet another new phone and contact had been re-established, refusing to explain the nature of the strings she'd had to pull or how vigorously she'd had to yank on them. It was for Jeff's own protection that he languish in ignorance.

No doubt remained, however, that it was an exploit never to be repeated. And that coolness was phony. Big time. You could hear the tension in her voice, the tightness in her throat. She planned to travel around, she said, for the next few weeks. Okay, he'd said; good idea. She was too good to lose; she was priceless.

Then you had the parents, Roy and Peggy. Which other retired celebrity academics could you rely on to ferry you from, say, Saint Vincent, the current stop-off in their never-ending Island Adventure (we're seriously considering Cuba, Jeff!), to a secret conclave of menacing plutocrats and mendacious politicians at the megalomaniac beach house of a rising talent in the alt-country charts? Exactly. It could only be them. And which other elderly couple would lecture you on Marx, Gramsci and the Italian Euro-communism of the mid-nineteen-seventies, while simultaneously plying you with expensive liquor on the upper deck of their eighty-foot motor yacht and narrowly avoiding collision with two cruise ships and a coast guard cutter? No other such couple, of course.

The family had left Scotland in the nineteenth century. And Scotland had been a tad less exciting ever since.

The arrangement was that he'd call Katherine when they reached the coast. Now seemed like a good time. He swallowed the last of his beer and picked up Roy and Peggy's satellite phone.

"Jeff?"

"Yup. We're here."

"How're mom and dad?"

"Just great."

"Did they hit anything with the boat?"

"No. Not even close."

Roy and Peggy's idea of *close*, and what was clearly the considered opinion of the cruise line industry, differed. But that wasn't important right now.

"I've got the GPS coordinates. Write them down."

She gave him the location of Reagan Pruett's beach-side mansion. He scribbled it down on a beer mat.

"Thanks. Where are you, by the way?"

"Where? Gee, let me think. I'm gonna say Disney World, Florida."

"Say hi to Goofy for me."

"You got it."

A thought occurred to him.

"Speaking of crazy characters..."

"Yes?"

"I forgot to tell you earlier — I mean, I don't see what we can do... But, based on what Moreland said, I think they're going for another coup. Any day now. In Ecuador."

"Oh, great. Venezuela was such a cakewalk. But nobody cares about Ecuador."

"That's what *he* said."

"Really? Too bad. Okay, gotta go. Good luck."

"Thanks. Stay away from the haunted castle."

"I will."

He ended the call. Immediately, he felt a sharp prod in the back. It was Isabel. She was wearing a red designer bathing suit, expensively purchased for her in Saint Vincent by Roy and Peggy, that made her look terrific. But, behind her over-sized shades, she didn't look happy.

"*What* did you just say?"

"Huh?"

"You said another coup. Another *Yankee* coup. In Ecuador!"

"Well, yeah, but —"

"Give me that."

She snatched the phone and made off for the lower rear deck, moving as fast as she could in her jeweled, high-heeled sandals.

Fine, he thought. Whatever. He gathered up his beer mat and picked his way down to the boat's flying bridge, where, somewhat to his relief, he found Roy at the wheel.

"Hey, Roy! Got this for you," he said, producing the beer mat with a jaunty flourish.

"What's that?"

"The GPS coordinates."

"GPS?"

"Yeah. D'you wanna input them?"

"Input?"

Roy was a sturdy seventy-eight-year-old, about half a foot shorter than Jeff, who looked like he worked out and who compensated for a tanned but shiny crown with white, shoulder-length dreadlocks. His features were pronounced and mobile, rather like those of a gregarious gnome who was always being surprised by things. Right now, he looked taken aback.

"Input?" he repeated.

"Input the coordinates," Jeff said. "Have the boat steer itself —"

"Oh, I don't use that!"

Well, this explained a few things.

"You don't?"

"Steer by the sun! By the stars!"

"You do have one, right? I mean, how much did this boat cost?"

Roy indicated a bank of computer screens.

"It's one of those. Do you know, the manual's three hundred pages long? I'm seventy-eight. I haven't got time for that."

"All right. Where's the manual?"

"Behind that box of weights."

"Okay. Nice evening, huh?"

"Beautiful. We have a life, don't we?"

"You certainly do."

Jeff located the Quick Start Guide at the front of the manual and punched in the coordinates.

"Okay, Roy. Let it steer itself. But keep an eye —"

"You think I'd trust that box of tricks? Phooey."

"Mm..."

He was pondering a pretext for lingering on the bridge when he heard a voice.

"Jeff! Come down here!"

It was Peggy, summoning him. He found her in the master stateroom. She was a delicate, slim woman of seventy-three, with what he suspected was a full-body tan and, surgery notwithstanding, the undisguisable sagginess that resulted from half a life in the sun. She had wide, fun-loving, green eyes and a bob of blond hair like a thatched roof. As he entered, she pretended to frown at him.

"Now have you thought about what you're going to wear?"

"What?"

He saw that Peggy had laid out a collection of suits and shirts on the bed.

"Don't tell me you're going like *that*."

"Well, I —"

"We've been to a lot of parties, Roy and I. Well, okay, not exactly like *this* one. But let me tell you something. Down here, people like to dress up."

"Dress up?"

"That's correct. Now, if you're going to go in there and mingle with these shitheads, you've got to look the part."

Shitheads? These academics knew how to nail an idea, didn't they? And she was right. He would stand out in the baggy orange shorts and white vest he presently wore.

"Okay then, Peggy. What do you suggest?"

"Well, just how smart a function is it? Are we talking about a power crowd?"

He began to wonder what exactly Katherine had told her parents about the mission.

"Power? I guess you could say that."

"Then you gotta go for the tux."

"The tux?"

Peggy handed Jeff a suit.

"Here."

He inspected it.

"Um, Peggy. This is Roy's."

"So?"

"I'm six inches taller than he is."

"Don't worry about it. It won't show. Just hoick your pants down a bit."

"I don't know..."

"Trust me. I know clothes. Okay?"

"If you say so."

"You'll look marvelous. Can you do the tie?"

"No."

"I'll do it for you. Now then — shoes."

Together, they looked down at Jeff's feet. He was wearing the ratty, jungle-stained white sneakers that had accompanied him all the way from Rancho Colorado.

"I think we got a problem," Peggy said. "We should have shopped for you. But with your girl, Isabel... Hmm. Go away. I'll think about it. Go!"

On his journey back up to the main saloon, as footwear worries vied with infiltration strategies for the attention of his mental processes, he once again found himself in demand.

"Mr. Jefferson Crockett! Please report to the rear deck! Immediately! I repeat..."

It figured. Roy and Peggy's boat was so big it had a PA system. But what did Isabel want now? He reported as commanded.

"Now what?" he said.

"Here," Isabel said, offering him the satellite phone. "He wants to talk to you. You must tell him everything you know."

He took the phone.

"Huh? Who the hell is it?"

"The President of Ecuador. He called me back. You better talk fast, he's paying."

"The *President?*"

"Yeah. Talk now, he's waiting!"

"You called the President of Ecuador?"

Isabel made a face — about a seven on the sour scale.

"I called the Vargas people in Guayaquil. *They* called him. Talk!"

Jeff put the phone to his ear.

"Er, hi there..."

The President of Ecuador — if indeed it was he, and Jeff felt increasingly certain that it was — spoke with gravitas, concern, and a certain understated indignation. His staff had performed some hasty research — a quick Internet trawl, Jeff guessed — and had concluded that he, Jeff, was to be taken seriously. In fact, his information was consistent with rumors floating around Quito, and the cocky behavior of certain unpatriotic business cartels. The President wished to remind Jeff — and the world at large, for that matter — that, when it came to fending off coups, he was not inexperienced. This time, however, given what had recently transpired in Venezuela, he was forced to admit that the matter was serious. Jeff said he agreed. Therefore, the President explained, he had appointed a Special Deputy, a trusted lieutenant from the old days, to fly immediately to the Caribbean, collect both Jeff and his girlfriend, and return with all possible haste to Quito. Here, Jeff, with his particular knowledge of the plotters and his bitterly–acquired and profound understanding of the ways of American imperialism, would assist the Special Deputy and a hand-picked brigade of loyal troops in their patriotic duty to defeat this monstrous assault on the rights and liberties of the peoples of Ecuador.

"Er, yeah," Jeff said. "That's great. Only thing is, I've got a party to go to." He let the *girlfriend* thing go.

The was a pause at the other end of the line.

"A party?"

Jeff explained the nature of the party and its attendees, omitting, for the sake of brevity, his intentions regarding *Faith Boy*, aka Number Two. The President sounded impressed, and congratulated Jeff on his initiative and his selflessness.

"Thanks," Jeff said.

The upshot was that Jeff undertook to gather as much intelligence as possible, both about the coup and the fate of Leo Vargas, and then swiftly make himself — okay, Isabel, too — available at Grantley Adams International Airport, where a discreet jet with Ecuadorian markings would be waiting, engines running.

After the conversation finished, the President signing off by declaring that Leo Vargas and Jefferson Crockett were the kind of upstanding global citizens the world needed more of, Jeff returned to his hammock in something of a daze.

While it was evident, despite the enormity of her sunglasses, that Isabel's reaction to this latest twist comprised one part triumph to two parts smugness, Jeff was interested to note that his own take was at first more, well, ambivalent. His whole career had been one of struggle — against unyielding authority, unaccountable power, and meager resources. Though he had, in his own way (the power of words, remember), fought against the coups, invasions and power-grabs of the past quarter-century, he had never expected to experience the prospect of actual *success*. And now here he was, allied with a Head of State, furnished with Presidential planes, and with brigades of *hand-picked troops* at his disposal.

Who would have thunk it? It would take some getting used to, but already he felt more pumped about the challenges the night was sure to bring. He had gotten some decent hammock action going, and was musing on whether, as a reward for services rendered, the President would be prepared to instigate proceedings in respect of Number Two at the International Criminal Court, when Peggy swung into view. She was holding up a pair of black dress shoes.

"Bingo!"

Jeff stilled the hammock. They were the biggest shoes he'd ever seen.

"Try them on!"

Peggy handed him the shoes, and spoke in a low voice.

"These belong to Brinsley. He won't mind. He drives the boat for us sometimes. You know, if we've had a drink or two. Roy's not as young as he used to be."

Jeff slipped the shoes on. To his surprise, they were comfortable. But the toes continued for some considerable distance beyond the point where his feet stopped. He composed a mental image of himself in Roy's tux pants and Brinsley's shoes. He was going to look like an elongated penguin. Well, what the hell. Once, he'd had to dress up as a gorilla. This time, he had the President, his cabinet, and the armed forces of Ecuador on his side. What other penguin could say that?

"What can I say, Peggy? Marvelous!"

"You're embarrassing me."

Jeff realized that the boat had come to a stop. Casting his gaze across to the shore, he was able to perceive, despite the failing light, a wide stretch of palm-dotted private beach, lit by flickering lanterns, behind which lurked a substantial white mansion with a double-decker veranda. It was possible to discern that quite a crowd had gathered. Waiters darted. The sound of a steel band drifted across the water. There was some pretty obvious security on the beach. This had to be it.

"Drop the anchor, Roy!"

It was time to suit up. By the time Jeff was ready, and had made his way to the jet-ski dock at the rear of the boat, darkness had fallen. Of course, his plan of infiltration did not involve the jet-ski; he would be using Roy and Peggy's inflatable paddle-dinghy.

As he was lowering himself into this craft, he felt the jab of something metallic in his back. Turning around, he saw that Peggy was holding a gun.

"We thought you might need this."

Jeff ducked into the dinghy.

"Jesus, Peggy — point it over there! Is that thing loaded?"

Peggy looked uncertain.

"Roy? He wants to know if it's loaded!"

"Of course it's loaded!"

"He says it's loaded."

Jeff nodded to Isabel. Isabel got the message and took the gun from Peggy. She examined it briefly and gave Jeff a meaningful scowl.

"Why d'you have a gun, Peggy?"

"Why? We're two old people. Alone on the ocean! You've got pirates, you've got drug-runners. You want us to be defenseless?"

"Well, no. But..."

"Do you want it or not?"

"No thanks. Look, I'm going now. Remember what you have to do?"

"Yes, we remember."

"Okay, good."

Jeff took up his oar, pushed back from the mother ship and paddled away into the night. The plan was simple; he'd learned the hard way that complicated plans never worked. The key thing was to evade the security goons on the beach. After that, he would lurk and loiter as necessary, keeping to the shadows, the penguin suit providing all the camouflage he required. He would reconnoiter, eavesdrop, take photos with his phone, search the property where possible, and even engage in conversation if he dared.

The mansion to the north of R-Pru's pad appeared unoccupied. There were no people visible, and though there were lights, they switched on and off in a style that suggested computer randomization rather than the human touch. He paddled past and then doubled back, closer to the beach. Sure enough, the house was empty. He hit the beach, jumped out, fell in the water, got up again, and dragged the dinghy into the shadow of a palm tree.

Well, okay, he was wet. But it was really too dark for it to be obvious, and the warm night air ought to dry him out quickly. Not far from the boundary with R-Pru's property was a row of bougainvillea bushes. He positioned himself alongside them and waited for Phase Two of the plan to commence.

But Phase Two did not begin on schedule. Jeff waited, keeping an eye out for the goons on R-Pru's beach. At length, just when he was on the point of aborting the mission, he saw all the lights on the mother ship come on, one by one. Then he heard the engines fire up. The boat began to move in a course parallel to R-Pru's beach, first north-to-south, then south-to-north, and so on, inching closer to the shore on each iteration. Colored lights began to flicker rhythmically — did they actually have a mirror ball on that thing? And then the music came on, at full volume. He'd told them to put on some kind of noisy, pounding, rave or club music. What he believed he was hearing was *Abba's Greatest Hits*; "Dancing Queen", if he wasn't mistaken. Well, it would probably do.

He observed the two goons, studying their body language. As the boat ploughed closer to the beach, their attitude transitioned from amusement to bemusement; from interest to concern; from alarm to panic stations. At the point where they ceased yelling and waving at the boat from the beach and ran back into the house, Jeff shook the excess moisture from his trouser legs and strolled calmly into R-Pru's domain. As he did so, he noted with satisfaction and relief that Phase Three had kicked in with military precision, and the mother ship was now heading due west at a rate of knots.

Sauntering up the beach toward the house, he caught sight of his reflection in the water of an ornamental pool. To his private hilarity, he resembled nothing less than a lanky, hand-me-down James Bond in clown shoes. Except, of course, that he was unarmed, not licensed for anything at all, and took his orders not from the Queen of England but the President of Ecuador. As for the girl — well, she'd stayed on the boat, and he was happy about that. What a hoot.

But then, reminding himself that he was on deadly serious business, Jeff slipped through French windows into what appeared to be a beach-side study, full of furniture, objets d'art, guitars and musical memorabilia. Above the fireplace was an odd heraldic device. There were two nattily-dressed party-goers on the far side of the room, one facing him, the other not. The first was unfamiliar to him — a smooth-faced, slightly chubby guy with supercilious eyebrows, who looked like an English butler. His conversation partner did not turn around until Jeff accidentally tripped over his own feet and toppled a framed gold disk from a poorly-positioned occasional table.

It was War Criminal Number Two.

CHAPTER 31

The former PM looked like he'd seen a ghost. Dolt had been pleasantly engaged with the Caribbean buffet on the garden terrace when the cry had gone up for his assistance, but he'd instantly dropped his spicy crab with pineapple relish and hastened to the scene. What he discovered, on arrival, was a tableau of angst and confusion.

Like a nervous spinster recovering from a Halloween prank, or a top banker suffering through the after-effects of a bonus tax demand, the former PM sat shivering and gibbering in an antique armchair while Gideon fanned him with a handkerchief and pressed a large beaker of what looked like brandy into his trembling hands.

As Dolt hove into view, the former PM gave a piteous start and lifted his head; there was a pleading look in his eyes.

"John! Thank God you're here."

"What happened? You look like you've seen a ghost."

"It's *him*. He's *on the premises*. Please, you've got to *do something!*"

"Who's that again?"

"*Him*. The one I told you about! *Crockett!*"

"What, that stalker bloke?"

"Yes!"

"The one who thinks you're a war criminal?"

The former PM choked on his brandy. It was mischievous, of course, for Dolt to bring the issue up, but it was also essential to the on-going psychological manipulation of his target.

While the former PM spluttered into his glass, Dolt drew Gideon aside.

"Did *you* see anyone?"

"Some chap came in through the French windows. He knocked *that* over."

Dolt crossed the room to the scene of the crime, scooping up the gold disk R-Pru had been awarded for her song, "Your Sub-Prime Heart's Gonna Foreclose On Our Love," and restoring it to its place of honor. More curious than R-Pru's homely metaphors, however, were the wet patches on the floor. And the

257

enormous, sandy footprints that connected them. This Crockett had to be some sort of giant.

"Right," Dolt said, for a subtle plan had already suggested itself to him, "I'm taking charge. We have a possible intruder situation. But it is vital that we keep this information to ourselves until my initial investigations are concluded."

Gideon was giving him a funny look, but he ignored it.

"Step one. We relocate to a secure location. Both of you, follow me."

Whereas Dolt, Gideon and most of the other guests were lodged at a swanky resort just up the road, the former PM, Rand Purdo and a handful of bigwigs had been selected to enjoy Reagan Pruett's personal hospitality. The former PM had been assigned an upper-floor suite on the garden side of the mansion, overlooking the terrace.

After they entered, via an outdoor staircase, Dolt ordered Gideon and the former PM to wait in the safety of the vestibule, while he put on a show, under Gideon's suspicious gaze, of checking each room. He found what he was looking for — the laptop — on a coffee table in the lounge.

Back in the vestibule, Dolt indicated the former PM and instructed Gideon in confidential tones.

"Escort him into the bedroom. Let him have a little lie-down."

Gideon gave Dolt a narrow-eyed look.

"Are you quite sure you know what you're doing, John?"

"I am, yes."

"You don't think, for example, that we should alert security? There's at least a dozen of them down there. They could help you look for your possible intruder."

"No. This has a bearing on the GPQ. It's top secret. I need to tackle him alone." Dolt glanced meaningfully at the former PM. "We had certain conversations on the plane that were for my ears only."

It was a bluff — and a pretty good one too, Dolt felt. Gideon folded his arms.

"Oh, that's right isn't it? While I was sitting at the back."

Dolt waited while Gideon inspected the ceiling and twiddled his fingers.

"Well, all right, John. Do it your way."

"Go in there with him, close the door and just keep an eye on him, okay?"

"Very well."

The former PM was muttering to himself — something to do with Dangerous Persons, by the sound of it. Gideon took him by the elbow and led him down the hallway to the bedroom. Dolt waited for the door to close, then raced back to the lounge. Which was when things started to get even curiouser.

The laptop was gone.

Had he been mistaken? No, you could see the little marks made by the laptop's rubber feet on the glass top of the table. Had one of the former PM's staff nipped in and grabbed it? No, they were all splashing about in the pool at the far end of the garden. Dolt slumped on to the sofa in frustration; spying just wasn't as easy as he'd begun to assume.

So who else could have taken it? He got up and went to the French windows that opened on to the upper deck of the veranda. They were locked. There was only one other exit from the lounge — the door to the vestibule. Which could only mean...

Dolt scanned the lounge, on high alert for hiding places. There were none — save the heavy curtains on either side of the French windows. Glancing down to his right, he spied a trickle of water that seemed to leak from the curtains on to the marble floor.

With maximum stealth, Dolt stepped back, selected a heavy object from a sideboard — it was another of R-Pru's gold discs, this one in recognition of "Baby, You Can Be My Drone" — and hurled it at the center of the curtain.

"Ow!"

There was a gentle thump as the laptop slid to the floor. Dolt sprang forward and snatched it. But before he could make good his escape, the curtain disgorged its secret inhabitant and Dolt found himself on his back, pinioned to the cool, marble floor by a soggy streak of vengeance in a penguin suit that was absolutely more than a few sizes too small. This, combined with the avenger's flipper-like footwear, made for a vision at once so discomfiting and pathetic that Dolt felt all the fight go out of him.

"Are you Jefferson Crockett?" he said.

The avenger looked surprised. His grip on Dolt's wrists loosened a bit.

"How did you know that? Who the hell are you, anyway?"

Dolt contrived to look as dignified as any person could, who happened to have a giant, damp, angry penguin squatting on his chest.

"I am John Dolt," he said.

This turned out to be the wrong thing to say.

"Dolt! You mean you're that friggin' brain-dead idiot who's been mouthing off —"

"Now, now — let's not jump to any —"

"— about immigrants and welfare and spending and foreigners and —"

"— conclusions. I'd just like to point out —"

"— shilling for the fat-cats and the turbo-capitalists, and trying to start another mindless, friggin' war and —"

"— that all is not necessarily as it seems."

"It isn't? Yeah, you bet it isn't! No kidding! You're just a fucking glove puppet, aren't you?"

"No, no. You see, what's actually happening is —"

"So who's got his hand up your ass, then? Oh, let me guess. Maybe it's Rand Purdo? Huh? So how much are they paying you, asshole?"

Dolt couldn't help but feel disconcerted — and a little hurt, too, to be honest. Well, all right, looking at things from a certain perspective... But *glove puppet?*

"No," he said. "They haven't given me any money at all. They said they would, but..."

"Oh, stop it. You're gonna make me cry."

This was mere sarcasm, of course.

"All I really wanted," Dolt said, "was to go on an island —"

"You *are* on an island."

"But things got out of control, and it got complicated, and then there was Aisha, and the big drone, and the motorcycles, and Des said I had to —"

"Wait. Hold it. What did you say?"

"The motorcycles?"

"No, no. Back up. You said something about a big drone."

"Oh, that. That's for the GPQ. You know, the March to War and so forth. Des wants to stop it."

This brought the conversation to a halt. Dolt took the opportunity to breathe heavily.

"They're going to use drones?"

"Yes."

"Big ones?"

"Huge."

For some reason, Jefferson Crockett decided to release Dolt's left wrist so that he could smack himself across the forehead.

"*This is huge!*"

He seemed to be talking to himself. All in all — look at those trouser legs — he was obviously a bit of an eccentric.

"And this guy Des wants to stop the war?"

"Yes. I'm helping him, aren't I?"

"But you're *in favor* of war."

"Oh, no. Not really."

There was another pause.

"Who's this Des guy?"

"He works for... Well I don't know, but his bosses are Oxbridge. He's supposed to be my Head of Security, but actually..."

"He's a spy?"

"Basically."

"Okay. Back to the drone. What do you know?"

"Um, look, Jefferson —"

"Just call me Jeff."

"Right, Jeff. Why don't we go somewhere private and have a little chat? You know, in comfort. Without anybody sitting on anybody else. I think we might be able to help each other."

"Oh, really?"

"Yes. I mean, the people who murdered Aisha had you on their enemies list, didn't they?"

"Aisha? Enemies list?"

"Yes. It's on the laptop. With a ton of other stuff. I'll show you. So we're really on the same side, kind of. Plus I stopped them alerting security after you blundered in and —"

"Wait. Are you saying you're *faking* all that populist shit?"

"Sort of. Up to a point. *They* do most of it for me."

Jeff looked baffled. He let go of Dolt's other wrist and shook his head slowly.

"But why would you *do* that?"

Dolt rubbed his wrists.

"It was my big chance. I've never had a big chance before, so..."

As rationales went, Dolt realized, it wasn't great. But it was the truth. As if by mutual consent, they let it hang in the air for a moment.

"All right," Jeff said, getting to his feet — not a trivial matter, given his choice of footwear. "Let's go talk someplace." He picked up the laptop, which appeared undamaged, and helped Dolt to his feet.

"There's a pagoda sort of thing," Dolt said. "Down by the pool. We can sneak up through the trees."

*

Jeff Crock realized, as he examined the contents of the laptop, that he'd struck the mother lode. He also understood that, without Dolt, he would, in all probability, have dumped the laptop after a cursory examination of the Internet, document and email folders. These contained ample evidence of Number Two's well-known and abiding fascination with ritzy international real estate, but absolutely nothing of interest. As he and Dolt huddled together in the pool pagoda, and Number Two's staff and Purdo's minions splashed and cavorted before them in Reagan Pruett's guitar-shaped pool, he admitted as much.

"Shit, John. It was only a spur-of-the-moment thing. I just hoped I might find some evidence."

"The war-crimes thing?"

"Yeah."

"But how did you know it was *his* suite?"

"He signed the guest book."

"Oh, right."

"That's a useful spy-tip for you, right there."

"Thanks."

Jeff pulled up one of the document files that Dolt had pointed out.

"Wow. There's some hot shit here. I mean, look at this. Fair Meadow Solutions, the drone people. I was actually there, in South Carolina. *He* was there! Green Lake Robotics, they do all the avionics."

"Howard Hooper," Dolt said. "Funny bloke. Smoker. Met him at the Global Faith Initiative. Kept going on about some Libyan thing."

"Libya? Fuck! *That's* where they're basing the drones. You know, I actually flew one — on a cell phone! They told me it was a *big empty country!* He's* had his hooks into Libya for years. He was the one who opened the door! Jesus!"

"You *flew* one?"

"Yeah, they got an *app.* And guess what? Look here, in this folder. There's a whole bunch of apps. Okay, here we go..."

Jeff whipped out his new cell phone and kicked off a set of wireless file transfers. Dolt looked on, as if transfixed.

"What are you doing?"

"File transfer."

"Can I do it, too?"

"Yeah, why not? Give me your phone."

Dolt handed it over.

"Let's see what else we got."

Jeff clicked back to the list of companies that appeared to have dealings with the Global Faith Initiative.

"Look at this one! Boschenkop. Whoa! Do you know what they do?"

Dolt looked blank.

"No idea."

"South African operation. Mercenaries. Logistics. Weapons. *Banned* weapons, allegedly."

"What, like WMD, you mean? Chemicals?"

"Well, they're kind of evil, but even they wouldn't —"

"Can I show you something?"

"Sure."

A beach-ball bounced in from the direction of the pool. Jeff jumped from his seat and hurled it back. When he sat down again, he found Dolt peering at some kind of technical diagram.

"At first I thought it was a vacuum cleaner."

Jeff examined the diagram. Then he studied Dolt's face. No, he really wasn't joking, was he?

"But it's not, is it?" Dolt said.

"I'm gonna say no. It's definitely not a vacuum cleaner."

But it *was* something that Katherine had to know about, right now. He picked up his phone and dialed her new number. The call didn't connect. He sent her a *call me* text message.

"What about these apps, then?" Dolt said.

"Shall we try one?"

"Is it safe?"

"Don't really know."

"Go on, then."

"There's one called *BaseCam*. Shall we try that?"

"All right."

Jeff activated it. A black window opened up. After a moment or two, the window filled with the image of a dark and unlit parking lot — a parking lot full of armored vehicles. Wherever it was, it was night-time. He flipped to the next screen, and kept flipping. A series of scenes presented themselves: The front of an enormous building, like an aircraft hangar; a flat stretch of desert; an empty control room full of computer screens; a very long runway; a view from above of a man with thick, black hair and olive skin, slumped in the corner of a tiny, unfurnished room; a selection of empty stairwells; some kind of armory, full of rifles and machine guns.

"Who was that bloke?" Dolt asked.

"I don't know," Jeff said. "But I have my suspicions."

"What are we looking at?"

"I think we're hooked into the security camera network at the drone base."

"In Libya?"

"Uh-huh. Let's see what else we've got."

He flipped again.

They saw two human figures in a dimly lit room that looked vaguely industrial — women, Jeff realized. From the way they moved, it was clear that they were in some kind of distress.

"What's happening?" Dolt asked.

"I can't tell."

"Can you zoom in?"

Jeff made the standard zoom gesture and dragged the picture to frame the faces of the two women. The camera angle was high, but the picture quality was good. More than good enough. After about a minute, he realized that Dolt was looking at him strangely.

"Who are those women?"

Jeff rubbed his fist across his forehead.

"Well," he said. "*That's* my mother-in-law, and *that's* my wife."

CHAPTER 32

Could there have been a safer place to hide from the battle than an underground bunker packed to the roof with poison? They couldn't find a way to close the outer door — the one that masqueraded as forty square feet of innocent desert — but, together, they managed to shut the inner one.

Then they sat at the desk with the red phone and the green folder and listened as the fight ebbed and flowed.

Bonnie opened the green folder. Boschenkop clearly knew their chemistry. They had an address in Johannesburg and a web site. What might the web site offer? It was easy enough to imagine. Pictures of Land Rovers and promises of unparalleled expertise. Not drums of nerve agent.

She touched her daughter's hand.

"Well, I don't know what we do next."

Annie withdrew her hand and looked up at the security cameras.

"They'll see off the insurgents. Then they'll check all the cameras."

"Perhaps we shouldn't stay here."

"There's nowhere to go."

Going nowhere seemed preferable to Bonnie than trysting anew with Mr. Andrew Willoughby-St. John, the master of the skies, and General Kadiya of Mogadishu, the lord of the earth. But this attitude held little worth for Leo. Hope lay with the *insurgents*, hitherto known as local residents. There could be but one explanation, to be sure, for their *new tactics*. How would Annie feel about that?

"You know, these *insurgents* — they're just a bunch of kids. Their leader is some kind of building contractor. If they're putting up a decent fight now, it's only because of Jay. I think we'd better go out there and find them."

Annie didn't reply.

"Come with me."

"Go on your own."

"Annie, how many lies must they have told you?"

"Everybody lies about everything."

"You can't continue with this. They're a bunch of war criminals."

The rattle of machine guns and the straining of engines sounded closer now. Annie stood up.

"War's just war. It's what it is. You win however you can. It's not a crime to win. You can't talk about crime if the ends are..."

"If they're what?"

"If they're right in the long run."

"How long is that?"

Annie didn't respond.

"How long do people live? How do you measure their suffering?"

"What would you know about that? You're out of your element here. You live under the protection of the strong, but you don't know it. People live. Or they die. Someone has to decide."

"Who?"

"Whoever's most fit. Whoever's proved their fitness."

Annie unlatched the inner door and swung it open.

"You can go now," she said.

She waited by the door with her arms folded. Bonnie picked up the green folder and stood.

"Change your mind? Please?"

"Go."

She stepped past her daughter, climbed the steps back up into the desert night and stood immobile, breathing the chilled air and trying to focus her recalcitrant eyes. It must have been two or three minutes before she knew for sure that the white lights bouncing towards her belonged to one of the Colonel's technicals, and not one of the General's toy tanks. And it was Jay on the gun in the back, and two of the Colonel's kids hanging off the sides.

"I guess I must apologize," he said, as he jumped down. "I *did* go back for you. But you'd gone."

"Better late than never."

"That's right."

"What about the people in the truck?"

"Gone. On foot."

"Where?"

He sighed.

"Doesn't really make any difference."

"Ah."

"Sorry."

She rubbed her bare arms, to warm them.

"So are you done fighting for tonight?"

"Oh, yeah. We shook 'em up a bit. They've gone to lick their wounds."

"Did you kill anyone?"

"Don't think so. We were aiming at their comms gear."

"Did you get Leo?"

"He's here?"

"Cells under the command block."

"We'll put it on the to-do list."

She saw that he was looking over her shoulder at the entrance to the bunker.

"Mind if I ask what you've got there, Bonnie?"

"Can't you guess?"

"Found it all on your own?"

"Not quite."

The look on Jay's face made her turn around. Annie stood at the foot of the stairwell. For a moment, no one spoke.

"I'm picking up on something kind of weird here," he said.

That was his idea of diplomatic language, she thought.

"Jay, this is my daughter, Annie."

"Your daughter?"

"She used to work for Andy, but I really think she ought to come with us."

Jay looked from mother to daughter and back again.

"Okay."

So he was freaked, but he didn't want to show it. Bonnie offered him the green folder.

"Check this out."

"Ah, Boschenkop. Figures. Okay, let me take a quick look down there, and we'll be going."

Jay signaled to the two kids to accompany him.

"Bring her with you," Bonnie said.

"She's not armed, right? Your daughter?"

"No. But be careful."

When he returned, he looked ill. Annie came with him, silent and stony-faced, but compliant.

"Well, now we know," he said. "How do we shut this thing up?"

Bonnie showed him. After the doors had closed, he kicked at the sand to obscure their outline. His shoes, she noticed, hadn't been cleaned in days.

He put Annie in the cab with one of the kids and the driver.

"You and me, we'll have to ride in back."

They drove slowly parallel to the runway for some distance, then turned perpendicular to it.

"We have to make a dash across the strip to get to Kufra," he said. "Hold tight."

But a moment later he was on his feet, banging on the roof of the cab. The technical stopped. Its engine switched off and its lights went out.

"Look at that," Jay said, pointing to the far end of the runway.

She could see small, red and green lights; they were moving, speeding up. Two small, propeller-driven drones took off, in parallel. They banked to the right, heading off in the same direction that the technical was pointing.

"Reprisals," Jay said. "Taking it out on Kufra. Didn't wait long, did they?"

"Reprisals? Against whom?"

"Doesn't matter, to them. They think this'll alienate the local population — turn them against the *insurgents*. That's their mentality. I think they read it in some book."

"People will blame the Colonel. And *you*."

"Yeah. Except they don't. They know what's happening. Oh wait — what's this?"

In the dark, at the far end of the runway, jet engines roared. Sharp, blue lights appeared, as if to pick out the extremities of some vast shape. The noise mounted, and the lights began to accelerate.

"What the heck are they doing?" Jay said. "These things are crashing in *daylight*."

"One of the big guys."

"Yeah."

They watched. The big drone made a perfect take-off. It rose and banked confidently, and made two steady circuits above the base. Then it descended and made a low, ground-shaking pass along the length of the runway, maintaining its height perfectly. Rising again, it made two further, precise circuits of the base, and then started into a series of breath-taking dives and maneuvers — the kind of thing, Bonnie felt sure, that no human pilot could endure. Finally, it made a second, even lower, pass along the runway, blasting out sand from the margins, before pulling up sharply, banking to the southwest, leveling out, and vanishing into the inkiness of the Saharan night.

Jay kicked his heels against the gun mounting.

"That don't look good," he said.

CHAPTER 33

John Dolt had wanted to ask his newest friend, Jefferson Crockett, the oddly-dressed but well-informed and passionately self-styled truth-seeker, anti-war campaigner and *blogger*, what had moved him to dispatch his female relatives, unprotected by all appearances, into the War Zones. But it had become apparent, as they watched the live feed from the Libyan drone base play out on Jeff's phone, that this was a touchy subject. Dolt decided not to go there.

Instead, as they hunched together within the dusky interior of the pool pagoda — and lanterns twinkled, a steel band played selections from Broadway, and the happy cries of bathers rose upon the scented Caribbean breeze — he filled Jeff in on the particulars of his own peculiar rise to the summit of populist demagoguery: Big Builder, the lacrosse mothers, Weese and Gunner, the Atlantic Affairs Institute, Gideon, Des, Jacqueline, K-Pru, Red Ron, the Global Faith Initiative, Aisha, the motorcyclists, the Greater Persian Question, and his mission to spy on the former PM — the whole twisted tale. Jeff, though understandably preoccupied by the plight of his wife and mother-in-law, listened in awe.

"Wow," he said, after his wife had disappeared from view, accompanied by a grim-looking, shaggy, middle-aged bloke in grubby clothes, and two gun-slinging teenagers, "you've been having quite the time of it, haven't you? What's your exit strategy?"

This, of course, was the question that Des kept flinging at him. Dolt had no idea.

"I'm working on it. It's coming along."

The party in the garden beyond the pool now began to crank up; the steel band had played their final request, and it sounded like R-Pru's backing musicians were tuning up.

"Glad to hear it. You'll need one."

"What about you, though? What's your next move?"

Jeff scratched his head and tapped his flippers on the pagoda's coconut matting.

"Well, John. First up, I'm wondering what the hell my mother-in-law is doing in some kind of bunker on a secret drone base in Libya."

Fair enough, Dolt thought.

269

"So, um, what about your wife?" he said, feeling emboldened.

"*That*, I can just about figure out."

"Right... How about that bloke who took her away?"

"That was interesting wasn't it? Who d'ya figure he was?"

"Dunno."

"Know what I think? There's a whole bunch of them. Dissidents, I guess you could call 'em. Some are still on the inside. Some are doing their own thing. Older guys, mostly. They look like movie actors. They have a weird sense of humor. Know what I'm saying?"

"Not really."

"Never mind, huh? You asked about my *next move?*"

"Yes."

"Well, one thing I have to do is go mingle with these people — I got it on the proper authority, by the way, that the correct term for them is *shitheads* — and find out what they know about up-coming coups in Central and South America. Did I mention that I'm on a mission from the President of Ecuador?"

Well, why not?

"And then there's this drone war that you, John, have done so much to promote, even though, you say, you're opposed to it. We gotta stop that. I need to talk to my boss, but she's not picking up."

"What, the President of —"

"No, different boss."

Jeff pointed at the laptop.

"And I've got to look at all the stuff on that. Maybe there's some evidence..."

He tailed off, a look of wonder or entrancement on his craggy face.

"Oh my God!"

"What?"

"Don't you realize what we've got here?"

"Well, actually, Des needs me to copy it and —"

"Think about it. Money gets funneled in from somewhere to the GFI. Goes into a slush fund. Then it goes out again, in lots of little payments — supposedly for *personal security* — to Boschenkop. They're a South African company. If they're running guns or mercenaries to another African country, let alone WMD... And *he* has to know about it! I knew it! They just keep coming back for more. John!"

"What?"

"Did you show him that diagram?"

"Yes."

"How did he react?"

Dolt recalled his in-flight interrogation of the former PM.

"Definitely looked a bit shifty. He said they'd war-gamed it with the PNC guys and —"

"The Persian National Congress? They're Moreland's stooges!"

"Who's Moreland?"

"Purdo's friend. Used to work for War Criminal Number One. What about the PNC?"

"He said it was the only option that worked. And Andy had tested the clean-up."

"Clean-up! Okay, okay..."

Jeff seemed excited — almost as if he were forming a plan.

"Here's the plan," he said. "What we need to do —"

"We?"

"Yeah. We need to get him to South Africa, somehow."

"Who?"

"Number Two. And then we have to get through to someone high up in the ANC. Those guys *hate* mercenaries. They got all these laws against them. They'll have his ass under house arrest before —"

"You said *we*. No offense, but what with the populism, and Des, and the exit strategy, I've got quite a lot —"

"*You've* got a lot? *I'm* trying to save two continents, and —"

"I mean, all this spying really takes it out of you —"

"You don't look so tired to me. All I'm asking is —"

"What about my exit strategy? How about helping me with that? Because I'm struggling, to be honest!"

Jeff paused for a moment, looking thoughtful in his own beaky way, and resembling an over-enthusiastic penguin which had been forced to consider the realities of its position. Then he spoke calmly.

"Look, let's not bicker. Let's help each other out. I'll work with you on the exit strategy. You help me with the Ecuador thing, the Libya thing and the South Africa thing. Sound fair?"

Fair? It sounded like his life-story again, Dolt thought. Was there any point in trying to resist? Then again, this bloke was the only person he'd encountered, since his entry into the world of politics — with the dubious exception of Des — who sounded like he didn't want to live in a world ordained, ordered and paid for by Rand Purdo. That had to be worth something.

"All right. What do you want me to do?"

"One, pump Faith Boy on Boschenkop. Two, get out there and mingle. Listen for stuff on Ecuador and Libya."

"Mingle. Right. We're both mingling."

"Yeah. As for South Africa... Oh, of course! The climate conference! Find out if your pal's going. If not, talk him into it — you seem to have a lot of influence over him. Cape Town. On the twenty-eighth. Oh wait — the twenty-eighth? Whoa..."

It was necessary, Dolt realized, to put his new partner on the right track.

"The trigger," he said. "It's happening on the twenty-eighth."

"The *trigger?* You mean..."

"For war. Prickler told me."

"Prickler?"

"Drake Strickland. Wanted to make me a millionaire. Told me before he crashed his plane into the Bureau of something."

"He did? Jesus!"

"Something to do with a memorial."

"Whose? Where?"

"He didn't know. He thought Rand might."

"Put that on your list."

Dolt sighed inwardly.

"What about my exit strategy?"

"I'll give it some serious thought. In the meantime, just carry on with the populist crap."

"Don't have much choice, do I?"

"Hey, don't be like that. Trust me. We'll meet up at, uh, let's say midnight. Behind the bougainvillea bushes, top end of the beach."

"I need to copy that stuff off the laptop."

"Leave it to me. I'll make you a copy. Go mingle."

"Midnight?"

"That's it. Go!"

It was, Dolt found, something of a relief to detach himself from his subversive taskmaster and fold himself suavely into the elegant, sophisticated and highly coiffured company that he encountered on the lawn beyond the pool — even if he were now spying not merely for Des but also for Jeff. Did that make him a double agent? Or simply overworked?

Everyone knew who he was, he noted; they all had the same tight little smile for him. But no one seemed to want to talk to him. All he got was the smile, the nod and the turned back. Until, that is, he descended, via an extravagant rockery, from the lawn to the terrace at the rear of the house.

"Hey!"

The voice seemed to emanate from above.

"Up here!"

He looked up. Above him was a large, twisty tree of some luxuriant tropical variety that Dolt couldn't identify. It spread out over the roof of the house. Hidden in amongst the branches and leaves was some kind of structure.

"There's a ladder round the back."

Dolt located the ladder and ascended into what looked like a tree-house. But it wasn't one of those self-assembly death-traps that were always on sale at Big Builder. This one had a couch, a TV, Wi-Fi, a built-in mini-bar, a gas-powered barbecue and an open-air shower. Draped across the couch was a rangy figure with a loosened tie and a cigarette. It was Howard Hooper, the loose-lipped supremo of Green Lake Robotics.

"Come on up!"

He made room for Dolt on the couch, poured him a glass of champagne and lit up a second cigarette.

"Here," he said, offering it to Dolt. "This is the only place it's allowed."

Dolt took the cigarette, sat and sipped his champagne.

"What a hero!" Hooper said. "Boy, do we owe you!"

"You do?"

"Big time. This is just between you and me. Andy was crappin' himself. Don't tell anyone I said that. He was telling the big shots everything was fine, but it wasn't. We were losing control of the big guys, they were crashing — and all because of one rogue programmer."

"Fancy that."

"Yeah! One guy!"

Hooper, rather like Prickler, sounded as if he'd started the night early, so Dolt decided to push his luck.

"I suppose you had to fire him. What was his name, again?"

"Fire him! You're a funny guy."

"Fred, was it?"

"What? No, no. Some Arab name. Abdel, that's it."

"But everything's fixed now?"

"Perfecto. I just got a message from our people. They ran a complete level-five test. Hundred per cent score."

Dolt took a long puff on his cigarette. He'd given up, obviously — but this was work.

"Great," he said, with fake enthusiasm.

"If you hadn't intercepted that memory stick, well, I guess we'd be pulling the plug right about now!"

The memory stick? A queasy feeling rose in Dolt's stomach, and it wasn't the cigarette.

"We were *that* close," Hooper said, leaning towards Dolt and slopping his champagne on Dolt's knee.

"I expect a lot of people would've been upset."

"Upset! You English guys, with your understatement. You crack me up. Can you imagine? Purdo? Moreland? The whole Rancho Colorado crew? They're invested up to here!"

Hooper made a descriptive gesture with his cigarette hand. Dolt brushed the ash off his shoulder.

"Well, I'm glad," Dolt said, subtly, "that you found what you needed on the stick."

"You mean the original code? Well, duh. That fucker Abdel deleted all the backups. Or maybe it was that sister of his. Don't matter now, anyhow. It's time to celebrate. D'you like country music? Have some more grape juice."

"Thanks."

The truth hurt. Aisha's brother had nobbled the big drones. But he, Dolt, had put them back in business. The thought of what Des would say when Dolt reported back caused him to tremble inwardly — until he recalled that it was Des himself who'd ordered him to hand the stick over to *Faith Boy*. And as for Jeff...

As he pondered the enormity of this, Dolt was distracted by the sound of boots on the ladder. A pink cowboy hat rose into view. Prettily arranged underneath were blond curls, blue eyes, and what was probably a scientifically-enhanced pout.

"Hi there, boys."

It was — who else could it have been? — Reagan Pruett, guitar-shaped-pool-owner and mistress of revels.

"You boys like to hear some country music?"

"We can hear it just fine up here," Hooper said.

"Oh no. You got to come down, so's you can hear it proper."

"You gonna make us?"

"I know what you bad boys are doing up here."

"Oh no, you don't."

"With your smokes, an' stuff."

Oh stop it, Dolt thought, his mind full of drones and motorcycles, and the image of Aisha, still warm and sticky on a London pavement.

"How about you, John? You're Rand's special guest tonight. What do y'all wanna hear?"

"Huh?"

"What're your absolute favorite songs, John? I'll sing 'em special, just for you."

"My absolute favorites? Er, how about 'Baby You Can Be My Drone?' And, um, the one about the sub-prime heart?"

"Oh, I love to sing that one. Are you coming to Freedom Aid?"

"Freedom Aid?"

"I'll get you a back-stage pass. We got so many acts signed up. They're world-class, every last one. Maybe you can make one of your little speeches while they're changing sets?"

"It's a concert?"

"For charity. We're doing one show in Houston and one in London. It's to spread freedom in the War Zones."

"Freedom? In the War Zones?"

"I knew you'd agree to help. Here's a list of who's playing."

She handed Dolt a flyer and turned her attention to Hooper.

"Now then, Howard. You put that dirty cigarette out and come with me."

"Okay, darlin'. Whatever you say. I'll go down first."

"Oh no, you don't. *I'm* goin' first."

They descended the ladder, leaving Dolt alone with his flyer. Who were these *world-class acts?* He'd never heard of any of them.

But none of that mattered; what mattered were drones. Hooper had somehow uploaded the good code from the memory stick to Libya. And the drones, which had been grounded, were flying again. The March to War had stumbled, but regained its stride. What would it take to do another switcheroo and reinstate the nobbled code, if it were available? Could it be done? How? Dolt was hardly a computer expert; nor, he was sure, was Jeff. As for Des and his cheapskate masters — forget about it. There was, in fact, only one person Dolt had ever met who might have the remotest idea...

But before he could pursue this line of thought, the tree-house shuddered with the arrival of yet another visitor. It was Gideon.

"Ah, so *here* you are!"

"Hullo."

"Would you mind putting that out?"

Dolt stubbed his cigarette carelessly on the arm of the couch.

"What now?"

"Did you track down your intruder?"

"What? Oh, *that*. False alarm."

"Not that stalker chap after all?"

"No. Just someone who looked like him."

Gideon smiled one of his superior smiles.

"Jolly good. No need to inform security, then?"

"No. How's Faith Boy?"

"*What* did you call him?"

"That's his nickname around here. Didn't you know?"

Gideon frowned a superior frown.

"No. Anyway, he's staying in his room for now. He's going to listen to your speech from his window."

"Speech? What speech?"

Gideon flipped back to the smile.

"Rand has decided that, since you were the last person to see him alive, you should make some appropriate remarks in memory of Drake Strickland. A eulogy, as it were. And you can ad-lib on your own account, so long as you keep it brief."

"Must I?"

"I'm afraid so."

"Now?"

"Yes. Miss Pruett is waiting to perform."

The work never ended, did it?

"All right, then."

"Some good news from home, by the way..."

"Oh?"

"Your staff have been very busy on your behalf. Membership applications have surpassed all expectations."

"Membership? What of?"

"Your movement. There was a competition to pick the name. You selected the winner. John Dolt's *Home Guard*. What do you think?"

Dolt scrutinized his personal assistant. Was this a wind-up? No, apparently not.

"It has a very reassuring ring, don't you think?" Gideon said. "No doubt you'll achieve much with it. The first rally is already scheduled. But now we must move on. Miss Pruett is not a lady — as she puts it — to *mess* with."

Gideon began to descend the ladder. Dolt, in a spasm of moral weakness that did not accord well with his new role as the charismatic leader of a manufactured mass-movement, snatched up the cigarettes and lighter that Hooper had abandoned and stuffed them in his trouser pocket.

Back on the ground, Dolt was conducted by credentialed minions to a flag-bedecked podium, erected above the rock garden, facing the house. Below, on the terrace, an expectant crowd had gathered.

It was at this point that Dolt caught his first-ever glimpse of the man to whom he owed everything: His mentor, sponsor, booster, backer, guiding light and all-purpose sugar-daddy; the man who — to borrow Jeff's memorable phrase — had his hand up Dolt's ass.

Rand Purdo was a fine specimen, of something or other; it was impossible to deny that. He was older than Dolt — he might have been anything from sixty to eighty — but, compared to Dolt, he was taller, thinner, fitter and way more handsome. He had far better hair and more of it; his gray temples speaking to physical and mental prowess, rather than simple rattiness. His forehead, as smooth as the boardroom table in an investment bank, spoke of power; his granite brows, expertly tended, whispered of dominion; and his chin, fashioned from surplus battleship parts, told a tale of relentless, unyielding accumulation. Had Dolt ever seen colder, grayer eyes, or whiter, more inhuman teeth? Were those limbs robotic, like the drones? And where did all that animal energy come from? That supra-human potency? Some secret, priceless additive in the blood?

Purdo joined Dolt on the podium and, without wasting time on niceties, preliminaries or eye-contact, gave him a firm and proprietorial slap on the shoulder.

"You can say your piece now."

Dolt stepped up to the microphone. As he did so, he surveyed his audience. What he saw in their upturned faces was a mixture of curiosity, neediness, condescension and fear. Here was quite a contrast, he couldn't help but reflect, with the reaction he'd engendered in the riotous mob at the premiere of *The Face of Freedom*. These, of course, were people who felt no need to riot. Or who, if they did, would do so in quite a different way — beginning, perhaps, by calling their *brokers*. But why did they fear him — and they did, didn't they? Perhaps because he was like the tradesman called in to do a dirty job; they were afraid he'd leave a nasty mess behind.

"I have been asked," he began, "to say a few words. A few words about a man who was a glowing example to us all."

Dolt waited for a reaction from his listeners. There was a murmur of approval. At his top-floor window, the former PM nodded sympathetically. Dolt opened his mouth to resume, but hesitated, distracted by a movement at the far end of the upper veranda. A branch swaying in the breeze? Local wildlife?

"I did not know Drake Strickland as long as some of you here," Dolt continued, "but, by the end, he was a friend of mine, and I felt I knew what really made him tick..."

No, it was a human shape. Someone was crawling stealthily along the upper veranda — someone with very large feet.

"Drake was a bloke who wasn't afraid to give you a piece of his mind," Dolt went on, "whoever you were and whether he knew you or not..."

This crack got a few nervous laughs. What the hell was Jefferson Crockett doing up on the veranda? Did he have any idea he was about to crawl under the former PM's nose?

"Drake used to get some smashing new idea," Dolt continued, upping the volume slightly, "and people would say, *stop! Don't go there!*"

He paused to see if Jeff had got the message. But no — like a penguin that had missed its lunch and was eager to get back in amongst the fish, he was still on the move.

"But would Drake listen? No! You're *going in the wrong direction*, they used to tell him. *Turn around now*, or it's all going to *blow up in your face!*"

Jeff paused on the veranda. A shiver of relief ran down Dolt's spine. But his listeners, he noticed, were beginning to shuffle their feet. Then Jeff raised his hand, gave Dolt a furtive thumbs-up, and recommenced his slow advance on *Faith Boy*.

"And yet Drake," Dolt said, a note of desperation in his voice now, "*wouldn't bloody listen*, would he? Oh, no. Not even if he was *hurtling into disaster*. Not even if he was about to *crash and burn* —"

"Thank you for that," Purdo said.

Dolt felt himself propelled from the podium. Someone grabbed him by the elbow and dragged him into the shadows. It was Gideon.

"What was *that* all about? What were you thinking? Tact, John! Tact, for heaven's sake!"

Dolt didn't reply. As he watched, Jeff edged closer to the former PM's window. Meanwhile, a huge cheer went up from the crowd; Purdo had stepped up to the microphone.

"Friends," he said, "the moment we've all been working towards — you, me, and, uh, our wonderful new friend from England — is almost here. I hope you've all spoken to your brokers!"

A peal of laughter rang around the terrace.

"Seriously, though," Purdo said, "we stand on the threshold of a new era of liberty. Liberty in Central and South America. Liberty in the Greater Persian region. But that's not all. We're gonna have liberty at home, too!"

Dolt wanted to avert his eyes, but he couldn't; Jeff was almost within touching distance of the former PM.

"When I first heard the idea," Purdo said, "I thought it was crazy. But the more I thought about it, the more sense it made. This guy from England — he's... Well, whatever else he is, he's a genius. Let's just see how they all do without us! Who's gonna join me on strike? Put your hands up!"

A great roar went up. And a forest of bejeweled arms. Up on the veranda, Jeff crouched, momentarily distracted by the noise, right under the former PM's window. Dolt winced.

"Thank you," Purdo said. "Together we can make a difference."

He picked up his notes and launched into his prepared speech.

"There was once a time," Purdo said, and the pathos and incredulity in his voice were palpable, "when corporations were not considered people. Now, some may regard that as a dark stain on our history. I say, what makes our concept of liberty so exceptional is that we continue to perfect it..."

He tailed off because a shriek of terror had pierced the night. All heads swiveled in the direction of the upper veranda.

"Aargh! It's *him! Help!*"

Someone, somewhere, activated a spotlight. Caught it in, Jeff froze — all of him, that is, except his head, which jerked this way and that, as if he were searching, in extremis, for the one person in the mob who wouldn't vote to rip him to shreds on the spot.

"John," Gideon said, "I thought you said..."

Dolt's mind raced; could Jeff be saved? He'd barely begun to address this poser when he heard a *whump* from the far end of the terrace and felt a flash of heat on his face. The tree-house had exploded into flames.

He released himself from Gideon's grip and ran towards the house.

"FIRE!"

As he ran, he saw the tree-house topple out of its tree and strike the veranda, shattering on impact and scattering fiery embers in all directions. The veranda sagged. Jeff had vanished.

All was now commotion. But it was imperative, Dolt felt, that he give Jeff the news about the drones, unwelcome as it would certainly be. Dodging hysterical party-goers and frantic security goons, he took advantage of the general confusion to slip unobserved to the rendezvous site.

Jeff was already there. He was tugging at a bulky, black object.

Dolt yelled at him.

"Jeff!"

Jeff jumped back in alarm.

"Yes, I know, I know! I screwed up! You were trying to warn me. I get it now —"

He broke off, distracted.

"Wow. Look at that. The whole house is going up. Jeez. Wonder how that got started."

"*I* don't know," Dolt said. "Why are you looking at me?"

Yes, it was another mysterious blaze. So what?

"Get anything on Ecuador?" Jeff asked, tugging again at the black object.

"No," Dolt said. "What's that?"

"Inflatable dinghy. *I* got something. The coup's two days from now. I gotta get to Ecuador."

"What, in *that?*"

"No, idiot. In the mother ship."

Mother ship? Let it go, he thought. The thing was to give Jeff the bad news. For that, he would require another of Hooper's cigarettes. He lit one up.

"Um, Jeff? Bit of a problem. You know those drones..."

"Yeah?"

"Well, Abdel — that's Aisha's brother..."

"What about him?"

Jeff seemed to struggle with his dinghy.

"Want any help with that?"

"No. What about Abdel?"

"Well, he was some sort of programmer at the drone base."

"And?"

"He nobbled the code, didn't he?"

"Nobbled?"

"Yes. He made the drones crash. The big ones."

Jeff let go of the dinghy and approached Dolt.

"What? That's great news!"

"Not really."

"No? Why not?"

"They got the code back."

"How?"

"It was on the stick I gave to Faith Boy. Ow!"

He said "ow!" because Jeff had shoved him backwards. Luckily, the dinghy broke his fall.

"You stupid fuck!"

"I didn't know! Des told me —"

"Okay, okay. It wasn't your fault. I'm sorry."

For a few moments there was silence, but for the distant crackling of R-Pru's mansion. Then Dolt heard a flatulent *phut*, followed by a throaty whistling sound.

Jeff tensed.

"What was that?"

Dolt realized that his cigarette had burned a hole in the dinghy.

"Ah..." he said, standing and stepping lightly out on to the sand. Then they watched as Jeff's escape vehicle deflated.

"You really need to give up smoking," Jeff said — and it sounded like he meant it.

"Yes, well..."

"Just shut up a moment."

Jeff pulled out a mobile phone and dialed a number. While he waited for the call to connect he paced the sand and the dinghy breathed its last.

"Peggy? It's Jeff. Put Isabel on, will you? Thanks..."

"Who're you talking to?"

"The mother ship."

Right...

"Isabel? Yeah. No, look... Listen will, you? No. No, I need you to..."

Jeff wandered off into the shadows. When he returned, he looked subdued. Dolt glanced back at R-Pru's mansion. There wasn't going to be much left in the morning, he thought. Why hadn't the sprinklers activated? They were all over the place.

"Here's your copy," Jeff said, handing Dolt a memory stick.

"Thanks."

"How do we figure out if the *nobbled* code is on here?"

"Dunno."

"How do we *upload* it again?"

"No idea."

"Shit. We need a computer expert."

Dolt drew a circle in the sand with his toe — something Jeff would have found difficult at best.

"Well, there is this bloke I know..."

He was thinking of Lescek, of course.

"A bloke? Does he know what he's doing?"

"Oh yes. He does high-energy physics. And bathrooms."

"Bathrooms?"

"He has a thing about tiles —"

"Never mind the tiles. Get him. Give me your cell phone number."

As they exchanged numbers, Dolt became aware of a high-pitched buzzing. It seemed to come from the ocean.

"Okay, I got to leave you now," Jeff said. "I'll call from Ecuador."

"Say hello to the President for me."

"Yeah, right. Good luck with your populist bullshit."

"Thanks."

"Oh, and don't forget — South Africa!"

To Dolt's amazement, a girl in a red bathing suit had roared up on to the beach astride a power jet-ski. Jeff discarded his footwear and ran towards her. There followed a brief and vituperative argument, after which Jeff flung himself into the rear seat and the machine took off again for the open sea — presumably to dock with the mother ship, anchored unseen in international waters.

As he watched this craft and its quarrelsome crew disappear into the gloom, Dolt heard someone calling his name. Gideon, naturally. Dolt snatched up Jeff's abandoned shoes and flung them into the bougainvillea bushes — just in time, as it turned out.

"John — what are you doing here?"

"Just wanted to get away from the smoke."

"Get away for a smoke?"

"No — *from* the smoke."

"Oh. Pardon me." He seemed to notice the airless dinghy. "Is that yours?"

"No."

"Then whose..."

"No idea."

"Well, never mind."

"Shame about the house."

"Yes, isn't it? State-of-the-art sprinkler system, and yet... It appears the previous owner deactivated it and no one remembered to turn it on again."

"Oops."

"Quite. One sympathizes with Miss Pruett, of course, but our own fortunes are on the up."

"Really?"

"Yes. Excellent news, John. Someone — I couldn't possibly say who — relayed your tribute to the late Mr. Strickland to one of the social media outlets that Amber Pike's staff just happen to monitor closely. I'm told she was much moved. The upshot is, you're to be her guest of honor at the rally of the New Patriot Movement tomorrow."

CHAPTER 34

I t was too dangerous, Jay said, to go out by day. Even at night it would be hazardous. It wasn't so much that the big drones had regained their mojo; if Andy wanted to sterilize Kufra, he could. But he wouldn't. He didn't have the local resources for the clean-up, and it could give the game away too soon. The threat, practically speaking, came from your smaller, everyday drones. These, Jay said, were considered violent enough for most purposes.

On their way back to the Colonel's anonymous compound on the fringe of town, Bonnie DiAngelo saw the proof of this for herself.

So they stayed indoors. Jay and the Colonel discussed plans. The Colonel's kids did house-work and weapons-cleaning. Annie sat alone, still and silent. Bonnie prepared some food.

The small drones could erase a house or punch an eight-foot hole in a road. They flew very high, and you couldn't hear them. Rarely would you see them, either. But they could see you. They could zoom in on your phone and read the numbers you were dialing. At night, they could track your heat signature. So if you lived in Kufra, now, this is what you had to consider. Who fed the drones their targets? What was the quality of their information? Did you feel lucky tonight? And even now, as she stepped away from the kitchen counter with her tray of food, who could say that her journey to the dining table would not terminate in premature vaporization or dismemberment?

Not this time, at least.

As they ate, she asked Jay and the Colonel what they'd come up with.

"We can't destroy the base. We can't get to the drones. We can't disable the runway."

"What *can* you do?"

"Damage their communications. But they'll fix it in a couple of hours."

Bonnie looked at her daughter. She sat at the table, eating silently.

"Annie? How did Abdel pull off that trick with the software?"

Annie shook her head, without looking up.

"You'd need the source code," Jay said. "You'd need to know how to upload it."

"Jay, you remember that cell phone we found? In the wreckage, in the Danakil?"

"I still have the card from it."

"What's on it?"

"You know, I'm ashamed to admit it, but I haven't even looked. But even if I did — it's not exactly my field."

"But if it was Abdel's phone..."

"Uh-huh. Maybe. But we'll need some help."

Bonnie glanced at her daughter again. Annie continued to eat, head down. The Colonel had finished. He leaned back in his chair with his eyes closed.

"Jay," she said, "I've got an idea."

"Well, speak up. Let's hear it."

"The Colonel's in the concrete business, correct? Ask him if he's got one of those big trucks."

"You mean, like, one of those things where they pour —"

"That's it."

Jay pushed his plate away, leaned on the table and scratched his forehead.

"Okay," he said. "I'll ask him."

He prodded the Colonel awake and spoke to him in Arabic. The Colonel listened, replied briefly, then closed his eyes and rocked back in his chair.

"He says he knows where he can get one, but if you want a house there are plenty of nice ones for sale at good prices."

"Funny guy. Look, Jay — tell me something. You saw all that *stuff* in the bunker. How do you destroy something like that?"

"Not so easy."

"Drop a bomb on it?"

"Disaster. Air's poisoned for hundreds of miles."

"What, then?"

"Call in the experts from the UN."

"Or just bury it in concrete."

Jay smiled.

"Well, I like the way you think, Bonnie. But they'll dig it out in a couple of days."

The Colonel stirred and muttered something.

"Okay, he says three to four days, if you use the quick-setting stuff."

"As I see it," Bonnie said, "that buys us some time. Right?"

Jay started to clear the dishes.

"Well, you got me. I don't have any superior ideas. So let's do it. The Concrete King and I will see to it. You better stay here with your, uh, daughter."

"No, Jay. It was my idea. And I'm not letting you out of my sight again."

"Then what about *her?*"

"She comes too."

Jay looked at Annie. She had finished eating, but she hadn't looked up.

"Well, okay. Maybe she can help. Though she doesn't seem too talkative."

"She didn't know about the chemicals."

"She didn't? Huh."

"So when do we set out?"

Jay turned to the Colonel. The Colonel puffed out his cheeks momentarily, then gave his opinion.

"We reckon Andy has his dinner around eight," Jay said. "So, tomorrow, that's when we'll go."

"He won't be there."

Annie had spoken. Jay stared at her. The Colonel opened one eye.

"He won't?" Jay said.

Annie looked up.

"He'll be at his daughter's wedding. In South Carolina."

For a moment, no one spoke.

"Interesting thing to note," Jay said. "Even people like Andy have families."

Families, Bonnie thought. Did Jay ever have one?

"So who'll be in charge?" she said.

Annie turned to look at her mother.

"General Kadiya."

CHAPTER 35

John Dolt had no problem with the *land*; it lay plainly in sight — vast, brown, flat and empty to the horizon. But where was the *heart?* The atmosphere in the Senior Cabin, during the flight from Barbados to Kansas, had been subdued.

The former PM, having been frightened not once but twice in the same evening by the barging-in and popping-up of his gangly nemesis, the idiosyncratic leftist *blogger*, Jefferson Crockett, hadn't felt much in the mood for conversation. (Jeff's alarming attire couldn't have helped, Dolt felt.) Instead, having first secured Dolt's earnest pledge to *sort out* the Crockett issue once and for all, he'd buried himself in deep study — his chosen road to self-improvement on this occasion being Amber Pike's seminal masterpiece, *Exceptional*. He must have found it instructive: A snort of incredulity here, and a sniff of cynicism there — these told Dolt as much.

And, of course, the party at R-Pru's mansion had not ended well — especially not for the mansion, which had been utterly destroyed in a mysterious blaze. Nor had the flames spared Reagan Pruett's priceless guitar collection. This, and her consequent inability to perform "Your Sub-Prime Heart's Gonna Foreclose On Our Love," had understandably impacted her mood. She had pointed the finger of blame, according to Gideon — who seemed to take an odd pride in the fact — at Howard Hooper. Purdo, whose pre-victory speech had been curtailed, was equally displeased. Recriminations had abounded. None, however, had attached to Dolt, whose celebration of the life and self-sacrifice of Drake Strickland, aka Prickler, had necessarily to be considered the evening's high point and one true success.

Privately, of course, Dolt had achieved much more: He'd acquired a new and potentially useful — if eccentric — partner in Jeff Crock, the unlikely emissary of the President of Ecuador; he'd recovered Aisha's data; and he'd learned the awful secret of the drone code. This meant that he had to make two phone calls of the utmost delicacy when circumstances permitted — one to Lescek, and one to Des.

285

For now, though, as he and Gideon rode, once again, in the unarmored limo at the tail-end of the former PM's motorcade, and they exited the eerily uninhabited airport at Topeka and began to speed, in a straight line, across the great vacancy of the heartland, there was little to do but look out of the window.

The sky lowered, full of dark and impatient clouds. Gusts of wind blew puffs of gray-brown dirt across the flatness. Gideon turned on the limo's air-conditioning.

"Terribly warm here for the time of year," he said. "They can't say why, apparently."

A lone, desolate structure loomed at the side of the road.

"What's that?" Dolt asked.

"Looks like a grain elevator."

"What happened to it?"

"Must have had a fire."

Another mysterious blaze.

They drove for another hour until they reached the former cornfield that someone who knew about these things had selected as the site of the great pre-election rally of the New Patriot Movement.

What Dolt immediately noticed, as they encountered a traffic snarl of camper-vans, pickup trucks and RVs, and a policeman directed the limo into a special lane, was that there were two sorts of New Patriot: Ordinary Patriots and Very Important Patriots. Despite being foreigners, he, Gideon and the former PM fell into the latter category. They sped past the queues into the cornfield.

A vast open-air arena had been created. At its focal point was the stage — a flat-bed truck, decorated with flag-draped hay bales and agricultural implements. Behind the stage was a roofed, terraced stand containing what Dolt took to be the VIP seating. At the top of the stand were glassed-in boxes where uniformed staff busied themselves. To either side of the stage were towering walls of hay bales, bedecked with the largest flags Dolt had ever seen. These walls served a dual purpose, however: They screened the VIP village to the rear of the stage from the ordinary gaze of the Ordinary Patriots who were busy installing their tents, folding chairs and coolers among the stalks and clods of the former cornfield.

Once admitted to the VIP zone, Dolt and Gideon found themselves separated from the former PM.

"He's having a quick one-on-one with Amber," Gideon said, as they strolled along an aluminum walkway to the main hospitality tent, "then he's flying out again. He has an important function to attend."

"Oh?" Dolt said. "Not a memorial, by any chance?"

"No. Why would you think that? It's a wedding, if you must know."

"Who's getting hitched?"

"Grover Purdo and Amanda Willoughby-St. John."

"*Grover?*"

"That's right. Rand's son."

"What does he do?"

"He's Rand's son."

"Who's Amanda?"

"No one you need be concerned about."

It was disingenuous of Dolt to ask, of course; it was easy to surmise that Amanda was the daughter of *Andy*, the implacable and now fully-empowered master of the Libyan skies. Talk about keeping it in the family. But Gideon didn't know that Dolt knew about Andy.

"Quick dash down the registry office, is it?"

"Very droll, John. It's a rather lavish affair, as I understand it. In South Carolina."

South Carolina — the home of Fair Meadow Solutions, drone-makers to the stars.

"Why weren't we invited?" Dolt asked.

"It's a purely personal occasion. Friends and family only."

"Oh. Right."

Dolt might qualify, for now, as a Very Important Patriot. But he wasn't *friends* and he wasn't *family*.

Inside the hospitality tent, they were shown to a table and presented with a menu of complimentary selections. Gideon flapped a white linen napkin on to his lap and picked up the wine list. Dolt thought of the mob outside, with their coolers and paper towels.

"When do we get to meet Amber?" he said.

"She's busy with her foreign policy team until lunchtime."

"Foreign policy? But she's not actually standing for election, is she?"

"Oh no. No more than you are. Perish the thought."

"Then why does she need a foreign policy team?"

Gideon ordered a half-bottle of something fruity from Washington State.

"To help her decide on her choices."

"Choices?"

"Later today, she'll announce which candidates she endorses. And — more importantly — which ones she doesn't."

"So she's telling people how to vote?"

"Yes."

"But shouldn't they make their own minds up?"

"You have to remember, John, that we're dealing with *low-information* voters here. They need a little guidance."

That again. Gideon seemed to share the former PM's view.

"But how come they don't have any information? I mean, you've got media everywhere, these days."

"Yes. It's a paradox, isn't it?"

"What about the candidates? Do they have to do what she says?"

"If they want her endorsement."

"So she has power but no responsibility?"

"Ha, ha. Very funny, John."

"Is it? Why?"

"Never mind."

Gideon's merlot arrived.

"Like a drop?"

"No thanks. Know where the gents' is?"

"Over there."

"Back in a moment."

But the gents' was too busy for Dolt's main purpose. While Gideon was reading the label on his wine bottle, Dolt slipped out of the hospitality tent. With his laminated ID prominently on display, he roamed the village, looking for a quiet spot. Such was the level of activity, however, that he quickly despaired of finding anywhere suitable.

An inviting tent turned out to house an argumentative table full of men and women in suits. A single empty chair and a map of the Greater Persian region told him that this was Amber's foreign policy team warming up before the match.

Further on, in a trailer labeled Melmotte Global Capital, a raucous party was in progress. Four colorful wigwams constructed under a banner reading *Invest In Uzbekistan!* were guarded by two off-putting heavies. Finally, Dolt located a crack in the steel perimeter fencing, squeaked through it and scaled the outer wall of hay bales.

The signal on his spy-phone was barely viable by this point, so he crouched against the bales and started dialing.

"Lescek?"

"Who is calling?"

"It's me, Lescek. John. I need —"

"John who?"

"John Dolt. Um, Lescek, I know —"

The line went dead. Dolt re-dialed. No answer. He tried again. Busy — Lescek had put him on the reject list.

He sighed, switched to full spy-fi mode and waited for Des to call.

"John!"

"Hello."

"Where are you?"

"I'm in a cornfield in Kansas."

"Kansas! You mean you're at the rally?"

"Didn't you know?"

"System problems. Don't ask. What's the latest?"

Dolt took a deep breath and explained how it had come to pass that Andy's nobbled drones had gained a new lease on life.

"No one's fault in particular," he said, summing up.

Des seemed to consider this point for a moment.

"Oh, fuck," he said. "Oh, fuck."

"Yes, but all is not lost," Dolt said.

"Isn't it? I thought you just said it was?"

"No. You see, I've got the nobbled code — well, I think I have. We can upload it again. All we need is a computer expert."

From the far end of the line came a muffled groan of anguish.

"Let me explain something to you," Des said. He launched into an impassioned and semi-coherent tirade in which the words *budget*, *Oxbridge* and *bastards* featured frequently. Dolt held his spy-phone away from his ear.

"And that is why we are totally fucked," Des concluded.

Dolt let the air clear for a moment.

"I know a computer expert," he said.

"You do? Then why didn't you fucking well say so?"

"Well —"

"Name?"

"Lescek."

"Give me his details."

Dolt gave Des Lescek's phone number, email and address.

"There's just one problem."

"What?"

"He doesn't want to talk to me."

"Why not?"

"Is that important right now?"

"No. I can guess, anyway. Leave it to me. I'll have a quiet chat with him."

"All right. You won't..."

"No, don't worry. I'll just make it worth his while."

It was one of those tough choices, Dolt reflected sadly, that top leaders like himself were obliged to make.

"So your priority now," Des said, "is this memorial. We know when — although something smells a bit funny there. Never mind. Find out who and where."

"How?"

"I don't know. Just keep doing what you've been doing. I mean, it sort of works, doesn't it?"

"I suppose so. Do I have to keep on with the populist stuff? Because it's —"

"Yes. For now. But it would be remiss of me not to warn you..."

"Warn me?"

"Yes. There are concerns. In certain circles..."

Concerns? Circles? *Circles?*

"For fuck's sake, Des!"

"All right, all right. It's the military brass. Some of them are getting cold feet. So... Just watch yourself, right?"

"Yeah, thanks a lot."

"Don't be like that. How's the exit strategy?"

"I've got someone working on it."

"You have? That sounds like progress. Well done."

Sincere? You could never be sure with Des.

"Is that it, then?"

"Yes," Des said. "Expect a call from Lescek."

"Oh — I nearly forgot. Would you like some intelligence about Ecuador?"

"Ecuador? Who gives a shit about Ecuador?"

"Right. Okay. Bye, then."

"Bye."

Dolt ended the call and slumped against the bales. Des might be indifferent to the fate of Ecuador, but Jeff wasn't. Who was right? Among the challenges that came with politics at the top level was deciding who to ally yourself with. Whereas Dolt had once been intent on playing Des off against Gideon, he now faced a fully three-dimensional puzzle. And that was only if you didn't include the former PM, and — for all he knew — Amber Pike herself.

But, in moments of honesty like this, older, deeper allegiances tugged at him. What, after all, had really become of Hamid? What would Samira do? What did he owe to Aisha? What responsibility would he bear, should the Greater Persian region not enjoy liberty, democracy and free markets, but instead, by some mishap or other, turn into another War Zone? And what price might he have to pay one day for all the lies that had been told in his name?

The trouble with moments of honesty, he decided, was that they were a total downer. Did Amber Pike have moments of honesty? The evidence said no. Bottom line? You could let it get to you. Or you could, like Amber, and as Des had cynically recommended, embrace the *dark side*.

Behind the bales, the sounds of another party bubbled up — not raucous enough, Dolt judged, for Melmotte Global Capital, but too light-hearted for *Invest in Uzbekistan!* Perhaps Amber's foreign policy team had scored a victory.

But then, from his right, came a different sound — a growling, urgent rumbling. He looked. The noise got louder; it was the revving and idling of powerful engines. Then, from around a curve in the line of bales, they appeared: Two fearsome, American-style (of course they had them here — what had he been thinking?) motorcycles. The ones with the extra-long handle-bars. The ones with the enormous back wheels. The ones with tassels dangling from the handgrips, and skulls painted on the tank. Their riders wore aviator shades, black leather — no surprise there, really — and retro open-face helmets in patriotic colors.

Dolt didn't need to think. He took to his heels.

With his legs and heart pumping, and the blood pounding in his ears, he tore across the emptiness of the cornfield, stumbling on the parched dirt and scraping his ankles against dried-up corn stalks. Behind him, just on the edge of his vision, the motorcycles purred and zipped. They could have out-run him with a flick of the wrist, but they were toying with him, taunting him.

He tripped, fell and ripped his jacket — a lightweight, padded outdoorsman's number sent on ahead by Jacqueline. The motorcycles circled at a distance, like crows sizing up a wounded rabbit. He got up and began to run again, lungs aching. Why run when it was futile? It had to be pure instinct; he couldn't help it.

The motorcycles shot ahead of him and doubled back, cutting across his path and then skewing around, their back wheels flinging dirt in his face. They wanted to tire him out, he knew. But he kept going until his vision began to blur and exhaustion felled him.

As he lay on the ground, chest heaving, he heard the motorcycles swooping, closing in on him. At length, they puttered to a halt, one either side of him, and their engines shut off. There came the squeak of leather as the riders kicked their stands down and dismounted. Boots crunched over the crusty soil. Dolt froze and closed his eyes.

When he opened them again — nothing had happened and the suspense was killing him — they were standing over him, helmets off but shades still on. It was curious, Dolt thought, just how much they resembled aging movie stars; they looked like actors from a nineteen-seventies road movie.

"You are Mr. John Dolt of England?" one of them said.

Dolt hesitated — but it was obvious that they knew.

"Well, basically, yes."

There was an exchange of glances. Then the second motorcyclist spoke.

"And how are you enjoying your stay in our great country?"

The obvious answer, Dolt thought, was probably the wrong one.

"Um, having quite a good time, actually, thanks."

"We're sure glad to hear that. We wouldn't want you to have a *bad* time."

He turned to his colleague and they started into a kind of double-act.

"Would we?"

"Most assuredly not."

"It therefore behooves us, wouldn't you agree, to give Mr. Dolt here some helpful advice?"

"A travel advisory, you mean?"

"That's a neat way of putting it. Mr. Dolt needs to know where to go and where not to go."

"Because we would hate for him to get into trouble."

"We surely would. Shall we point out some places he should avoid at all costs?"

"Yes sir, indeed we should. It's only fair."

"Amber's cabin, for example. That's definitely a no-no."

Amber's cabin! How did they know about that? What were they getting at in their annoyingly sardonic and humorous way?

"You are correct, sir. But it would also be a mistake for him to get up on that big old stage over there and start blabbing on about things concerning which he has, in truth, very little knowledge."

"You know what they say about a little knowledge."

"Exactly. And the one place he should absolutely not go is..."

"The Greater Persian region?"

"That's right. Because..."

"It would be very perilous for him."

"We wouldn't want him to be imperiled."

"Not at all. And the best way not to be imperiled is..."

"To stop banging the drums of war? Just my opinion."

"You know what? I think you just nailed it. And when he goes home to England, what should he advise his pal, the Prime Minister?"

"He should advise him to shut the fuck up about being happy to participate in another American war. *Successful* or otherwise."

"Right. But he should say it nicer than that."

"Yeah. Sure. Pardon my French."

Dolt had had enough. He sat up.

"You two," he said. "Are you *dissidents?*"

The motorcyclists looked at each other again.

"Not as dumb as he looks, is he?"

"I guess not. Has he got the message, though? That's my concern."

"I think he has."

"Great. Want to take a ride into town, get a sandwich?"

"Sure. Do you think he'd like a ride back to the village?"

"Nah. Look at him. He needs to lose a pound or two. Ready?"

They started to put their helmets back on.

"Hang on a minute!" Dolt said.

But they ignored him, mounted their bikes and roared off across the cornfield, leaving twin clouds of dust behind.

Dolt struggled to his feet. He looked a mess, he realized — dirt, scratches, shredded clothing. More perplexing, though, was his new predicament. Both camps — pro-war and anti-war — were now threatening him. Both sides came equipped with motorcycles. The dissidents' bikes were cooler and more stylish, but that was beside the point. What was he supposed to do? Was he really going to stand on that *big old* stage, alongside Amber Pike, with the massed ranks of the New Patriot Movement hanging on his every word, and say that, oh well, perhaps war *wasn't the best option after all*, and what with one thing and another...

And it wasn't like asking Gideon or Jeff for advice would help. Purdo had referred to Dolt as a *genius*. What a joke. But if he ever needed a stroke of genius, it was now.

Doggedly, he slogged back across the cornfield to the village. But the motorcycle chase had disoriented him, and he couldn't find his way back in. Too weary to search, he simply clambered to the top of the wall of bales, finding himself just to the side of the VIP seating. The bales here were covered with some kind of cloth, so he sat and gazed down into the arena. A vast and enthusiastic crowd had gathered — and they were still coming. He'd never seen so many flags, portable barbecues or baseball hats. Music blared from loudspeakers; he realized he was listening to "Baby You Can Be My Drone." It wasn't that bad, he thought. As he listened, his feet began to tap. Then his phone rang. It was Gideon.

"John, are you all right? You're not still in the —"

"No, no. Just went for a stroll. Get some air."

"Where are you now?"

Dolt told him.

"What on Earth are you — Never mind. Just wait for me."

"Okay."

Dolt hung up. Then he pulled out Hooper's cigarettes from his trouser pocket and lit up. It was going to be one of those days.

Moments later, Gideon materialized on the VIP terrace. There was a stony look on his face.

"John," he said, "from where I'm standing, you appear to be sitting, in a warm and gusty breeze, on top of a very large, very publicly-visible American flag, which is itself draped over an enormous stack of tinder-dry bales of hay, with a lighted cigarette in your hand. Do you really think that's wise?"

"What? All right. I'll stub it out."

"No, no, no! Come here and give it to me."

"Fine."

Dolt clambered from the bales into the VIP stand. Gideon snatched his cigarette away and then took a step back, the stony look mutating into one of shock.

"What happened to you?"

"I, er, I fell over."

"Did you? You know, I've been getting complaints from Jacqueline. She's demanding an increase in the clothing budget."

"Sorry."

"Yes. Well, come and get cleaned up. You can't meet Amber looking like that."

Dolt permitted Gideon to lead him back to the VIP village, where Gideon extinguished Dolt's cigarette in an ornamental fountain. There followed a clean-up session in the gents'. Dolt couldn't help but be impressed: Gideon would have made an excellent butler, valet or nanny. Had he learned all these tricks at the knee of his own nanny or valet, perhaps?

On exiting the gents', they ran into the former PM, who now looked more like his old self.

"Ah, John! Just the guy I was looking for!"

There followed a polite tussle for possession of Dolt, which the former PM won. Dolt followed him back to his private trailer.

"Not bad, is it?" the former PM said, as Dolt made himself comfortable in a leather swivel chair. "Not as nice as Amber's, but, well... I suppose it's really *her* day, after all. Wonder how much they cost?"

"You wished to speak to me?" Dolt said, hoping to maintain the upper hand in this relationship by adopting a superior tone.

"Yes. Just a couple of quick ones. About Crockett. I was just wondering if you'd been able —"

"As it happens," Dolt said, "I have just had a quiet conversation with two of his associates."

The former PM seemed to be studying the scratches on Dolt's face.

"Really? Wow. I guess you warned them —"

"More or less. There was an understanding."

"Cool. Great. Er, where is he now?"

"My information is that he has gone into hiding. Somewhere in South America."

"Gosh, that's excellent. I mean, thanks — what can I say? You guys..."

"You're welcome."

"Can't understand how he disappeared like that, though. It was as if he beamed up into a spaceship..."

"It was something like that."

"I suppose you can't reveal —"

"No. What was the other thing?"

"Oh, right. Well, I just had — I guess you'd call it an *audience*, you know, with Amber. And, well, it's a bit difficult to understand her sometimes, but what I got was that she's a bit concerned that Downing Street isn't being supportive enough. You know, on the GPQ. Publicly, at least."

"Really? Go on."

"So, obviously, I said I'd been using all my influence. And she said she wanted to endorse the Global Faith Initiative as an official Freedom-Loving Partner of the New Patriot Movement — I can't tell you how much that would mean to us, obviously — but there was just this issue of the GPQ. Of course, I said to her, look — we're actually supposed to be in different parties and all that —"

"Different parties, yes..."

"But I guess that wasn't really what she wanted to hear. And, anyway, the bottom line is, I said *you* really have more influence than I do. And she said, well, get on to John, then."

"I see. And this endorsement for the GFI..."

"Would be magic. Brilliant. Do you think you could..."

"Get Downing Street to big up the GPQ in public?"

"Yes, a bit. If you wouldn't mind. If *you* tell them, they'll have to listen. I mean, they've seen the polls..."

Dolt drew a long, slow breath and clasped his hands together with exaggerated seriousness.

"I'll give it some serious thought."

"Great! Thanks!"

With the former PM feeling in his debt, Dolt realized, now was a good time to have a punt at doing Jeff Crock a favor and keeping him on-side. But he would have to lead up to it subtly.

"I hear you're going to a wedding?"

"That's right. Grover and Amanda. Great kids."

"South Carolina, is it?"

"Yes. The FMS campus — it's secure, they've got all the facilities. Parking. Chapel. Beautiful landscaping."

"Should be a fun day, then."

"Absolutely. Andy and Rand are pulling out all the stops. Southern barbecue, outdoor picnic, Reagan Pruett performing, bouncy castle for the kids. Aerobatic displays. You name it."

"Flying out soon?"

"Actually, we've been delayed. Some bad weather moving in, apparently."

Dolt saw his opening.

"Funny weather here for the time of year."

"Gosh, yes, isn't it?"

"Global warming, I suppose."

"Ah, well, some people would say so."

"Some people? Scientists, you mean?"

"Ha-ha, good joke, yes. Wouldn't try it on Amber, though! Friendly advice, know what I mean?"

"Amber not into science, then? Doesn't think it's important?"

The former PM cleared his throat and lowered his voice.

"Well, of course science is important, but, you know — if people have other views... What I always say is, you can't just ignore that."

The former PM flashed Dolt a cheese-eating grin.

"I suppose not. But you *are* attending the climate conference in Cape Town, I presume?"

The former PM hesitated. The grin froze on his face.

"But that's on the twenty-eighth."

"Yes."

"The twenty-eighth."

"Quite. Do you have a prior appointment?"

The grin faded from the former PM's face.

"As a matter of fact I..."

"You see," Dolt said, "I have been given special knowledge of a certain opportunity."

"Opportunity?"

Dolt paused strategically and narrowed his eyes.

"You are aware, I take it, of moves to encourage investment and economic what's-it in Uzbekistan?"

"Uzbekistan!"

"And you may, perhaps, have heard of a highly-regarded South African company by the name of Boschenkop?"

"Boschenkop!"

"And would it surprise you to learn that these two esteemed parties are currently seeking a trusted intermediary? Someone of high-class reputation and top-notch integrity, who could stitch a deal together? An international big-wig, as it were, with the appropriate contacts, who would be well-placed to manage certain sensitive aspects of the transaction? A transaction involving enormous piles of dosh?"

"Enormous!"

"It would be what you might call a *prestigious consultancy*."

"Prestigious!"

"Do you get my drift?"

He bloody well ought to, Dolt thought, after all that.

"Um, yes! Gosh..."

Dolt prepared the killer blow.

"But it has to be on the twenty-eighth. In Cape Town. Using the conference as cover."

The former PM's face fell.

"Ah. Right. Thing is, John, if Amber found out..."

Dolt folded his arms.

"*I* won't tell her."

"Wow, though. I mean, Uzbekistan!"

Dolt affected a frown.

"Isn't that the place where they boil people in oil?"

"Oh, that's greatly exaggerated. I always say it's better to engage with people, whatever the human rights lobby might want to moan about..."

"I'm sure you're right. All you need to do is book a flight to Cape Town and say you're observing the conference. Don't say a word to anyone. Except me."

"Right, right. Gosh, thanks, John! What would I do without you, eh?"

"Just doing my job."

Where had he learned such deviousness? In the pubs of Wembley and the lock-ups of Park Royal. The Club for Greed would have been impressed.

At that point, there was a polite tap on the door to the trailer. Dolt opened the door. It was Gideon.

"Amber's ready for you now."

*

Amber Pike's trailer was indeed much grander than the former PM's. She had an office area, a lounge with twin sofas, a kitchen, a bathroom, a large dressing room and, in one corner, a miniature basketball court with a hoop on the wall. Dolt found his gaze drawn irresistibly towards her as he entered. She sat behind an enormous desk on which there were three super-sized computer screens. Wearing her familiar deep-red suit, pearls and square glasses, she affected to study one of her screens and pretended not to notice Dolt as he approached.

Gideon had said that Amber didn't need glasses, but the glasses, nonetheless, performed an important function: They created a serious and intelligent *visual*, one that registered with people, regardless of any nagging disbelief they might have had in her seriousness or intelligence. It was one of those *subliminal* things. And the reflections prevented you from seeing her eyes too clearly — one's eyes being, of course, the windows to the soul. Dolt's view was simpler: They were a protective barrier, like double-glazing.

She let Dolt stand immobile before her desk for three perfectly-counted seconds before she noticed him.

"Oh, hi there! Didn't see ya come in! Take a seat on the sofa."

Dolt caught a glimpse of one of the screens. Amber, it appeared, had been checking out the latest customer reviews of *Exceptional*. He took his seat on the sofa. Amber made him wait for another minute, poking unconvincingly at her keyboard, before she joined him.

"So! You're that guy from England, then!"

"One of 'em, yeah."

"And how are you liking this, our great state that we have here?"

Gideon had warned Dolt that Amber's speaking style was more about imagery than syntax, so he was prepared for this.

"Can't get enough of it."

"That is so true. And how about this weather that is so strange that we are having?"

The temptation lay before him; he hadn't expected it quite so soon, but he remained strong.

"I know. Weird, innit?"

"This is a great honor that you, a foreigner, being here for our great rally today."

"Er, yes. Thanks!"

"We need, also, to stand firm, together on our freedoms and our democracies."

"Definitely. Couldn't have put it better."

Something drew Dolt's gaze to the window. The sky had darkened. Sheets of blue lightning flickered.

"And the Persians, also, are deserving our liberty and our freedom-loving."

"They are, aren't they?"

"And we should bring peace to them."

"Yes. In a way."

"After we have, also, defeated them. In the air, and surgically, also."

"Mm."

This was harder work than Dolt had anticipated. He felt compelled to take the initiative.

"About the GPQ. I've had my foreign policy team working on it, non-stop, and what they've come up with is rather interesting, I think."

Of course, Dolt's foreign policy team consisted exclusively of Dick, the rogue walrus at the Atlantic Affairs Institute, whose densely analytical emails, printed out for Dolt by Gideon, Dolt had cheerfully ignored. But Amber didn't know that.

"And how is it, that they are being interested?"

"The basic concept," Dolt said, "is nuance."

Amber tipped her head on one side, as if this were the new Word of the Day. "Nuance?"

"Yes. Instead of just banging the drums of war all the time, sometimes you bang the drums of peace. And you keep switching between 'em."

Amber was staring at him, mouth open, her eyelashes batting away behind their windshields.

"That gets 'em confused," Dolt said. "And, obviously, it works to our advantage."

His scheme, of course, was to get Amber confused, and thus evade the whole tricky GPQ issue. It seemed to be working. She shook her head.

"I'm not gettin' it."

Dolt indicated the basketball corner.

"It's like basketball," he said. "First you *dodge* this way, then you make a *feint* that way, and bingo. Ball in the net."

Amber perked up.

"Hey, wanna shoot some hoops?"

This wasn't the outcome Dolt had hoped for.

"C'mon! Scared a girl's going to beat ya?"

She leaped from her seat and grabbed a basketball from behind the sofa.

"C'mon, then! Show me what ya got!"

"Erm, all right."

Dolt joined her on the court and play commenced. He saw at once that it wasn't going to be an equal match. Despite her tight skirt and high heels, Amber rang rings around him — rather like the *dissidents* on their motorbikes, but with a lot more high-pitched laughter. Then, as he picked himself up off the floor for the fourth or fifth time, he remembered something. Many and tedious were the accounts in *Exceptional* of Amber's prowess in high school athletics. What was the punch line, again? Oh, right. Amber had been odds-on to win some trophy, but a jealous rival had bribed the judges. Naturally, Amber had burned with righteous anger at this injustice and had dedicated herself, etc., etc.

From outside came a rumble of distant thunder. A gust of wind rattled the trailer. Amber was leading eight-nil. Surely Dolt could score at least one basket, couldn't he?

Amber potted her ninth. As she was bending down to pick up the ball, Dolt accidentally-on-purpose bumped her on the hip and snatched the ball. Then he flung it with all his might in the general direction of the hoop — brute force, at this point, being his only hope. The ball cannoned off the ceiling, plummeted through the hoop, rebounded from the wall and the floor and, still traveling with an irresistible energy, rocketed directly towards Amber, striking her on the forehead with a convincing *thwack* and felling her in one.

She lay still, spread-eagled on the trailer's luxurious deep-pile carpeting. Another gust shivered the trailer. For one long moment, a sickly hand of dread gripped Dolt's innards and gave them a vicious twist. He hadn't felt anything like this since he got that last letter from Victoria's vile solicitor. But it quickly passed. Amber wasn't dead; she was dazed and considerably out-of-it, but otherwise unharmed. Well, all right, she had the letters "NBA" imprinted backwards on her forehead, but that would probably fade in time.

He knelt down.

"Erm, Amber? Are you okay?"

"Wha—? Who?"

On the sofa, he thought, *glass of water*. He scooped Amber up in his arms — she really wasn't that heavy — and stumbled towards the sofa. Having deposited her, he made for the kitchen, but Amber's computer screens caught his eye. Dare he? Well, a quick peek wouldn't hurt, would it?

On the first screen, it appeared that Amber had been *liking* and *disliking* reader reviews of *Exceptional*. The second screen showed the celebrity gossip page of some cable TV station. And the third displayed a mass of open windows. Dolt clicked through them. Upscale clothing retailers, various social networking sites, a blog called *LiberalsAteMyLunch* and a calendar. Dolt focused on the latter, flipping forward to October 28. And there it was: Great Leader State Memorial, London, England.

Great Leader? What Great Leader had snuffed it lately and yet needed to be remembered? It made no sense. Then Amber stirred; Dolt clicked away from the calendar and resumed his flight of mercy to the kitchen.

But then the trailer seemed to lose all sense of responsibility or proportion. The far end rose up, tipping Amber's computer screens off her desk. Dolt reeled backwards, bumping against the trailer's main door and popping it open. Amber flew from the sofa and rolled up against his shins. He scooped her up again. The trailer lurched once more. Dolt spun around and, hugging Amber tightly to his chest, jumped.

He landed on his back in a mess of hay, cushioning Amber with his body. A ferocious gale blew, the air full of dirt and hay. Amber's trailer rocked and strained against its moorings. And, through the murk, Dolt now saw what he was really up against: Descending from the torrid sky was a pulsating, black funnel. And it was coming straight towards them.

Dolt scrambled to his feet, bracing himself against the wind, and gathered Amber up again. Recalling in this moment of extreme danger the lessons of *London's on Fire* and his retrieval of K-Pru from her tree at *The Face of Freedom*, Dolt slung Amber over his shoulder and set off with all possible speed in a direction perpendicular to the path of the tornado.

All around was disorder and flying debris. He ducked and flinched as he stumbled through the wrecked village and out through a gaping hole in the perimeter wall. Glancing back, he saw the tornado rip into the village, deftly skirting Melmotte Global Capital, for some reason, but shredding *Invest in Uzbekistan!* without pity. When he could run no further, he collapsed among the cornstalks and laid Amber gently on the ground. He was — there were no two ways about it — knackered. This had been his second cornfield slog of the day.

Looking up, he saw that the tornado had lost interest in the village and had taken off in a new direction. Perhaps it was heading into town for a sandwich.

Anyway, it had hardly touched the arena itself, which was a relief. As for Gideon, the former PM and the rest of the VIP crowd — well, you had to wonder.

Then the wind dropped abruptly and Dolt realized that the temperature had dropped with it. Amber seemed more lucid now, but she was shivering. Dolt snatched up a flag that the twister had discarded nearby and wrapped her in it. Then he picked her up again and began the trek back to the remains of the village.

He was encouraged to see that a crowd had gathered at its edge. Their demeanor told him that injuries, happily, had been few. As Dolt drew closer, Gideon broke from the mob and ran to meet him. He looked ruffled but intact.

"John! Thank God!"

"Yes, you too."

"We thought... Amber's trailer — it's gone! The tornado just picked it up and... What have you got there?"

Dolt stopped.

"It's Amber."

Gideon's mouth fell open.

"But we thought... Is she...?"

"She's okay. Bit of a bump on the head."

"John! You saved her!"

"Well, I, er... Yes, I suppose I did."

Sometimes, Dolt reflected, you could really see Gideon's brain go to work simply by observing his face. This was one of those times.

"You saved her life, John! This is huge! Come with me!"

And so it was that John Dolt found himself standing on that *big old* stage, the flatbed truck, before the Patriotic multitude, an object of adoration. By his side were Amber herself, now firmly back on her feet; Gideon; the former PM; a host of Patriotic notables, preachers, talk-show hosts and entrepreneurial job-creators; and a clutch of dispirited refugees from Uzbekistan. As for Melmotte Global Capital — well, it sounded as though the party was still in full swing and its attendees had yet to catch up on events.

The atmosphere in the arena quickly became that of a religious revival; sure, you got a load of waffly speeches about Big Government, union bullies, unaffordable entitlements and socialized medicine, but the GPQ, to Dolt's relief, was side-lined. Adding to this sense of relief was the obvious fact that Amber remembered nothing that had transpired between Dolt's arrival at her trailer and his unfurling of her from her flag before a suitably-staggered Gideon. Amber still wore the flag around her shoulders as a kind of totem or poncho. She also still wore the tell-tale imprint on her forehead, but no one had noticed.

After the last preacher on the bill wound up (they all agreed on the facts: That God himself had sent John Dolt unto Earth, expressly to save the life of Amber Pike; that this constituted divine proof that America was uniquely blessed; and that America's exceptional destiny lay in Amber's hands, Dolt having fulfilled his bit-part in the Lord's plan) the speeches stopped and the music started. All at once, it was one big party. "Baby You Can Be My Drone" came on again, and Dolt's feet started to twitch.

"Hey!" Amber said. "Ya wanna dance?"

Dolt could no more dance than he could play basketball, but to refuse seemed churlish.

"All right."

They started to gyrate together. Amber moved decisively into Dolt's private space.

"How d'ya reckon I'm ever gonna thank ya?" she said.

"Oh, don't worry about it."

"Hey, I know! Ya like to hike?"

"Not really."

"Oh, you'll love it once you try it. We'll go to the mountains together. We'll stay in my cabin!"

Dolt froze.

"What's up? Y'okay, John?"

But before Dolt could respond, he felt Gideon's hand on his shoulder.

"Something's come up," he said. "The PM's calling out for you, John. He's desperate. Things are falling apart back home. You're his last hope. We have to leave immediately."

Dolt turned to Amber.

"What is it?" she said, the lettering on her head set into relief by the stage lighting.

"Sorry," Dolt said. "Gotta go. Bye!"

Amber looked crestfallen.

"Aw. Gee. See ya at Freedom Aid, then?"

"Yeah, sure, whatever."

As they hurried away together, Dolt had a simple question for his personal assistant.

"So. How d'you think that all went?"

"Not exactly the way I had it planned," Gideon said. "Then again, I suppose you might consider it a..."

"A what?"

"A *slam dunk?*"

CHAPTER 36

I t was as if the entire Earth had turned green. But the more you looked, the less it seemed like a forest; rather, it was some singular and gigantic organism, Jeff Crock thought, going about its private business while giving breath to those who would destroy it.

Here and there, giant trees poked above the uniformity of the canopy — kapoks, according to *Marco*. That being the name by which the President of Ecuador's Special Deputy wished to be known. Meandering across this verdant blanket were wide, twisty, milky-brown rivers. These channels, Marco said, drained the Andes and supplied the minimal nutrients that sustained the forest.

Like Jeff, Isabel had never seen the Amazon from the air before. She was entranced, and quiet. This, he thought, was to be welcomed.

Their escape from Barbados had been a close-run thing. The incineration of Reagan Pruett's mansion, with so many big-shots on site, seemed to have woken up the whole island, including what passed for its elite anti-terror squad. The airport — which they'd successfully located, despite Roy's navigation skills and Peggy's insistence on *riding shotgun*, as she put it, on the sundeck — had been surrounded by not one but two police cars. Luckily, Marco had thought ahead. He'd been on station outside Departures, diplomatic paraphernalia at the ready.

Now Marco returned to his seat next to Jeff; he'd been talking to the pilot. Marco was small and fit and about forty years old, with longish, well-tended black hair and a serious manner. He wore jeans and a short-sleeved white shirt. Jeff had gotten the impression that he meant business.

"We are going to descend," he said, "and follow the Napo river as far as Coca. Perhaps we will see something interesting."

The Napo was one of the widest of the milky-brown rivers. At this lower altitude, Jeff could make out the much smaller, darker tributaries that ran into it, draining the forest itself. Where the waters met, dark and light brown mingled along a jagged line.

Coca, Marco explained, was the only town of significant size in the Ecuadorian Amazon. Its official name was Francisco de Orellana, that being the name of the Spanish conquistador who'd founded it. Francisco had subsequently gone on to impress the indigenous people of the time — the Tupiguaranis, the Ticunasa and the Omaguas — by discovering the Amazon river itself. But everyone called the place Coca, because it lay at the confluence of the Napo and Coca rivers. It was the gateway to the Yasuní — the national park over which they now flew. And it was the base for the oil industry.

Oil exploration had begun in the nineteen-sixties, in Orellana and Sucumbíos provinces. A four-hundred-and-twenty-kilometer pipeline had been built across the Andes to the Pacific coast. Roads had been hacked through the forest. The roads brought settlers, and farmers — who cut down even more of the forest, for livestock and palm oil plantations. But oil leakages had poisoned water sources and killed cattle. And little of the oil money had remained in Ecuador.

Then, Marco said, in the nineteen-nineties, oil was discovered in the Pastaza and Napo valleys. One deposit, in a zone known as block 31, was thought to consist of more than 900 million barrels of heavy crude. But it lay beneath ecologically-priceless forest: The Waorani Reserve and the Yasuní National Park.

"Look at it," Marco said. "It's almost the last untouched place on Earth. If we dig it up and poison it, we can have ten billion dollars. That's pretty good for a poor country with twelve million people, yes? And four hundred million tons of CO_2. And the oil will keep the world moving for a week and a half."

Hence, Marco said, the big idea: A bunch of academics had proposed leaving the oil in the ground, forever. Ecuador would merely ask that the rest of the world stump up about half of that ten billion dollars. The Ecuadorian people overwhelmingly supported the idea. And the President himself had been persuaded.

So what had happened? Chile, Peru and Spain had made token gestures. America, Britain and other rich countries had called the scheme "impractical" and turned their backs. So the first attempt had failed. The President had tried again. And failed.

And, if the coup succeeded, the foreign oil men would be on this river tomorrow. If, that is, they weren't here already.

Jeff looked down. By the edge of the river were huts and people.

"The Kichwa people," Marco said. "They live here. For now, at least. They are experimenting with eco-tourism. With some success, I think."

They flew on, following the curves of the river.

"Do you know what has become of Leo Vargas?" Marco asked. "He was a big supporter of the no-drilling plan."

Jeff remembered the image of a dark-haired man in an empty room, as rendered by the BaseCam app.

"I think I do," he said. "I'll show you later."

But Isabel had seen something.

"There," she said. "Look!"

Moored by the side of the river were ten heavy barges. They were loaded with construction equipment — bulldozers, cranes, dismantled derricks, fuel trucks, drilling gear.

"They're just waiting," Marco said. "They don't even care that we can see them. Excuse me."

Marco left his seat and entered the cockpit. The plane ascended. When he returned he looked, if that were possible, even more serious.

302

"There is no time to stop in Quito," he said. "We will go directly to Guayaquil. Alvaro needs to talk to you."

"Who's Alvaro?"

"He's the one who will stop the coup."

The plane continued to climb, passing over the grid of low-rise streets and the long, riverside airstrip that made up the town of Coca; passing over the eastern edge of the Andes and the city of Quito, sprawling along its intra-Andean valley; then descending to the fertile Pacific lowlands.

When they arrived in Guayaquil it was midday.

*

E ventually Alvaro found what he needed. Hidden amid the data Jeff had stolen from Number Two's laptop — with the help of John Dolt, the semi-deluded glove-puppet — was an email containing the names of the coup ring-leaders. Alvaro — a stocky forty-five-year-old in a suit and tie, with a military bearing and a closely-trimmed beard — didn't seem surprised. He picked up a phone and gave the necessary orders.

"Usual suspects?" Jeff asked.

Marco nodded.

"Respected businessmen and media owners. Who spend too much time visiting think-tanks in Washington."

"Yeah," Jeff said. "Or maybe Costa Rica."

Alvaro looked up.

"You said these people have a base in Costa Rica? That is their command center?"

"That's right," Jeff said. "They've got a golf course and everything. All these corporate crooks —"

"Come with us," Alvaro said. "We'll walk. You, me and Marco. You can tell us all you know."

They left the hotel in which they'd gathered, leaving Isabel to sleep. Then they walked four or five blocks to the east, through the bustling central business district, to the Malecón, the two-and-a-half-kilometre-long promenade along the Rió Guayas. As they walked south towards the Mercado Sur — a century-old covered market made of steel, according to Marco — Jeff told his fellow coup-busters everything he knew about Rancho Colorado. He didn't burden them with the fact that Katherine's phone remained unreachable, or that the web site of The Liberal was currently inaccessible.

"Have you ever used a parachute?" Alvaro asked, when Jeff had finished.

"No. Why?"

"You'll find out," Alvaro said, as Marco looked on, a sly hint of humor on his serious face.

"Hey, we'll show you something," Marco said.

They left the Malecón, threaded their way through busy street markets and turned north. As they walked, Jeff took out his phone and activated the BaseCam app. And also, just for the heck of it, another one called DroneCtl. The dark-haired man still languished in his empty room. Marco and Alvaro looked.

303

"That's Vargas," Marco said. "Where is he?"

"Libya."

Their little procession came to a halt.

"What's he doing in Libya?" Marco asked.

"Got caught up in this Greater Persian thing, I guess."

They looked at him.

"What Greater Persian thing?" Alvaro said.

"Oh, there's going to be an attack. With drones. And WMD. Probably on the twenty-eighth. It's just something else I've been working on. My wife and mother-in-law are mixed up in it too. In Libya. You know how it goes."

Well, maybe they didn't; it looked that way. They resumed their promenade and Jeff tried to make sense of it all for them. It looked like they mostly got it — though it was tough to explain what the hell *John Dolt* was all about.

"And are these the same people?" Marco asked.

"Pretty much. Heard of a guy called Douglas Moreland?"

They had. That seemed to complete the picture for them. They walked a little further in silence and then entered a small park with ornamental gardens and mature trees.

"Here we are," Marco said. "This is the Parque Bólivar — also known as Parque Seminario. One of our great attractions, here in Guayaquil. What do you think?"

Jeff looked. On the pathways, on the grass, on the benches, in the trees; moving slowly, climbing over each other, fingers gripping, tails flexing, eyes swiveling — iguanas. Iguanas! Everywhere he looked — iguanas. In every size from large to XXXL.

"We're not supposed to feed them. But people do," Marco said. A boy was feeding the iguanas peanuts. They were climbing up his legs.

The light-headedness came on suddenly. Jeff selected an empty bench and collapsed on to it.

"Are you okay?"

"Yeah, it's all right, Marco, thanks. Bad memories, that's all."

"Bad memories? The iguanas?"

"Uh, don't really want to talk about it, right now."

"Okay. You want some water?"

"Thanks, yeah."

While he was drinking his water his phone bleeped. The DroneCtl app had activated. On the screen he saw something that looked very much like the app he'd played with at the FMS picnic. But this time he wasn't looking down at a desert. There were buildings, grass and trees. A parking lot. He zoomed in. Tents, people — and an inflatable castle?

"What are you doing?" Alvaro said.

"Uh, flying a drone, I think..."

"What? In Libya?"

"No, no... I think it's... South Carolina."

It was. He recognized it now. The FMS campus. What was going on?

"What does that do?" Marco said. He was pointing to what looked like a joystick icon.

"I don't know."

"Try it."

Jeff tapped on the joystick. Nothing happened. Then a window popped up. *Control override established,* Jeff read. The window faded and a new set of controls appeared.

"Can you steer it?" Marco said.

"I don't know."

"Try."

Jeff experimented with the controls. The drone responded, turning one way or the other, ascending or descending. His hands were shaky, but the drone's software seemed to be idiot-proof; it wasn't going to let him crash it, whatever he did.

He managed to turn the drone around and bring it down low across the lawns where the tents had been erected. Zooming in again, he saw a crowd of well-dressed people.

"Who are they?" Marco said.

"I can't tell."

"Go round again, lower."

Jeff maneuvered for another pass. He came in lower, over the inflatable castle — and this time, at full zoom, he understood what he was looking at: It was a wedding party.

He found that if he tapped the screen, the drone's camera would lock on to a position on the ground. When he did this, the drone seemed to circle automatically. He could drag and zoom — and see faces. And since everybody was looking up, it wasn't that hard to recognize some of them.

Rand Purdo. Douglas Moreland. War Criminal Number Two. War Criminal Number One.

Shit!

"What's that?" Marco said.

"What?"

"That." Marco was pointing to another icon. This one looked like a key inside a cartoon bomb.

No, he thought. They *wouldn't,* would they? An armed drone flying over a wedding party? *No way!* But there was a test range at the campus, wasn't there? Why not have a few fireworks to entertain the guests?

"Try it," Marco said.

His finger hovered over the key icon. Should he? He felt something heavy crawl over his foot. He tapped. They key icon turned red. *Ordnance enabled,* he read. A kind of bomb-sight now superimposed itself over the zoomed-in camera view. And a large, red button blinked at the bottom of the screen.

The noise of the square seemed to fade to nothing. Everything in his field of vision appeared to recede — the grass, the trees, the people, the iguanas. All he could see was the red, blinking button.

He could do it, couldn't he? He could really do it. A single tap.

One more wedding party? What was the big deal?

Oh, some collateral damage, sure. But how old-hat. What did it matter when you had a high-value target literally in your sights. Not just one, either. At least four. Should be a no-brainer, right? Crank up that body count. Go for it.

So easy, so tempting, so clean — on this little video screen. Click the button. Bug splat. High-five from the boss. Take a break, get a coffee, maybe a doughnut. Couple more hours, log off, drive home to the wife, the kids and the dog. Watch the news about the War on Christmas.

It looked different on the ground. And you had to bear the sounds and the smells, too. Someone had to clean up. You saw these scenes on Russian or German television, but not on American or British screens. He remembered the faces. And those not-quite-forgotten, disembodied voices now rang around the inside of his head again. What were they saying? What were they crying for? And what, if it were possible to ask them, would they have him do?

Just one more wedding party.

He felt something scrape at his ankles. Glancing down, he saw the iguana staring up at him with cold, glassy eyes.

Slowly and with great care, he reached for the power switch on his phone and turned it off. Then he stood up and detached the iguana from his foot. Marco and Alvaro were looking at him, silent.

"What was all that shit about a parachute?" he said. "Tell me more."

CHAPTER 37

If there were a single consolation to finding himself closeted once more with the Policy Steering Committee, John Dolt felt, it was the knowledge that Amber Pike's cabin lay at least three thousand miles away. Apart from that, there wasn't much to be said for it. Unless, that is, you were bitter and twisted enough to derive entertainment value from observing the many and colorful ways in which so much anger could disfigure the plumpest and best-fed of faces.

The PM and the *utopians* were beside themselves. By contrast, the *irreconcilables*, a harder, meaner-faced bunch, combining grimness and smugness in a sadistic symphony of self-satisfaction, insisted that they had seen it coming all along.

Not only had the disturbances stepped up to a new level, but someone — *someone* — had dared to organize an illegal general strike, and had gone right ahead and penciled it in for the twenty-ninth.

"How could this possibly have happened?" the PM demanded to know. "We *caught* Red Ron. John here found him, and we dealt with him. We cut the head off the snake. So I repeat: How can this be happening?"

One of the utopians reported a rumor that the new banking tax had proved unpopular.

"You mean the one *for* the bankers?" Dolt asked.

"Yes," the PM said. "But that doesn't make any sense at all. Everyone knows how vital the City is to the national interest. There must be something else."

One of the irreconcilables pointed out that, as far as they were concerned, it was a clear case of devious foreigners plotting to bring down the financial sector and the rest of the economy with it. Red Ron had been in league with them. Now that he was out of the picture, they would be forced to replace him.

"So you think there's a new Red Ron?" the PM asked.

The irreconcilables became animated. They were missing poor old Ron already, Dolt thought, bleakly. How long before they came up with a Red Roger or a Red Rita?

"Ron did not act alone. I can tell you that," he said, stirring the pot.

Up went the noise.

The PM banged his palms on the table.

"All right, we get the point. Whatever they're called, and however many of them there are, we need to find them. But what are we going to do about this strike? John?"

Dolt moistened his lips.

"Well, which strike are you talking about?"

There was a pause.

"What do you mean, *which* strike?" the PM said.

"Well, there's this illegal general strike, that you were just on about. Then there's the other one."

"What other one?"

"The one that Rand Purdo is organizing."

"Rand Purdo!"

"Yes, he's a friend of mine. Do you know him? Anyway, the basic idea is that all the top productive people are going to walk out. Starting on the twenty-sixth — right, Gideon?"

Gideon, sitting, as before, at Dolt's right shoulder, nodded.

"Top productive people?" the PM said — and you could hear the fear in his voice.

"That's right," Dolt said. "Your bankers. Your top corporate blokes. Libel lawyers. TV presenters. Lobbyists. Advertising big-wigs. Media magnates. Management consultants. Your hedge fund bosses. Private equity what's-its. Am I getting this right, Gideon? Yes? Anyway, you get the idea. Those sort of people. Here and in America. All out together. Nice little break in Costa Rica, possibly."

There was silence around the table. The utopians looked anxiously at the irreconcilables. The irreconcilables looked nervously at the PM. The PM sat slumped with his mouth open.

"Well," he said, at length. "That's obviously a very serious, um, decision that they've come to." He paused, apparently looking for inspiration, but finding none on offer from either of the factions. "Was this Rand's idea, John?"

"He says it was mine," Dolt said.

More silence.

"All the wealth-creators," Dolt said, helpfully, "and all the job-creators."

"Yes, yes, I get the idea," the PM said.

"They have a point to prove, apparently."

"Mm. Yes, I can understand that. It's just that... Well, obviously, it's their choice. They *are*, as you rightly say, John, the wealth-creators..."

"And the job-creators."

"Quite. Exactly. And if they choose to take a few days off... Even *en masse*, as it were... Well, I don't really see... I mean, they're only exercising their rights, after all. Aren't they?"

"Might be more than a *few days*," Dolt said. "I mean, it's not like they need the money, do they?"

Once again, the PM looked for inspiration, but found none. He shook his head, like a wet dog that had taken an ill-advised dip in a smelly pond and wanted to forget about it in a hurry.

"Well, there it is, I suppose. Let's move on, shall we?"

There were loud mumblings of consent and much chair-shifting from both factions.

"Now this strike — *this illegal general strike* — is absolutely intolerable. It is an insult to the hard-working families of this country. *What* are we going to do?"

"Can't we just shoot them?"

"Dan, you know the line we're taking on sanctions. That is *not* official government policy, but we *are* looking at all the options."

Dolt drew a long breath, noisily and provocatively.

"Can't trust the army," he said. "All those disgruntled squaddies with their rubbish kit, just back from the War Zones. *I* wouldn't rely on them."

"The police?"

"Outnumbered," Dolt said. "And routinely outwitted, to judge by their success with the disturbances."

"*What then?*" the PM insisted.

A pause. Then one of the irreconcilables nodded towards Dolt.

"Isn't it obvious?"

There was another outbreak of seat-shuffling.

The PM sniffed and looked at Dolt.

"You mean..."

"Yes, him. Dolt. This Home Guard of his. He's got more members than the bloody National Trust. And I wouldn't be surprised if they're better armed, as well."

This was news to Dolt. How many members? Five million? Six?

"You think they could..."

"Break the strike? You bet they would. They're angry, they're motivated, they hang on his every bloody word."

"Yes, but..."

"Why can't *we* generate that kind of support, by the way? Our policies are the same as his!"

"Not officially, Dan. Do I have to keep warning you?"

Another awkward silence fell. Someone tapped a pencil. Gideon whispered in Dolt's ear.

"Well," Dolt said. "All I am prepared to say, at this point, is that I am not willing to stand idly by while evil flourishes and dark forces run amok, undermining our values, subverting our liberties and destroying the country I love."

A bit wordy, he thought. But you could almost touch the sense of relief in the room.

"Whether," Dolt went on, "those dark forces be domestic — or *foreign*." As he spoke this last word, he caught the PM's eye and something unspoken passed between them. The PM looked reassured — although, if he'd known what Dolt was really thinking, of course, he wouldn't have been.

Gideon tapped Dolt twice on the shoulder. It was the signal.

"And now," Dolt said, "I'm afraid you must excuse me. I've got a lot on today, what with the Freedom Aid, the Home Guard rally, and er..." He turned to Gideon. "What was the other thing?"

"The War Zones tour".

"Oh, right. I'm going on this morale-booster thing, aren't I?"

It was a surprise that Gideon had sprung on him during the flight home from Kansas (no Senior Cabin this time; just Dolt and Gideon, side by side, in First Class). Dolt and a gang of ghastly celebrities had been signed up to conduct a lightning jaunt around the War Zones, their mission being to dole out hand-made crap from the viewers back home; to admire the world-beating quality and value of British military hardware; and to cheer the troops up and generally make them feel wanted. And, naturally, to get lots of good pictures.

"Of course, of course," the PM said. "We understand. And let me just say, on behalf of everyone here, how much we, um, appreciate all you're doing for the country." He looked from one faction to the other. "Am I right?"

There was a smattering of reluctant applause. Dolt stood and made for the exit, Gideon in tow.

"How did I do?"

"Very well indeed, John," Gideon said. "You're getting better all the time."

Outside the so-called Cabinet Room, Dolt made his excuses and sought out the gents'. He found it agreeably uninhabited. Which was just as well, because he had one other item on his agenda that he hadn't advertised to the Policy Steering Committee. He whipped out his spy-phone and jumped straight into spy-fi mode.

"Des?"

"John! You're back, I see."

"I want a meeting."

"Do you? Well, okay. Let's see... You'll be back at your hotel —"

"Not there."

"No? Oh, like that, is it? Okay — where?"

"The Royal Fusilier. Cricklewood."

Silence.

"Don't fuck with me, John. I'm warning you. I thought we had something good going here."

"We do, sort of."

"Then can't we —"

"No. The Fusilier. An hour from now."

Down the line there came a bitter sigh of resignation.

"All right."

"Good," Dolt said. "Oh, and *don't be like that*, okay?"

"Hah!"

"Yeah! Bye."

Dolt hung up.

"John," Gideon said, on Dolt's return to the lobby, "perhaps we should get you a check-up. You seem to need to *go* a lot."

"I'm all right."

"We'll discuss it later. Now, then. Next, you have an appointment with Jacqueline, to —"

Dolt didn't want an appointment with Jacqueline.

"What about that lawyer bloke? Why can't I have an appointment with him?"

"What lawyer bloke would that be, John?"

"The one who's managing my offshore account."

"Ah. That one. Well, he's not available just now, John. But I'll make a note."

"Jacqueline's off, by the way."

"Oh?"

"Yeah. Just got a message from you-know-who. Needs to talk to me now."

"Really? Well, I'll summon Des with the Range Rover and —"

"No, no. It's top secret. Just me. Need to know, and all that. Undisclosed location. Got any cash?"

"Cash? What for?"

Sometimes Gideon could be a bit slow. It was a common failing, Dolt had noticed, with your intellectual types.

"For a taxi."

"A taxi! John, you need to realize that you're extremely well-known now. You can't just wander around in public on your own. You are a national figure. You are ubiquitous."

He wasn't sure whether that last remark was a dig nor not, but it didn't matter.

"Gimme some cash."

Gideon hesitated.

"Come on!"

Gideon dug into his pocket and retrieved a bunch of fifties.

"Here you are. But I'm going to need a receipt."

"Yeah, yeah. Later."

"Please be careful out there. I'll see you at lunch?"

"Lunch?"

"In the Melmotte Global Capital box? At the stadium? Freedom Aid?"

"Oh, right. Yeah, see you there. Bye."

Dolt bounded out into the gray light of the street. What he sought was a black cab. There were plenty of them. But the weird and disturbing thing was that almost half of them seemed to have his face plastered on the side. He hailed the first empty one he saw; it came careening towards him. Was that really his face? Yes it was — though it bore none of his undisguisable defects and it wore an expression of menacing and overbearing vehemence that he'd never consciously adopted.

He jumped inside, bawled out his destination, and then immediately registered his error.

"You're *him*, aren't you?" the driver said, as his vehicle lurched back into the traffic. "You're John Dolt!"

"Yes," Dolt admitted. "I am John Dolt."

Then it began. Dolt closed his eyes and tipped his head back — a mistake, of course, because the jerking and wheeling of the cab made him feel sick. Or something did.

The driver was an enthusiastic member of the Home Guard. He had volunteered to organize his local neighborhood *squad*. Politicians — the lot of them — were useless, lily-livered bastards, just out for what they could get. Dolt was different. Dolt was just an ordinary citizen, like him. Dolt had made him feel proud to be English again.

The driver paused to make a crazy right-turn, then resumed.

Dolt was the only one willing to take a stand against hand-outs, and *human rights*, and political correctness gone mad. Yes, there was that bloke in the paper, but he was just doing it for the money wasn't he? Fucking millionaire. Didn't really mean it, did he? Not like Dolt.

It was about time all those lazy foreigners got what was coming to them. And the scroungers, and the gippos, and the blacks, and the homos, and the Muslims, and those fucking champagne socialists up in Hampstead, and...

And so on and so forth.

Dolt, in short, was the man for him.

By the time they reached the Royal Fusilier, Dolt was aching for a drink. Des, of course, had arrived early. No doubt he had vetted the bar staff and swept the pub for bugs. Actually, the pub could have done with a sweep. It was filthy. You could have written your name in the dust on the framed fake-imperial memorabilia that passed for decoration. To think that Red Ron had been reduced to living above this!

Des had secured a remote corner table and had constructed a kind of personal Green Zone out of spare chairs. Dolt clambered through with his pint of Old Grenadier.

"Why here?" Des said. "That's what I want to know."

"Red Ron used to live here."

"And?"

"You got me at a weak moment, didn't you?"

"So?"

"The motorcycles, and all that."

"They're still out there, John."

Dolt sipped his beer.

"The PM must love you," Des said. "Knocking off old Ron like that."

"Hasn't made any difference, though, has it?"

"No."

Des gave a bitter chuckle and slurped his orange juice.

"Orange juice?"

"Driving. You haven't been on public transport lately, have you?"

It couldn't be worse than the cab ride, Dolt thought.

"They just don't get it, though, do they?" Des said. "Yanks are the worst. Half a million dollars a pop. Maybe more, depending. One high-value target after another. And they wonder why things only get worse."

"Red Ron had a wife, didn't he?"

Des put his orange juice down.

"What's that to you?"

"I want her phone number."

"What could you possibly want that for?"

Dolt hesitated.

"Maybe I want to console her."

"But you're the one who shopped him!"

"All the same."

"What's got into you? Just give me your latest intel. I heard you got very close to that crazy Pike woman. What have you got?"

312

Dolt finished his pint, taking his time.

"Give me the number."

"Are you serious?"

"Yes."

"All right. I haven't got time for this. At your own risk, John."

Des whipped out a ratty notebook, flipped though it and showed it to Dolt. Dolt memorized the number.

"Is it bugged?"

"Not any more."

"Thanks," Dolt said. "Here's what I've got."

He gave Des an exhaustive update on his adventures with Amber, not neglecting — indeed, enhancing — his tornado-related heroics.

"Great Leader?" Des said. "What fucking Great Leader?"

"I dunno."

"Didn't you ask her?"

"No. I couldn't, could I?"

"Oh, right. Because the tornado sucked her out through the window and —"

"Wait. Look."

Dolt had seen something on the TV screen above the bar. Coverage of cricket from Sri Lanka had been interrupted.

"Oh!" Des said, and there was an extended holding-of-breath while they both took in what they were seeing. "*That* Great Leader. Jesus! How long have they been planning this? How come we weren't told?"

Dolt recognized the Great Leader, though not with much fondness. If he remembered correctly — Gideon would know — this particular Great Leader had been very hot on the GPQ. Though it wasn't called that back then, of course.

Des, his features immobile, appeared to have vacated the pub temporarily, leaving his body behind while he explored caverns of deep thought.

As he waited for Des to re-emerge, Dolt listened to the clipped and respectful tones of the TV announcer as he described, in the mournful cadences normally reserved for royal stiffs, how it had been decided that what the nation yearned for, in its time of trial, was a Great Moment of National Unity. Thus there was to be, every year, a National Day of Remembrance in honor of the Great Leader.

For who could forget how the nation had rallied in its time of sadness? Politicians and people alike had been pole-axed by grief and united in sorrow. And yet, though the memory of the Great Leader was venerated by all, what was deemed to be lacking was a *focus*.

And so, in accordance with the wishes of family and friends, the monarch, the PM, the Policy Steering Committee, the investment banks that sponsored the Great Leader's Foundation, and in recognizance of various affairs of state that didn't need to be gone into, there would be a State Memorial, culminating in the erection of a statue of the Great Leader in Parliament Square. It would take place next Friday. The twenty-eighth.

"What a fucking stitch-up!" Des said, surfacing once more from the depths.

"How? What's it all mean?"

"Don't you see? This so-called State Memorial. It's perfect. You couldn't come up with anything better."

"Huh?"

"There's going to be some kind of provocation. That's got to be it."

"Like what?"

"I dunno — a siege, a suicide bomber. Something violent, probably."

"Violent?"

"Yeah, it would have to be."

"So then..."

"There would be instant retaliation."

Des stabbed a finger at the TV.

"Listen to all that crap. This is all we're going to get until next Friday. Perfect conditions. Then, bang — it happens. What a fucking outrage! So then the friends of the Great Leader — especially the *American* friends of the Great Leader, the *private-sector* American friends of the Great Leader..."

"Drones away."

"Before anyone can say, for example, *are these terrorists for real?*"

They sat in silence in front of their empty glasses.

"What do we do, then?" Dolt asked.

"Well, now we've got two problems. Or opportunities, if you think there's any use in being optimistic. The drones and the provocation."

"What about Lescek?"

Des groaned.

"He's a tough nut, that one. I'm having one last go at him. This afternoon, while you're laughing it up with Melmotte Global Capital."

"What?"

"You're in their sky-box at this Freedom Aid shit-fest. Along with Kenny Pruett and your BFF. What's that you call him again?"

"Faith Boy?"

"Faith Boy! Nice. He's gonna have a ball at the memorial."

"Maybe. Maybe not. But what about this provocation, then?"

"I'm running out of ideas, John. You're the one with the private army. Maybe you can think of something."

A *private army?* Composed of *squads* led by idiots like that taxi driver?

"Are we done here?" Des asked, a note of weariness in his voice. "I hate this dump and that effing TV's getting on my wick."

"I suppose so."

"Want a lift to the stadium?"

Dolt recalled his taxi ride.

"Yes. Please."

*

Rather like the party-goers at Reagan Pruett's mansion, Dolt noted, the Melmotte Global Capital crowd didn't really want to socialize with him. But then, they hadn't been much interested in Amber, either, had they? On the positive side, they seemed in good spirits. Dolt got the impression that — as the late, great Prickler would have wanted — they had spoken to their brokers and had come away feeling pumped.

As was his style, Dolt slipped away to the gents' before Gideon could lock on to him. There he took out his spy-phone and dialed a number in the unstylish 0208 zone.

"Is that, uh, Mrs. Red Ron?"

From the other end of the line came a sigh that sounded like the death of hope.

"Yes, this is Mrs. Red Ron. Who the fuck is it now?"

"This is... This is a friend. A friend of Red Ron."

"You mean Barry."

"Yes, right, Barry. How, um, is he, by the way?"

"How would I know? He's a *Dangerous Person*. You know what happens."

"Um, yeah. Sorry. Look, there's something I need to tell you. It's important."

"He didn't really have any friends."

"No? I thought we got on quite well. We had an ice cream together."

"An *ice cream?*"

"Yeah. Okay, that's not really important right now. I want to talk about the strike."

"I don't know anything about that."

"No. But I'm guessing you know someone who..."

"Guess away."

"Okay, look. The thing is this. I think you — I think *the strike* should be moved up to the twenty-eighth."

"The twenty-eighth? Why?"

"I can't say why. You have to trust me. It's just that things will work out much better if you do. I mean, if it is."

"Not much to go on, is it? Your say-so. Whoever you are."

"But it has to be a total surprise, right? Last minute change of plan. Catch 'em all off-guard. Complete secrecy."

"Who *are* you?"

Dolt agonized. He had to give her *something*, didn't he?

"Can you see out of the window?"

"Yes."

"See any black cabs?"

"I'm on the twenty-third floor. And the lift doesn't work."

"Ah."

"It's all right. I've got binoculars."

"Have a look. What do you see?"

A pause.

"No! I don't believe it."

"Yes, really! Don't believe the hype, and all that."

Another pause.

"Did you honestly have an ice cream with him?"

"Yes."

"What's his favorite flavor, then?"

"He had a tutti frutti. I had a raspberry ripple."

"How many scoops?"

"I had one. He had a Triple Deluxe."

Another sigh.

315

"I used to worry about his weight. Don't suppose that's a problem, now."

"So, you heard what I said, right?"

"I heard what you said."

"Good."

"Not that any of that's anything to do with me, of course."

"Course not."

There was a meaningful pause, then the line went dead. Would Dolt's game-plan, still hazy as yet, make it to the kick-off?

It all seemed to hinge on that Super-Kone Triple Deluxe.

CHAPTER 38

The Colonel, Bonnie thought, was a man who wore his professional pride as conscientiously as his civic duty. You couldn't have picked a superior fellow in all of Libya, she was content to believe, if your purpose was to encase a chemical-weapons bunker in quick-setting cement. Not only that, but he'd given Jay a break on the price and thirty days' grace in which to pay up — cash only, of course. Jay, the Colonel accepted, was good for the money. And even if, as Jay claimed, he was no longer a contributor to the CIA's pension plan — well, the Colonel knew for a fact that no one who'd once had access to the agency's bottomless bank account would ever lack for retirement funds.

She tightened the scarf around her face. The desert had favored them tonight, in the only way it could. A sandstorm had blown in from the southeast, and the base languished in a an opaque, shifting, abrasive fog. Kufra felt locked down. Even the drones were grounded. Jay had located the bunker by GPS. A solitary, unlucky vehicle — one of Andy's toy tanks — had been on guard; General Kadiya didn't want Andy's poison going missing on his watch, she supposed. It hadn't taken much for Jay and the kids, riding in the technicals, to tease Andy's expensive armor away into the flying sand. After which, the Colonel's truck had lumbered out of the murk and set to work.

Now, his special commission completed to his obvious satisfaction, the Colonel attempted to defy the desert by lighting a cigarette in the lee of his truck. They could not leave until Jay returned. Jay had the GPS.

She felt her daughter's hand on her shoulder.

"We could do it now, if you want," Annie said.

"Do what?"

"Get your friend out."

"Leo?"

"Yes. I know where he is. I know how to get to him. This storm — it's the only chance."

"But Jay —"

"Doesn't trust me. But you do, don't you?"

Bonnie shielded her eyes with her hand and looked at her daughter.

317

"Tomorrow," Annie said, "they're moving him out. There's going to be a coup in Costa Rica. They'll hand him over to the new régime."

"Tomorrow?"

"Yes, Mom. Tomorrow."

"But how do we —"

"With that."

Annie pointed at the Colonel's truck.

"Come on."

Annie glanced at the Colonel, still battling the desert for his job-done smoke, then she ran to the truck and climbed into the cab. Through the scouring haze, Bonnie saw her daughter struggle to hold the door open against the wind. She ran to the truck. Annie pulled her in.

"Put your seatbelt on," Annie said. "You're going to need it."

The truck lurched forward. Annie switched the lights on, but all they could see was a shimmering wall of sand. She turned them off again. The truck wallowed and bumped through the sand, the engine screaming and choking by turns.

"All we need," Annie said, "is to find the runway. The command block is right there at the end."

As the truck clawed and ground its way forward, and the sand forced its passage through a crack in the windshield in order to implant a colony of miniature dunes on the dashboard, Bonnie wondered what it would do to the Colonel's standing in the building trade to have his valuable cement truck stolen by two crazy women in a sandstorm.

Then they hit the runway. Annie shifted gear and accelerated.

"Are we going the right way?"

"Don't know, Mom. We'll find out. Watch out on your side."

The truck picked up speed. They were driving blind at eighty kilometers an hour. When the edge of the runway became visible, at three meters or so, Annie swerved back towards the center. On the instrument panel, an amber light flashed. There was a smell of hot rubber.

"Overheating," Annie said. But she didn't slow down. The Colonel, Bonnie recalled, had blocked the radiator grille with nylon sacking, to keep the sand out. And he'd driven slowly.

Then the markings on the runway changed abruptly. Annie braked hard and the truck skidded to a stop, sideways on. She put the truck in low gear, pulled it back into line and crawled forward. A faint oblong of light formed above them, suspended in empty space.

"Control room," Annie said. "We go to the left."

Carefully, she brought the truck close to the gray walls of the command block and drove in parallel. The amber light on the instrument panel went out. At regular intervals they passed through the dirty, orange cones of light given off by the command block's security lights. Then a square indentation appeared in the wall. It looked to Bonnie like a steel roller-shutter — the kind of thing you saw in the loading bays at the rear of Home Depot.

"That's it," Annie said.

She hauled the wheel to the left, so that the truck stood perpendicular to the doorway.

"Ready?"

"Ready for what?"

"Put your head back. You might want to hold on to the seat."

"Are you —"

"Yes, I am."

Annie put the truck in reverse. Bonnie felt it tug against the brake. Turning her head, she saw that Annie had closed her eyes. She had one foot on the brake and the other on the gas. There was an instant of protest from the engine, and then they were in motion.

The shock of impact brought a moment of silence and weightlessness. Then she heard the rending of metal and felt the seatbelt bite against her chest as the truck recoiled and its gears clashed.

Annie pulled the truck forward.

"Okay?"

"Yes."

"Again?"

"Go."

On the third attempt, they broke through.

Then they were out of the truck, on their feet, and Bonnie found herself running after her daughter, dodging through the debris field, then following full-pelt down a steel staircase and headlong through a concrete corridor.

Jay didn't *get* Annie, Bonnie thought as she ran. Annie, to whom people with the wrong ideas were hardly people at all — until the ideas changed, which, every so often, they did. How could Jay know *that?* All he knew was that even people like Andy had families.

Bonnie stopped. Annie had vanished. A metallic rattle came from a room on the left.

"Annie?"

"In here."

It was an armory. Annie snatched a rifle from a rack and slammed in an ammunition cartridge with the same distracted impatience she used to display when told to tidy her room.

"Leo's downstairs. Come on!"

Annie took off again, rifle at the ready, finger on the trigger.

"Annie, wait!"

But she was already half-way down into the basement. Bonnie took a deep breath and ran to the head of the staircase.

Annie had once been the soccer team's secret weapon, only to be dismissed from the field for unprovoked violence. What would she do?

Gunshots boomed against the concrete.

"Mom!"

Down the stairs into a long, empty corridor. A steel door with a keypad. Annie punching in a number.

She hadn't killed anyone — had she just scared them away? Well, she knew how to do that.

The door swung open. And there was Leo, his face frozen behind a ratty beard and uncharacteristically unwashed hair.

Annie yelled at him, but Leo backed away. He was looking for something.

Did he want out or not? What was the problem with these men? Bonnie pushed her daughter out of the way.

"Leo, Jay's not here. It's just us. Come on!"

"Bonnie?"

"Now!"

Annie led the way. Leo followed. Back at the armory, Annie pressed a rifle into Leo's hands. Had he ever held one before?

Then up, and up again, into Andy's realm, where the style was corporate-military.

Bonnie wondered where the General was. Out hunting ghosts in the sand? And what of the General's crack troops, imported at Andy's expense from the finest military schools that Mogadishu could provide? Keeping out of Annie's way, for now? So much for male valor.

Annie kicked in a pair of double doors. Leo politely held them open for Mom.

This was *it*, she thought — that ethereal rectangle with its face set against the desert: The control room. Low lights, computer screens, air-con. A bunch of paunchy, surprised, thirty-something white men in short-sleeved white shirts — rising from their seats, which might have been recycled from fighter jets, or else ordered online from some boys' toys web site.

One glance at Annie's gun and they were holding up their hands. Were they thinking about their insurance?

Annie tore into the place. She was looking for something, rearranging the furniture, making a mess.

Bonnie looked at Leo. Annie expected him to hold the fort, but he looked scared; he knew how to love-bomb his audience, but what if he had to shoot these guys?

There was a corner office with thick glass and blinds. It had to be Andy's private domain. Annie was trashing it.

Then she emerged, rifle in one hand, a tablet computer in the other.

"This way. Run!"

She led them to a fire escape. They descended into the pelting sand. Bonnie gripped Leo's hand. And, half-blind, they ran after Annie.

"Where are we going?"

"We borrowed a truck. It's right here, somewhere."

And there it was: The Colonel's truck, or the shape of it, thick with smoke and resolutely on fire despite the deadening sand.

Annie had stopped.

"You came in *that?*" Leo said.

"It's what we had."

Annie started off again, skirting the burning truck. They followed.

"You know that she's —"

"Yes, I know," Leo said. "She told me... A lot."

"Can you run?"

"No, can you?"

"Not any more."

"Where is she going?"

"I don't know."

"We'll follow her anyway?"

"Yes."

They walked out on to the runway. Ahead, Annie faded and rematerialized. Behind, Bonnie saw the dim oblong of the control room window, with its human shadows. A few steps later, it had gone.

The storm intensified. Annie vanished into a swirl of orange fog. Leo stopped to clear the sand from his eyes and nostrils.

The desert, Bonnie thought, was the master here, not Andy. It could blow over Andy's base and bury it; it could choke the drones out of the sky, if it chose to. But, of course, it wouldn't choose, and Andy would simply wait — as perhaps he did now, bored in Tripoli, say, on his way back from his daughter's wedding.

"Leo?"

"I'm okay. But I don't like this desert. We are going to have too many deserts, soon. I also want to say, thank you for finding me. And I have still not forgotten your birthday."

"Oh, I have."

"Should we continue?"

"I think so."

They began to walk.

"Your daughter said she chose to come here. I don't understand that."

"I do."

"Then you are wiser than I am."

"Yes, I am."

A splutter of a laugh from Leo.

"Then you should have this."

Leo offered her his rifle. She took it.

"I'll do the shooting, then?"

"You do it."

"You don't think the sand..."

Well, it probably didn't matter, she thought. Ahead were two low, square shapes, side by side. They stopped and waited. There came the sound of a door opening — more like the creak of a battered pickup than the clang of a baby tank. And those clicky footsteps...

"Welcome back, Mr. Vargas," Jay said. "Mrs. DiAngelo, you may lower your weapon at this point."

"Ah. Sorry."

"No problem. But we need to go. Andy's guys are all over at the bunker — nice job, by the way. Though you are going to have to explain to the chief what happened to his truck."

"Annie can tell him."

Jay hesitated.

"Well, okay. But where is she?"

"She's not here? She was ahead of us. You must have —"

"No. Haven't seen her."

"But we can't leave without —"

"We'll drive a hundred meters back down. Then we'll turn around."

They drove. But Annie wasn't there.

CHAPTER 39

If he could point to one thing that Gideon excelled at, Dolt mused — apart, of course, from all those activities that were routine in his profession, and essential to the art of politics: Distortion, subterfuge, provocation, demonization, mock-outrage, flattery, the whipping up of base emotion and the flat-out telling of porkies — it was frowning. The man was an expert. He could do two at once — one per eyebrow, in effect. And what Dolt spied on his personal assistant's face, as he exited the gents' in the Melmotte Global Capital sky-box and the sound-tests of Freedom rose up from the stadium below, was a composition to rival them all.

Frown number one spoke of concern tinged with suspicion: Once again, Dolt had absented himself from public view; did Gideon suspect something more than a minor medical condition? Frown number two registered suspicion too, along with impatience and a certain controlled alarm.

"Anything the matter?" Dolt said.

"Well, I certainly hope not, John. I've booked you a check-up. But there's something else..."

"What?"

"Do you, by any chance, know a girl called Samira?"

"Samira!"

"Well, I see you do. She's been detained by Security, downstairs. Causing a bit of a fuss. Says she's got some very important information for you, but won't say what it is. I don't suppose you would have any idea, would you?"

Dolt considered. Samira — to borrow from the language of politics — had made her position very clear at their last encounter, at the Brit Arse. What more could there be to add?

"No."

"Sure?"

"Well, she might be worried about her dad."

One of Gideon's frowns softened — a hint of sympathy?

"She does seems a little emotional. One understands. The pressures on the family these days, and so on... But it's hardly your problem, though — is it, John?"

Did Gideon really not know Hamid's fate? For all his elegant jokes about the *dirty* business of politics, Gideon was very careful to leave the really grubby stuff to the likes of Des, and to make it plain that whatever Des *was*, in fact, *like*, he, Gideon, wasn't. Gideon liked to waffle on about the benefits of *compartmentalization*. Perhaps he truly meant it.

But what if Samira really did have something to tell Dolt?

"Um, perhaps I'd better have a word with her."

Gideon's other frown hardened into something prohibitive. With a generous gesture, he indicated the contents of the sky-box: The Melmotte Global Capital mob, in freshly-purchased chinos and designer-check shirts, keeping it all in-house as usual, piling in on the hors d'oeuvres; the Pruett sisters, Reagan already in her spangled cowboy hat, glittery boots and make-up; a couple of the younger *irreconcilables*, in corduroy jackets; Rand Purdo, already installed in the best seat in the house, taking in the scene, attendants at his elbow; four lumpy, short-haired blokes in dark suits who were probably something to do with Des; and a selection of what Dolt took to be Anglo-American high society, charity on their minds, dipping into the popular arts for a change. As far as Dolt could tell, there were no members of the Home Guard.

"Well," Gideon said, "she can't come up *here*."

"I'll go down there."

"No, you've got to stay put for now. There's been a threat."

"Threat? What threat?"

"Tell you what," Gideon said. "We'll keep her in the wings. You can have a quick chat just before you go on."

"Go on?"

"To introduce Miss Pruett. She's the first act. I'll go and tell them."

"You didn't say anything —"

"I believe I did."

Oh, but Gideon was right, wasn't he? Dolt, under the influence of one too many celebratory sherries, had agreed to perform the opening ceremonies and stand in as Reagan's warm-up act. Hang on, though — what about that *threat?*

But Gideon had gone. At once, seizing the opportunity, the Pruett sisters pounced.

"Hey, John!"

"Hullo, Kenny."

"How about you, then!"

"What about me?"

Coy laughter. Reagan pulled her hat down over one eye.

"So, are you, like, the boss of England, now?"

"Not really."

Reagan addressed her sister.

"He's a *dic*-tator. They gotta have a *dic*-tator, 'cause they're in such a mess. I mean they're, like, in deep shit."

"He's not a dictator."

"He is, too. You know, like... Who was that guy?"

"Hitler."

"No, the other one. The other guy who was a *dic*-tator."

A pause.

"Mussolini?" Dolt said.

They looked at him.

"Nah," Kenny said. "Some other guy. He had a good economic policy. Rand says so."

"Made the trains run on time, did he?" Dolt said.

The girls looked at each other.

"I guess," Reagan said. "But it was all worth it. Because of the economic growth, or whatever."

"*What* was worth it?"

"Huh?"

"You said it was all worth it."

"Well, duh. But Rand says they have to learn the lessons all over again."

"Do they? Who, exactly?"

"Like, the South Americans, and people like that."

"Right. Gotcha."

Kenny Pruett seemed to have something else on her mind.

"Um, John?"

"Yes, Kenny?"

"You remember Brandon, right?"

She meant Burrito, film auteur extraordinaire.

"How could I forget?"

"Could you, like, talk to Rand? You know, about the movie?"

"You mean *The Amber Pike Story?*"

"Uh-huh. Brandon's had the script rewritten? And it's like, you're in it now? And there's a scene with you and Amber, and you're goin' up in the tornado together, and —"

"Don't worry. Leave it to me."

Could Dolt think of anyone more likely to do justice to the material? No, he couldn't. There was just one thing...

"Um, Kenny..."

"Uh-huh?"

"How, erm — how does it end?"

Embarrassed mutual clutching and swaying on the part of the Pruett sisters.

"Oh, it's, you know... Just you and Amber, up in the mountains, in her cabin..."

Inwardly, Dolt shuddered. But this detail clinched it. If any single person could guarantee that the movie would, were it to be made at all, flop instantly, Burrito was that person.

"I'll see to it," Dolt said.

"Wow, thanks, John! You're cool. You're like the dictator of cool!"

It was just as well, Dolt thought, that Samira had not been present to hear this. But now, just at the right moment, Gideon returned.

"Ah, Miss Pruett!" he said, addressing Reagan with one of his most condescending frowns. "I'm to say that you are on in twenty minutes." And with that, he shooed the sisters away.

"Right. Come along, then, John. Let's find out what this Samira girl wants. This way..."

G ideon, understandably distracted, perhaps, by the Samira issue, had neglected to fill Dolt in on the running order. Thus it was that Dolt found himself at the edge of the great stage, in full view of the freedom-loving multitudes, enduring two long minutes of silence in honor of the Great Leader, while Samira, restrained at a safe distance by Security, put everything she'd got into a stare of such vengeful reproach, Dolt felt, that even the Great Leader couldn't have matched it. He couldn't meet her gaze. But he could feel it on the back of his neck, like twin laser-beams, exquisitely tuned to whatever frequency it was that said *I accuse!*

He tried to divert himself by studying the faces of the crowd. All those damp eyes. All those quivering lips. Not quite North Korea, he thought. But not far off. Would this be his own posthumous reward, one day? Should he switch role models, dumping Amber in favor of the Great Leader? Yeah, right. He and Amber might traffic in the same goods as the Great Leader, and peddle them in the same bazaar, but the bosses at Melmotte Global Capital weren't going to put Dolt on their board of advisors, or pay for *his* memorial. And Dolt's career would not last nearly as long as the Great Leader's. He was pretty sure of that.

The silence came to an end, accompanied by cheers and applause — either for the Great Leader or for the applauders themselves; it was hard to tell. A video presentation now lit up the big screens on either side of the stage: It was a black-and-white, slo-mo montage of the supposedly *iconic* moments in the Great Leader's life, set to plaintive piano chords. The late afternoon light was fading, and the mass holding-up of candles, but for intrusive fire regulations, would surely have broken out. Instead, people held up their mobile phones, many of which had been respectfully equipped with video loops of a flickering flame. Samira strained at the leash.

"Well, then," Gideon said, indicating Samira, "shall we find out what *this* is all about?"

"All right. But what was that about a *threat?*"

"Oh, you get threats all the time, John. Goes with the job. Don't let it get to you."

"But I thought I was really popular."

"You are. Success inspires envy, I'm afraid. I think we covered that — remember?"

Yes, he remembered. He got it. In a weird way he felt envious of his own success. Something to do with that elusive off-shore bank account, possibly.

"Let her go," Gideon said.

Samira was unhanded. She shook herself, like an angry swan looking to pick a fight with an insensitive park visitor. Then she advanced on Dolt. Gideon intervened.

"No," Dolt said. "It's all right. Gideon, wait here. Come on, Samira."

He led her to a remote corner filled with cables, speaker cabinets, fire-extinguishers and drum kits. For a few awkward moments, Samira said nothing. He could hear her breathe — slow, deep, and loud. Then the laser-beams switched off and her eyes seemed to turn a dreadful, empty black.

Dolt had expected anger, and perhaps even violence — he was prepared to take it on the chin, kneecap or elsewhere if he had to. But *this*, whatever it was, felt worse. His spine froze.

Samira took a deliberate step towards him. Dolt stumbled backwards.

"I know what this is all about," she said.

"Oh?"

"Some of my dad's friends. They found out where he is. Everyone over there knows what's going to happen."

"Mm. And, er, how is your dad? Is he okay?"

The darkness in Samira's eyes darkened again. Which hardly seemed possible. But there it was.

"No John, he's not okay. He's bad. Really bad."

Had Dolt promised to intercede on Hamid's behalf? He seemed to remember that he had.

"Um, Samira — I haven't forgotten that I promised... It's just that —"

"Too late, John. Doesn't matter any more. *Really* doesn't matter."

"No? I, er —"

"My dad just wants you to know that he hopes you die knowing what you've done. Okay? That's his message to you."

Jesus!

Frozen spine and trembling limbs notwithstanding, Dolt felt that the time had come to *explain*.

"Look, Samira. I know this sounds corny. But all is not as it seems, and —"

"Oh, right. And that's not your fucking private army outside this fucking stadium, with their guns and their knives and their baseball bats and their *disgusting* slogans."

"Guns?"

Samira stepped forward and poked him once in the ribs with her forefinger. It was just a tap, but he staggered backwards.

Then she spoke quietly, and with a terrible calm.

"That's all I have to say, John. You can go now. Go out on that stage and do your act. I'm done."

Samira turned her back and shoved her hands into the pockets of her oversized duffle coat.

"But that's just it, Samira! It *is* an act! Listen to me..."

Samira began to walk away. Dolt grabbed at her coat. There was something heavy in her pocket.

"What have you got in there?"

Samira stopped and turned around.

"Nothing. Bottle of water."

"It's an *act*, Samira! I'm not a bloody dictator!"

"No. You're not that good. You're just a —"

"It's *me*, and Des, and this American bloke called Jeff, and also the dissidents, and we're just trying to find out —"

"*Dissidents?* John, you're so full of —"

"Wait a minute. Back up. You said —"

"You're full of —"

"No, hang on, you said that *everyone over there* knows what's going to happen."

"Yeah."

"So what's going to happen?"

"Like you don't know!"

"It's the memorial, isn't it?"

Samira stared at him, the darkness in her eyes now turning watery.

"Samira. What's going to happen at the memorial?"

Dolt kept his gaze focused on Samira, but he saw now that Gideon was bearing down on them, Security in tow.

"Samira!"

Samira turned her back.

"All sorted out?" Gideon said, arriving on the spot with breathless officiousness. "Everyone happy?"

Dolt nodded.

"Miss Pruett hates to keep her fans waiting, John. So, if you wouldn't mind..."

"Yes, all right."

"No need to detain this lady any longer?"

"No."

Dolt turned and walked out on to the vastness of the stage. Glancing back he saw that Gideon had vanished — presumably to rendezvous once more with the complimentary comforts and superior society of the sky-box — but Samira hadn't. She stood, frozen, in the wings, no longer considered a security threat, apparently, but merely one hanger-on among many.

As he approached the microphone, Dolt tried to remember the script he'd been shown. Reagan's band had assumed their positions, but the singer herself waited off-stage, astride the battery-powered mechanical bull that lent a flash of style to her trade-marked stage entrance.

"Hullo, and welcome to everyone here; to our sister celebration in the great city of Houston; and to viewers all across the free world and beyond!" Dolt said, with somewhat less enthusiasm than the script had called for.

"This is Freedom Aid, everybody!"

He must have got the name right, because a huge roar rose up from the roiling mass before him.

"What do we want?"

Freedom!

"When do we want it?"

Now!

"How do we get it?"

Democracy and free markets!

"What do we need first?"

Deregulation and privatization!

Some of these slogans hadn't been thought out properly, Dolt felt, but he slogged through them all the same. Out of the corner of his eye, he saw that the mechanical bull was under starter's orders. Reagan was in the saddle, guitar slung around her neck, and two heavy stage-hands stood ready to propel the beast into the limelight.

"And now," Dolt said, "get ready to do The Surge..." The Surge was a form of country line-dancing, he'd been told. "...because, all the way from South Carolina, here she is..."

The mechanical bull, now fully powered-up, trundled into public view. Reagan whooped and waved her hat in the air.

"...it's Reaa — gaan Pruu — ett!"

But it wasn't Reagan Pruett, or her steed, that caught the public's attention. It was Samira. She ran to the microphone where Dolt stood and kicked him to the ground. Winded, he rolled in agony. Samira snatched the microphone from its stand.

"This is for John Dolt," she said. Then she threw the microphone to the floor and pulled out the water bottle from her pocket. The crowd gasped. Lying on his back, Dolt saw Samira empty the water over her head and shoulders. Some of it splashed on to his face. It wasn't water.

When you worked with people like Hamid, with his dodgy vehicles, or Lescek, with his poorly-maintained power tools, there were many skills you had, of necessity, to acquire. And you also had to learn to act quickly in an emergency. So it didn't surprise Dolt at all that the next thing he knew was that he was standing over Samira's blackened shape, an empty fire-extinguisher in his hands, and the stench of Samira's cheap, acrylic duffle coat in his nostrils.

He dropped the extinguisher. It rolled off the stage on to the camera track. He knelt down, ignoring the pain in his gut.

"Samira!"

No answer.

"Samira! Please!"

"No, John. Too late. Watch out for your... Your cross girls."

Cross girls?

Paramedics arrived. Dolt felt himself lifted from the floor, then hustled into the wings, where Reagan's mechanical bull stood, smoldering, under the anxious protection of its traveling technicians. Gideon burst on to the scene. His face was white — unlike his shirt, which bore the tell-tale stains of a recent wine-spillage.

"My God, John! Are you all right? I *knew* that woman meant —"

"I'm fine."

"Des is on his way."

Yes, Dolt thought. He would be.

From the stage, came the sound of Reagan Pruett's voice. He really couldn't focus on her individual words, but it seemed to Dolt that she was calming the crowd and generally rescuing the occasion. Not only that, but she was talking about *him*. *What* was she saying?

John Dolt had saved her sister, Kenny, from being torn apart by a murderous mob!

Not really true, of course. He'd just plucked her from her tree. And the banker-bashers were probably some of Kenny's biggest fans.

John Dolt had saved Amber Pike from a tornado!

Again, an exaggeration. A game of basketball gone wrong.

John Dolt had saved this *poor, sad, deluded girl* from *self-immolation!* You saw it with your own eyes! Didn't you see how fast he moved?

True? How he wished it would prove so.

And now — on with the show!

Reagan's band started into her latest release — it sounded as if it might have been called "Like A Smart Bomb, Baby, I'm Burnin' Up For You."

"Ah, here's Des," Gideon said. "Where's your jacket?"

Yes, good question. Where was it?

"I must have used it to..."

"Oh, of course." Gideon made a face.

Screw Jacqueline, Dolt thought. Then he gave himself up to Des, and his attendants, and allowed himself to be escorted out of earshot of the jaunty sounds of Freedom.

As the light failed and the black Range Rover edged its way through the sullen, pinched throng outside the stadium, Dolt peered out at his private army and wondered how many of them really had guns.

The dark side had never looked quite so dark, had it?

"Where are we going?" he asked Des.

"It think you call it the Brit Arse, don't you? Funny."

Revenge, Dolt thought. Revenge for the Fusilier.

"What? Why there?"

"You've got an appointment."

"Who with?"

"Lescek."

"Lescek!"

"Yeah."

Des smacked his lips.

"Just don't freak out when you see him."

CHAPTER 40

In his dream, Jeff Crock has that *locked-on* feeling. And, like a knot in the stomach — a knot of anticipation, excitement, triumph and latent validation — it's physical, visceral, a taste on the tongue and not to be denied. He circles, performing the final calculations and calibrations. Far below, beyond human sight but well within the resolution of his optical systems and digital image enhancers, the high-value target goes about its business, relaxed, careless, and — for a moment or two yet — innocent of the content of the unappealing — and, frankly, unappealable — decision of Jeff's recently-upgraded Battlefield Legality plug-in. It's version 2.0: The best Conventions you can buy, and certainly the upgrade of choice for those seeking to bolster that all-important body-count. All the privilege and immunity you could ask for, plus real-time technical support and no questions asked in Congress.

And so what time is it now, Jeff? Bug-splat time! Jeff arms his ordnance. But wait — sensors indicate that the high-value target is not alone. Who's that with him? The iguanas! Everywhere, the iguanas! This can't be right; the system has made an error. But it never malfunctions! The President himself says so, and his lawyers agree. And that high-value target isn't a high-value target after all — it's Eric! You can't get more low-value than Eric. This is *so* wrong, but the system won't abort. Poor old Eric's organized a wedding party, he's put on his best vest and sandals and he's invited the iguanas — look, there's nothing wrong with that, what century are we living in, people? — but who the hell does he think he's marrying?

"Wake up!"

Isabel yanked the sheets from the bed. Jeff sat up in a panic and rubbed his temples.

"Whuh? What?"

"Hey. It's Marco and Alvaro. Something's happened. You've got to come. Get dressed."

Isabel handed him a pair of jeans. He glanced at the clock on the night stand: 5:00 am. Where was he? Oh, right — fancy hotel, business district, Guayaquil, Ecuador. Good. And why was he still here? In order, according to Marco, the

President's special deputy, and Alvaro, his military sidekick, to assist in a *special operation*. Jeez, and there was something about a parachute, wasn't there? Shit...

"Here. Come on."

Isabel handed him a T-shirt. It featured a satirical cigar-smoking iguana in a Che beret below the legend *Hasta la victoria siempre!* Jeff hesitated.

"Put it on!"

He slipped the shirt on and followed Isabel from the room. She led him down to the mezzanine level and into one of the business suites. Marco and Alvaro, looking suspiciously fresh and, in the case of the former, particularly serious, sat at the conference table.

"What's up?" Jeff asked.

Marco pointed to a chair.

"Take a seat. We're having a videoconference."

"Really?" Jeff said. "Sure. Why not?"

He sat. Isabel took the chair next to him. Then he noticed what was on the screen.

"Uh-oh, fuck."

Alvaro rubbed his beard and leaned across to Jeff.

"We think they traced your phone."

Jeff stared at the screen.

"I just want you to know, Mr. Crockett, that your bloody wife made a hell of a mess in my office."

Andy Willoughby-St. John sat with his feet up on a table, his sandy soles close to the camera. So much for local mores, Jeff thought. Andy wore a maroon track suit with white piping and what Jeff took to be some designer logo. He was sipping a cup of tea — that silky string with its gold tag said as much.

"Like the shirt, by the way."

Jeff looked at Marco.

"What does he want?"

"We don't know. He wanted to talk to you. Says he's heard a lot about you."

Isabel poked Jeff in the ribs.

"You have a wife? How come you never said anything?"

"Well, it didn't seem relevant at the —"

"*Relevant?* You're talking about *relevant?*"

"Look, Isabel —"

"I don't get this *relevant*."

Jeff glanced at the screen. Andy smirked as he drank his tea. Then he put his cup down, noisily.

"All right. That's enough fun. I've got a jolly busy day today, and I'm not really in the mood for any more nonsense. It's not just your wife, Mr. Crockett. I really don't know what's got into her, by the way. She was doing quite a good job, I would have said. At least until your blasted mother-in-law arrived. Have you any idea what she did to my extraordinarily expensive bunker? It gets on one's tits, it really does. I mean, honestly! Well, never mind. We can fix everything. It's just a question —"

"Wait, wait, wait," Jeff said. "Where are they?"

Andy looked put out.

"Your family members, you mean? We'll come to that. First, I want to spell out a few things for you. Okay?"

Jeff said nothing.

"Firstly, congratulations. To your action-man friend there with the beard. Plucky little Ecuador gets to play at socialism and thumb its nose at Uncle Sam for a little longer. Enjoy it while you can. Hasta la victoria, for Pete's sake. You know that Douglas doesn't give up on these little tasks, don't you, Mr. Crockett? He just reschedules them."

Something told Jeff that Isabel might be tempted to raise a point or two at this juncture, so he placed a gently pre-emptive finger across her lips.

"Say hello to Douglas for me," Jeff said.

"Of course. I'm sure he'd love to catch up with you. Now, about your little stunt at my daughter's wedding."

"Oh, that."

"Yes, that."

Jeff remembered flying the drone above the wedding party at the FMS campus; he remembered locking on to War Criminals One and Two; he remembered those disembodied voices.

"That was a bloody silly thing to do."

"I guess."

"You'll find that all those remote app thingies have been disabled."

"Shame."

Thingies? Andy wasn't a nerd. He wasn't a techie. He was a murderer.

"How did you get hold of them, by the way?"

"Uh, let me think..."

"We know you were in Barbados."

Careful, he thought. Don't drop John Dolt in it. The guy was, well, basically a fuck-up. But not a total fuck-up. He might yet serve some purpose. And, in the end, he would certainly drop *himself* in it, unassisted. They always did.

"Oh, oh! That's right. I got 'em from Faith Boy."

Andy affected a look of lofty disapproval.

"That's not a very respectful way to speak of one's most loyal ally."

"No. It isn't."

"Dear me. Well! Oh, and just so you know. Whatever you may have seen on your screen, there was absolutely no live ordnance involved. So don't bother sitting around, thinking of what might have been. If you follow me."

A murderer and a *liar*.

"Sure. Whatever you say. Are you just calling to be an asshole?"

Andy bristled. The feet came down off the desk and the tea cup went flying.

"You listen to me. All of you."

Once again, Jeff dissuaded Isabel from comment.

"No one is going to stop this operation. The drones are flying again — very impressively, may I say — and no one, not even Mr. Crockett, is going to commandeer them. Thanks to, ah — I'll just call him a very sound, helpful fellow — we have retrieved the computer code that was stolen from us. We —"

"Where's Annie?" Jeff said.

"We have taken all appropriate measures —"

"Where is she?"

Andy paused and folded his arms.

"You want to see her? Oh, very well. General? Would you mind?"

Jeff pushed his seat back, stood, and took a step closer to the screen. A tall, sunken-eyed man in military fatigues — not Libyan, Jeff thought; Sudanese? Somali? — moved into frame and placed a second chair alongside Andy's. Then he moved out of frame again, to return moments later with his second payload, which was Annie. Her wrists were bound with shiny white plastic. Jeff took another step towards the screen. Behind him, he heard Isabel gasp. He was aware that Marco and Alvaro were looking at him. Annie's face was a mess.

"No gang of senile, superannuated *dissidents* is going to spoil the party," Andy said. "No special ops for them. They're finished. It's social security and the early-bird special, if they're lucky."

Jeff held his breath. Annie looked down at the table, silent.

"No campaigning liberal journos are going to blow the whistle. Your pathetic web site doesn't even exist any more — have you noticed? Shut down. Just like that. You don't even have a pension, do you?"

What about Katherine? He wanted to ask, but restrained himself.

"The public doesn't give a flying toss about whistle-blowers. Not any more. Discredited. The lot of them. Good job there by someone, I don't know who."

Annie lifted her face an inch — not enough for eye contact. Jeff took another step towards the screen.

"The great American public doesn't even know where the Greater Persian Region is. As for the Brits — well, I've never seen anything so splendid. What is it Mr. Dolt says? We don't want them all coming over here and... Well, whatever."

Annie tilted her head on one side. It was as if she were looking at something on the table.

"And no tin-pot South American demagogue is going to stand against the tide of history. Just so you know."

"Okay. Got that," Jeff said.

"So, Mr. Crockett. Here is my advice. Give up. Go away. Abandon the civilized world. Live a quiet life somewhere. Paraguay, perhaps? Laos? Mozambique? Some place that no one cares about. You know, I'd be jolly inclined to give the same advice to your wife here. With me?"

"Yeah. I'm with you."

What was Annie looking at?

"Good. Well, I think that's all. Nothing to add, General? No? Well, I didn't think you would. He's more a man of action, you see. Well, that's all. Goodbye."

The screen went blank. The atmosphere in the room condensed. Jeff realized that he'd been sweating. Marco and Alvaro were out of their seats, walking it off. Isabel shouted abuse at the darkened screen.

"Marco?" Jeff said.

"Yes?"

"Did that get recorded somehow?"

"Let me see."

Marco poked at the laptop through which the video conference had been conducted.

334

"Yes, it's here."

"Can you wind back about a minute from the end and pause it?"

"Okay."

Jeff looked at the frozen image of his wife on the laptop's screen. Annie was looking at a flat, rectangular object.

"Is this high-def?"

"I think it is," Marco said.

"Zoom in on *that*."

"Okay."

The object was a tablet computer. That's Andy's morning, right there, Jeff thought. Cup of tea, check your email, beat up your enemy's wife.

"Zoom in some more."

Marco zoomed.

"What's all that stuff in Spanish?"

Marco peered at the screen.

"Well," he said, "it sounds like *everything* is *go* for *tomorrow* in Costa Rica."

"Shit!"

"Yes. I agree. Alvaro?"

Alvaro looked at Marco and rubbed his chin. Then he picked up the phone.

CHAPTER 41

Lescek looked as if he'd accidentally fallen downstairs. After that, he must have accidentally walked into a closed door. In fact, it looked as though his day so far had been one long series of painful calamities, culminating, from all appearances, in his having stepped on the wrong end of a garden rake several times in succession.

Dolt took this in for several moments.

"Don't throw a wobbly," Des said.

"You said you weren't going to —"

"Well, fuck me," Des said. "I forgot to keep my election promises. What a bastard. Oops!"

They were in the Karaoke Lounge at the Britannia Arms in Wembley. Des and his short-haired assistants had secured the lounge and the stickily-carpeted corridor that led to it. Lescek cowered in a red-velvet booth beneath a picture of Madonna in her *vogue* era pomp.

Des activated the karaoke system. Lights began to flash. A mirror ball jerked into motion. Dolt realized they were listening to "I Get Knocked Down, But I Get Up Again," by whoever the hell it was. Had Des really lost it this time — or was this some pathetic shred of fuck-you spy-craft?

"Lescek here's agreed to help us," Des said.

"Fuck off out of it!" Dolt said. "Go on! Get out of my face for a minute."

"All right, all right. Nothing to wig out about."

Des retreated to the bar and pretended to study its inventory of trendy, TV-advertised beverages.

Dolt slumped on to the banquette alongside Lescek. Lescek flinched and held his hands in front of his face. Those scratches — tile-related injuries? Dolt didn't think so.

"Lescek. I, er..."

He was going to say that he didn't know what to say. But that was the problem. He didn't.

A long moment passed. Lescek lowered his hands.

"I can do whatever you want, okay?"

"Um, sure, Lescek. But —"

"I can figure out this code for you. Hey, remember that vacuum cleaner you showed me? Big joke, huh?"

Dolt looked down at his shoes. Along the bottom edge of the banquette was a loose piece of gilded trim. He began to tug at it.

"Yeah, I know. Hilarious. Look, Lescek —"

"You gave me the complete on-board system code for some new American drone. But I have no sense, of course. I'm just a stupid idiot. I should have sold it to the Russians, or the Chinese."

"Er, no, you wouldn't want to do that, Lescek. Cause —"

"But your friend over there, Mr. State Security, he says there's a deliberate bug in the code. You find it, he says. And then tell me how to upload it."

Dolt ripped another six inches of trim from the seat.

"Did you find the bug?"

"Oh, sure. But not so easily. This particular programmer is a very smart guy. Do you know him?"

Dolt ripped off another foot of trim.

"Not personally."

"Okay," Lescek said, tipping his head back and slipping down in his seat. "So far so good, you see?"

"Yeah. Then what?"

"Well, we have a problem. I asked your friend — I said, what happened to this guy? He has no good answer, so I ask myself a question. What happens to a guy who uploads bad code to a top-secret American drone? All the comments in this code are in Arabic, okay? But the guy puts his name in the code change history. Very professional. So then I search online and I read about you and this terrorist girl. Aisha, yes? Same last name as the guy. She's from Libya. Fine, now I can put it all together. So I tell your friend here to fuck off, because I've got enough trouble without pissing off the Americans. I just want to go back to my tiles."

Dolt snapped off the trim and threw it on the floor.

"And that was when —"

Lescek pointed at his face.

"Yeah, sure."

"I told him, I absolutely told him —"

"Whatever you say, John."

"Lescek, you've got to believe me. I swear I didn't —"

"Yeah, yeah. Just don't make me a *Dangerous Person*, okay? Please?"

"Is that what Des..."

Lescek nodded.

"Fuck *him*," Dolt said. "But you know what we're trying to do, right? The Greater Persian thing?"

"If you say so."

"It's fucking WMD, Lescek!"

"Yeah, that's bad."

"Aisha had some pictures. You should have seen them!"

"I'll take your word. Tell me what you want."

338

Dolt stood, kicked over the cocktail table in front of the booth and paced the dance floor. Beneath his feet, multi-colored plastic squares flickered and pulsed. The music had changed. He was listening to "Go West" by The Pet Shop Boys.

Some primordial, unsummoned impulse animated him, and he made for the karaoke control desk, visions of ruin trembling before his eyes. But Des grabbed him by the elbow and hauled him back to the booth where Lescek languished, mute and limp.

"Lescek's going to provide us with a... What is it, again?"

"A loader program," Lescek said.

"Right," Des said. "It loads the what's-it into the drone. You following me?"

Dolt nodded.

"There's only one problem."

"Only one?"

"Yeah. They've shut off all their external... What d'you call 'em?"

Lescek sighed.

"Network application access points."

"Exactly," Des said. "Which means that..."

"Someone must go on site."

Dolt looked at Des.

"What does he mean, *on site?*"

Des licked his lips.

"Libya. The drone base. What did you think he meant?"

A sense of unease began to seep up into Dolt from the jittery floor. It didn't help that the karaoke system had now selected "I Would Die For You" by Prince.

Dolt hesitated.

"I know what you're going to ask me," Des said.

"Who's going?"

"You."

"No, fuck off. Send one of your sodding agents."

"Firstly, John, they're not my sodding agents. And, secondly, to be honest, I'd rather put my faith in you, bizarre as that may seem. You may not know this, but the clueless toffs who —"

Dolt wasn't in the mood for another of Des's rants about *Oxbridge*, so he put his foot down.

"I'm not going to Libya."

"Yes, you are."

"No way."

"You're flying out tomorrow."

"I'm going on this flaming War Zones charity tour."

"Exactly."

"Libya's not on the list."

"It is now."

"How?"

"You're going to put it there. I'll explain in a moment,"

Des turned to Lescek.

"Now *you* — get out of here and get to work. And don't forget that tweak we talked about."

Lescek didn't move.

"Now!"

Lescek struggled to get up. Dolt lent him a hand and escorted him to the door.

"What a friend," Des said when Lescek was gone.

Dolt said nothing. Des looked at his watch.

"Oh, look at the time. You've got a night-time rally to go to, haven't you?"

The karaoke system started playing "Candle In The Wind" by Elton John. Des groaned.

"Let's get out of this dump. We'll talk in the car. Come on."

Outside, in the car park, the air felt chilly. Cold air, hot blood, Dolt thought. Would the pubs empty for his searchlight rally?

Which was more intoxicating — a five-quid pint of Old Grenadier, or a free bucket of Dolt's trademark *dark-side* bile?

The black Range Rover lurked in the shadows. On Dolt's side, someone had parked an antique motorcycle-and-sidecar contraption. Such a relic seemed out-of-place, here. The Brit Arse was more your entry-level-BMW or obscure-Asian-SUV kind of establishment. Weird.

"Here's what you do," Des said, as he flung the car on to the public road and pointed it towards the North Circular.

"You get on the blower to your pal, Faith Boy. I believe you have his private number, don't you?"

"Yes." The former PM's people had passed it on to Gideon's people.

"Tell him you're worried. Your sources tell you there's a danger that forces opposed to the liberation of the Greater Persian region are plotting a black propaganda campaign. In the aftermath, that is. They intend to accuse the liberators of war crimes. Got that?"

"I suppose so."

"Therefore, you feel it is imperative that you are in a position to refute their slanderous lies. Right?"

"Right."

An idle glance in the Range Rover's nearside door mirror told Dolt that the antique motorcycle had elected to join them in the outside lane. Well, why not?

"So you want him to arrange a visit for you. To the drone base. No cameras, though — we'll say you're dropping in on British Special Forces engaged in sensitive operations. Don't want to endanger our brave lads, do we?"

"No."

"Then, when you get back, you're in a position to say, if it comes to it, that you inspected the base thoroughly, and — be careful how you phrase this next bit — you saw absolutely no evidence of inappropriate substances."

"Inappropriate substances?"

"Yeah."

Des seemed to have spotted something in his rear-view mirror. A mirthless smile flashed across his lips.

"What?" Dolt said.

"Nothing. Did you get all that?"

"I think so."

"Call him after the rally."

They rode for a while in silence. Then Dolt decided to ask Des a question.

"Why are you doing this, Des? I mean, really?"

Des turned and stared at Dolt. The Range Rover began to drift into the center lane. Horns blared.

"Because I love my fucking country, don't I? Can't stand any more of these bloody disasters, can we?"

"Only asking," Dolt said.

They drove the rest of the way to the stadium without speaking.

"One thing," Dolt said as he stepped out into the clamminess of the underground car park. "What was that you said about a *tweak?*"

"John? Don't worry your pretty little head about that, okay? Go and do your rally."

"Hmm."

Dolt scanned the car park. No antique motorcycles. No side-cars.

"You just go over that way," Des said. "Gideon's waiting. He's polished your jackboots for you. Enjoy!"

The car door slammed and the Range Rover roared away. Dolt saw Gideon marching towards him.

Tweak? What tweak?

*

T he rally passed as though it were happening to someone else. And perhaps, he thought, it really was. From the very beginning, he felt a sense of dislocation and detachment. Behind him on the great stage, set up in preparation for Day Two of Freedom Aid, were the props — hay bales, fake chickens, watering cans, sunflowers, a cardboard-cut-out tractor and a scarecrow — that belonged to tomorrow's opening act, some country-rap outfit he'd never heard of.

Just to his left was Samira's burnt patch.

He couldn't tell how large the crowd was, because the searchlights at his feet rendered it mostly invisible to him. But he could hear it. And what he heard frightened him.

Yet this fear served only to distance the real John Dolt from the great stage and the great stadium that contained it. And, as he receded, so his doppelgänger — the one that lived in the pages of the tabloids; on *John's Jury*; in the guilty nightmares of the *utopians* and the wet dreams of the *irreconcilables* — so this alternate Dolt stepped into Jacqueline's smart-casual loafers (that crack about jackboots was Des's idea of a joke).

He listened to his other self speak. He listened to his other self exhort and demand, wheedle and cajole, damn and exalt, vilify and threaten.

After a while, he tuned out. You would, wouldn't you?

When he left the stage he was steaming with sweat.

"How did I do?" he asked his personal assistant.

Gideon looked at him.

"I'll take you home, John," he said.

CHAPTER 42

S ome small decisions are definitive, and may be fatal. Bonnie DiAngelo had traveled enough in Africa to know this. So she had to allow that Jay's moral credit, in some limited sense, had been restored to a positive balance — a supply of capital surpassed, perhaps, only by the shed full of dollars he claimed to keep at that farmhouse of his in Namibia.

They had lost Annie, and Jay hadn't wanted to look for her. It was his decision. Likewise, they had not returned to the Colonel's compound — because, as Jay had pointed out, as a matter of dumb fact, *Annie knows where it is, doesn't she, Bonnie?*

And the Colonel wouldn't be going back there any time soon; his compound had been pulverized, and much of the street with it. Like children kept indoors during a thunderstorm, Andy's drones had gone back out to play the moment the sand had stopped flying.

Jay had made the right call.

For a while, Bonnie, Jay, Leo, the Colonel and the kids had holed up in a house belonging to the Colonel's eighty-five-year-old mother. Now they were in a meeting hall attached to a mosque; it was considered a neutral place. But the meeting, at first, was noisy and fractious.

It so happened that the street on which the Colonel's compound once stood was also a boundary between zones of influence. Did Andy know that? Furthermore, *all* of Kufra's power-brokers — community leaders, bosses, barons, chieftains, warlords, businessmen; call them what you want — and their friends and associates, all the way up to Tripoli, had gotten to the point where it was generally agreed that Andy was just a bit too much trouble.

That's what the meeting was about. Jay had predicted, correctly, that there would be an impossible argument about *who* was to contribute *what* to the effort. And so, approaching the problem in the way that can-do men so often chose, he proposed to throw money at it.

He already owed the Colonel for the hire of the cement truck, the *replacement* of the cement truck, and the loss of the compound, so Jay had decided to fling open his vaults. But he had to convince the meeting that the vaults actually existed. That was why he'd hooked up the mosque's laptop to its video projector.

The picture, when it finally came through, was jerky but clear. The noise in the hall dropped almost to nothing. Jay declared that the meeting would now be able to observe his farmhouse in Namibia — not the original one, southwest of Windhoek, but the new one, up near the Waterberg plateau. Evidently, it was wired for video. Jay flipped though several static perspectives. It felt like a real estate viewing.

Finally, he came to what the meeting really wanted to see: A room full of wooden crates. Standing in front of the crates was an elegant, fit graybeard in a suit and open-necked white shirt.

"Hi there, Walter," Jay said. "Thanks so much for doing this."

"You're welcome, Jay."

"Good trip up from Jo'burg?"

"Pretty good."

Walter, Bonnie thought. Jay's so-called boss in South Africa. But if those crates were really full of dollars, why did he need a boss? Why didn't he just retire? The Waterberg was a nice place to live.

"Want to open one up for us?" Jay said.

"Sure."

Walter picked up a small crowbar and jimmied open one of the crates. He put the top of the crate aside and picked out two small, polythene-wrapped bales.

"Want me to unwrap these?"

"If you wouldn't mind."

Walter unwrapped one of the bundles, advanced towards the camera, and held up a fistful of hundred-dollar bills. A murmur of approval ran around the hall. Walter picked out a single bill and held it up to the camera — first one side and then the other.

"How can we tell it's real?" someone yelled.

"How can you tell it's not?" Jay said. "What's the difference?"

But of course it was real. She couldn't doubt it. Every dollar bill the CIA ever printed was real, wasn't it?

"Walter? Just tip that box over, so the folks here can see inside, would you?"

"You got it."

Walter flipped the crate on its side. It was full of money.

Jay addressed the meeting.

"Any questions, gentlemen?"

"How soon?"

"To Tripoli? Walter — how long to ship it?"

"Maybe three days."

"Okay. Gentleman in the green shirt?" Jay said.

"How much in one box?"

"Uh, I forget. Couple million, I think. Maybe three."

"How many boxes?"

"How many have I got, or how many are you getting?"

This caused a stir; Jay was pushing his luck again, she thought.

344

"You guys can have three. How's that? No? Okay, okay — four. What? Come on, you're killing me here. All righty — five. Final offer. No, no — five it is. Deal? I said, deal? Okay, done. Thank you very much, gentlemen. A pleasure doing business with you. Go start getting ready. Meeting over, people!"

The crowd began to disperse — in a happy mood, it seemed. A nice little windfall for some of Kufra's leading citizens: All they had to do was storm Andy's castle. But what about Annie?

Leo had sat beside her during the meeting, silent. What, she wondered, did Mr. Corporate Social Responsibility think of Jay's business methods?

"All that money," she said. "You know, back home, they're turning off the street lights."

Leo made a noise — somewhere between a cough and a snort. Sometimes he could be a drama queen — in a strait-laced sort of way.

"This is not the right way to behave."

"No. It isn't."

"Your friend has his own agenda."

"I guess he does."

"He is not much better than *them*."

She let that go. Jay approached.

"That seemed to go okay."

"You're really giving them the money?" she said.

"Sure. Deal's a deal."

"What about Walter?"

"He won't take any."

"No, I mean... Never mind."

"So everything's cool. Hey, Leo?"

Cool?

She got to her feet.

"You know, I wanted to talk about my daughter. But she's irrelevant. I can see that. There's a fight, and she's in the way. The fight goes on, doesn't it? There's always a fight. I was the only woman in that meeting. Where are the women? You men are the problem. With your wars, your exploitation, your machines, your poisons. You fight each other. You fight the planet. Even when you say you're fighting *for* it. You fight for power, even when you have no use for it. You build and you destroy. But what do you create? You're going to have to change. You're all going to have to change. I mean it."

She stopped talking, but her words echoed on around the empty hall. Then, for a while, there was silence.

"I know," Jay said. "Can we go now?"

"Yes," she said. "We can go now."

CHAPTER 43

Though his alter ego slumbered — sated and spent, at least for now — the real John Dolt found no repose. Here he was, back in his Afro-Swiss hotel suite, restless, wakeful and anxious. The Tanzanian chocolates on his pillow did little to calm him. He found no solace in his freshly-laundered Egyptian cotton bathrobe; or in his complimentary voucher for a head-and-shoulder massage in the hotel's Lac Leman Spa and Sauna; or in the upgraded artwork on his walls (portraits of great British statesmen of the nineteenth century); or in the tributes submitted by the van-load from chapters of the Home Guard all across the land — some floral, some poetic, others plain crazy; or in a voicemail from Amber Pike commending him for *stickin' it to the secular elites that are coming down our throats, also.*

According to the itinerary Gideon had left for him, Dolt was to be collected at 6:00 am by Des, who would transport Dolt to the military airfield at Northolt, whence his flight into danger would begin. It was now 2:15 am.

He couldn't sleep, and there was nothing for him to do. Unless, that is, he wanted to watch his performance at the rally; Freedom News UK was running it on the hour, every hour. But he didn't. He would have been happy to do his own packing, but Jacqueline had done it for him. In her note, she explained that she'd gone for earth-tones and understated military chic. If Dolt elected to visit any battle-zones, however, he'd need specialized gear; Jacqueline had forwarded his measurements and requirements to the relevant military authorities.

To ease his agitation, Dolt paced in his business den. His phone call to the former PM had gone well. But there was something faintly off about the alacrity with which the former PM had received his request to visit the secret drone base. Was Dolt missing something there? Perhaps. On the other hand, there seemed little doubt that the former PM was girding himself to stiff the Great Leader's memorial in favor of a new flowering in Anglo-Uzbek relations. In fact, the former PM was eager to know who exactly he should be hooking up with in Cape Town. Dolt had been forced to prevaricate; instructions had yet to arrive from Jefferson Crockett. Perhaps the accident-prone American had got himself lost in the jungles of Ecuador, or offended its President and been cast into a dungeon; who could say?

But it wasn't the fate of the lanky leftist, or the possible wiles of the former PM that haunted Dolt. Nor was it entirely Des's brutal treatment of Lescek or Samira's desperate act that presently bothered him — though even now he felt the scars knitting on his soul.

And it wasn't the prospect of venturing into the War Zones. After all, his celebrity companions comprised a goateed fashion stylist who told fat women they were gorgeous; a posh woman who found big houses for rich families too lazy to look for themselves; and a footballer-turned-entrepreneur who wanted to help poor kids to learn to dance. What could possibly happen to *them?* Road-side bomb? Inconceivable.

No. It was Gideon's *threat*. And Des's *tweak*.

He shambled over to the window and looked down into the street. All was quiet. Well, all right, the distant wail of sirens and the thumping of helicopters told him that the disturbances hadn't taken a night off after all. But it all depended on what you were used to, really, didn't it?

And, of course, if there was one thing he *didn't* want to get used to, it was being pursued by motorcycles. Yet there it was, parked not quite out-of-sight: The antique motorcycle, with its equally decrepit sidecar.

Enough was enough, he thought. He discarded his bath robe and flung on the first outfit he pulled out of Jacqueline's matching, personalized luggage set — some kind of beige linen safari outfit, with fake-leopard lining and trim.

In the lobby, he brushed past Des's dozy minions and ordered them to stay put. Then, like a portly, middle-aged cheetah trying to recall its old tricks, he slunk along the pavement, keeping to the shadows, until he was within shouting distance of the motorcycle. There, he stopped and observed.

A tell-tale quiver on the part of the sidecar confirmed his suspicions. He rose up to his full height and advanced. On reaching the sidecar he proceeded to hammer on its roof with his fist. This produced a reaction. A small window opened.

"Hey!"

Dolt peered in. The occupant of this absurd vehicle was an elderly gent with white hair and an over-trimmed moustache. He wore an olive-green jumper with patches on the shoulders and had been engaged in swilling from an old-fashioned thermos flask. It smelled like onion soup.

"Let me guess," Dolt said.

He recalled Des's warning about *military brass* who were getting *cold feet* about adventures in the Greater Persian Region, and his sneery, dismissive smile upon spotting the sidecar in his rear-view.

"You're *dissidents*, and you've come to warn me off?"

The gent in the sidecar didn't reply. He was looking at the empty space above Dolt's right shoulder. Dolt dodged to the left, spun on his heel and wheeled around to face his attacker. It was a second old geezer, dressed like the first, armed with a cricket bat.

"Oh, for fuck's sake!" Dolt said, snatching the bat away and flinging it into a handy skip.

"You, sir, are a disgrace!"

"No, I'm not."

"You drag this nation into dishonor!"

"No, I don't."

"We didn't fight the Nazis and the Soviets so that people like you could —"

"Course you didn't. Look, mate. You're barking up the wrong flag-pole. We can sort this out very easily. Are you familiar with a bloke called Desmond Crabtree?"

There was a pause. The first geezer emerged from his sidecar and mopped the spilt soup from his jumper.

"Crabtree, you say?"

"Yeah. Hang on, I'll give him a bell."

When Des answered, Dolt handed his phone to the second geezer, folded his arms and waited. Des's laughter pierced the night air.

"Good night, Des," Dolt said, when it was over, "and fuck you, too."

Then he addressed himself to the geriatric generals — for that was surely what they were.

"Got the picture, now?"

"Well, yes. Indeed. Different complexion, and all that. Sorry about the, er..."

"Don't worry about it," Dolt said. "How'd you like to do me a favor?"

"Well, what sort of favor?"

Dolt indicated the sidecar.

"I need a lift to West Hendon."

*

The lights in Lescek's attic flat, as Dolt had anticipated, burned brightly. He ordered his motorcycle detail to loiter inconspicuously in the street — a big ask, but never mind — while he wore his thumb out on Lescek's doorbell. Eventually, Lescek agreed to admit him.

The state of the flat, Dolt felt, spoke to the disorderly drive of its occupant. Lescek had been slaving at his keyboard. He had three large computer screens on his desk. There were multiple windows open on each. Dolt inspected them. Each window contained line after line of gibberish — weirdly indented and highlighted in various colors — that consisted of round, square, angle and curly brackets, mathematical symbols, and the odd recognizable word. The most popular word was *if*. It was appropriate, Dolt thought. The whole thing looked extremely *iffy*.

Dolt collapsed on to Lescek's two-seater sofa-bed, having first removed the Polish newspapers and pizza boxes.

"Is that it, then?" he asked.

"Yes. This is the code."

"Looks complicated."

"Maybe, to you."

Dolt pointed at one of the windows.

"What's that bit do?"

"That? Nothing. Just the declaration of some abstract base classes."

"Thought so."

Lescek started to type. Dolt took a moment to survey the contents of Lescek's studio flat. Either the bathroom business wasn't paying as well as Dolt had always assumed, or else Lescek was sending all his dosh back to Poland. What would the other John Dolt have said about *that?*

"Lescek?"

"Yes?"

"Mind if I ask a question?"

"No, John. Ask your question."

Dolt shifted on his sofa-bed.

"Um, it's just something Des said. At the Brit Arse."

"Yes?"

"He said something about a *tweak.*"

Lescek stopped typing and turned to face Dolt.

"Don't ask me about any tweaks."

"Yeah, but I just did, though, didn't I?

Lescek shook his head.

"Did Des tell you not to..."

Lescek nodded.

"Lescek, you can't trust that guy. *I* don't trust him. I mean, look what he did to you."

"Yes, look."

"What is this tweak? What is he making you do?"

Lescek turned back to his screens but didn't resume his typing.

"Honestly, Lescek — Des is never going to help you. I'm the only one who can."

Lescek's head seemed to sink into his shoulders.

"Okay. I'll show you. Come over here."

Dolt followed Lescek into the kitchen. On the table was a map of Africa.

"See this?" Lescek said. He drew an imaginary line with his finger from south-eastern Libya to the middle of the Indian Ocean.

"Huh?" Dolt said.

"Your friend — Des — wants the drones like fly like so."

"Into the sea?"

"No. There's an island. Look, here."

There was indeed a speck of land.

"He wants the drones to land on *that?*" Dolt said.

"No. Not land. Crash."

"*Crash?*"

Lescek nodded.

"Can you make them do that? I mean —"

"Sure, it's simple. I override some virtual functions. Then I hard-code the navigation vector array. And I —"

"Yeah, yeah. I get it. But why?"

Lescek shrugged.

"He didn't say?"

"No."

Dolt looked again at the map.

"What island is that, anyway?"

"It's called Diego Garcia."

"What's so special about it?"

"I don't know. I don't *want* to know, John."

Well, it wasn't hard to grasp Lescek's reluctance. And though a quick Internet search might have told them much, Dolt sensed that here was an issue that cried out for informed, expert — and, possibly, unconventional — opinion. And there was only one suitable expert he could think of. Not Gideon. Not the former PM. Not those self-deluding twats at the Atlantic Affairs Institute.

"Um, Lescek, can I use your phone?"

"What's wrong with yours?"

"I, er, left it in the car. I mean the... Never mind."

This was untrue. But he didn't want to risk calling Jefferson Crockett on his own phone. Lescek's would be okay, wouldn't it?

"Okay. Here."

Dolt took Lescek's phone and, at least partly out of habit, he supposed, adjourned to the bathroom.

"Jeff?"

"John!"

"Where are you?"

"Military airbase near Guayaquil. Where are you?"

"Flat in West Hendon."

"Cool. How's it going with Faith Boy?"

"Great. Got a contact for me yet?"

"Still working on it. Saw your friggin' rally on Freedom News. Boy, you're somethin' else, ain't ya?"

"Thanks. Question?"

"Yes?"

"Diego Garcia. What is it?"

There was a pause.

"Why do you ask, John?"

"Cause Des wants to crash the drones on it."

"He *what?*"

For the next few minutes, Jeff did all the talking. He had quite a lot to say, and altogether it was, Jeff asserted, an *ugly story*. Diego Garcia had been part of something called the British Indian Ocean Territory. But, in the nineteen-sixties, the British government began kicking the local inhabitants off, and handed over the island to the US military. A vast air base had been constructed. The location was, obviously, *highly strategic*. The locals had been rounded up and dumped in the Seychelles, or somewhere, then left to rot. Their pet dogs had been gassed. Decades of legal appeals had come to nothing. Rumor had it that the island now harbored an illegal *black-site* secret prison.

But Jeff was firm.

"John, you can't let him do that."

"But you said the locals aren't there any more."

"Those military guys are people too, John."

"Ah. Right. What, then?"

"Give me a moment. I need to talk to Marco."

"Who's Marco?"

"My new best buddy."

"Okay."

Best buddy? Where did that leave Dolt? Oh well...

"John?"

"Yeah?"

"Listen carefully. Get your guy to program the drones to fly towards Diego Garcia. Don't crash. Don't land. Keep going south. Stay over the ocean. Got that?"

"Yeah. Then what?"

"Land 'em at the main airport in Cape Town."

"Bloody hell."

"You got it, buddy."

CHAPTER 44

Two twin-engined propeller planes, bearing the logos of a fictional Ecuadorian tour company, headed out over the Pacific Ocean in the direction of the Galapagos Islands. Once out of sight of land, they turned to the northeast. In the first, rode Marco, his team of diplomats, and Isabel. Their ultimate destination was the United Nations in New York, but they would not be going there directly. Jefferson Crockett, meanwhile, his newly-issued diplomatic passport notwithstanding, rode in the second plane, along with Alvaro and his team of aerial commandos. Their immediate target was the Osa peninsular of Costa Rica, and the bolt-hole *de luxe* of North Atlantic plutocrats known as Rancho Colorado. Jeff now understood all that talk about parachutes.

Some assumptions had been made. Assumption (a) was that Jeff's half-day of training would prove adequate and he would pull the right string at the right moment; assumption (b) was that the management at Rancho Colorado hadn't — yet — installed anti-aircraft guns; assumption (c) was that Jeff would find some means of getting from Rancho Colorado to the airstrip at Puerto Jiménez — which was located, Jeff might find it helpful to remember, right next to the town cemetery — where Marco would await him; and assumption (d) was that Alvaro knew what the hell he was doing. There had been keen discussion of assumptions (a) through (c), but no one had dared to raise assumption (d).

To pass the flight-time and keep his mind off *the jump*, Jeff reflected on the essential mystery of the man who called himself John Dolt.

Here was a man whose self-proclaimed ambition — to *go on an island* — was modest and, arguably, had already been achieved. And though he had professed, in passing, some frustration concerning an *offshore bank account*, he hardly seemed to be motivated by financial gain. His public performance as populist rabble-rouser and right-wing demagogue was near-flawless. Clearly, the invisible apparatus that supported and groomed him was formidable. But there was something else. During a lifetime spent observing the habits of political fakers and hypocrites, Jeff had never seen anyone fake authenticity so well. Sure, War Criminal Number Two had been a world-class act, for a time. But the odor of political insincerity is strong stuff; you just can't keep it bottled up for long.

Dolt, though he waded with abandon into swamps of muck that his predecessors and competitors would dance around, somehow smelled sweet. No dog-whistle for him. No weaseling. No compromise and no retreat. In fact, if you were his handlers, wouldn't you be getting a little uncomfortable at this point? You know — that whole *Frankenstein* thing?

In private, the man was an ordinary goof, an everyday fuck-up. He wasn't a thinker, or even a dreamer. He was barely political at all. How did this separation of spirit come about? How long had it taken? Years? He seemed, after all, to have taken to his new avocation with only minimal instruction. Who had done this thing — whatever, precisely, it was — to him? It was worth finding out, Jeff thought, because someone, somewhere, had committed a great crime.

In the meantime, though, Dolt was *the man who mattered*. His plan, he'd told Jeff, was to infiltrate the drone base in Libya, essentially on his own. Jeff's warning had been stern: Dolt would be going up against Andy Willoughby-St. John and some guy who looked like Andy's pet warlord. Without backup. Unarmed. Dolt proposed — somehow — to reprogram the big drones not only to crap out, but, at Jeff's suggestion, to land in Cape Town at the very moment that their faithful sponsor, Number Two, swept into town powered by dreams of Uzbek gold. (Memo to self: To close the deal, Jeff still needed the help of some sympathetic South African politico.) And sparing the cooks, drivers, grunts, and — perhaps? — political prisoners of Diego Garcia was not merely a happy side-effect, but a moral imperative. Dolt was going to do all this. But why had *Des* — some kind of double- or maybe even triple-agent in the Dolt camp — wanted to crash the drones on the island? The reason remained obscure, perhaps obscene.

More: Dolt had pledged to help Annie, if he could. He would *keep an eye out*, he promised, for Jeff's mother-in-law. And how pathetic had it sounded for Jeff to plead like that? Yes, exactly — *that* pathetic.

Well, look, Dolt wasn't the only one taking risks. There was still *the jump*. Yes, the jump. Which string was it, again?

*

In the event, tumbling out of the plane proved to be a simple matter, especially when you had Alvaro's boot on your ass. What's more, there was only one string available to pull, Alvaro shrewdly having stowed the others. Jeff simply had to yank on his when the others yanked on theirs — easy. All that remained was to steer towards the landing site — the lawns in front of the glass-fronted building where all the coup magic happened. This, despite yesterday's crash-course, he found more challenging. The main thing, he reminded himself, was to land on something soft. The golf course — if it came to it — would do.

As he floated down, he took in the scene around him. According to the indefatigable Dolt, Rand Purdo, the ultimate Seignior of Rancho Colorado, had been inspired by Dolt to declare a strike of all the *truly productive people*. This had fazed the British PM somewhat — which Dolt seemed to find quite funny. But the strike had begun, and you could see the results here: There was what you might call an *influx*. Marco had said that every corporate jet in the western

354

hemisphere was either heading south, or was stacked up above San José. Here, helicopters queued up to land on the pad behind the main building.

And from his airy vantage point, Jeff could now appreciate that Rancho Colorado was, in fact, far larger than he had realized. Those idiosyncratic villas around the edge of the golf course comprised only the *front line* of what had to be the most seriously-gated community in the world. Even so, you had to worry about the extent of the accommodation available. Had any of these militant arrivees — or their people — thought to book ahead? How many bankers were prepared to bunk up? It was the age-old problem of resource distribution.

He would have dwelled on these pleasant thoughts if he had not noticed that his path of descent had diverged from that taken by Alvaro and his men, and that he was, indeed, destined to come to Earth on the fairway of what looked like the second hole. No amount of tugging or twisting could amend this fate. And, if Jeff had never seen a golf buggy with his name on it before — well, he was seeing one now.

Furthermore, as luck would have it, he *did* land on something soft. It was Elliot Tucker, the Medicare fraudster, discreetly on furlough from that coma clinic in Switzerland.

As per his training, Jeff detached himself smartly from his chute. It blew across the fairway to a neighboring green, where it intercepted a long putt by — could it be? — Morrison Tweed, the careless coal-miner. Protests rang out from the frustrated putter and his partners. But Jeff was ready for them. At Marco's insistence — and Jeff, still sore at the fate suffered by his spy-camera on his first visit to Rancho Colorado, had readily agreed — Jeff had been outfitted with a secret, helmet-mounted, high-definition, audio/video recording system. He now activated this device.

Tucker had gotten back on his feet and now glared at Jeff with such a tidal-wave of entitled anger that, were it only to be harnessed somehow, Jeff felt, it could have powered an entire fleet of golf buggies for the duration of a major tournament.

"Hey, Elliot! How's it hanging? Shaken off that coma yet?"

"Who the hell are you?"

"I'm your worst nightmare, Elliot. I'm your nemesis. I'm the angry guy on the subway. I'm the patient who didn't get the treatment I needed. I'm the Chinese worker who killed herself in your factory. I am vengeance. I am your Angel of Destruction. I am the ninety-nine per cent."

Okay, so he was getting a little carried away here. And he really ought to be catching up with Alvaro and the guys. But it just felt so good, fuck it!

"Got something to say to the FBI? Speak now."

Tucker, mouth open, jaw trembling, seemed to struggle to comprehend. He looked — to borrow one of Dolt's epithets — *gob-smacked*. But then he must have spotted Alvaro's troops assembling on the main lawn.

"Who are those men?"

"They are the shock troops of the revolution."

A shudder traversed Tucker's well-padded frame.

"Oh my God... Morrison! Morrison!"

Tucker dropped his five-iron, turned and fled. Jeff recorded the scene for posterity, then ran as fast as he could to the main lawn. Alvaro was waiting for him.

"You. Lead the way."

Jeff's role in the mission was multifaceted and, according to Marco, pivotal. First, Jeff was to direct Alvaro's forces to the control center from which coup operations were conducted. This was easy; all he had to do was point and say *in there*. Next, he had to locate Rancho Colorado's all-important communications gear — dishes, antennae and so on. Again, this was simple; they were *up there*. Jeff had already pointed out the beach-side sentry-boxes from the air; Alvaro now dispatched a small contingent to persuade their occupants to remain inside and contemplate the soothing motion of the waves. More crucially — and perhaps this was what Marco was getting at — Jeff needed to determine whether drone operations in the Greater Persian Region were to be controlled from Rancho Colorado (this was Marco's belief) and, if so, to make sure that they couldn't be. Jeff knew about drones; he'd used the software; it was all up to him.

There was one more task for Jeff to perform before he headed out, by means yet to be determined, to rendezvous with Marco's diplomatic corps at the airstrip in Puerto Jiménez. He was to identify for Alvaro any *persons of interest*. Marco didn't mean corporate crooks like Elliot Tucker and Morrison Tweed. And he didn't need to spell it out. Jeff knew exactly what he meant.

There was a suspended moment of impending resolve, in which Alvaro's men appeared to commune with the spirit of something or someone — Simon Bolivar? Leo Vargas? — and then the action began.

For Jeff, to begin with, it was all a discomfiting blur of the counter-intuitive, a physical contradiction of a lifetime's experience. The *goons* were supposed to burst in on *Jeff*, not the other way around. It should have been *Jeff* that got man-handled to the floor and sat on, not these nice, clean people in their chinos and polo shirts.

But he got over it.

The control room was in a ferment. The operation in Costa Rica looked like it was about to start. All the computers were on. The big monitors were busy. Radio communications buzzed. People ran to and fro on the mezzanine level with cell phones and print-outs. Ferment turned to commotion as Alvaro's men set to work. It was a bit like the finale to a James Bond movie — but with cable-yanking instead of shooting, and a smart-casual vibe in place of those color-coded boiler suits.

Things got a bit more hectic when Alvaro's men decided to clear the mezzanine by letting off a couple of smoke grenades. No doubt they also felt that it added to the action-flick atmosphere.

Remembering his mission, Jeff began to hunt among the workstations for signs of drone-related activity. Finding nothing on the lower level, he headed up into the smog and confusion of the mezzanine. On one screen, just before it went blank, he glimpsed a map of the Greater Persian Region. *Getting closer*, he thought. At the rear of the floor, obscured by filing cabinets and potted plants, was a single, closed, handle-free door. Jeff approached. Next to the door, at eye-level, was a weird, glassy panel. Jeff squinted into it. A red light flashed three times.

Okay, he thought, now we meet high-tech with low-tech. He rapped on the door with his knuckles. Nothing happened. He pounded with his fists. No response. He kicked with the heel of his German army-surplus paratrooper's boot.

The door flew open. He felt himself gripped by the throat, hauled inside and flung into a leather swivel-chair. When the chair stopped revolving, he got a look at his new office-mate.

Yes, okay, he thought — a *person of interest*. Possibly *the* person of interest. Douglas Moreland.

Obviously, they had much to catch up on. But before either could speak, the monitors turned black, the computers died, the air-con shut off and the lights above the door went out. Alvaro's men must have found the generators. Moreland swore. Jeff swiveled tentatively in his chair. They regarded each other in silence for several moments.

"I bumped into Elliot on the golf course," Jeff said. "Remember him? He's looking good."

Moreland said nothing.

"So why did you wanna take over Costa Rica? Was it the fruit?"

Moreland calmly selected a chair, placed it behind a desk and sat, facing Jeff.

"Seriously, though," Jeff said, "that whole drone thing's a bust."

Moreland leaned forward. He shook his head.

"What could it possibly be?" he said. "What in damnation is that thing on your head?"

"Oh that? That's like, a parachute hat. I guess."

Moreland made a face — kind of like a family patriarch on Masterpiece Theater contemplating an unsuitable son-in-law.

"Oh, so you came by parachute?"

"We did, yeah."

"Who are your friends?"

"I don't really want to say."

Moreland leaned back and took a deep breath.

"You realize that door doesn't open without power? It's a security feature."

There were no other doors, just two frosted-glass windows that did not open.

"And those are bullet-proof."

The room, Jeff realized, was practically air-tight. Some smoke from the grenades had blown in during his enforced entrance, and the air-con was off. It was going to get hot and unpleasant — never mind the company. How long would the batteries in his helmet-cam last? Would Alvaro come looking for him, or assume he'd set off for Puerto Jiménez?

"Huh," he said. "How 'bout that? What are we going to do?"

Moreland slid open a desk drawer.

"Well, I know what I'm going to do."

He reached into the drawer and took out a heavy automatic pistol.

CHAPTER 45

John Dolt, like movers and shakers the world over, was time-poor. Specifically, he had lacked for time in which to study the fine detail of his pollsters' daily reports. Had he been able to do so, he now suspected, he might have discovered an anomaly. His stock had never been higher, he was certain, with taxi-drivers, tabloid newspaper-readers, lovers of law-and-order, haters of hand-outs, fearers of foreigners, skeptics of Science, and — of course — all those *truly productive people*. (The great walk-out, or jet-off, had begun, and much was anticipated from it — though the results were yet to be felt.)

And the anomaly?

As he shifted on his bench-seat and his military-chic combat trousers chafed against his thighs (either Jacqueline had miscalculated, or Dolt had put on weight) it stared him in the face. No, it wasn't Gideon. Dressed not for adventure but in his customary suit and tie, he looked serene — though he was, Dolt felt, keeping one of his frowns on standby. It had been that way ever since Gideon drove Dolt back his hotel after the rally.

And it wasn't Dolt's companions on this voyage to the sharp end of democracy: The stylist, the house-hunter and the ex-footballer seemed content enough, either studying their scripts or investigating their VIP lunch packs.

Nor was it the heavy-weight correspondent from Freedom News Network, the mallet-headed Flint Gunner, or his off-screen, camera-unfriendly side-kick, the mullet-headed Nigel Weese. These gentlemen sat on the opposite side of the cabin from Dolt and beamed at him in a hearty manner that made Dolt wonder what they had in store for him.

No, it was none of the above. And, to be honest, Dolt couldn't say he hadn't been warned, could he? Hot looks. Cold shoulders. A certain brusqueness. He hadn't even got his VIP lunch pack. The geriatric generals — the ones who'd smuggled Dolt to his secret West Hendon rendezvous with Lescek, in their eccentric motorcycle-and-sidecar combination — had been right.

Ginger and *Snowy* — there'd been an argument about whether *Monty* and *Gordon* were better names, but Dolt had settled it — had laid it out for him after they'd delivered him home from Lescek's West Hendon eyrie. The Policy Steering

Committee, the Home Guard, certain financial interests and the public in general — mainly thanks to Dolt — might be up for smiting the Persians. But the military weren't. If, the two generals insisted, Dolt would only look at things from the point of view of the average young captain or major, he would understand that professional and regimental pride precluded what these dedicated young warriors regarded, almost without exception, as another politically-driven military disaster. Their men were morose. Their NCOs trembled. The senior ranks fumed. Mutiny? Of course not. But that just meant they were all looking for someone to take it out on.

That someone would be Dolt.

Now of course, Ginger and Snowy understood that Dolt could not announce his true intent. That meant he would have to watch himself. He should avoid walking in front of heavy military vehicles; he should not wander off on his own, especially not on to inviting sandy paths that appeared freshly raked; he should only eat what other people were eating; and — if absolutely necessary — he should seek the society of his fellow celebrities. Dolt had heard the expression *human shield*, hadn't he?

It rankled that this valuable advice had come not from Dolt's personal assistant or his head of security, but from a pair of onion-soup-guzzling, cricket-mad pensioners who puttered about town on a death-trap motorcycle-and-sidecar combination. But Dolt had learned by now that, in politics, friendship was a commodity, and each participant had their own agenda. Even Amber Pike's outdoorsy solicitations had their purpose.

On a more positive side-note, however, Dolt had a shrewd intuition that the sidecar, if not the onion soup, might just come in handy later.

Already weary of avoiding the hostile gaze of the uniformed men and officers who comprised the larger part of the plane's pay-load, and deterred from conversation with Gideon by the roar of four enormous propeller engines, Dolt pretended to study his itinerary.

He was to drop in on Camp This, Camp That and Camp The Other. Variously, he was to admire the sterling work of provincial reconstruction teams; be impressed at the rapid progress made in training fresh recruits to the new non-sectarian national defense force; and marvel at the enthusiasm and hunger for knowledge of school children — girls especially. Though he knew from Des that the same stretch of road had to be reconstructed over and over again; that, due to some mysterious wastage, the need for fresh recruits never let up; and that the girls were doomed, he felt he could make a more convincing stab at these tasks than at *cheering up* the troops and making them *feel wanted*.

His true mission, of course, depended on three things. Lescek had to complete his coding — substituting Jeff's *tweak* for Des's; Des had to get the code and the *loader program* to Dolt; and Dolt, somehow, after being separated from the stylist, the house-hunter and the footballer, and being spirited to the secret drone base, had to nobble the drones without being rumbled. Easy, right?

If only these dour squaddies knew what perils lay before him, and what he was about to risk on their behalf, they wouldn't be giving him those dirty looks. It was frustrating — a form of agony. In the end, though, he supposed, it would all come out and he would be a hero, wouldn't he? Almost as if he'd gone on that island and been the last contestant standing.

For a moment or so, he let his mind wander. The thrumming of the engines filled his ears. Of course there would be life after politics. He could see his way to it, now. It had been necessary to embrace the dark side; that much was clear. But after the drone attack was foiled, and the whole Greater Persian fuss had blown over, and things had begun to calm down — after all that, he would — gently, subtly and patiently — re-educate the Home Guard. They would listen to him. He would explain why he'd done what he'd done. They'd understand. The general public would sympathize. After a decent interval, he would step aside. Lessons would have been learned. Politics, and society, would move in a new, better direction. Oh, he had no illusions about changing the world. But he would have made a difference, wouldn't he? People would be just that little bit nicer. The Persians would reach out. The Policy Steering Committee would sit down and ask itself if it was really helping. And Dolt would become a — what did you call it? An *elder statesman*, that was it. Only not like the former PM, obviously. There were things that lay beyond even Dolt's genius.

The engines thrummed soothingly. Dolt's breathing slowed. But then he remembered something — something Samira had said.

Cross girls.

What the flip had she meant?

CHAPTER 46

J eff Crock felt sure that he'd seen this movie. He knew, in principle, how it was supposed to end. The problem was, he couldn't remember what he was required to do. Some kick-ass stunt, he guessed. Did it involve martial arts? Kind of a non-starter, given his unwieldy frame. More likely, he ought to be preparing to activate, unbeknownst to his antagonist, some miniature yet devastating device; it would be concealed in a ring or fountain pen, and would involve lasers or steel darts or titanium trapeze wires. Or something. But Katherine had neglected to equip him with any such gizmo. He didn't want to blame her; she probably had issues of her own right now. But all Jeff had in the way of secret-agent toys were his helmet-cam and his cell phone. Talk about suspense.

Moreland, meanwhile, was holding up his end of the drama — along with that heavy, shiny pistol of his. More prolix by far than the average super-villain, he explained to Jeff not only the mechanics of his plot — all drone command functions would now automatically be transferred to Libya, for example — but also its moral, political and economic justifications; its historical and philosophical context; and its private meaning and value for him, personally, as one who had dedicated his entire public service career to the furtherance of that incontrovertibly desirable global beneficence, a second American Century.

Well sure, Jeff thought. Yadda, yadda. You could hear this stuff, dumbed-down to third-grade level, any night of the week on Freedom News. The question was, would Moreland actually shoot him?

Were he one of those blowhards from Freedom News, the answer would have been yes. And he probably would have missed, at least at first. But Moreland was an intellectual. He was unpredictable. He might do it, or he might not. But if he did, he wouldn't miss.

Moreland was a graduate of the class of Vietnam — not in the sense of having gone there or worn a uniform, but in the sense of having paid his dues to the Domino Theory, a deeply religious belief that clearly informed his present assessment of the Greater Persian issue. Like many of his persuasion, he'd had *other priorities*. The difference between Moreland, however, and his contemporaries, especially the ones who now occupied the CEO suite, was that he *really did* have other priorities. And he pursued them still.

Weirdly, Jeff felt sorry for him — kind of in the helpless way that you lament the descent of a neighbor's kid into the grip of a flying-saucer cult. But this sympathy dripped away when he remembered that Annie, too, had beamed up into this particular brain-fuck.

And he started to feel anger.

Moreland was still talking.

"Am I making sense? I think I am. Do we need to justify ourselves to anyone? On what basis could they assert their superiority? Do they even believe in it? You should ask yourself that. The exceptional cannot be but self-evident, wouldn't you agree? How else —"

He was starting to sound like Amber Pike. If he was going to die, Jeff decided, let it be now. He angled his swivel-chair, lifted his feet, kicked off against Moreland's desk with all his might, and sent himself spinning off towards the far end of the room. Moreland stopped talking and took aim. Jeff tumbled from his chair and crammed himself under a desk. Moreland fired three times; Jeff heard the desktop crack and splinter an inch above his head.

Then something unexpected happened. It began with a hissing, whooshing sound, followed by a *clunk*. Jeff found himself first ankle-, then knee-deep in white foam. Moreland's gun — either the flash or the smoke — must have activated the fire suppression system, which, as you'd expect in a building of this quality, had its own battery back-up. And that *clunk* had to be the door popping open.

How about that! Someone must have decided, as Rancho Colorado rose from its jungle soil, that, even in the innermost sanctum of the super-villain's lair, building codes were important. You could only salute their judgment.

Jeff waited momentarily, while the foam rose to chest-height, then he began to crawl. He heard Moreland curse and, with curious trepidation, lifted his head to take a peek. Moreland had removed his glasses. Like his head and shoulders, they were covered in foam; he was struggling to clean them.

Jeff submerged again and, navigating slowly so as not to leave any tell-tale wake, headed for the door. As he bore down on it, he glimpsed the hazy verticals of Moreland's legs. Should he go for it? Tackle the guy, wrestle the gun from his grasp and...

No. He knew what Katherine's advice would have been. *Get outta there, Jeff! Run! Now!*

He took it.

Outside, it was instantly apparent that Alvaro's men had seized the hour. Satellite dishes lay, smashed to pieces, on the lawn. Smoke rose from behind the main building, where the helicopter pad and, Jeff guessed, the generators were located. The Ecuadorians had secured the main building, but had made no advance into the residential quarter. The beach and the golf course were deserted, but there was quite a tumult on the roof terrace of the club-house. Helicopters queued up to pluck the fortunate away from the Fall of Rancho Colorado. It all looked a bit disorderly and, well, bad-tempered.

"We let them go."

It was Alvaro.

"Why are you... Never mind. Give me your report."

Jeff recounted his near-death experience in the grip of Moreland's megalomania.

"Ah. A *person of interest.*"

Alvaro issued orders in Spanish. Two of his men headed back into the main building.

"He's armed."

"Don't worry. Now you must go to Puerto Jiménez. You can go from the beach."

The *beach?* Did Alvaro expect him to swim? Actually, it might be preferable to dragging himself through the jungle again, even without the gorilla suit.

"Look," Alvaro said.

Jeff looked. There were two abandoned jet-skis on the sand. Well, *no problem!* He started towards the beach, but Alvaro held on to him.

"Wait."

Alvaro took out a handkerchief and wiped the foam from the lens of Jeff's helmet-cam.

"Now you are good."

"Thanks. Catch you later!"

He'd never driven a jet-ski before, but Isabel had proved it was easy, hadn't she? He dragged the first one he came to into the water, jumped on and powered it up. Then he yanked back on the throttle. The machine shot out from under him, flipped over and landed upside down in the surf. The engine gurgled to a stop. *Shit!* Hey, at least he'd washed all that foam off, right? He hoped the helmet-cam was water-proof.

Second time out, he did it right. Within minutes he was skimming the coast, clocking the scarlet macaws in the trees and the pelicans on the beach. Presently, he rounded Cabo Matapolo, taking care to avoid the surfers — the rich kids with beach houses that Eric had talked about.

Not much later, he was puttering up to the water's edge in Puerto Jiménez. Shortly after that, he was jogging down the street that led to the cemetery and the airstrip.

He found Isabel in the back garden of a sleepy café located right at the edge of the airstrip. She was sitting under a wild plum tree, drinking a beer. She looked him up and down.

"What happened to you?"

"You wouldn't believe it."

"No shit! Here, have a beer."

He took the beer and drank, astounded to discover how thirsty he was.

"Marco is coming, soon."

"Cool."

Jeff tipped his head back and savored his beer. From above came a rustling sound, and then a *thunk*. He looked up. The tree was full of iguanas. They were jumping on to the tin roof of the café.

He reached for another beer.

365

CHAPTER 47

John Dolt had never doubted that life in the War Zones was hazardous. He genuinely felt for those young men and women — and, bloody hell, they really *were* young, weren't they? — who got shipped out to Camp This, Camp That and Camp The Other. Those weekly announcements on the TV news got to him. He felt guilt. Shame, too.

Well, not any more. Now he knew a political lever when he saw one. The Policy Steering Committee might witter on about how important it was to *show that we support our troops*. The other John Dolt — the one who was Leader of the Home Guard — used grimier language. But it was the same thing. And Amber Pike might struggle to compose a lucid sentence, but she was fluent in low-end emotion. The PM and the former PM could emote like they meant it about *our troops*. But *those kids* were something else — other people's children, a burden on the welfare state just waiting to happen. Lever-pushers, all.

Dolt might have fancied himself an advocate for the enlisted man or woman. But he feared his situation would prove sticky.

It did.

During a layover at a gigantic American airbase in War Zone A, Dolt was obliged to visit the gents'. He immediately found himself sandwiched at the urinal wall between two towering squaddies. At first, no words were spoken. Then a conversation started up. The two soldiers seemed exercised by the lack of spare parts at Forward Operating Base So-And-So. As they spoke, they naturally turned towards one another. And something warm and pungent began to seep through Jacqueline's mercerized cotton to caress Dolt's hips.

"Oops! Sorry, mate!"

Thus began Dolt's initiation into the hazards of war.

At Camp This, Dolt posed for photos with a multinational road-building crew consisting of one Swede, one Australian, two Brits and about fifty Yanks; got his military-chic combat trousers laundered; was instructed in the art of changing a wheel on a thirty-ton truck; narrowly avoided being crushed by same when someone backed a tank into it; volunteered to accompany the stylist, the house-hunter and the footballer on a night patrol, even though he was totally knackered, for fear of being the only one sleeping in his designated tent.

At Camp That, Dolt participated in a video segment for Freedom News called *Texting for Victory,* in which he read out messages from military families, then responded to questions from Flint Gunner on his experiences so far, recounting anecdotes scripted for him by Nigel Weese; succumbed to a vicious stomach bug and had to get his trousers laundered again; attended a passing-out parade of newly-trained recruits, where he accidentally threw up on the host country's flag; flew in a lurching helicopter, despite his crushing nausea, with the stylist, the house-hunter and the footballer, to a meeting of village elders where he was accorded the honor of slaughtering a goat; was almost flattened by an armored Land Rover when someone gave him mistaken directions back to his tent.

At Camp The Other, Dolt told Gideon he felt like staying in his tent today, but then changed his mind when informed that the stylist, the house-hunter and the footballer were all heading off to Forward Operating Base So-And-So to be shown how computerized logistics had enhanced battle-readiness; fell into a latrine, after someone gave him the wrong directions to the mess tent; discovered that Forward Operating Base So-And-So had no laundry facilities; failed to hit it off with a classroom full of girls studying nutrition and basic hygiene; got half-way down a freshly-raked sandy path before realizing his error and retracing his steps in a panic; nearly perished in a midnight fire-fight because someone had removed the sandbags from his end of the tent.

And so it was with considerable relief that Dolt received from Gideon the news that he, Dolt — and he alone, to the bafflement and resentment of the stylist, the house-hunter and the footballer — was to *drop in* on British Special Forces on a *top-secret mission* behind enemy lines in an *undisclosed country.*

Gideon also gave Dolt a small, sealed, padded envelope. Inside he found a memory stick and a note. The note said *Good luck and fuck you — Des. PS Lescek says fuck you too.*

Dolt couldn't have been happier.

But there was just one thing — he'd been thinking about it a lot during the past few days of torment and soiled trousers. He didn't want to go to the drone base alone. He wanted Gideon to come with him.

And, no, it wasn't just the *human shield* thing; Dolt's sentimental attachment to his personal assistant was, in a querulous, desiccated and nagging way, a thing of beauty in a world of rigged perspectives, political commerce and Big Lies. It was like a pressed flower found between the pages of a tabloid newspaper. They'd been through so much together — the candy-counter siege at *The Face of Freedom*; the obliteration of Reagan Pruett's beachside mansion; the tornado that had boosted Amber Pike to the top of the American political charts — and through all this, and more, despite the stark discrepancy in their origins, they had bonded. Gideon had opened Dolt's eyes to The Possible. And, even though Dolt understood that The Possible was a very different beast to The Probable — especially when it came to offshore bank accounts — there was no going back. Gideon had liberated the confidence and sense of self that Dolt now had to assume he'd somehow always had. Gideon had improved Dolt's vocabulary beyond recognition. He had introduced Dolt to the pleasures of sherry, and showering *every day.* He had protected Dolt from — well, who knew what? That was the whole point of *compartmentalization* — another gift. Gideon had made him *participate* in life. And he'd loaned Dolt that cash for the taxi.

Did he trust his personal assistant? Not really. But you couldn't have everything. Nonetheless, Dolt was inflexible: Gideon would accompany Dolt to the secret drone base.

On his second layover at the ginormous American airbase — which seemed to have undergone a growth spurt during his absence — he avoided visiting the gents'. But he did check his email. Someone called JHanCock wanted him to know that NEW AFRICAN SEX PILLS WILL MAKE YOU HARD HARD HARD. It was a bugger, he thought. No matter how top-secret or not-to-be-divulged your address was, the spammers got it.

"Something amusing?" Gideon said.

"Spam! Would you believe it? Sex pills."

"Really? I never get those. Don't know why."

"No? I used to get these ones, they —"

Dolt hesitated.

"They what?"

"Oh, you don't want to know."

"I don't suppose I do, actually, John."

But it wasn't spam, of course. It was Jefferson Crockett telling Dolt that drone command was reverting to Libya. Jeff must have been successful in *nixing*, as he'd put it, the Costa Rican end of things. Good for him. But where would all those *truly productive people* go if Jeff had blitzed their time-shares? What about that Big Builder bloke? Perhaps he'd stashed some spare bricks somewhere. He could start again from scratch.

A thought struck Dolt.

"Gideon? How d'you think the strike's going?"

One of Gideon's frowns came out of hibernation.

"I really couldn't say, John. Early days."

"So, no crowds in the streets, pleading for 'em to come back?"

"Not yet, John."

Time would tell, wouldn't it?

*

They landed in Libya under cover of darkness. This was fortunate, Gideon intimated, because it meant they didn't have to wear blindfolds, and they were just in time for dinner.

The room they found themselves in, Dolt thought, looked more like an executive dining room — the sort of thing Melmotte Global Capital probably had — than a military mess hall. But he wasn't complaining; he hadn't eaten well at Camps This, That and The Other, and his stomach, not yet recuperated, yearned for the rich but gut-assuaging West End cuisine that he'd begun to appreciate at Gideon's elbow.

And, weirdly, that was exactly the sort of food they got. Dolt hadn't tasted anything quite as good since the time — the *only* time — that Gideon had taken

Dolt to dine at his *club*. (Dolt had seen the inside of a few clubs — mainly those dodgy, after-hours places in Willesden — but Gideon's had been something else. Alas, Gideon, ever optimistic about his pupil, had misjudged Dolt's culinary learning curve. Some senior members had been alienated by Dolt's way with his knife.)

He'd expected military rations tonight, not a dinner party. Yet here they all were. Dining with the drones.

At the head of the table sat the boss. There hadn't been any formal introductions — just a panicky rush from the runway into this building, whatever it was, and then straight into dinner — so Dolt assumed that this bloke, with his wispy fair hair and peevish manner, must be Willoughby-St. John, the Drone King. Des, the former PM and Jeff referred to him as Andy. But Gideon called him *Andrew*. Interesting.

Dolt had been given the seat of honor, at the King's right hand. Opposite him was a rangy, African bloke who looked about sixty but was thin and wiry and therefore probably younger. He hadn't spoken yet. There was an air of violence about him; he looked like he would have done a far more efficient job of slaughtering that goat than Dolt had done (he'd chickened out, of course). Could this be Jeff's pet warlord?

Next to him, and avoiding everybody's gaze, was a woman with short, dark hair. She didn't look happy. Her face reminded Dolt of the off-side rear quarter of the Jobba van, after he'd accidentally reversed into a skip down at Big Builder and had got as far as applying the first layer of repairs. Like Lescek, she must have fallen down some stairs. Was this *Annie?* Dolt thought it must be. But Jeff hadn't said anything about the stairs.

So far, only the King and Gideon had spoken. *Andrew?* Did they know each other? Dolt now knew that people of Gideon's class often went to the same school — there were only six or seven of them, apparently, so it wasn't surprising. Some history there, perhaps?

By the end of the second course, Dolt's stomach had settled, his nerves had calmed — perhaps the Tunisian wine had helped — and he felt able, just about, to contemplate his mission. What he needed to do — this was Des's advice, not Jeff's, and was therefore probably sound — was *reconnoiter the terrain* and *gather information*, prior to *going for it*. It was time to pipe up.

"So, um, *Andrew*, how's it going with the drones, and all that?"

Andy stopped in mid-chew and glared at Dolt. Then he glared at Gideon. After that, he took a moment to swallow, then put his cutlery down with a clatter.

"Why are you two here, again? Remind me, would you, Gideon?"

Gideon coughed, like a determined sheep girding itself to see off a bothersome fox.

"Andrew, it was decided that it was in everyone's interest for John to make a quick visit. Our esteemed sponsor approved it himself. It's really all about the post-liberation news management scenario. Surely your PR people filled you in about —"

"Didn't get a bloody sniff. Ask her yourself. She's sitting right there."

He meant Annie, if the dark-haired woman was Annie. Annie was silent.

"Whose bloody idea was it anyway?" Andy demanded, picking up his fork and jabbing it at Gideon.

"Does it matter whose idea it was?"

It was Dolt's, of course. Or Des's, rather. But Dolt let it go.

"I'm just here to have a quick look around," he said, adding, for extra reassurance, "won't get under your feet, or whatever. It's just the *substances*, though, innit? I'll have a wander, and not find any evidence. Know what I mean?"

Andy looked at Dolt as though he'd done something really beyond the pale with the butter knife.

"Gideon. Is this really your —"

"Yes, it is, Andrew. John has performed beyond all expectations. We're all extremely happy with his —"

"This is him?"

"Yes."

Andy toyed with his fork, moodily, while the dishes were removed and the main course arrived. The African bloke now examined Dolt, through narrowed eyes, as if he suspected he was looking at a man who might not be sound on goats. The woman who was probably Annie stared into her lap, not eating. Even Gideon, whose joie-de-vivre had reignited upon sight of tonight's menu, now began to flag. This was a party, Dolt decided, that could do with a kick up the arse. And, in honor of Abdel, Aisha and JUSTICE, he, John Dolt, would be the one to put the boot in.

"So, *Andrew*. Funny story. I'm at the GFI with Faith Boy, and —"

"*Faith Boy?*"

"He means you-know-who," Gideon said, helpfully.

"— I'm at the GFI, and I pop outside for a puff. I mean, I've given up, obviously, but you know how it is. Anyway, I'm out there on the steps with this American bloke, the one who does the robots, and he's having a smoke as well, and — stop me if you've heard this one, by the way — and this girl comes up and starts hassling me. And the cops are just standing there laughing, of course, useless sods. And then she's all sort of, *oh, you've got to help me, I need JUSTICE, I trust you* and blah-blah and yakkety-yak. Foreign girl. Says her name is *Aisha*. Like I say, stop me if you've heard it. Anyway, there's a bit of a *fracas*, and *I* get your code back for you, and *she* runs off, and the *cops* are still pissing themselves, and then *vroom*, up comes this motorbike and... Well, you know that bit, don't you?"

Dolt paused for effect, and to get his breath back.

"*Anyhoo*," he continued, "here's the funny bit. Ever since then, wherever I go, it's like, bang — motorbikes."

Gideon was looking at him strangely, both frowns at three-quarter strength.

"Kansas — motorbikes!"

Gideon opened his mouth to speak.

"Barbados — motorbikes!" He was thinking of Jeff's girlfriend's jet-ski, but it was close enough.

"New York — motorbikes!" Okay, he was making that one up.

"London — motorbikes!"

"London?" Gideon said.

Dolt nodded.

"Yup."

He scanned the table. Probably-Annie had lifted her head and was looking at him for the first time, her face white behind her camouflage make-up. The African bloke was playing with the rings on his fingers. Gideon had notched one frown up to maximum. Andy's face was red, the dimples in his cheeks verging on puce.

"Well, it makes *me* laugh," Dolt said. "Hang on, I've got another one. Remember the robot bloke? Well, I'm up in this tree-house with him, and —"

There was a pounding boom. The room shook, rattling the cutlery on the table. Dust descended from the ceiling.

Gideon was on his feet.

"My God, Andrew, what the —"

"Sit down."

Andy turned to the African bloke.

"I thought you told me —"

But the African bloke was on his feet and out of the room. Andy called after him.

"What the bloody hell do you think I'm paying you for?"

Dolt stood and rubbed his ears.

"You!" Andy said. "Sit down. And you, Gideon. Sit down, blast you. We're going to finish our bloody dinner!"

He actually meant it, Dolt thought. And that's what they did: They finished their dinner, right up to the point where Andy banged down his dessert spoon and chugged something pale and syrupy. Meanwhile, it was obvious to Dolt that the drone base was under assault. By whom, he could only guess. As they ate, the bombardment mounted, and the building shivered with each explosion. It was like something from a Carry On film.

Then, without a word, Andy got up and strode from the room. Dolt turned to his personal assistant.

"Old friends, by any chance?"

Gideon made a sucking noise that was hard to interpret. The explosions seemed to be coming closer.

"D'you think we're safe in here?" Dolt asked.

"Possibly not."

"Perhaps you should go and ask Andy."

"Or you could go..."

"I don't think he likes me. You seem like you're old pals."

"Well, it's... All right."

"I'll wait here. With, um, with *her*."

"Fine. Yes. If it gets worse, you could get under the table."

"We could, yes."

"Mm."

Gideon hesitated, then got up and stole out of the room. Dolt immediately switched seats, parking himself next to the dark-haired woman.

"Annie, right?"

Her eyes widened and her mouth fell open. But she didn't speak.

"Don't say anything," Dolt said. "Just listen."

372

Fearing Gideon's return, Dolt attempted to bring Annie up to date in the fewest words possible. She struggled to comprehend the whole Barbados thing, but that couldn't be helped.

Dolt brandished his memory stick.

"Just tell me where to shove it," he said, instantly regretting his phraseology.

"I... You... Oh, what the hell," she said. "Come on."

Now they were running — along corridors, up staircases, through a maze of high-tech offices. They must have looked an odd couple — damaged Annie in her lavender track suit and Dolt laboring to keep up in his safari outfit. But no one challenged them; it was a right old after-dinner panic.

"Get many attacks, do you?"

"Not like this."

"Jeff didn't tell me..."

"Tell you what?"

"Who hurt you?" Dolt asked.

"General Kadiya."

"Was he the —"

"Yes, him."

The African bloke — a *general?*

"And, um, don't mind me asking, do you, but..."

"But what?"

"Jeff wanted me to find out, you see..."

"What?"

"Where's your mum?"

Annie stopped dead and flattened her back against the wall of the corridor, breathing unevenly.

"Mom?"

Dolt waited. A long moment passed.

"Well, I guess she's probably dead."

"Probably?"

"We got Leo out, Mom and I..."

"Who's Leo?"

"Leo Vargas."

Had he heard that name? He didn't think so. Who was Leo Vargas?

"But then we got separated," Annie said. "They brought me back here. Made me sit in front of a screen. Drone targeting screen, you know, with a satellite map. Jay and the Libyan guy, the Chief — they had a compound. In Kufra. Andy made me point to it."

Dolt's face must have betrayed him; Annie gripped the crumpled lapel of Jacqueline's stay-pressed, anti-wrinkle safari jacket.

"They *made* me — you understand?"

He nodded.

"So then the drones..."

"Ripped up the whole street."

"Ah."

Annie looked at him. Then she smiled.

"So come on, Mr. Populist. What have we got to lose?"

She began to run again.

Who was *Jay?* No one had ever mentioned a *Jay.* Not Gideon, not Des, not Jeff, not Ginger and Snowy, not the former PM — no one. Nor this *Leo Vargas.* So it was uncharted waters from now on, wasn't it?

Shit!

CHAPTER 48

Bloody Lescek! Dolt couldn't believe it. He read it again. Was Lescek serious? For *fuck's sake!* He and Annie stood in Andy's office — Andy wasn't there, luckily; perhaps he was having an after-dinner cigar, or cheese and biscuits, or yelling at his *General* — and they were looking at his computer screen.

According to Annie, only Andy's computer would do — and she knew his password. Dolt had had to fumble underneath Andy's desk to find a socket for the memory stick. Then Annie had run Lescek's *loader program*, and *this* had popped up.

They were looking at a dialog box. At the top was a picture of Lescek. He had a happy, slightly crazy smile on his face. And, in a carefree, jaunty kind of way, he was giving Dolt the finger. Yes, okay, fair enough, Dolt had thought at first. But the devil was in the small print.

Lescek wanted a million euros. If he didn't get a million euros, the drones would do their owner's bidding. If he did get a million euros, the drones would become Dolt's playthings (Jeff's actually, but Lescek didn't know that). There was more. Shortly after take-off, the drones would — get this! — *phone home* to Lescek's flat in West Hendon. If Lescek did not lift his receiver and tap in the correct PIN number, Dolt was out of luck. Lescek had chucked in his own tweak!

"That's pretty fucked up," Annie said.

"Tell me about it!"

"Is this guy pissed at you about something?"

Dolt didn't reply. He hit the carpet again and retrieved his memory stick.

Lescek, idiotically, seemed to assume that Dolt had euros stuffed down his socks. Actually, he was, as far as he could tell, broke. And he'd never worked so hard in his life! How come Amber Pike had millions and he didn't? Was anyone even paying the mortgage on his half-a-house? What's more, the window of opportunity was coming to an end. Then what?

A million euros? Did Lescek think he could fuck off back to Poland and live happily ever after? Perhaps Des could persuade him to divulge his stupid PIN number. For a moment, Dolt savored this prospect. Then he glanced at Annie's face and changed his mind. Budget issues or not — Des would have to cough up.

"We should get out of here," Annie said.

The sounds of battle had faded, Dolt noticed. And Annie was right. The smart move would be to dash back to the executive dining room; with luck, they might be seated again before coffee was served. Dolt spun around and launched himself towards the door — only to come to a carpet-wrenching halt. The doorway was blocked by a tall, angular man with sticking-up blond hair, dark glasses, black T-shirt, tight jeans, and shiny wing-tip shoes. Across his hips he held what Dolt took to be a handbag-size designer machine gun.

"Pardon me," this interloper said, "but I had a mind to use that computer."

"Jay!" Annie said. "I thought..."

So this was *Jay*, Dolt mused — American, armed, a bit weird.

"Your mom's fine. We left her someplace safe."

"That's good," Annie said. "That's, uh, really good. Thank you for that."

Jay stepped into Andy's office and swung the door to.

"Who's this guy?"

"That's John Dolt."

A pause.

"He just flew in, with some other guy. Listen, you won't believe what he just did."

"Isn't he the guy that —"

"Yeah, that's him."

"The guy that saved Amber Pike from —"

"That's him!"

"Huh. So what's he doing here?"

"Tell him, John."

Dolt sighed.

"Right. Here we go again."

The coffee would be getting cold, but it couldn't be helped. He spun his tale once more. When he was done, Jay turned to Annie.

"Is he for real?"

"He's friends with Jeff. The Cape Town thing — it's Jeff's idea."

"And it's a heck of an idea. I guess I should tell Walter." Jay indicated Andy's computer. "I had some vague idea about screwing with the system, but you know what? Your idea is better. Congratulations."

Dolt poked at the carpet with his heel.

"There's a bit of an issue with a PIN number, but —"

"A PIN number?"

"But it's solvable."

"Sure?"

"Mm-hmm."

"Then Annie and I should get out of here. I guess *you'll* be staying?"

"Have to, really, don't I?"

Jay swung the door open but, once again, an unexpected visitor blocked the exit. This time it was Gideon. He held a cup of coffee in each hand.

"I heard your voice, John. What are you doing in there?"

Jay sprang out from behind the door. Gideon stumbled backwards, spilling his coffee. Jay grabbed him and hauled him into the office.

"Who's this?"

"Gideon."

"*Gideon?*"

"Yeah, I know. You get used to it. He's my personal assistant. Um, Gideon, how long —"

"Was I standing outside? Long enough, I would say, John. Long enough."

Well, this was embarrassing, wasn't it? Talk about an awkward moment. Fortunately, the eccentric American gunslinger had a solution. Dolt and Gideon were to be *kidnapped by terrorists.*

Jay pulled a radio from his belt and began talking in some funny foreign language — Arabic? Dolt heard the sound of boots in the corridor.

"Okay, people," Jay said, "follow me."

Gideon resisted, but Jay's reinforcements — a bunch of skinny kids in camouflage trousers and dark sweatshirts — hustled him out.

Then they ran.

Into the corridor, down the stairs, down again, a commotion behind them, shouts, Gideon stumbling, Gideon dragged by his collar, more shouting, Annie yelling back — then out into the darkness and the chilling air, and two gun-laden pickup trucks wheeling out of nowhere. Dolt and Gideon into the back of the first pickup, Gideon losing his left shoe. Two gunshots from behind and above and Dolt flinching on the floor of the pickup as it fishtails away.

Then more gunshots, lots more, and Jay's voice and the *terrorists* shooting back, the second pickup accelerating, and then floodlights, brightness and shadows. Now Dolt on his knees, looking up, and Andy's warlord general on the roof with a rifle, and Annie on her feet in the second pickup, her hands on the machine gun, twisting it up to the roof. Then the pickup lurching over a bump, two shots from the roof and Annie falling back — collapsing backwards, tipping over, down into the sand. The second pickup skids to a stop and reverses. A moment. Then it's tearing after the first again, and Dolt is on the floor, his hands trembling, practically nose-to-nose with Gideon, who closes his eyes.

*

At a crossroads, two cars waited. Jay directed Dolt to the second. "You're in that one, with the Chief."

Dolt climbed down from the pickup, then looked up at Gideon. Gideon met his gaze and turned away.

"We'll keep him a few days," Jay said. "He'll be okay. *You're* on your way home."

"But —"

"You *were* kidnapped," Jay said. "But now you're escaping."

"But me and him, you see..."

"Don't you have stuff you need to do back home?"

"Yes, but I just wanted to explain to him why —"

"Later, huh?"

"Right."

Dolt climbed into the back of the car. He found himself seated next to an elderly woman. She acknowledged him with a faint smile but said nothing. He could see that this was Annie's mother, Jeff's mother-in-law. She seemed in semi-robust shape, though she was thin and her face looked drawn and weary. How old was she? Seventy?

Jay shut the door. The car pulled away, following the first car, but at a distance. Jay hadn't spoken to Annie's mother. Dolt began to feel sick. How long would it be?

It was about twenty-two minutes. Then he heard her take a long, deep breath, hold it, and then let it out slowly.

"Did you see my daughter? Do you know where she is?"

Dolt looked at her. The darkness and the motion of the car prevented him from seeing her clearly. But the shape of her mouth and the way she clasped her hands together told him that this was a question he would have to answer.

So — slowly, simply, and quietly — he told her. She didn't reply, but turned away from him and leaned back in her seat.

"General Kadiya?" she said.

"Yes."

Presently, the car stopped at an intersection. Calmly, as if she'd just taken a taxi to the station, she opened her door, got out and began to walk briskly back down the road.

Dolt tapped the Chief on the shoulder and pointed. The Chief sighed, then hauled himself out of the car and jogged after her. Dolt watched. The Chief caught up to her. He remonstrated. She kept going. He took her by the wrist. She shook him off. More remonstration. No good. The Chief flapped his arms above his head, turned and trudged back to the car.

As the car pulled away, Dolt watched Bonnie DiAngelo vanish into the night and the desert.

*

I n Tripoli, Dolt waited in an empty warehouse while five crates full of American dollars were emptied out, the resultant pile (minus a bonus for the Chief) split up into twelve equal shares, and each share stuffed into a heavy plastic sack; was introduced by Jay to an elderly South African politico, name of *Walter*, who said he'd flown the cash all the way up from Namibia, wherever that was, and who was highly intrigued to learn all about Jeff's scheme to trap the former PM; wondered who the dark-haired, olive-skinned bloke in the other car was; got dumped outside a fortified seaside apartment block with the information that this was the British Embassy and good luck.

CHAPTER 49

J eff Crock strolled down Fifth Avenue as if it were the last time he would ever do so — and, hey, it just might be, right? He'd given up the lease on his Park Slope pigeon-hole; the Upper West Side office of The Liberal had been re-let to a nanny agency; and Katherine Jane McPherson might never have existed. All the more reason for doing this, then: One last promenade down the Avenue of Dreams, with the late-fall sunshine and that invigorating little bite of winter in the air. He felt like flaunting himself — and Isabel had wanted to go shopping.

In order to minimize the chance of some legal, law-enforcement, diplomatic or extra-judicial mishap or ambush, he and Isabel were accompanied by two *special assistants* from the Ecuadorian embassy. Marco, currently engaged in delicate negotiations over at the UN, had made Jeff promise to *not do anything stupid*.

And so Jeff and Isabel had but a single free day in the city. Tonight, he, Isabel and Marco would fly back to Quito — via Mexico City, as on the way up — then Jeff and Isabel would make the long, slightly dangerous drive south to Cuenca, where Marco had found them an apartment. Cuenca, Marco assured them, was a pretty, safe, historic city; it was popular with American retirees. And Annie and her mother could live there too, should they so wish.

But Jeff, Isabel and Marco absolutely had to fly out tonight, because tomorrow was the twenty-eighth.

At 34th Street, they headed west: Isabel wanted to see Macy's. While Isabel shopped for winter coats — Cuenca was up in the Andes and got cold at night — and the Ecuadorians considered scarves for their wives, Jeff checked his phone.

He had two new messages. The first, from Marco, said that negotiations had been *difficult*, but a deal was shaping up. Basically, Douglas Moreland would be dumped across the Nicaragua-Honduras border, in return for the funding of the reforestation of Rancho Colorado and diplomatic denial all round. *Difficult?* No kidding. Marco said that Jeff should think about heading back over to the UN.

The second message, whose subject-line was *This is your captain speaking*, simply told Jeff that his *flight* had *arrived safely*. Well, this had to be the movie-pilot — the guy who'd flown Jeff and Isabel from Costa Rica to Saint Vincent. And he seemed to be saying that Katherine was safe, somewhere. Good news. Really, really good news. Well done, captain.

He'd been hoping for a message from John Dolt. But there was nothing. Perhaps later.

Isabel didn't like the coats at Macy's; she wanted to check out Bloomingdale's. So they all went back out on to Broadway and began to walk north.

The news crawl on the big screen in Times Square declared that Amber Pike's *slate* was expected to *win big* in the upcoming elections. How would she wield her power? *Nnngh*, he thought.

A movie theatre was showing Kenny Pruett's *The Face of Freedom*. There didn't appear to be any ticket-buyers in line, but there was a compact, noisy demonstration outside. Jeff felt a small, warm glow somewhere deep in his chest cavity. The young people! Of course!

"Hey, kids!"

The young people stopped chanting and looked at him.

"That's one hell of a shit movie, ain't it?"

They agreed that it was.

"You kids ever read The Liberal? Uh, maybe you checked out the web site?"

They hadn't. What was the web address?

"Actually, the site's not up right now. My name's Jeff. I used to write —"

Oh, okay, one of the girls remembered her father talking about The Liberal. Great, great — did he enjoy it? Oh, he was a conservative. Never mind.

"You kids — you all have blogs, and all that good social stuff, right?"

They certainly did.

"Okay. Well, in that case, I've got something for you."

Now they were excited.

"Ever hear of a couple of guys called Elliot Tucker and Morrison Tweed?"

They weren't sure. Half of them reached for their hardware.

"Corporate crooks. You can search 'em later."

How about Douglas Moreland — had they heard of him? Well, duh.

"Okay, kids, here you go!"

Jeff pulled out a memory stick and offered it to the girl nearest to him.

"It's all on here. Photos, video, documentation. Corporate crooks! War criminals! WMD! All kinds of shit. Listen, you might be hearing, any day now, about some stuff going down in, let's say, Central America, or Libya, or the Greater Persian region. It's all on *that*. You're looking at the mother lode."

The kids looked skeptical, but the girl took the stick.

"Put it on your blogs, your social widgets, whatever. Spread it around."

Isabel was tugging at his sleeve. The Ecuadorian guys were getting antsy.

"Okay, I gotta go now," he said. "Jefferson Crockett leaves the stage. He hands his torch on to you. Be good!"

Isabel fastened herself on to his arm and propelled him forward, in the direction of Lincoln Center.

He thought about his encounter with the kids.

Did that count as *stupid?*

Nah.

CHAPTER 50

This was to be a glorious day. It was official. Sad, yes — but also stirring; melancholy, but moving; grave but not glum; lachrymose and yet uplifting; heart-rending and soul-wrenching, of course, while also still a good day out for all the family.

Or so it said on the radio.

John Dolt sat in the front passenger seat of the black Range Rover alongside Des, his head of security. Des had parked the car, nearside wheels up on the curb, adjacent to a burger van in his home patch of Streatham. They were having breakfast.

"No news about your pal, then?"

Des meant Gideon.

"No."

"Pity. You must be worried."

Dolt sucked his lips in and nodded.

"What I really don't get," Des said, "Is why they let *you* go, these terrorists — but they kept *him.*"

Dolt sniffed.

"I escaped, didn't I?"

"John. *John.* This is me you're talking to. People like *you* don't escape from people like *that.*"

Dolt shrugged.

"Look, I know it's fucking great for the image — the fearless Leader of the Home Guard smacking a bunch of towelheads around and stealing their camel, or whatever it is you reckon you did. That's lovely. I get it. But you're not fooling me."

Too true, Dolt thought. It was tough to put anything past Des. Tough, but not impossible. He chewed slowly on his ham and cheese croissantwich. It tasted vile. Why didn't they have any oat bran and blueberry muffins on this stupid van?

Des took a resentful bite out of his egg, bacon and sausage bagel.

"Maybe they thought *he* was the important one," Dolt said. "Cause of the posh accent."

381

"*Posh accent?*"

Des shook his head with incredulity. A squirt of egg issued from the corner of his mouth and splattered the collar of his black leather jacket.

"What do these dickheads know about posh accents? I tell you what, though. They watch TV all the time. They're all over the net. They know who you are."

"Just a theory."

Des stared at Dolt. Dolt turned his head to watch a man in a football shirt walk by with a greyhound on a lead.

"All right," Des said. "Have it your way. You obviously don't want to tell me. I thought we didn't have any secrets."

There followed a frosty but also noisy interlude in which they finished their breakfasts.

"Right," Des said, balling up his carton and bag together and lobbing them into the roadway, "Down to business. What a glorious fucking day it's going to be."

Glorious day, Dolt thought. Actually, now that he looked, he could see that it was, indeed, a fine, crisp, late-autumn day — one of those days when it felt like someone had given the city a bloody good valeting, and had then gone on and re-sprayed the sky. The life of the city presented itself on parade, in a way. People walking their dogs. Girls jogging. Mums with kids in strollers, not as stressed-out as usual. Special offers in the pubs tonight. Not a holiday, exactly, but a day of national communion, and everyone — *nearly* everyone — in a good mood. On a day like this he almost might not have minded having to drive one of Hamid's creaky minibuses, or even his horrendous old open-top Routemaster (which Dolt didn't have a license for, but never mind).

"Oi! Are you listening? Earth to fucking John!"

"Yeah, yeah. I'm listening."

"Go and wake up old Lescek, shall we?"

"Suppose so."

Amongst other virtues, Des's plan for the day possessed the advantage of brilliant simplicity. He'd settled on it quickly — once, that is, he'd dismounted from the roller-coaster of anger and outrage that he'd hurled himself onto upon hearing from Dolt of Lescek's treachery and greed. It had been quite a ride. When it was over, though, Des had begun to see the funny side. *Silly old Lescek, eh? What a bastard!* It turned out that a million euros wasn't that big a deal, so long as Lescek — or *Home Run*, as he would thenceforth be known — was prepared to sign on as a *secret source* at the Polish embassy having access to classified materials pertaining to American military arrangements on the Belarusian border. This, Des felt, was something Lescek would leap at, as soon as he saw Des's Tesco bag full of cash. Dolt didn't doubt it either. Thus they would present themselves at Lescek's West Hendon residence; get him to sign on the dotted; hand over the bag; then turn on the TV and observe the day's solemnities and festivities while waiting for the phone to ring.

Of course, Des didn't know that his tweak had been superseded by Jeff's. Nor, for that matter, could either Dolt or Des be certain that Lescek hadn't instituted yet another tweak of his own. Lescek was known to harbor a grudge against the Driver and Vehicle Licensing Centre; would chemical death rain down on Swansea?

Des, though, seemed happy, mostly. The million euros weren't coming out of his own pocket; his rival, Gideon, was out of the picture — albeit in suspicious circumstances; his plan to wipe out Diego Garcia — which, he obviously assumed, Dolt hadn't worried his *pretty little head* about — was afoot; and he could look forward to spending the day with his feet up, watching TV.

By contrast, Dolt felt acutely on edge. What would happen when Gideon was released? And when, exactly, would he regain his freedom from Jay, the mercurial American freelance spy? How much time did Dolt have left? What about that offshore bank account?

There was more. As part of the day's obsequies, Dolt was to address a special gathering of the Home Guard; would he have the nerve to go through with his plan — the great *switcheroo*? And, if he did, and the Home Guard did what he asked of them, how upset would the PM and the Policy Steering Committee be? Would Mrs. Red Ron deliver? Would Walter, the ANC elder statesman and part-time pan-African money-launderer, successfully put the kibosh on the former PM, as Jeff so fervently desired? Or would the former PM, in typical style, slip the bonds of JUSTICE, and, enraged at missing out on both the Uzbek gold and the Great Leader's memorial, enlist his many powerful friends against a newly-powerless Dolt?

And there was one more thing, wasn't there? What to tell Jeff — and how.

It all made him feel a bit tense, to be honest. One thing he didn't have to worry about, though, was the strike of all the *truly productive people*. A glance out of the Range Rover's window suggested strongly that life went on — more spiffingly yet than before, perhaps. Even the disturbances had taken a break. According to the radio, banks continued to operate their day-to-day services, thanks to back-office staff, despite the closure of the speculative markets. The great corporations continued to function, thanks to middle-managers, in spite of the absence of their CEOs and boards of directors. And it went without saying, the newsreader seemed to imply, that the net effect on society, so far, of the loss of all those hedge fund managers, private equity bosses, management consultants, brokers, advertising executives, libel lawyers, celebrity chefs, fashion designers, consultants, columnists, presenters, editors, stylists, house-hunters and foot-ballers... was nil.

But there remained one issue, above all, that pressed heavily on Dolt's consciousness: The *provocation*. The incident that would spur the drones into flight. The outrage — violent, according to Des — that would start it all. It would happen today. But what was it? Tellingly, Des had lost interest in it. But Dolt hadn't.

He became aware that Des was talking to him.

"Had any more thoughts about the exit strategy?"

"Not really."

"Got it in hand, though, have you?"

"More or less."

Des swerved past a dawdling Toyota.

"I hope so, John. I mean, you realize, don't you? Whatever happens to your pal, your usefulness to them, as of tomorrow, is considerably diminished. Innit?"

"*Them?*"

"Yeah, you know. Rand Purdo, Faith Boy, all them plutocratic Yanks. The so-called Atlantic Affairs Institute. The whole, vast, bleeding right-wing conspiracy. You're what they think of as a short-term asset."

It hurt to hear Des say it out loud. But Dolt had known the truth of this for some time now, hadn't he?

"Exit strategy," Des intoned, musically, "gotta have an exit strategy." Then he began to hum to himself.

"Des?" Dolt said.

"What?"

"There's something..."

"On your mind? Speak now, John."

They began to traverse Tower Bridge. Dolt glanced out between flags at the river, and the patriotic flotilla heading upstream to Westminster.

"Well, it's just... It's something Samira said."

"Samira! Ooh, that was nasty, wasn't it?"

"Yes, it was."

"What did she say, then?"

"Well, she said *everyone over there* knew what was going to happen."

Des chuckled.

"Yeah, they would think that. Might even be right. So?"

"She said something else. Right at the end. When she was..."

"On fire?"

"Yes."

"What did she say?"

"Something about *cross girls.*"

"*Cross girls?*"

"Yeah. What did she mean?"

Des furrowed his brow.

"Dunno, John."

"I've been trying to work it out. I mean, is it *Kings* Cross? *Charing* Cross? *Brent* Cross?"

"Beats me."

"Maybe we should ask her?"

"Don't think she's in any state, John."

"Oh."

They drove north, then west, then north again, up the Edgware Road. It was still early; traffic was light. When they bumped up on to the curb outside Lescek's abode in West Hendon, they could see that the lights in his attic flat were on.

But when they buzzed him, Lescek didn't answer. Eventually, Des persuaded a downstairs neighbor to admit them to the communal hall, and they piled up three flights of stairs to Lescek's door. Des pummeled on it. He yelled Lescek's name. No answer.

"Wait here," Des said.

He returned, a minute later, with a little two-man battering ram of the type used by police when raiding drug-dealers or anti-war protestors. Presumably he stored it next to the jack and the spare wheel.

"Grab hold," he said.

384

Then they smashed Lescek's door open. Lescek wasn't at home. The lights and the TV were on; all Lescek's computer gear had gone; and everything else was a mess.

"*Shit!*" Des said. "They've fucking found him, haven't they? How did they know?"

He now gave Dolt one of his ugliest looks.

"Who did you tell?"

"Me? No one!"

"Nobody else knew, John."

"I didn't tell anyone. Why would I?"

"Not even your pal?"

"Especially not him."

Des picked up the battering ram by one of its handles and swung it, with deliberate menace. Trusting that his political education would not let him down now, Dolt summoned every last drop of mendacity at his command.

"*I didn't fucking tell anyone!*"

Des paused. Then he dropped his weapon on to the remains of Lescek's rickety coffee table.

"All right, all right. Fuck! What are we going to do?"

Dolt didn't answer; his mind was elsewhere. He'd made a call, hadn't he? From right here, to Jefferson Crockett, using Lescek's phone. *Stupid idea, dumbo!* Anyway, someone must have bugged that, or traced it. So they would have connected Jeff and Lescek. Maybe they also knew Lescek was tweaking the drone code. But they didn't necessarily know that Dolt had uploaded it, on site in Libya; or that Lescek had come up with his PIN code wheeze. Dolt looked about the room for Lescek's phone. There it was, on the floor. Surreptitiously, he stepped towards it. It appeared to be in perfect working order.

Des sounded disconsolate.

"Well, come on, then," he said, picking up his ram again, "let's see if we can find the bastard."

He crunched his way out of the flat. Dolt waited. When he heard Des descending the stairs, he pounced on Lescek's phone. A few moments of tapping and bleeping later, he had it forwarded to his own mobile.

When he got downstairs again, he found Des waiting in the Range Rover, passenger door open, engine revving.

"Drop me back at my hotel," Dolt said.

"Why?"

"I've got an idea. It's a long shot but…"

"What idea?"

"It's a bit difficult to explain…"

Des stared at him, misery and skepticism combining to distort his features.

"Okay. Fine. Whatever. Get in."

They headed south again. As they drove, Dolt took out his phone, dialed a number from memory, transmitted a text message and erased all his call logs. Des glanced over at him but said nothing.

Then, moments after Des had deposited Dolt on the pavement outside his hotel and had roared off again in the direction of the river, Ginger and Snowy hove into view, traveling in the style for which they were renowned. They pulled up to the curb and removed their goggles.

To Dolt's unexpected pleasure, Ginger and Snowy were in uniform, medals and all. Defiantly, they wore berets in place of crash helmets. It was less in honor of the Great Leader, they explained, than that they so rarely got a chance to dress up any more. In a gesture of restrained patriotism, they had attached two small, triangular union jacks to the front of the sidecar, one on each side.

They dismounted and presented themselves to Dolt, on parade, as it were, but at ease.

"So you —"

What should he call them? *Chaps? Fellows? Blighters? Men?*

"— so you guys know what it's all about today, right? I *think* I nobbled the drones, but I can't be certain..."

They nodded.

"This provocation, though," Snowy said. "What is it?"

Dolt shifted his weight.

"Ah, well, that's the problem. I've got a clue, though."

"What's the clue?"

"*Cross girls.* Mean anything to you?"

"They're all cross these days," Ginger said. "Well, they are with me."

Snowy polished his goggles, thoughtfully.

"My granddaughter..." he said. "Now what is it she and her friends... Oh, that's it — *lacrosse!* Could it be *lacrosse girls?*"

Something started pinging at the back of Dolt's brain, like some hard-to-trace rattle at the rear of the Jobba van.

"They're part of the parade," Ginger said. "But then — who isn't?"

"What?" Dolt said.

But Ginger had to be referring to the Great Patriotic Parade that someone — the PM himself, Dolt suspected — had decided ought to trundle after the Great Leader's memorial procession in order to round off the day in the right mood.

"Saw it on the idiot box," Ginger said. "Been all round the world. Won a trophy. Got themselves an open-top bus. Dare say they deserve it, but what do I know?"

The pinging got louder — and Dolt realized where it was coming from. *Lacrosse girls. Open-top bus.* Could it be?

"Got an idea," he said. "Let's hit the road."

He gave Snowy directions to the premises of the Super Westway Limousine Company, then crammed himself into the sidecar for what he suspected might be a journey into infamy. But he had to take a moment to congratulate himself on his prescience: The whole antique motorcycle thing was brilliant. Nobody could tell it was Dolt in the sidecar. And not even the most officious cop was going to challenge Ginger and Snowy on a day like this.

When they got to Hamid's yard, nothing looked amiss. The business had obviously shut down. The corrugated iron gates were chained and padlocked. Weeds were starting to grow underneath. Dolt wasn't surprised; Hamid *was* Super Westway. Samira couldn't have run the business, even before... Well, anyway.

386

Dolt squeezed out of the sidecar and reconnoitered the gates. Then he performed a reckless chin-up in order to peak over the top. And that was when he saw it. Or, rather, he didn't — Hamid's nasty, old, red, open-top Routemaster bus. It was gone. All of Hamid's other crummy vehicles were there, though — slumbering under a cozy layer of dirt and leaves.

Dolt dropped to the ground. *Lacrosse girls.* In a stolen bus. Part of the Patriotic Parade.

"Snowy?" he said, deliberately injecting a note of steely urgency into his voice, "This Patriotic Parade. Where's it assembling?"

"Hyde Park."

"Oh, right."

It made sense. The route of the Parade, then, was obvious: Park Lane, Hyde Park Corner, Constitution Hill, Buck House, The Mall, Admiralty Arch, Trafalgar Square, Whitehall, Parliament Square. In Parliament Square, the Patriotic Parade was to pass between the Great Leader's statue — parked up temporarily on the grass next to Winston — and a viewing stand packed with VIP mourners. It was a pretty evil idea, Dolt thought, even if these lacrosse girls turned out to be the very same ones he'd had to ferry to Heathrow, way back at the beginning of his rise to eminence. As a *provocation*, though, you couldn't fault it.

But before he ordered the advance on Hyde Park, he wanted to check in with Des.

"Des?"

"I'm in a meeting, John."

A *meeting?* What the fuck! But Des sounded wound-up; was he on the carpet, getting a telling-off from his Oxbridge bosses?

"Listen, Des. Super Westway. Hamid's minicabs. There's some funny business about a —"

"Funny business?"

"There's a bus missing."

"A bus!"

"Could be in the parade, I'm —"

"Shit!"

"— I'm on the case."

"Fuck! All right, John. Oh, by the way — Lescek? Some *idiot* — yes, that's right, I said *idiot* — decided to deport him. Some bollocks about a driving license. He's in Poland. Nobody knows where."

"Ah."

"Just... Just do what you can, yeah?"

Des hung up.

PIN number, Dolt thought. What could it possibly be? What would Lescek have chosen? Was there any chance that Ginger and Snowy could guess it?

"Problem?" Snowy asked.

"Yeah, but... Hyde Park first. Let's go."

On the ride to the park, Dolt spotted a line of buses parked in a side street. The shabby appearance of these vehicles told him that they'd driven down from the north. What's more, their occupants didn't look like mourners, or families on a day out. They looked grim. Could it be?

What remained of the regular police force had been devoted to protecting the Great Leader's procession from sections of the population too numerous to list without embarrassment, so Dolt wasn't surprised to find that the entrance to the park was guarded by a pair of private security goons. Goons such as these were no match for Ginger and Snowy. After barely more than some terse observations and a smart salute, the motorcycle combination hit the grass. Then they cruised between rows of trucks, vans, and coaches, and Dolt popped his window open to scan the horizon for Hamid's bus.

As they passed a troupe of patriotic morris dancers, Dolt's phone rang. He recognized the number.

"Yes?"

"Is that the fearless Leader of the Home Guard?"

"Uh-huh."

"This is Mrs. Red Ron."

"Ah!"

"You asked for it. You got it."

The line went dead. Presumably she meant that the illegal general strike — the one that had so offended the Policy Steering Committee — had been moved up to today. It *was* what Dolt had asked for. That Super-Kone Triple Deluxe had paid off, after all. Those northern buses! More pressure!

Someone — probably Ginger — rapped on the roof of the sidecar. A gloved hand appeared in front of Dolt's face, its index finger extended to the right. Dolt craned his neck and looked. There it was: Hamid's bus. Dolt responded with a thumbs-up. The motorcycle combination swung right and wobbled up to the bus.

Dolt eased himself out of the sidecar. It was Hamid's bus all right. Someone had cleaned it and attached a banner that read *Varsity League World Lacrosse Champions*. And over there were the girls, milling about on the grass, talking on their phones. In truth, to Dolt, these lacrosse girls could have been any lacrosse girls. But he recognized the mothers. He felt a little kick of fear in the gut.

"Snowy?" he said. "What d'you reckon?"

Snowy considered.

"If you're right, then it's imperative that this bus be driven to a place of safety. We'd be talking about a volunteer."

"A volunteer?"

"Quite. But first, I suggest we let Ginger take a look."

Snowy gestured to his comrade. Ginger commenced a flanking maneuver to the far side of the bus.

"What if it's not a bomb?" Dolt said. "What if it's —"

"Have no fear. Whatever it is, Ginger'll —"

"You can't park that object there!"

They turned and looked. One of the lacrosse mothers was bearing down on them. She pointed at the motorcycle combination.

"This is *our pitch*. Get it off this minute, do you hear?"

"No, hang on a minute," Dolt said. "Where did you get that bus?"

A pause. A widening of the eyes. A pinching of the mouth. The fists on the hips.

"It's that man! Look, everyone, look!"

The girls ignored this injunction but the mothers all stopped what they were doing and stared.

"Isn't he that awful squirt they sent us when —"

"That's him!"

"Is he the same dreadful oaf who —"

"Puffs himself up as some kind of popular leader? That's him!"

"Odious little oik."

Dolt took a step forward.

"I *said*, where did you get that bus?"

A second mother maneuvered forward to reinforce the first.

"Good lord, just look at him!"

Well, all right, Dolt looked a bit rumpled on account of riding in the sidecar, and he'd spilt some of the salad cream from his croissantwich on his shirt, but he wasn't going to be deflected.

"This fucking bus. Where'd you get it?"

"The language! Did you hear that?"

"Georgina, tell him to go away!"

"I'm telling him, Antonia! He won't listen!"

"Tell him again!"

"You tell him. I don't even want to talk to him. He's just a ghastly, grubby, lower-class fascist. Thinks he deserves to be a dictator? Thinks he can order people around? Even our Prime Minister? All those horrible things he says! He disgusts me!"

An awkward pause. A couple of the girls looked up from their phones. Dolt waited to see how much moral support this stance would elicit. Not much, as it turned out. Would there be a back-track?

"Look, I'm not saying I *disagree* with what he says — it's just, well, he's such a common little man."

Dolt took a deep breath.

"All I want to know is, who got this bus for you?"

"Well, if you absolutely must know, it was Jerry. Jerry Aylsham. *Lord* Aylsham, to you."

Dolt felt a tap on his shoulder. It was Ginger. He shook his head slowly.

"Nothing?"

"Nothing."

Snowy gestured towards the motorcycle combination.

"Need to regroup," he said. "New battle plan. Tactical withdrawal. Come on."

As they retreated from the fray, Dolt asked himself where he'd heard that name before. *Aylsham. Lord Aylsham*, no less. Where was it? If only Gideon were here, he would certainly... Oh, right! Gideon's beaky-faced, so-called boss at the AAI! Dolt poked his head out of the sidecar window and issued new orders. Snowy kicked down a gear and accelerated in the direction of Mayfair, and the headquarters of the secretive, exclusive and distinctly dodgy think-tank that called itself the Atlantic Affairs Institute.

Though they clearly hadn't been expecting him — never mind Ginger and Snowy, in all their finery — the girls on the front desk recognized Dolt, and put on for him what Dolt took to be their second-best or business-class smiles. They directed him to the Institute's media center, which was named, by chance, after none other than the Great Leader. Ginger and Snowy elected to loiter in the lobby, so as to keep an eye on Vera — their pet name for the motorcycle combination. Ginger gave the girls a wary half-salute. They beamed back at him.

The media center resembled a small but very posh cinema: Chunky recliners with side-tables but no popcorn. Dolt slipped in silently and stood at the back. There were about two dozen cinema-goers in the stalls, suspending their disbelief while a corporate-style presentation rolled on the big screen. It was dark enough, Dolt calculated, for him to lurk in the shadows unrecognized.

Up on the screen, he saw a familiar face: Seated at the dinner table in his executive dining room was Andy Willoughby-St. John, who had skipped lunch, it seemed, in order to deliver some form of status update. Dolt listened.

Minor collateral damage, Andy said. More a *nuisance* than anything. *Not a scratch* on the drones. *Blasted Libyans* ganging up, for some reason. Otherwise, everything in *splendid shape*, just waiting for the off. Yes, yes, there *was* the annoying issue of *that Gideon chap*; Andy had someone looking into it.

He followed up with a check-list of drone-related technical stuff, a bitter complaint about unreliable supply convoys, and a few pithy observations on the wisdom of *parachuting in* a *pair of idiots* who had nothing better to contribute than getting themselves *kidnapped by terrorists* and wasting his time.

But now General Kadiya entered the frame. He whispered into Andy's ear. Andy stood and declared his performance over. The screen went blank and the lights came up.

Dolt slipped into a seat in the back row and, while pretending to adjust his shoelaces, covertly monitored the audience as it exited: Eva the vampire economist, looking quite well now, by her standards; Dick the foreign-policy walrus; a pair of top *irreconcilables;* a bunch of people Dolt didn't recognize; representatives of Melmotte Global Capital; Rand Purdo, looking pumped; Howard Hooper, the robot guy, already fumbling for his smokes — and then, bringing up the rear, a stringy, hatchet-faced bloke who just had to be Aylsham.

Dolt tailed Aylsham to the gents' and then proceeded to surprise him with a tap on the shoulder from behind.

"Are you Aylsham?"

"What the... Yes, of course I am."

"I'm Dolt."

Aylsham looked Dolt up and down.

"Yes."

Dolt subjected Aylsham to a challenging eye-to-eye.

"Did you steal a bus?"

"Did I what?"

"A red, open-top, vintage Routemaster bus. With the open deck at the back. Property of the Super Westway Limousine Company?"

Aylsham rolled his eyes.

"Oh, *that!*"

"So you *admit* you stole it!"

"Well, really, that's hardly the way I'd —"

"Did you or —"

390

"Yes, yes. All right. So we had someone *liberate* the bus. So what? We'd already paid for the damn thing. I'm not *made* of money. It's not my fault if that blasted Hamid chap runs off and —"

"So you haven't put a bomb on the bus?"

"A *bomb?*"

Aylsham looked puzzled, as if Dolt were bothering him with some mundane technicality best left to the staff.

"Did you or did you not place a bomb on that bus?"

Aylsham seemed to find this all rather ridiculous.

"For heaven's sake, man — Toni and Georgie will be on it!"

Dolt mulled this. It was conceivable, he supposed, that Aylsham had some sentimental attachment to Antonia and/or Georgina. It was a whole different world, wasn't it?

"But that bus is part of the provocation, right?"

Aylsham shrugged this off with a superior smirk.

"*Provocation?* I'm afraid I don't follow you at all. Don't you have a speech to give to your, ah, *followers?*"

Well, he did, of course. Time was dribbling away. But if there wasn't a bomb on the bus, then what had Samira meant?

"Um, Jerry..." Dolt said.

Aylsham scowled.

"Jerry... Are you by any chance in the viewing stand? You know, for the big parade down —"

"As a matter of fact, I am. Guest of the PM, if you must know."

"So *he's* there, too?"

"Naturally. Fancies himself as the *heir.*"

"Ah."

Dolt had to admit it: Even a twat like Aylsham wouldn't conspire to blow himself up. While Dolt scratched his head — not really, just *metaphorically*, as Gideon would have said — Aylsham finished his business and sidled out of the gents', a sly and wistful smile on his lips.

Watch out for your cross girls...

It still had to be *something* to do with the bus, didn't it?

Just then the door to the gents' cracked open and Snowy's head appeared, followed by his left forearm. He tapped the hefty, commando-style watch on his wrist. Dolt nodded.

They rode Vera east and south to Trafalgar Square and parked her up alongside one of the lions. The square seethed with those members of the Home Guard lucky enough to have won a ticket in a specially-organized lottery. They were excited. There was a smell of, well, *something* in the air: Greasy, earthy, stale, sooty, leathery, chemical, yeasty, dank and yet pine-freshened — the smell of England?

A platform had been constructed at the foot of Nelson's Column, facing north towards the National Gallery. As Dolt ascended to his podium, accompanied by Ginger to his left and Snowy to his right, a great roar went up. Dolt raised his arms to acknowledge the acclaim of his followers. They returned the compliment: A forest of raised fists. Directly below, Dolt saw TV cameras. Des leaned against

391

the base of the Column, talking on his phone. And there, too, were Flint Gunner and Nigel Weese. What a surprise. Gunner stared up at Dolt, blank-faced. Weese grinned, winked and gave Dolt a satirical thumbs-up.

"Just in time," Snowy yelled in Dolt's ear. "Look!"

Glancing back over his left shoulder, Dolt saw a formation of motorcycle outriders — the advance guard of the memorial procession — emerge from the shadows of Admiralty Arch. Then came guardsmen on horses, and a military band. After that, more soldiers, sailors and airmen. Next up, a clutch of somber dignitaries in long black coats. Finally, the statue itself appeared, shrink-wrapped for its own protection in transit, and loaded up like a new fridge-freezer, on the back of a black-draped gun-carriage.

From his speaking platform, Dolt watched the procession emerge from the arch, clip-clop around Nelson's mini-roundabout, and turn right down Whitehall. The Home Guard fell silent. They looked cowed, Dolt thought. They cringed. They were almost afraid to look up, these dauntless English yeomen. Well, he'd see about *that*, wouldn't he? He wasn't supposed to begin his address until the last blinkered and patriotically be-plumed horse had cleared the burger bar on the left. But he felt like pushing his luck. Why not? Once you'd embraced the dark side you couldn't un-embrace it. You'd made a lifetime commitment. He decided to begin his speech *now*.

"Is this not a glorious day?" Dolt thundered.

No reaction.

Down below, he saw Weese wrinkle his nose and cup both hands to his ears. Dolt switched on his microphone.

"IS THIS NOT A GLORIOUS DAY?"

The result this time was a howl of approval — almost as if Nelson himself had guaranteed all present fifty per cent off their car insurance.

Dolt started in on the warm-up section of his speech. He noticed that his voice sounded clear, calm and implacable. It was the sort of voice, he mused, that hadn't been heard in the public sphere for some time: Neither the tetchy confidence of the current PM, nor the unctuous defensiveness of the former PM.

"For a while now," Dolt said, "people have been asking: Who is this John Dolt bloke? Well, that's me, innit? I'm the bloke who says it like it is, and doesn't take any crap. And I'm here today to give it to you straight. Whether you want it or not."

Cheers, yelling, hooting.

"You may have noticed," Dolt said, "that we've been having what you might call a bit of a moral crisis. Well, I'm here to explain to you what it's all about."

A glance back over his shoulder told Dolt that the Patriotic Parade had begun. How long before the red bus arrived? He decided to skip the remainder of his warm-up remarks and just go for it.

He told the Home Guard that the rulers of the world had decided that *they* were *no longer needed*, and this explained why their miserable lives got ever shittier. He backed this up with many colorful examples, touching on Melmotte Global Capital, amongst others.

He explained that people like himself, and Amber Pike over there in America, were in the business of getting ordinary people to vote against their own interests

392

by playing on their fears and turning them against each other — the age-old divide-and-rule trick, for fuck's sake. Again, he illustrated his point with a number of striking anecdotes, including the fraud of *John's Jury* and his PR trip to the War Zones, and also Amber Pike's book full of ghost-written lies.

The parade advanced at a stately pace; no sign of the red bus yet. The crowd seemed to hang on his words — but he sensed uncertainty; they weren't quite with him yet.

He informed his listeners that the tabloids were poison, written by people who despised them.

He told the Home Guard that war was about money and power and not patriotism or duty or democracy or values or *defending our way of life*. Did they *really* want to defend their way of life when, to be brutally honest, it sucked? Whose way of life was being defended, then?

Glancing down at the press pen, Dolt spotted a look of open-mouthed ecstasy on Weese's face, and one of limp-jawed bafflement on Gunner's.

Then something bulky, ponderous and red loomed in Dolt's peripheral vision. He broke off from his speech and turned his head. There it was: The red bus, with its world-beating cargo of sporty young English womanhood — and their mothers. The upper deck shuddered with patriotic athleticism, girlish enthusiasm and the fresh new hope of the nation. Hamid wouldn't have approved, though; you weren't supposed to stand on the upper deck. Alone on the open platform at the back was the conductor.

Wait a minute. Conductor? Why did they need a conductor? And why did the conductor need a broom? Why was he holding it up like that? What was this weird red spot on Dolt's chest?

He was on the point of connecting these observations when Ginger, in an exercise of pre-emptive military might, felled him to the floor as brutally as if he were a migrant burglar on *John's Jury*. The stonework of the Column proceeded to explode above his head. He felt shards in his hair, spiky dust in his eyes.

Then it stopped. Next came the sound of a powerful motorcycle, screaming off in the direction of Northumberland Avenue.

Snowy crouched by Dolt's head.

"All clear. They missed you. Good work, Ginger."

Dolt sat up.

"The motorcycles!"

"Well, *a* motorcycle. Shooter was on the bus, another chap comes along on the bike and —"

"We've got to get after them!"

Snowy shook his head.

"On Vera? Out-gunned, I'm afraid."

"Then what should I..."

"Calm the crowd. Then finish your speech, perhaps? You were raising some interesting points."

Dolt got to his feet and shook the debris from his hair. On the platform now, getting a first-hand from Ginger, was Des.

"John! Fuck! It was you all along! The provocation, the trigger and all that —
it was *you!* You know, it *did* occur to me. Perhaps I should have said something?
Anyway, no harm done — right?"

No harm?

But before Dolt could even think of lashing out at Des, he felt himself gripped
from behind. It was Snowy's voice in his ear.

"Not wise, John. Speak to your people."

Dolt took in the scene. The rifle shots themselves had been barely audible.
The crowd looked restive and confused. To Dolt's rear, the parade continued as
if nothing had occurred. The red bus and its jaunty crew now approached the
burger bar, where staff stood ready to lob them complimentary snack bags.

What should he say? There remained so little time in which to *re-educate* the
Home Guard. Inspiration arrived.

"I *knew* Red Ron," he said. "Red Ron was a friend of mine."

He proceeded to detail the injustices of Ron's life and downfall, not omitting
a long digression on the subject of the former boss of Big Builder, and how he'd
buggered off to Costa Rica.

"They've got this amazing fucking palace in the jungle," he said, recalling the
description Jeff had given him. "You wouldn't believe the sort of people, what
they've been getting up to..."

Then he remembered where he'd meant to go with the Red Ron thing.

"There's a national strike going on today," he said. "They say it's illegal, but
I say stop us if you can! I want everyone here — everyone in the Home Guard,
all over the land — to join the strike! Today! And then together — *together!* —
we can *take back our fucking country!*"

Down at the base of the Column, Dolt saw Weese talk into his mobile. He
listened for a moment, then lowered his phone and looked up a Dolt. A big, queasy
grin spread across his face.

But Dolt felt certain that he had the crowd on his side now. Their mood,
originally dour, pinched and fearful, was now one of light-headed jollity, mixed
with a boisterous punchiness and possibly even a carnivalesque gaiety. Dolt
capitalized on this by telling tales from his former life — rather as he'd done for
the Club for Greed in New York — except with the opposite spin, obviously. For
a while, this went very well indeed.

But then something began to distract the crowd. You could see it spread —
glance here, an elbow there, the urgent thumb-scrolling, the double-take, the
have-you-seen-this? It grew into a kind of sentimental flash-flood.

Dolt turned to Des.

"What's happening?"

"This."

Des held up his phone. On the screen was the headline news page of a tabloid
newspaper.

PERSIANS IN MEMORIAL OUTRAGE, Dolt read. HERO DOLT DEFIES TERROR
PLOT. PM VOWS ACTION.

After that came sports news. Then...

DOLT IN PAEDO SHOCK. LEADER'S "VILE" SNAPS. DOLT NAMED IN ABUSE
SCANDAL. SEX SHAME OF HOME GUARD "MONSTER".

Dolt looked at Des.

"Surprised?" Des said. "Have a look down there."

He tipped his head in the direction of Weese. Weese gave Dolt another cheery thumbs-up. Then he slapped his stony-faced side-kick, Gunner, on the back and, together, they began to shove their way through the crowd.

It was, in a way, fascinating to observe, in the aggregate, the mentality of the masses. Gideon, once, after a few sherries and just prior to their Kansas trip, had entertained Dolt with some of the hottest bits from the theory of evolution. An *exogenous shock*, some said, could accelerate the process to lightning speed. Something similar was happening now. To think of it in another way, it was a bit like watching someone do a handbrake turn in the Jobba van — not that such a thing was possible in reality, or that the handbrake really worked. From HERO to "MONSTER" in about half an inch...

But Des had decided to focus on the practical.

"Time to leave, John."

Aided by Ginger and Snowy, Des ushered Dolt to the black Range Rover. Given the evolving mood of the mob, the intent to which it now gave voice, and a mounting fusillade of rubbish, the farewells were short.

"Snowy? Um..."

"Can't win every battle, John."

"Er, Ginger? Thanks, mate."

"It's the training. Pure instinct, after a while."

Des powered the Range Rover the wrong way around Nelson's mini-round-about then thrust it under the Arch and on to The Mall.

"This exit strategy of yours," he said. "I've seen better."

Dolt hammered at the Range Rover's glove box with his fist. It sprang open. An A-to-Z, a half-eaten Toblerone and a toy gun fell out. Or was it a toy?

"Pictures?" Dolt said. "What fucking pictures?"

"On your computer. The one you let me take."

"There weren't any *pictures* on my computer!"

"No. But there are now. Ooh, look at that!"

Des meant Buckingham Palace. It was on fire.

"Look what your pals have done!"

"What pals?"

"The strikers."

"I didn't tell them to do that."

"No. And they didn't. Today isn't just about the Persians, you know. I mean, you didn't intend it to be, did you?"

"Well, no, but —"

"We need somewhere to hole up," Des said, as the Range Rover punched a tunnel through the smoke that billowed across Constitution Hill and into Green Park. "I know the perfect place."

As they drove north, the light began to fail. The streets were full of people, angry faces on all sides — but were they strikers, or disenchanted Home Guard members, or had the disturbances got their breath back? Here and there mysterious fires burned, but none of them had anything to do with Dolt.

Des's idea of a good place to hole up turned out to be the Royal Fusilier. To protect his identity, Dolt agreed to don the black hoodie and NYC baseball cap that Des kept under his seat. They needn't have bothered; despite its patriotic decorations and two-pints-for-the-price-of-one special offers, the Fusilier was all but empty. Des directed Dolt to the darkest corner available and made a token purchase of two halves of Old Grenadier.

"Cheers," he said. "Now tell me I should have warned you."

Dolt drank his beer in silence.

"What cliché do you want, John? The one about living by the sword? The one about reaping what you sow? The one about shitting where you —"

"They tried to *kill* me, Des."

"And your point is?"

"After all I did for them."

"No gratitude in politics, John."

"Gideon betrayed me."

"Maybe. Maybe not quite. You lucked out with the old soldiers, though."

"No thanks to you."

"I haven't asked for any thanks, John. Even though, as I recall, I tried to make you understand, right from the beginning —"

"Now what?"

Dolt's attention had been captured by the TV above the bar. Coverage of rugby from New Zealand had been interrupted for a newsflash.

"Ah, shit," Des said. "Here it comes."

The PM had called for firm and immediate action against the Persians — and he had urged that *anyone* with the will, determination and ability to act should immediately undertake *all appropriate sanctions*. The Persians had attempted to assassinate a leading British citizen — on a day of national mourning, no less! And no one had been more steadfast in condemning Persian duplicity and aggression than this very same citizen.

Now it had to be admitted, unhappily, that certain facts concerning the aforementioned citizen had just come to light. Unsavory facts, to say the least. But that did not affect the principle of the thing. Furthermore, many people were now asking whether this person — given the extreme views he had so recently voiced, and his association with Red Ron and the illegal general strike — might not have been a Persian stooge all along. Either way, the right course was clear.

Then a Global Terror Analyst came on to explain, with the aid of computer graphics, how long-range stealth bombers based on Diego Garcia were rumored to be revving up in order to bomb the shit out of the Persians.

In other news, the strikers had *stolen* the Great Leader's statue, and were demanding a ransom, plus also the re-introduction of the minimum wage.

"Heads they win..." Des said.

"Is that it, then?"

"That's it."

They sat in silence for a time.

"Want another beer?" Des asked.

"No thanks."

A heavy pause.

"Don't suppose you have any idea about that PIN number, then — do you?"

"No. And I don't suppose you have any idea about my offshore bank account, either — right?"

"Nope. Sad, innit? Means our association is at an end."

"Really?"

"Yeah."

An even heavier pause. Dolt considered pleading with Des for assistance, but feared a not-my-job-any-more rebuff featuring *budgets* and Des's *Oxbridge* bosses.

"So what's going to happen to me?"

"Something horrible, I expect. Want a lift anywhere?"

Most of Dolt's meager possessions were back at his hotel.

"Well, all my stuff is —"

"Nah, you don't wanna go there. Not unless you're in the mood to give your pal *Nigel* an exclusive. They'll have the hotel staked out by now."

"Oh."

Where else could he go? Home? Where was that, now? Back to the half-a-house? It was all he could think of. As the sound of cheering rugby fans blared from the TV, they exited the Royal Fusilier, climbed back into the Range Rover, and headed for the North Circular.

As they approached Hangar Lane, Dolt's phone rang.

An international call! The drones! Were they *phoning home?*

It turned out to be Gideon. He'd heard the news. Jay had granted him a phone call, under strict conditions.

"But John — are you safe?"

"Er, well…"

"John, it's important that you know this. I had no idea that they meant to… I thought it was just to be a piece of theater."

"Theater?"

"I was misled, John. Grievously misled."

"Uh-huh."

"To be fair, though, you weren't entirely honest with me either — were you?"

"Mm."

"Not that it matters now, of course. It's all out of our hands."

"Right."

"Distressing all round. I may have to consider another career."

"Yeah, bummer."

"I heard your speech…"

"Yup."

"In a way, I suppose, I understand."

"Do you?"

"We seemed to complement each other so perfectly… And yet, it always felt a touch —"

"Too good to be true?"

A sigh from Gideon.

"I worry about what will happen to you, John."

"You don't need to worry about me."

"These situations... There's often such a ruthlessness. Someone like Des, for example. I hesitate to —"

"I'm not scared of Des."

A pause.

"Perhaps you should be, John."

"Up to a point."

Gideon paused. When he spoke again there was a tremor in his voice.

"I know things can never be the same for us," he said. "We came from utterly different worlds, and something special happened, but it was always inevitable that we should be torn apart again, one day. But I just wanted you to know that, whatever happens from now on, wherever we end up and whatever the fates have in store for us... That we'll always have —"

The Range Rover plunged into an underpass. Dolt's phone signal cut out. *What?* What would they always have? *We'll always have...* Paris? No, they hadn't been there. Kansas?

They emerged from the underpass. But Gideon had gone.

"What a prat," Des said.

Dolt's phone blipped.

A message had arrived from Amber Pike. Her car-crash syntax rendered it largely unintelligible, but what Dolt took away was that Amber had been saddened by the *switcheroo*, and Dolt's standing invitation to *the cabin* had been rescinded.

He made Des stop the car at the end of his road. They sat for half a minute in silence. Then Des flipped open the Range Rover's glove box and began to rummage. The gun fell out again. Des retrieved a pen. Then he ripped off a piece of the Toblerone wrapper and scribbled something on it.

"Here. Best I can do."

Dolt took it. Des had written down an address — somewhere on the Isle Of Wight.

"What's this?"

"Victoria's address. Your wife. She's not in Spain. I lied."

Dolt stared at the chocolaty scrap in his hand. Des's blocky script seemed to blur in front of his eyes.

"They'll be cutting off her payments. Maybe the two of you can... Who knows?"

"Victoria?"

"Kids too. Tamsin and..."

"Tamara."

"You go down there and you lay low. Keep quiet. They really just want you to go away, at this point. Got a war to think about, haven't they? Understand?"

"Yeah. Got it."

"Okay. Get out of the car, then."

Dolt opened his door and dismounted.

"Des?"

"What?"

"Is that a real gun?"

"Yeah."

"Wow."

"Exactly. One last thing, John. Next time, *get yourself a fucking exit strategy!*"

Des slammed his door. The Range Rover spun its wheels on Dolt's greasy road and snarled off again towards the North Circular. Dolt tucked his wife's address into his trouser pocket and began to walk.

Dolt's half-a-house had been fitted with steel shutters; they now smothered its doors and windows. A security company notice warned that the property was under *constant surveillance*, and implied, fraudulently, that Alsatian guard dogs patrolled its interior. It looked as though the upstairs neighbors had moved out.

The easily-reachable portions of the house had been sprayed with graffiti — mostly personal, not political. And someone had even gone to the trouble of imprinting the chimney stack; while they were up there, they must have helped themselves to the satellite dish.

The skip had been repossessed by its owners, but the Jobba van remained, moldering like the funerary pyramid of a minor pharaoh. It retained three of its four wheels. That figured; there'd only been one good tire. Like the house, it had attracted comment, but not recently — the layer of grime had grown too thick. There were no leaves; except for the flimsy willow once favored by next-door's cat, Dolt's road was treeless.

He tugged at the passenger door. It swung open. The inside of the van was a mess. It looked as though someone had been sleeping in the back. There was a tabloid newspaper on the seat. He retrieved it.

DOLT SLAMS PERSIANS, he read. HOME GUARD LEADER BLASTS APPEASERS. He flung the newspaper back into the van.

Just then, the upper hinge on the passenger door gave way and the door tipped at angle, slicing Dolt across the left knee. He limped to his front door, sat on the step and writhed for a minute or so.

Then he became aware that his phone was ringing. It was another international call. He pressed the answer button and held the phone to his ear. At first he heard only static. Then a series of beeps. Then...

"Enter PIN."

It was Lescek's voice.

More beeps.

"Enter PIN."

Oh, Lescek... he thought.

"Enter PIN."

Four numbers. But which?

"Enter PIN."

He stared at the back of the Jobba van. His gaze fell upon the steel bar and padlock that Lescek had made him have welded to the van's rear doors. Lescek always worried about his tools, even though they were rubbish.

The padlock didn't have a key, though, did it? It had a combination. Four numbers. Lescek knew them. Dolt knew them. What were they?

He strained to remember. They came to him. He tapped them in.

"PIN verified."

The line went dead.

Dolt sat on the front step of his half-a-house for a few minutes more, until his leg felt viable. The he got up and hobbled slowly in the direction of the A40.

When he got there, he stopped at the very edge of the pavement and watched the traffic. The big day was over and, out here where the political air was thinner and people breathed oxygen, things were getting back to normal.

White vans, like his own before it died, just trying to earn a living.

Crappy, twelve-year-old hatchbacks, hoping not to break down half-way home to half a house.

People carriers, full of tired children or despondent pensioners, desperate to get the journey done.

Taxis — many with the advertisements ripped from their doors or painted over.

Pricey German limos, each with a single *truly productive person* in the back.

Black Range Rovers, heading for Knightsbridge or Chelsea or even, perhaps, the heart of political power.

He could end it all here, couldn't he? And look — a flat-bed truck, loaded with bricks. How appropriate. People could stop asking *Who is John Dolt?* and get on with their lives.

But then he thought of Jeff Crock (he still hadn't made that call, had he?) and Jeff's mother-in-law, and he let it pass.

If only there had been a desert here, instead of a dirty arterial road, would he have walked off into it? He thought he might.

To the east, where the political heart of the nation pulsed anew with the hot vanity of war, the glorious day now ended in expectations of triumph and validation.

But John Dolt now knew that he wasn't cut out for glory, or even petty tragedy.

He turned his face to the west, braced himself against the chill, stuck his hands in his pockets — in one of which he clasped a scrap of paper — and began to walk.

His mission: To go on an island.

CHAPTER 51

Leo Vargas stepped out of the Cape Town International Convention Centre, squinted up, briefly, at Table Mountain, then slid into the chilly interior of an air-conditioned taxi. He checked the message on his phone, then asked the driver to take him to the Victoria and Alfred Waterfront. It was a very short ride, and not at all ecologically sound, but it was a hot day, this was Cape Town, and he had resolved to worry more about his personal security in future.

As he rode in the taxi, he glanced up again at the mountain — a special place, like the Corcovado. *Yes*, the driver said when Leo asked, it *was* hot for Cape Town at the end of October. Bad for the fynbos, Leo said. The driver agreed. Who was going to save the fynbos?

It was a ridiculous question to ask, now. The climate conference, held practically within sight of this biodiversity hotspot — this *World Heritage Site* — had collapsed. The Cape Floral Region would be less floral in future. Two thirds of the fynbos would die off. And perhaps forty per cent of the proteas.

Apparently, it was not possible to discuss such matters while war raged in the Greater Persian region. The speed with which certain delegations had packed their bags had been unseemly. But where did these people think they were going? The airport was closed. Three enormous drones, tanked up with chemical weapons, had parked themselves there. And no one knew what to do about it.

At the waterfront, he walked among tourists, sight-seers, and off-duty office workers, looking for the coffee shop in which Walter Gabo awaited him. He thought he detected a fragile sense of normality — certainly, everything looked very normal here: A little bit of Euro-America at the very tip of Africa — but his experiences in Ethiopia and Libya, he suspected, had eroded his ability to make these judgments. What was normal? Why not deserts in Spain and Italy?

In Ethiopia, a new drought loomed. And Eritrean bandits had killed five Dutch tourists in the Danakil, so Bonnie DiAngelo's great hope was dead. As for the woman herself — well, perhaps Walter had news.

And there he was, sitting under an awning at an outdoor table in a straw hat with a wide brim.

"Leo! Sit! Have some coffee."

Leo sat, poured himself half a cup of black coffee and forced himself to sample it, sucking it in between his lips and letting it hit the back of his mouth. Thin and watery, he thought; a bitter edge, no sweetness, no oils, no body; dry, stale, powdery beans, under-roasted. Too much Robusta.

"Thank you," he said. Then he waited.

"We're trying to find out, Leo, but you can imagine the difficulty. She got out of the car and... As far as we can tell, nobody has seen her."

"You'll keep looking?"

"Oh, we shall, yes."

"Can't that American find her?"

"Jay? No, he's... Now, how did he put it? He's gone on sabbatical. Indefinitely. I can't contact him. I don't know where he is."

"Namibia?"

"No. I don't know."

Leo sipped at his coffee. How could people tolerate this stuff? The level of ignorance... For example, Ecuadorian coffee was at least as good as Columbian, but all people wanted —

"Well, at least you're getting your forest back," Walter said.

"It will take years, but... Yes."

And in what condition, he wondered, would he find the Pelican Lodge? Could he afford to repair it? A loan might be necessary. Or perhaps a mortgage would be preferable. Maybe a combination...

But Walter was talking again.

"I'm sorry?" Leo said.

"We're giving in. The pressure's too much. You wouldn't believe the threats. We're not a powerful country."

"Giving in? What do you mean?"

"Well, at least we arrested him. In front of the cameras. That was something. We had everything documented — the front organizations, the money trail, Boschenkop, Libya, those *things* out at the airport..."

"Oh, *him*."

"So he's acquired a medical condition — one that can't be treated in South Africa, I suppose — and we're saving face."

"What did you expect?"

"Mm."

They paused for a moment to watch a pair of pretty girls walk past.

"But what are we going to do with those *things*?" Walter asked.

"Don't they want them back?"

Walter spluttered into his coffee cup.

"They're not getting them back. You know whose idea it was to send them here? Listen to this. Jay told me..."

But Jay's agenda no longer interested Leo. His mind fled, until it was twelve thousand kilometres away. The problem with the eco-lodge, he decided, was that it was *too* luxurious. The guests were still too *insulated*. He could save money and improve the quality of the experience by...

But Walter was staring at him.

"*John Dolt!*" he said.

Leo finished his terrible coffee.

"Who is John Dolt?"

Also by Rory Harden

Who thinks running guns to Africa should be a nice little earner? Who's accidentally acquired a soccer-mad private army of child soldiers? What happened at the Glue Factory? Who forgot to switch off the fountains? Oh, and by the way...

Why is Africa's richest country so poor?

A deceptive plot to take over the "richest country in Africa" in the name of Democracy. An ethically-challenged businessman on a voyage of self-discovery. A glimpse into the dark heart of the "New Democratic Consensus".

Also by Rory Harden

Who really won the Presidential Election? What's the true purpose of the Chinese moon landing? Who's building big in Madagascar? Who's on a mission to *disrupt?* America won't be the same again. In fact...

Will it even be America?

A third-party candidate to be US President. An exclusive hedge fund with *consistent* returns. Naval conflict in the South China Sea. An underground battle over secrets. Unrest in Hong Kong. A destitute woman with nothing but the key to unlimited power.

About the Author

Rory Harden lives in London with his wife, Nancy, and two adopted cats, Spike and Monty. He enjoys travel, books, music and computer programming. And he plays guitar and bass – not too badly, sometimes.

www.ingramcontent.com/pod-product-compliance
Lightning Source LLC
Chambersburg PA
CBHW070902260626
47162CB00007B/2538